Sons of Fate

The Last World

Part I

By

L. J. Hennes

Dedication

For Victor, Lisa, and Tobin, who led my team at McGilligan
Publishing.

You made this possible.

Acknowledgment

To formally acknowledge everyone who has helped me with this series would probably end with as many pages as the books themselves. To my friends and family who have stood by all the shenanigans, you know who you are, and you know my gratitude.

There is one, however, who doesn't, and is worth mentioning.

In the year 2019, I was scrolling through Facebook and came across a snippet of a fantasy story from a website ad. The story featured all the fantasy romance we know and love. The story was decent, full of mild tension and romance that centered around the main character waiting for graduation so they could move away from the house they lived in, only to discover they are the fated mate to the son of the leader. Classic. Loved it.

That story inspired me to write the original draft that later devolved into this series. The story you are about to read is leaps and bounds away from where it started six years ago, but I remember the moment I started to write my first paragraphs, wanting a wolf-based story of my own. When it began, there weren't gods and monsters and witches and slaves, but it evolved, as all things do, into the monstrosity of events that you, my great reader, are about to put yourself through.

I don't remember the name of the story, the name of the website on Facebook, or the name of the author. I search to discover it again, that I might find it and seek out that person to thank them for their inspiration. For their story has become part of me and has led me to publishing my first book series.

To the author out there who gave me the first ideas for the story that has devolved into this madness, I long for the day to find your story again so that I may learn who you are and thank you properly. Until then, I give you my gratitude.

May the Fates bless you.

Contents

Dedication i

Acknowledgment ii

Trigger Warning 1

Prologue… 2

Years Prior… 6

Present Day… 27

Trigger Warning

The following content contains depictions of mental, physical, and sexual abuse, as well as graphic violence. These themes may be distressing or triggering for some readers. Please proceed with caution, and prioritize your well-being. If you find any of this content overwhelming, consider taking breaks, seeking support, or choosing not to engage with it.

Prologue...

They stood together as they always had. Their backs pressed against one another in the veil of white that surrounded them. In any direction they would look if they chose to, they would only see the void, the great expanse of nothing that enveloped creation. Or marked the lack thereof.

The first man was dressed in black. Long flowing clothes that hung in the emptiness around them. His hair was nearly as dark as the fabric that covered and hid his small frame. Everything about him was young and still hopeful. His onyx-black eyes looked up as if there was such a direction in the expanse and around the space around him as he visualized the potential of what would soon be the new world.

The second man had his eyes closed. His head tilted down in exhaustion. He didn't want to see the emptiness of where they were. The failure that it marked. He was swathed in cloths of white, styled and draped in nearly the same fashion as the man in black. He was taller and older, with dark olive-tinted skin and narrow eyes. White hair nearly faded into nothing, nearly blinding him when he finally opened his pale grey eyes. He didn't look around with hope and wonder like the younger man did. He could only feel what was lost. The souls that were supposed to have been given back had been seized, frozen in an unnatural limbo that kept them from reaching their much-needed peace.

Time would have passed, if there was time in that space between spaces. The man in black could still feel his heart and used the beats to measure the minutes that would have passed if they had been standing somewhere in time. He nodded with a smile, more to himself as he knew the man in white couldn't see him. "I know what to do this time."

The man in white resisted a flinch that threatened to twist his face. He had heard those words before. He took several deep breaths as his own form of time before he spoke, "What makes this time any different?"

The man in black turned, and the man in white did the same, nearly mirroring his movements as they faced each other. Their expressions reflected the other's intensity, but as with so many things about them, they held opposing emotions. The man in black smiled while the grimace on the man in white intensified. "It will be." When the man in white shook his head, the man in black reached out and touched his face. After a moment of silence, he spoke with a gentler voice, "It will be."

The man in white leaned into the hand that caressed his face. When he finally met his counterpart's eyes, tears fell. They streamed down his skin, falling from his chin, the water dissolving into whisps of black mist that faded into the rays of white that absorbed everything around them. "Why can't we just let them be?"

The man in black shook his head, his expression shifting quickly as the gentle smile faded from his mouth. His voice turning insistent, the darkness in his eyes shined with a glimmer the man in white knew all too well. "Don't you want them to live?"

The man in white answered quickly. He knew what the question was, just like the man in black knew what his own response was going to be. A conversation they had over and over, as their attempts all ended in failure. Any changes they made or didn't make, the results would nearly always be the same. "Of course, I want them to live." Moments passed, and he asked, "How many times are we going to try?"

The man in black let out a sigh. He held up the palm of his hand and said, "This time will be the last. It will work. Trust me."

It felt like a long moment; the man in white took in a full inhale and released the breath in just as much time. He spoke simply, a whisper against the emptiness around them. "Last time." When the man in black nodded, he took the hand.

The nothingness around them began to move and shift. From their feet came the ground: rocks, dirt, and sand that allowed their foundation to stand strong. The sky formed above them, clouds, storms, and stars that would shape the wonder and beauty of the seasons. The elements yielded to their creation, forming the oceans, rivers, volcanos, mountains, and valleys they had grown to know so intimately.

The man in white let out a heavy breath, almost relieved, as he looked around at the forest they stood in. As much as it was a part of him, the hollowness of the void was something he did not long for. The emptiness between worlds continued to haunt him since he had first entered it lifetimes ago.

Before their eyes, the seasons in the forest changed. Waves of storms and wind colored the sky in endless rounds of blue, black, and grey as day turned to night. Leaves and plants sprouting, shining in the sun before turning glorious colors and falling to the ground to be covered in snow. Only to regrow again when the snow melted.

The man in white closed his eyes as the life began to form. He could feel all the lost souls appearing on the earth as the man in black pulled them from purgatory and gave them life once again. When his eyes met the man in black once more, he gave a smile. A sight that seemed to be a rarity as time went on.

The man in black returned a thankful grin. He stretched his arms out to the side, his palms warming in the sun that glowed above them. In his mind's eye, he envisioned the life that began to sprout across the world. The histories, cultures, territories, and peoples all emerged as they were designed. Once more, the man in black held out his hands, both this time, in offering to the man in white as he repeated his words. A mantra he seemed to have adopted throughout the ages, "This time, it will work. Trust me."

The man in white nodded and spoke with as much confidence as he could muster, "I trust you." He took the hands of the man in black. A shroud of black smoke emanated from him, enveloping their forms and swirling like a windless tornado. When the smoke cleared and tendrils of mist had disappeared into the earth, they had vanished.

Gwen took several deep breaths as she drove down the packed city streets. She grumbled softly, cursing with faded words as she changed lanes once again. "Merciful Fates, how am I supposed to find a parking spot in this mess?"

She had only been in the city for a week and hadn't fully had time to explore her new surroundings of the Newaygo Territory. Born and raised in the state of Montana, she had recently been forced to relocate. She had petitioned several different cities in four other states; the city in Michigan was the only city to respond to her request.

From the backseat of the small car sat her eight-year-old son, Halius. His face was buried in a tablet as he played one of the mind-numbing games. She heard his sarcastic snicker followed by an equally snarky question, "Do you even know where we're going?"

Her eyes flashed to him in the rearview mirror. Her glare did little against his growing attitude. She snapped back at him, "Of course I do! I have the address here in the GPS." She shook her head as if to throw the anxieties from her mind and spoke more to herself than to her son. "We'll be on time if this fucking traffic ever lets up."

Halius's voice was small as if he was falsely attempting to hide the statement. He knew how to prod his mother's patience. "Doesn't matter anyway."

Gwen's voice barked at him with an echo from the wolf that her body contained. "Be quiet! I'll take that tablet away!" While sitting at a red light, she turned over her shoulder and placed her arm on the passenger's seat. Her eye color shifted to a golden yellow as her wolf's rage burned against her irises. "Behave yourself. I am not kidding."

His eyes looked up at her. For a moment, Gwen thought he was going to argue with her more as his fingers flexed against the tablet. Halius remained silent as his eyes turned back to the tablet. A momentary guilt flashed across his face before his irritation returned.

When Gwen was able to find the café she was looking for and a parking spot that was as close as she could park to the busy city café, they were nearly an hour late. Gwen threw off her seatbelt and yanked her purse from the passenger's seat. Her movements were manic and hard as she pulled open the rear door. "Alright, Halius, let's go."

He slowly took off his seatbelt. His eyes never left the tablet screen as he leaned forward and said, "Yeah, hang on. I'm almost done with this level."

Unable to stop herself, a growl escaped her lips. The sound echoed by the wolf that was threatening to overtake her body. She ripped the tablet from his hands and ignored his protesting cries as she yanked her son from the car. The slam of the door rocked the sedan as her fingers crushed his bicep.

He was practically dragged along as she briskly walked them down the sidewalk, nearly three blocks from their destination. Her voice rumbled with an irritated snarl, "We wouldn't be late if you had listened to me when I told you to get ready the first time! This is the first territory that would even *think* of letting us move here." She stopped them only for a moment, just enough time to pull up his eyes and allow her glare to cause the fear she wanted to start to emerge across his face. "Do not ruin this."

Halius could barely keep up with her when she started to pull him down the street once more. His legs practically dragged across the pavement. "Why do we even have to do this? I saw some territories where we don't have to be part of a pack to live there. We wouldn't be Rogues either; they're called Sanctuary Cities. I found them on the internet when we were in Chicago!"

Gwen clenched her jaw and hissed, "I know what they are, Halius! We are not living in one of those wretched places."

Halius tried to keep the whimper from his voice when he said, "Mom, you're hurting me."

She stopped them at the door of the shop. Taking several deep breaths as she tried to soften her face. She knelt, adjusting his buttoned shirt, and spoke as gently as she could muster. "This was part of the deal the Alpha of this territory gave me. We are Betas; Halius, the Alpha's Prime-Beta, has no mate. If this works out, we'll never have to worry about anything else. OK?" She managed a half-smile. "It will be like it never happened."

He held her gaze for a long while before he said, "But it did happen. Dad's dead, mom."

Gwen wanted to be angry. She wanted to scream, to lash out at him for his rude remarks. Instead, she let out a sigh and said calmly, "I can't change what happened, Halius. We will never forget him. But life moves on, and we must move with it. Less we get caught in Death's wake." She took his small hands and said, "Now, we are going to go in there and I am going to talk to the Prime-Beta if the Fates are kind and he is still there. Then, hopefully, we can find ourselves a new home and we can try to put this behind us."

To her surprise, Halius nodded. He quickly swiped his hand across his eyes, causing guilt to stab at her chest. Halius flinched slightly when she reached out and brushed her fingers against his cheek. She felt no remorse for his response to her touch. "Behave yourself for me, and I'll get you a muffin before we leave."

A smile pulled the corner of his mouth. A rare sight for him. "A blueberry muffin?"

Gwen stood, her face twisted as she said, "Yes. Behave yourself, help me make this meeting go well, and I'll get you your disgusting muffin." She felt her heart grow warm at the sight of his growing smile and ushered him inside.

She wasn't sure what emotions her wolf was pressing into her logical human mind when they walked into the café. The smells were all a mix of various coffees; the noise level was lower than expected, considering the moderate crowd between the counter and the tables scattered across the floor.

A smile came to her face as they made their way across the shop. She recognized him from a single picture that was sent to her from the Prime Alpha of the Newaygo Territory. The photo did him no justice.

He sat at a booth that was against the wall, sporting a casual dark grey blazer jacket over a white buttoned shirt. His dark eyes were turned down, focused on a tablet that he read from that was propped by its case on the table. His brown hair was neatly slicked back, the style accenting his hard jawline.

Next to him, sitting on a flower-printed cushion on the floor, was a young girl. Roughly the same age as Halius, her legs were folded in front of her. Her face was plain as she played a game on a cell phone. Hair the color of mud covered the majority of her face.

Gwen tried not to make a face at the girl. An Azure, marked by the metal, thick banded bracelets she wore on her wrists. The intricate designs carved into the metal were almost invisible against the glare of the fluorescent lights. The bracelets seemed a little large for the girl, sliding down to almost her mid-forearm.

When they approached, his eyes went up to her. A courteous smile on his face and he patted the shoulder of the girl. She quickly jumped to her feet and placed the phone on the table. She pulled out Gwen's chair on the opposite side of the table and then Halius's. She noticed the smile that Halius gave her in the form of thanks. Gwen did not give any kind of gratuity.

Gwen did spend entirely too long watching the girl's bracelets but offered no emotion towards her. Thankfully for her son, she didn't see him smile at her before she sat back down on the cushion.

The Azure was a race of people who had been bred for enslavement. Generations of servitude, along with the bracelets they were forced to wear continuously, left them to be little more than glorified magicians. Made of a combination of Copper and Iron, the bracelets inhibited strong spell casting, or spells over long durations of time. It was through the magnetism of the bracelet metal that some of the energy from their bodies was absorbed and left them with minimal abilities they could only perform with permission. Powers were ranged, but the most common ones were tracking, elemental manipulation, communicating with animals, and healing. The bracelets were often carved with a design made by the Prime Alpha of the territory, as well as a phone number where the owner could be reached.

Upon the sale of an Azure, the engravings on the bracelets would be ground down and restamped with new information. Usually causing burns and lacerations to the arms and hands of the Azure and were generally worn so tightly around the wrists they could not be removed. However, this girl's bracelets were oversized and potentially could slip off.

Gwen resisted the urge to tell him her bracelets needed resizing, but she was not yet his wife and had no place to tell him how to treat his property.

The man took her attention when he placed his tablet down on the table. He took another sip of his coffee before smiling at Gwen and saying, "You must be Gwen." A moment passed, and he added, "Your picture does little to favor you."

She returned the smile, a slight color coming to her cheeks as she said, "I am. And you must be Beta Liam. Thank you for meeting with me."

His eyes flashed down to the girl, who looked up at him and smiled as if they shared an inside joke. "Well, I don't know if I *must* be, but I suppose." He leaned onto his forearms, his gaze turning to

Halius. The smile never faltered as he said, "That makes you Halius, doesn't it? I've heard a bit about you, too."

Halius slumped down in his chair. His eyes lowered to his fingers that he twisted nervously in his lap. He remained silent as the few moments passed. Normally, a sign of submission from children to their superiors, but for Halius, in that moment, it was to hide tears forming in his eyes. He did not want to be there.

Gwen attempted to pull the conversation back towards herself. She kept her voice light as she said, "I don't want to complain, but finding this place was a nightmare."

Liam sat back against the booth and chuckled. His hand returned to the hair of the girl as she continued to play on the phone. "I thought about warning you, but that would have taken away some of the fun." He paused, looking outside over Gwen's shoulder before he continued, "There is not one summer where part of our city isn't under construction. A new road, repairing an old building, the advancements of the inner parks and trails…" He trailed off, his voice lowering to nearly a whisper as he said, "Keeping tabs on all of it is quite exhausting."

Gwen nodded understandingly. She knew from experience that the Prime Beta was responsible for several aspects of the territory on behalf of the Alpha. Security is one of them, as well as approval of infrastructure changes and upgrades. She kept the smile on her face and said, "Well, a heads up would have been nice. Maybe we wouldn't have been so late."

Liam looked down at the girl once more, "We didn't mind, did we?" Before Gwen had a chance to ask him any questions about her, he continued, "So, my Alpha thinks it would be a good idea for us to get married. Seems a little abrupt, doesn't it?"

Gwen shrugged a shoulder, her smile disappearing as she spoke. "Well, logic dictates we give it a try. I'm not of Beta blood myself, but my True Mate was one. Halius has a very strong will, and he will require a father when he comes of age. Since I… hope to be new to the territory… well…" She hesitated. Her voice trailed off as her wolf started to whine in the back of her head.

Liam's smile had slipped away as well. His brow turned down. The play vanished from his voice, making his words sound like an order. "Finish your thought, Gwen."

She took in a long breath, letting it out in just as much time. Her fingers picked at the edge of a napkin. "Your Alpha made it sound like if we didn't do this, then I wouldn't be permitted to live in the territory. There's a lot on the line for us. He was the only one who returned my residential application."

Liam's confusion seemed to surprise her. "He was? How many did you apply to?"

Gwen shook her head. She tried to keep her mind from trailing back to those awful days. She and Halius had lived in a small territory in Montana. The pack she was in was set to take over the territory when her Alpha, Eli, was ready to ascend. His father had prepared to step down within the next two years until they found out that Eli's True Mate was an Azure.

It didn't happen often, but there were times of confusion for Lycans—the wolves that reigned supreme on the planet in their own forms of government—when they had spent too much time around the Azure that served them. The battle in the Montana territory lasted three days. Riots and fights tore apart the small city as Lycans took the side of Sympathizer towards the Azure.

The chaos was only put down when the Nexus of the state had intervened. In their attempt to flee, her whole pack lost their lives, with her only able to save herself, Halius, and the three Azure children owned by her late husband.

Gwen quickly rubbed her eyes before tears could fall. She pulled herself from her spiraling mind and cleared her throat to give her an extra few seconds to remember the question, "I… um… Seven.

Seven territories in four different states. I sent in the applications when we made it out of New Salem."

Liam's brow raised. His voice was calm and gentle when he asked, "New Salem? What kind of Territory name is that?"

Gwen let out an involuntary chuckle. She saw him return the smile, and for a moment, she felt her chest tighten. A flutter in her heart she had not felt in a long while. "Well, Alpha Eli's family was from Jerusalem. His father's great-great-grandfather founded the settlement with the intention to rebuild the great city in America." She looked down at Halius for a moment. A sigh escaped her mouth, and she shook her head, "The conflict is probably why the other territories I applied to didn't respond."

Liam was nodding, but he didn't seem to be paying much attention. At some point, while Gwen was trying to speak, he looked down at the girl once again. He didn't look up at her when he said, "A lot of Alphas don't want refugees from other packs in their territories. There was a stigma around them for a while, at least here in Michigan. Where if you got enough of them together, they would form some kind of Rogue pack." When he did look up, his eyes circled the café. His voice turned mocking as he continued, "They would be full of sympathizers who would tear down this oh-so-fragile hierarchy that we have worked so hard to achieve." He saw Halius smile, though the boy attempted to suppress the action.

Liam leaned onto the table once more, his fingers leaving the girl's hair and lacing it together as he said, "I see you smiling over there. Are you one?"

Halius looked up at his mother. A flash of fear came across his eyes before he looked at the man and asked in a small voice, "Am I one, what?"

A sneaky grin came to Liam's face. "Are you a sympathizer of the Azure? Have you come to tear down our structure and throw our territories into anarchy?"

Halius let out a small chuckle. He should have said yes. He should have made up some kind of elaborate story about how it was his life's work. His father would have. They always played those games with each other and with unsuspecting people.

Halius's humor was killed by his mother. Her venomous eyes stabbed daggers into him as if she could predict his thinking. Constantly, on the drive over from their hotel room, she stressed that he mustn't do anything to ruin the meeting. He lowered his eyes, forcing himself to stay quiet, and shook his head.

When Gwen met Liam's eyes once more, he didn't look amused. He sat back against the booth. His hand returned to the girl's hair as he took another absent-minded sip of his coffee. Fear itched Gwen's mind as her wolf began to whine. What was that look on his face? Disappointment? Was that because he didn't get the answer he wanted, or because Halius didn't act the way he liked? Her words were sharp and fast as she tried to recoil the horrid turn the conversation seemed to have taken. "I apologize, Beta Liam. My son is… difficult. Obnoxious and… well… he's a deviant at times." Her tone became more desperate as she continued, "I can assure you, he's not a sympathizer. I'm not either and—"

Liam had opened his mouth to speak. However, he never got his chance. To Gwen's dismay, her words were cut off when Halius decided to speak. "Dad was."

Eyes fell on the boy. Liam's brow raised again, the shock in his voice accentuated by a laugh that escaped his throat. "What was that?"

Halius looked at his mother for a moment. Her head whipped around so fast he was almost hit by her braided hair. He was able to look past her anger. Somehow, somewhere, he found the strength to push passed his mother's hatred, irritated by her statement. Ever since they had to flee, she had been cruel to him. Cruel to the Azure children who lived with them, it was unnecessary and wrong. He wasn't difficult, and she was just a bitch.

Halius squared his shoulders and locked eyes with Liam. "My father, Terrance Usoro, was a sympathizer. He stood by his Alpha when he announced the Luna of the pack was going to be an Azure." His words were strong, and he saw a smile tugging the corner of Liam's face as he held the man's attention, "During the fights, he defended that stance against the Alpha, even though—"

Gwen broke through his words when she erupted from her seat. The chair skidded on its feet and clattered against the floor in a shockwave of sound in the otherwise quiet café. She snatched the boy by the collar of his shirt and dragged him to the door as she hissed her displeasure at him through gritted teeth.

Her hand struck the back of his head after she had shoved him out the door. Outside, her volume grew. "I cannot believe you just said that in front of the Prime Beta!" Her fingers dug into his shoulder as she shoved him down onto the sidewalk. "Sit there! What were you thinking?"

Halius opened his mouth to respond, but before he could, her hand struck him again. The blow to the side of his temple nearly knocked him over.

She continued to scream at him as he sat up with his back against the building, "You know better than to discuss such things! If the Alpha refuses us, do you know what will happen? Are you *trying* to turn us into Rogues? Do you think we'll survive like that? Lycans do not survive without packs!"

Halius returned the glare his mother was giving him. She knelt as her eyes shifted to the venomous yellow. He held her stare as long as he could, feeling himself start to shake as he resisted her influence over him. After several long moments, his eyes lowered.

Gwen leaned close to her son, her furious breath hot on his face as she whispered with an intensity he had never heard, "Do. Not.

Leave. This. Spot. I will deal with your insolence later." Upon standing, she added, "Do you understand?"

Halius managed a nod. He managed to speak, his voice a whimpering croak, "Yes, Mother."

Gwen tried to walk strong as she headed back inside. However, no one was looking at her except for Liam.

For Lycans, the punishments used to keep the young in line were often violent and extreme. It was expected to hold ranks and prevent things like rebellion. Horrific stories from the earliest civilizations would speak of enough Rogue wolves joining together after they had left their families. The Rogue packs would destroy entire bloodlines, often aided by Azure, who murdered their owners to set themselves free.

Such monstrosities were all in the past. Society had moved passed such threats, all thanks to the constraints placed around the Azure in the form of their copper and iron bracelets and the Lycan adults' willingness to keep their children in line. Although to some, it often felt like an excuse to abuse the children and the Azure for the sake of it.

Monsters never truly disappear; they simply evolve as time does.

When she returned to her seat, Gwen shook out her hair, running her thumb and forefinger over the corners of her mouth, and waited for Liam to speak.

He had watched the entire scenario unfold before him. His face was unchanged as he watched Gwen strike her son. He had seen Halius's failed attempt to keep his eyes locked on his mother through her wolf's piercing gaze. Liam didn't see her look flustered until she returned to the table.

The chatter of the coffee shop was worse than a ticking clock as Gwen continued to wait. No one else in the shop had turned an eye towards what she had done to her son. Such behavior, because it was so normal, drew little attention.

Gwen bit the inside of her lip. She folded and unfolded her fingers, scratched the back of her head, and took several deep breaths. All in the silence of Liam's empty stare. How could things have gone so wrong for her? What must Liam be thinking of her? Would he believe that Halius was going to grow up to be a sympathizer? The Midwest states were not known to embrace the cause of the Azure. Rogues were common and forced to try and live outside the territories established by the Prime Alphas.

Most of the time, the Rogues died in the forests between the territories, unable to survive without the bonds of a pack.

Gwen couldn't let that happen to her or her son. They were no sympathizers; if she had to spend the rest of her life proving that to him, she would. She couldn't let him reject her. It had to go well. There was no other choice.

With the silence digging into her mentality, she blurted out, "I promise he's not a sympathizer!" She saw his brow raise at her. Her cheeks reddened as she averted her eyes from his gaze. Looking down at her hands as she felt his studying eyes. "His father was… um…" Liam smiled as if he thought he knew a secret. His eyes glanced to the girl, who smiled up at him for only a moment. The movement is unbeknownst to Gwen, who had her eyes on the table. "Sympathetic, perhaps?"

Her eyes snapped up. The hostility overtaking her voice caught Liam off guard. His smile vanished as she snipped, "Stupid." She watched his expression recoil; the sensitivity she thought she had unlocked slammed shut before her at that moment. But she could take no risks with the meeting; she had to be abundantly clear of her intentions, "He picked the losing side. Intentionally. And now I and his only son are paying the costs for his decisions."

Liam sat back against the booth. He tipped up his cup as he drank the last of his coffee. His head seemed to tilt with an expression Gwen couldn't fully read. His eyes looked away from her, out the windows to the horizon hidden behind the downtown skyscrapers, as he thought about what she had said. The silence lingered for another long moment.

A heavy sigh escaped his lips, one that Gwen finally noticed. She nervously rubbed her hands together underneath the table. Had she said something wrong? Was he trying to think of something to ask her? She couldn't risk him getting up and leaving. She spoke, with a nervous twitch to her voice as she tried to smile, "I don't want you to think I hate the Azure. I see you brought one with you." She motioned down to the girl.

Liam looked down at the child. He saw the gesture for what it was, how shallow it seemed. But it was an effort, so he indulged it. "Yes, this is Sydney." He gave her a warm smile and spoke with a softness that Gwen didn't seem to appreciate. "Say hello, Sydney."

The girl looked up, gave a respectful bow of her head, and said in a quiet voice, "Good afternoon, Mistress Guinevere."

Gwen tried to keep her voice light on the topic. She needed to pull him back from the sour turn the meeting had taken. "She seems very well-behaved." He nodded once, and she said, "I have three, myself." When his brow pulled together, a nervous breath caught in her throat. "Mostly for… um… for Halius's sake. The parents of the Azure… his father… my late… um… Terrance owned them. I promised him I would take care of them. The family had served him for generations."

When Liam's eyes returned to hers, her stomach turned. Something behind his eyes made her feel uneasy. There was a type of sympathy there, an understanding of their importance, but the hardening of his jaw made her blood turn cold. She could hear her wolf whimpering in the back of her mind as he said, "I'm sorry to hear that, but I have no need for more Azure. If we marry, you'll have to be rid of them."

Gwen felt her heart drop. Finally lost for words as her jaw dropped. Was that truly going to be what decided if they could stay in the territory?

Liam reached down and took the phone away from Sydney. "I know of a few pairs of Lycans who purchase Azure for the sake of raising them as children. They cannot have kids of their own; every decade or so, they get a new set. Good people, for the most part."

Gwen's head rocked back and forth. "I... I can't... they are..." She was able to steady herself enough to look at him, "There is no reason to get rid of them. They are well-behaved; they are excellent at cleaning. One of them can cook. The oldest one is tall enough to drive; he's ten. The only reason they didn't come with me today is because I wasn't sure how they would react to the Metropolis. The city we came from only had twenty thousand people in it. Nearly a quarter of the size of Newaygo."

Liam shook his head. "I'm sorry, there isn't room in my home for three more. I have Sydney, that's enough."

Gwen's brow turned down. "Your home? The... the pack house... I've seen pictures of the pack house. There is plenty of space, your Alpha assured me. It's a mansion because of how big the territory is."

Liam stood from the table, seeing the distress come across Gwen's face as his irritation began to radiate from him like heat on glass. His words were low, the tone sharp as he almost growled, "I do not live at the pack house. I have no need, and no room, for more Azure. Nor do I have the patience for a wife who does not know when to relent." He snapped his fingers, and Sydney silently got to her feet. She handed him the pillow she had been sitting on that he quickly tucked under his arm.

Gwen watched Liam take the girl's hand and tried not to flinch. She turned in her chair when he walked past her, "Is that it, then? I won't sell my Azure, and you're not even giving me a chance?"

Liam paused; he pulled open the door with his free hand and propped it open with his foot. He looked back at her, contemplating for a moment his position with his Alpha. He did not allow himself to look down at Sydney before he responded to Gwen. "I will consult with my Alpha. Someone will be in touch." With that, he left.

She turned back around in her chair and pressed her palms to her temples. She leaned forward, her elbows resting on the table as she tried to steady her breathing. Her wolf began to whine as her thoughts spiraled out of control. Had she ruined it? Would she be able to face anyone again if she couldn't even convince this man that she was worthy of being his mate?

She couldn't stay homeless forever. Not with four children to take care of. Where was she supposed to go if this pack rejected her? Would the Alpha be kind enough to let her stay even though she would be unmated? It would make her an Omega again, as she herself did not come from Beta blood. But Halius did, and because of their differences in rank, the Alpha could deem her unfit to raise him and could take him away from her.

She couldn't let that happen. She had lost too much already.

Gwen jumped at the sound of someone clapping their hands. Her eyes snapped up to the corner of the large booth Liam had been sitting at. The slow, sarcastic clap immediately set her teeth on edge.

When he knew he had her attention, he rested his arm on the back of the booth. His ankle was resting on his knee in a pose that seemed far too casual. He looked exactly like she remembered him. Distant, faded images slowly crept into her mind the longer she stared at him. Mid-thirties, white messy hair that was shaggy around his face. He wore a plain white T-shirt with a black open sweater overtop. A white design decorated the sweater in a sort of fleur-de-lis pattern stretching over his shoulder. Clean blue jeans accented by perfectly clean white shoes. Topping the look was steel-grey, nearly white eyes that looked pale in the light and off-place against his olive-tinted skin.

Atlas.

He didn't look threatening, but Gwen knew better. The very image of him made the hair on her nape raise in alarm. Her wolf rumbled a low growl in her mind that was a mix of fear and anger.

With his eyes on her, she could feel a dread building in her chest. The air suddenly felt heavy as the aura of the calm café began to change. Lycan customers suddenly became irate about small things, barking their displeasure at the Azure baristas who were attempting to serve them. The baristas turned more frantic as their masters came from the office after hearing the disgruntled customers.

Gwen looked over her shoulder, seeing the sky begin to darken as clouds rolled over the sun. Clouds that weren't in the forecast for that day. She turned back, her chest struggling to expand enough for a full breath. "Showboating a little hard, aren't you?"

Atlas shrugged one shoulder. "What's wrong, Guinevere? There was a time you were happy to see me."

Gwen rubbed her thumbs against her eyes. The terrorizing thoughts were pressing into her head. He looked so strange, but why?

She didn't have to think too hard about that thought. She knew why. She remembered. She remembered because they made her remember. She heard death echoing in her ears. The screams, the blood, the murder of her husband, her pack, fresh in her mind's eye. She had to close her eyes as the images intensified and changed.

Gwen saw her husband, his friends, and his brothers. She felt a heat rising around her as if the table were on fire. The images of her memory shifted with each pound of her heart, changing little by little until the world she recognized had nearly vanished. She tried to ground herself, opening her eyes and attempting to speak through heavy breaths, "I haven't…. been happy to see you… since… the…. Since… um…"

A touch on her arm brought her back to the quiet of the café. The horrors of her mind receded into obscurity until it was exactly what she thought it was. Her pack was murdered during their attempted escape from the territory in Montana. Nothing more.

The touch on her shoulder came from a man who sat down across from her. Although she didn't want to see him either, his presence felt like a gift. A flood of calm pulled back the hostility that had taken over so quickly. Tensions in the café died down; the sky lightened slightly as the sudden storm threat broke apart.

The young man sitting before her did not look older than twenty. If he were even that old. Midnight black hair was swept to the side in his long bangs. His pale skin seemed to glow against the black of his clothing. His eyes were also dark, nearly as infinite as his pupils, which made the shining white of his eyes even more luminous. However, that was also accented by black eyeliner that winged from the corners of his eyes to the edge of his temples. Unlike Atlas, who seemed to be much cleaner, this man's clothes seemed to come from a yard sale. An old black shirt with cutoff sleeves hung around his thin frame like rags on a drying rack. The cutoff sleeve showed a black mark against his forearm, an uneven circle, hollow in the center and broken in two points as if someone had poured oil on water and tattooed its silhouette on his arm. His jeans were also a dark color, with several tears and scruffy edges. He also wore no shoes and had thin leather cuffs adorning his wrists that had a stripe of silver down the center. Seemingly styled after the Azure's bracelets.

Niklas.

He leaned onto the table and laced his fingers together. Not bothering to smile when he asked, "Since what, Gwen?"

Her mouth opened, but she found no words. Her mind went blank as she tried to finish a thought she knew she wasn't supposed to have. She remembered them but could no longer discern from where. The calming influence was making it hard to think. She should have panicked. She should feel her heart thrumming in her chest, her wolf uneasy as they manipulated her thoughts.

It took all her willpower; Gwen gritted her teeth as her fingers gripped the table, and she forced herself to growl, "Stop it."

Niklas looked to Atlas, his smile vanishing when Niklas asked, "Are you done?"

Atlas shifted a bit uncomfortably. He nodded, his face twisting into a pout as if he were a child who had been screamed at. He pulled a cell phone from his pocket and busied himself playing with it, allowing Niklas to turn his attention back to Gwen.

Niklas let out a heavy breath and said, "You have to try somewhere else."

With their influences subsiding, she was able to respond. "No, I don't. I have to get rid of their kids."

Niklas's eyes held firm as he said, "You can't do that."

If he hadn't kept her under control, she would have attacked him there. She would have shifted and attempted to rip out his throat. Her eyes flashed the golden yellow of her wolf as she said, "Oh, and you'll help me with that, will you? Will you just *make* us another place to live, then?"

His tone was steady. His voice was never quavering even through her agitation. "Don't try and blame this on us. You have your own blame in this."

She responded quickly, "I told them not to go! I told Terrance we would never survive long enough to make it to the Sanctuary state!" Her palms slammed against the table. "They didn't listen to me! You made them not listen! This is *your* fault! Just as much as it is mine." Tears pooled in the corners of her eyes as she spoke. The recollections of Montana were overshadowed once more by memories of a world that was long gone.

She saw fire. She felt the heat of explosions caused by earthquakes. Tidal waves erased coastal cities, and thousands of souls perished in a war across the world that no one could fight. She saw herself sobbing in the chaos, clutching her child as the world was destroyed around them.

A temple sitting in ruins.

A gunshot echoed through the air.

Darkness.

Niklas's voice found her through the cacophony of horrific images, "Gwen, you know you can't give them up. They're not just Azure, you know that."

She leaned back in her seat, shaking her head aggressively as the tears streaked down her face. "They're nothing. I know they're nothing." She said it over and over in a faulty attempt to convince herself. Eventually, she bit her lip. Her voice was a whisper when she said, "Their parents were Azure. The Azure are nothing."

Atlas sat forward and nearly screamed, "They were not *nothing*, Guinevere!" He sat back only when Niklas raised a hand to him. With a grumble, he murmured to himself, "How dare you speak of them that way."

Gwen shook her head. "I can't do this, Niklas." The sound of defeat entered her voice. Her anger giving way to a sorrow she had not felt in lifetimes. "I can't live like this. If you want me to try and keep the children, if you want me to be able to… to…" She cleared her throat. "To live. Take it from me."

Niklas was silent for what felt like an eternity. He glanced back at Atlas, who did not meet his eyes. When he looked back at Gwen, he subtly shook his head. "Gwen, you agreed—"

She quickly cut him off, nearly shrieking, "I didn't know *what* I was agreeing to!" She leaned forward, her words hissed through clenched teeth, "I have watched worlds *burn* because of you. You tricked me; I didn't agree to any of this." Her eyes moved to Atlas, who looked up at her when she said, "You should know all about that."

Silence overtook the café. An eerie, thick hush encompassed the world around them. Gwen never looked away from Niklas as the world seemed to freeze around them. There was no sound from the café, no other voices, no traffic outside.

Even Gwen's voice seemed to disappear before it reached them. "I know what is supposed to happen next. How am I supposed to live like this?"

Niklas answered with a voice that could have been remorseful. The tone was nearly believable, though it didn't seem to fool Gwen. "Just like you have before. Continue to fight, live on, and when the time is right you…" He let his voice trail off.

Gwen scoffed and shook her head. If it was so difficult for him to say, why would they make her relive it over and over? Did they enjoy it? Anytime she tried to ask the question died in her mouth. This time would be no different. She folded her arms over her chest and leaned back in the chair. Unable to hide her exhaustion, tears finally dropped down her face. "I need to think of my son. Niklas, please, take it away from me."

Atlas was the one to ask, "And put it where?"

She paused. His words shocked her as if he were considering it. She attempted to respond quickly, though the time had already passed for that. "I don't care. Anywhere. Make it anything, anything you want." A single, airy laugh escaped her lips, "It's your world, after all."

Niklas looked at Atlas. They stared at one another, seeming to have a whole silent conversation in a matter of seconds. When he looked at her again, he whispered his only demand, "Promise to keep the children."

Gwen's face was calm, her words almost cold when she responded, "I will do what I can."

They knew they shouldn't have, but they took the answer. Niklas let out his breath and whispered, "Close your eyes."

Gwen obeyed.

When she opened her eyes, she was alone at the table. She looked at the clock, seeing thirty minutes had passed since Liam had left.

She must have been deep in thought and lost track of the time. Her mind had been cleared of the torment she had lived with, and now she had no memory of it. When she thought back to Montana, all she knew was the tragic slaying of her mate and her pack. There was no underlying torment, no altered history.

Nothing.

She gathered herself, wiping the tears from her eyes as she rose from the chair. She left the café without a word to anyone. She reached down to her son, who waited patiently on the sidewalk and led him back to their car. From there, they returned to the hotel room and waited to hear about the decision that would decide their fate.

Present Day...

"Get up, Halius!" Gwen's shrieks echoed through the house as she pounded on his bedroom door. He had locked it once again, preventing her from her usual maneuver of going into his room and literally rolling him off his mattress to wake him up. She tried the knob once more, but it wouldn't turn. She slammed the side of her fist on the door and continued to scream, "Halius! I will break down this door!"

A moment of pause as she pressed her ear to the wood. Hearing shuffling from inside the room before her son's groggy voice. His croaky tone made it clear she had woken him up with her barrage. "I'm coming! For Fate's sake, mother, stop."

He struggled to sit up and let out a groan. Tangled in a mess of his comforter and sheet from a night of tossing and turning. When he was able to free himself from the web, he massed the fabric against the wall his bed was set against and stood on stiff legs.

From his floor, where multiple sets of clothes were scattered, he picked up each item of clothing one at a time. He dressed quickly in clothing that didn't seem too dirty. Nothing smelled, no stains. Clean enough.

Halius was just pulling his buttoned collared shirt over his arms when he heard his mother's piercing voice once again, "Halius Usoro! Get out of bed, *now!*"

Had he been in the same room as his mother, she would have used her command against him. He could nearly hear it in her voice, trying to burst through the door. The command was a power all wolves held over their subordinates. A strange connection that broke the will of the one being subdued and made them almost incapable of disobeying the order. Because he was her son, it would have worked on him even though he was eighteen. The only saving grace was eye contact needed to be held for the command to work.

He sat down on his bed and pulled on his socks. In a moment of poor judgment, Halius snapped back, "I'm getting dressed! Give me a fucking minute!"

Gwen sharply inhaled as Halius opened the door. Stepping out just in time to see her shocked face, she asked, "Was that a *curse* word?"

Halius turned away from her before he rolled his eyes and walked into the kitchen. He could smell the breakfast being cooked and it was too early to deal with his mother.

The house they lived in was small. A three-bedroom, single-story, ranch-style house that sat on the outer edge of the city. The main room of the house was nearly fully open, apart from the u-shaped kitchen that put a wall up between it and the living room. The nearly completely square space was broken up by furniture that was gracefully arranged with a series of sofas and chairs, as well as a large dining room table that was nearly four feet from a kitchen island that held a bar with four stools.

The table was a mess, halfway covered with books and binders of paper that consisted of Halius's homework from school.

Liam sat at that table. He had cleared part of the chaos to allow space for the small family to sit for breakfast. He had agreed to his Alpha's demands to marry Gwen after she had sold her Azure children to a couple who also lived in the territory. Gwen had told Liam how much of a fight Halius had put up when she had found the Omega couple who purchased her three Azure.

That arrangement was nearly ten years ago.

Liam sat in the chair closest to the sliding glass door that led to the patio outside. Sipping a coffee Sydney had placed in front of him minutes earlier. He was reading, as he often did in the morning, news stories off his tablet from the surrounding territories.

Halius gathered up the books and papers, stuffing them into his backpack that was in the chair at the foot of the dining table. He zipped it closed just as Gwen came out from the hall.

She adjusted Halius's shirt as she walked by. When he protested she said, "Sorry, I just don't want my son looking like a deviant." She watched him fidgeting with his bag before she snipped, "Did you just pack your backpack?"

Halius paused, glancing at Liam, whose eyes had shifted up to his wife. When he looked at his mother, he said, "Uh… yes. Why wouldn't I? I have to take this to school, you know."

Gwen let out a huff as she sat at the bar. She threw her hair back over her shoulder as Sydney attempted to give her a cup of coffee. Gwen tapped the countertop with her nail and waved dismissively when Sydney placed the cup on the granite. She began to play on her phone that was up on the counter. Without looking at the Azure, she spoke to the girl in a condescending tone. "Did you not get up on time, Sydney?"

Sydney looked up from the stove. Her schedule was the same each day, and she always got up at the same time. Her morning chores usually consisted of opening the shades in the main room, making the coffee and breakfast, and making sure their shoes and keys were in the same places each morning, no matter where they were thrown the day before. Sydney looked to Liam, whose eyes were heavily fixed on Gwen. "I… I woke up on time, Mistress Gwen. 4:30, as always. I have done my morning chores." She risked a look at Liam.

Gwen's eyes snapped up. Her eyes burned into the eighteen-year-old girl with a contempt the Azure should have been used to after the years she had been married to Liam. "Why did you not pack Halius's backpack? This is a precious time when he could be mentally preparing himself for school. The moon is a waxing gibbous and his training is going to become extensive in the next week."

Halius rolled his eyes again. When he sat at the table, he left a place between himself and Liam. "Mom, I am more than capable of packing my own bag. The only reason I didn't do it last night was because I was trying to slam for a test we have today."

Gwen took a big swig of her coffee. Her lips smacked as she said, "You shouldn't have to be as focused on cleaning up. Isn't that why we have Azure in the first place? They are servants, after all."

Liam dropped his tablet to the table. The loud *thwack* made Gwen jump slightly, though she tried to brush it off quickly as she took another drink. She didn't turn from the bar, unwilling to meet her husband's eyes. He remained silent, his eyes moving to Halius for a moment. The look was unseen by the teenager as he shook his head at his mother.

Halius pulled his phone from his pocket, "They're not supposed to wait on us hand and foot, mother."

Gwen scoffed lightly. She roughly took a plate of food that Sydney had held out to her. But even that made Gwen sneer as she muttered, "You're supposed to serve your Master first. He is the head of this house, after all."

Sydney bit her lip as she moved on. She gently placed the second plate she held in front of Liam. He didn't speak, only giving a short smile and a nod before he held out his tablet for her to take.

Sydney moved quickly, placing the tablet on the bar opposite where Gwen was sitting, and grabbed the two other plates for herself and Halius. Hearing a reflexive "thank you" from Halius when she placed the food in front of him and sat down between him and Liam.

Gwen took her plate from the bar and joined them at the table. She held her tongue about her disdain for Sydney eating with them at the table. An argument she had lost years ago with Liam insisting he preferred Sydney to sit next to him. She smiled at her husband for the first time that morning. "Was there anything noteworthy in the news?"

Liam reached over his plate and tapped the screen on the phone. He sipped his coffee, almost purposefully taking extra time before he spoke. Throughout his actions, he did not return her smile. "Most of the others are reporting about the riots along the Pacific. The stories are dying down, though. Either they've calmed down, or people are tired of talking about it."

The conversation, as it continued, between Gwen and Liam only consisted of a few topics. A few more comments about the news from other territories and how their own Alpha was responding, what Liam was doing for work that day in regard to Enforcer training and routes and infrastructure reviews for the city, and what Gwen would be occupying herself with. Her schedule often varied depending on the needs of the pack.

Liam glanced at Halius; when the conversation died with him and Gwen, he said, "The Alpha and I will be at your school today, Halius." It took a moment, but Halius nodded wordlessly and returned his focus to his food. "How's your training going for the Annual Games?"

The Annual Games was a collection of competitive sports played between all the territories in the state. Each state had its own version, and it was a way for the modern-day Lycans to appease their aggression without outright violence between territories. The rise in popularity of the games ended centuries of territory wars and disputes in the country, both between states and the packs within those states. It was considered a high honor for a young Lycan to be chosen to compete.

Halius only shrugged one shoulder and said lowly, "Fine, I guess."

Gwen took the opportunity to respond, her smile beaming as she boasted, "The Luna and I are going to start working with the Gym classes for the senior students to prepare for the games. She told me yesterday that things are looking quite promising for our students."

Liam smiled for the first time that morning, though it still seemed a bit forced. "Good. Perhaps this year we will win the Relay if you compete, Halius. You're finally old enough."

The Relay was one of six events in the games that would be held in the state capital at the end of November. It was a race that consisted of four participants across varying obstacles. It wasn't the most prestigious event, but it was one that many enjoyed. More seemed to do it for fun than the glory that came with some of the other events.

Halius shrugged once more. He spoke with a mouth full of food as he scraped his fork across his plate, finishing much faster than the rest of them. "Yeah, maybe. I guess it depends on how much training I get. I'd rather do the Gauntlet."

Unlike the Relay, the Gauntlet was a heavy contact game and one with the most prestige. Fighters would compete head-to-head in fights, with the winner advancing through to the next bracket. Four brackets made the Gauntlet, each with its own class of weaponry and rules that needed to be followed. Although some referees and judges kept the fights as fair as possible, they were in no way considered safe.

The games took many lives in the past; those who fell were often remembered in glory.

Gwen waved a passive hand as she said, "Well, don't worry about that. I'll be there to facilitate your training." She watched him step away from the table before she added, "And there is no way you're entering that Gauntlet."

Liam looked at his watch. He tapped Sydney's arm and pointed to the time without speaking.

She nodded, finishing the last couple bites of her food before she stood. She took the plates to the kitchen and said, "It's time for us to go, Halius. Otherwise, you will be late."

Gwen let out an irritated sigh as she leaned back in her chair. "You should have been watching the clock a little closer so you could get those dishes done before you leave. Now my kitchen is going to be nasty by the time we all get home."

Halius scoffed quietly as he threw his backpack over his shoulder and mumbled, "Hard to call something yours when you don't use it."

Gwen gripped her mug so tightly she felt the ceramic begin to crack. All Lycans had a superior hearing, and she was able to pick up his attitude in the quiet of the house. The growl was evident behind her words as her head snapped in his direction, "What did you just say?"

Halius pushed his feet into his pre-tied shoes. A habit that he had picked up because of how quickly it deteriorated the back of his shoes, to the detriment of his style-obsessed mother. He spoke quickly, in a voice that was lighthearted enough to further dig into Gwen's irritation. "Nothing. I agree with you; everything you say is one hundred percent correct all the time."

Gwen's sharp breath burned her nostrils. The house was almost vibrating with tension as she held back her anger. Lashing out at him would only make him late for school. She smirked to herself as she remembered what her day was going to be: leading the training at the school. She closed her eyes and calmed her breath, imagining how she would turn his training into punishment.

Halius pulled his car keys off the hanger. "You ready, Sydney?"

She nodded and finished putting on her own shoes and joined him at the door.

Gwen let out a dramatic sigh when Halius put his hand on the door. "Oh, Halius, did you forget something?"

He glanced at Sydney before subtly rolling his eyes. He saw Sydney hide a smirk by swiping her hand across her mouth in hopes the emotion would go unnoticed. Halius walked back to the table as Liam passed him to meet Sydney at the door. Halius kissed his mother's cheek and quickly said, "Love you, mother." He left her side just as quickly, moving passed Liam and Sydney out the door before he could be stopped again.

Her attention returned to her phone as she said, "That's better. I'll see you later, dear." She tried not to look over to the door at her husband, who was giving the Azure attention. It seemed that Liam was always giving Sydney attention that Gwen deserved better. She knew he was whispering something in the girl's ear, for when their interactions ended, she would nod subtly, and the kids would leave. But not before Liam would take a moment to adjust the ribbons that decorated Sydney's hair.

It was one of the many things that bothered Gwen. How Liam always treated Sydney with some kind of undeserved reverence. He would style her hair each morning with ribbons and bows that Sydney was allowed to choose. She never did as many chores as she was supposed to. The Azure even had her own room in the house and her own cell phone that was nearly as unlocked as Gwen's own phone. Privileges that were practically never awarded to an Azure, even the ones who were treated well.

She tried to focus on enjoying the rest of her coffee without looking into the kitchen. It would be dirty all day because Sydney didn't take the time to clean it before she and Halius left for school. Gwen felt the irritation building in her mind once more. Her wolf stirred uncomfortably in her mind as she tried to push back her frustration.

To the dismay of Halius, Gwen had succumbed to Liam's demand prior to their marriage and sold the three Azure children she had in her possession. Those three Azure would have been perfect for keeping up the house. There was room in the backyard for a shed that would have housed them if Liam was so against having them sleep inside due to the special constraint. They would have been no bother, and he still would have been able to favor Sydney the way he does. Instead, she sold them to an Omega family that lived on the opposite side of the city from them.

Liam remained in the doorway and watched Halius drive away from the house. It almost made him laugh whenever he saw Halius get in the driver's seat. Gwen was adamant against driving himself anywhere and often gave the teenager lectures about how Sydney should drive him so he wouldn't have to worry about something so trivial.

When the car was out of sight, Liam closed the door and returned to his morning routine. He stepped over to the table, where Gwen was getting to her feet, and gave her an emotionless kiss before he headed into his home office to find out what few things he needed to take with him.

He emerged from his office with his satchel over his shoulder. "I'll probably see you at the school tomorrow. I don't know if I'll make it there today."

Gwen nodded, "That's OK. I'll get a start on the kids with the Luna. I'm meeting her at the pack house."

At the mention of the pack house, Liam seemed to flinch. The subtle flex of his cheek that Gwen knew was a sign of disgust. Throughout their marriage, Gwen had asked him several times why he had moved out of the centralized pack house. It was expected that the Prime pack in a territory all live under the same roof, or at least in some kind of proximity. A Prime-Beta, the second in command, was never far from the Alpha.

Liam had never told Gwen why he moved to a house on the outer rim of the city. She had even gone so far as to ask the Alpha why he had moved out. But the Alpha provided little answer himself, leaving Gwen to her own speculations. His words pulled her from her thoughts when he said, "I'm headed out. Have a good day." He kissed her cheek and added, "Love you."

Gwen smiled at him. "I love you too. I'll be heading out in about an hour." She followed him to the door and waved goodbye as he got in his car and drove away.

*****

Halius and Sydney didn't often speak on the drive to school. The ride was smooth and quiet in the four-door Dodge that Liam had bought Halius when he got his license. The only noise was the occasional engine rev and the sound of the low radio music that played in the morning. Halius's drive to school was nearly forty minutes from Liam's house.

Halius often considered trying to have conversations with Sydney. He didn't share his mother's opinions about the Azure, and he hoped that Sydney would know that. He didn't try to treat her poorly, but there was an awkwardness that hung between them like a curtain that kept him from interacting with her.

He gave full blame for that to his mother. He blamed her for selling the three Azure he had been raised with, whose parents were owned by his own father. The three siblings were very close to his age; they might as well have been siblings. When they were sold so Gwen could marry Liam, Halius was crushed. But he was able to see them at school, thank the Fates because the Omega couple who bought them had the intention of treating them like their own children.

Sydney was sitting quietly, not even playing on the phone that was tucked into the pocket of her sweater. She never played on it while away from Liam. Instead, her eyes were out the window, watching the world fly by as Halius drove down the expressway across

36

the upper edges of the city. She could see the skyline of the skyscrapers as Halius took the exit and into the suburbs.

The city itself was quite large. Nearly the entire population in the territory lived in a single city, as close to the center as possible. Skyscrapers separated the businesses and more luxurious housing from the Omega suburbs, which made up the majority of what was called the "Outer Ring." After the ring was a large expanse of farmland and—depending on the territory's economy—manufacturing plants.

Highways and trains connected the territories, with the trains being the preferred mode of transport for those traveling. Between the farms and factories of the territories was a massive expanse of forested land. Kept as natural as possible, with scatters campgrounds and recreational areas for the Lycans to enjoy. There were a few roads that would go out to the wilderness, often to dead ends, for the Lycans to immerse themselves away from the noise of the city. Although, in comparison to some of the neighboring territories, Newaygo was not that loud.

The territory held 50,000 Lycans, and did not count the owned Azure as part of the population. Unlike the Kent territory, the county to the south held a registered population of over 652,000. The Muskegon territory to the west held a registered population of 177,000, a much more realistic number since Muskegon—much like Newaygo—only included Lycans in the population count.

It was always at the discretion of the Alpha on how to best run the territory. No matter how big or small the population, everything focused on the Alphas. The pack houses also resided in the center of the city or as near the center as geographically possible.

Halius glanced out the window of his car as he drove over the final bridge before reaching the school. A large and flat river snaked through the territory and led to the lower edges of the border. Two dams were used to generate power for the city and created lakes that the Lycans loved using for recreation. The city's edge could be found at the first dam up the river, and across the large lake that had been formed over the centuries of the river's blocking was the training camp for the Annual Games.

The training camp was for teenagers who were not yet old enough to compete in the games. They had mock events that gave them a sense of what the sports would look like and provided a safer environment for the young Lycans to determine which event would suit them the best to represent their Alpha. Halius, because he had enraged his mother one weekend, was not allowed to attend the camp for the last couple of years. However, he could still compete in the games if he could pass the entrance test and had permission from the Alpha.

He pulled the car into the parking lot of the school. The massive building was something to behold. The massive structure was divided into four wings: Primary, Elementary, Middle, and High School. The Primary was mostly preschools and daycares for the small Lycans who needed interaction, as was most of the Elementary with a few introductions to language, reading, and math. Most of the core classes weren't introduced until the middle school ages, when the students could focus a little more because sometimes, keeping control of a kindergarten class of Lycans was a lot for the teachers to handle. Each of the schools had multiple floors, with nearly fifty classrooms on each floor.

Halius parked where he always did, in the senior High School section of the parking lot. Other students were arriving in their own vehicles. A little less than half of the students drove themselves, with many finding it easier to take the numerous busses that routed the inner and outer suburbs of the city. The majority of those who did drive were either from the pack house itself or from the outer farms that the busses didn't quite reach.

When he turned off the car, Sydney looked over to him. Her eyes quickly averted when she knew she had his attention, and she asked the question she asked every morning. "Would you like me to stay in the car today?"

Halius sighed. Another common Lycan practice he didn't fully care for or understand. Many of the Lycans who went to school had Azure following them around as attendants. They usually drove the cars, cooked the food, cleaned, and would even take notes for the Lycan in classes. Anything that could be seen as a mundane activity that was beneath a Lycan, the Azure was put to task. Such was their function in the eyes of the Lycans.

Servitude. Nothing more, and never less.

Halius preferred to drive himself; he liked the freedom it gave him. As close to freedom he could feel without running through the woods in his beastly form. His response to her question was also the same as it was each day. The same rehearsed conversation that set the tone of their interactions, "Did Master Liam tell you to wait in the car today?" When she shook he head, he opened his own door and said, "Then let's get inside."

Sydney caught up with him quickly. Hearing the car behind her lock as Halius hit the button on his remote key. She carried a bag of her own that held school notes Liam required her to write down. He would often tell Halius it was to supplement his notes in case he missed something in class—which he did more often than he admitted—but part of Sydney always knew it was because Liam wanted her to learn at the school as well.

It was a subtle way of her getting an education that was normally not afforded to the Azure. They were trained to scribe the information and sometimes parrot it back if a Lycan asked about it. Once a class was over or a test had been taken, they normally didn't have the chance to study deeper into any topic.

Before they got to the door, a small cluster of boys hooted at them as he approached. Three of them were waiting for him. One of them was the Alpha-Prime's son, Maddox Neway, and the other two were Omega-Primes, Elliot and Ezra Galloway. When Liam had adopted Halius as a Beta-Prime, he was introduced to them in hopes of joining the young pack that had just begun to piece itself together. Their ranks were defined by their parents but could be in flux depending on if or when they found their True Mates. However, rank-switching was quite rare.

They quickly became friends and were not always the greatest influence on one another. Focusing on pranking people within the school and trying to pass their classes with minimal effort.

Halius was greeted by a chorus of cheerful colloquial greetings from the three of his brothers and his usual one-armed bro-hug from Maddox. "What's up, guys? How was the weekend?"

Elliot was the one who answered. He was older by a year, although he was in the same grade as the rest of them. Save for Ezra, who was a junior that year, while the rest of them were seniors. Elliot had been held back a year, to not advance faster than his Alpha. "We made it to level four on the new Halo. You should have been there, man!"

Traditionally, the Alpha would be the oldest member of his pack. Rank was established at every possible moment the Lycans had. When Elliot was born, the Alpha of the territory had full rights to kill him because his own baby had not been born. It caused quite a controversy when the Alpha allowed the baby to live.

Halius sighed as he watched his packmates high-five each other while Maddox and Ezra agreed with Elliot. "I know, I wanted to, but… you know… my mom."

A ruckus laugh sounded from Maddox and Ezra as the former smacked his palm against Halius's shoulder. "That's right, mamma's boy." His voice raised to a mocking baby pitch as he said, "Still need her to tuck you in at night?"

Ezra spoke between his laughs, "Yeah… can't sleep without… without you're… the lullabies from her?"

Elliot was hesitant, but he was chuckling as he added, "Does she lay out your clothes too?"

While they took turns high-fiving one another again, Halius gripped the strap of his backpack. He closed his eyes for a moment and took a long, deep breath to keep himself calm. He threw a glance over his shoulder to where Sydney was standing. She was trying to keep her eyes down but managed to slip him a concerned look.

He saw something glint in the light coloring of her eyes. A look, subtle, nearly imperceptible that reminded him of something. With a grin, he turned back to his friends. "She's going to be here today, you know." His smile widened, shimmering his eyes as their laughter quickly died. His packmates were freezing in place as their eyes locked on him. "She and Luna Erika are starting our training today for the games."

Slowly, the other three exchanged worried looks, their jaws opening and closing as they tried to speak but couldn't.

Halius walked past them and returned the hit to Maddox's shoulder. "Don't worry, I'll make sure she isn't too mean. I am her baby, after all." He pulled open the door without looking behind him, "Come on, Sydney."

She quickly followed him inside without looking up at the others.

For the students in the school, the schedule was divided into two structures. Everyone's hours at school were 8 am to 4 pm, with a half-hour lunch for everyone from 11:45 to 12:15. The day was evenly split between regular school classes and half a day of gym classes.

Halius and the rest of his pack all had the same schedule. By design, of course. With their book classes—as the rowdy kids called them—in the first half of the day and their gym class, or "Rec Class," being after lunch.

He headed to his locker, throwing in some of the books that he wouldn't need for his first two classes. He held the sack out to Sydney, "Can you hold this for me for a second?" Without responding, she took the bag and held it open so he could use both of his hands to sort and organize the papers.

Sydney took a moment to look around as the hall filled with students. Many of them, probably a little more than half, had Azure accompanying them. It was very common for Lycans to send their children to school with an Azure servant. Most of the time, they were older women, ones who had served a family for a while and would assist the kids with homework and tests during classes.

Some considered it cheating, with parental controls set in place on how often their kids could use Azure during class. There were a few sets of kids who were not allowed to use their Azure at all during class, while others were allowed to have their Azure take the tests for them. It didn't fully matter how the children got good grades. Most of them remembered the material when they were asked outside of the pressure of class, school was more used to teach the Lycans structure and scheduling to better prepare them for adulthood.

What Sydney often noticed the most was how the other Azure were treated. Some were told to remain in the car during class, especially if the kids couldn't use them during class. Others had to carry all the heavy books and bags, even for multiple children. They were yelled at, struck, and even humiliated to varying degrees. Anything the Masters wanted, the Azure had to do.

She was never treated as poorly as they were.

Halius never struck her. He never yelled at her for any reason. Sydney didn't know if it was because Liam had told Halius never to treat her that way or if it was just Halius's nature. She, of course, had to follow every order Liam gave to her. But others knew that she was not their property, although she did have a list of things she could do for Halius. Taking notes, helping with tests, and carrying his bags. Not much else.

The warning bell sounded, and they headed to class. He had taken back his bag before they headed down the long and crowded hallways. As they walked, she could hear the ridicule while they walked by. Other Lycans spoke their disgust that Halius had to carry his own bag while a perfectly capable Azure followed him. That part didn't bother her as much, what did get under her skin was the dirty looks from the other Azure. She knew they resented her for how she was treated.

Occasionally, Halius would overhear one of the other Lycans and would respond with equal amounts of hostility, "She's not for that. I can carry my own bag."

Sydney would try not to think too deeply about what Halius meant by that. Did he know what she was for? It certainly allowed the imagination of his classmates to run wild when he didn't elaborate. Perhaps that wasn't always a good thing.

Halius took his seat in class. Sitting closest to the window in the middle row of the room. Often, he would look out the window into the trees that lined the back of the school grounds. A small set of woods divided the school from the river down a slight embankment. Ecology and Biology classes would use those woods, as well as the river and its inlets around the school, for some of the classes with weather permitting.

That semester, he didn't have any of those classes. He let out a regretful sigh, preferring the classes that allowed him outside.

Sydney wasn't sure if she felt the same way because it made Halius happy or because she also loved the outdoors. She had more autonomy when the classes moved to the outside. Being able to walk around and interact with the other Azure so long as they were not disruptive and away from the class. While inside, they had to remain quiet. The Azure were required to sit against the back wall and wait until they were called upon by their owners. Large cushions were provided, although it was often thought the comfort was to keep them from shifting around and distracting the children who were trying to learn.

The class they sat in was very standard. The English teacher wrote on the board as he gave the lecture. With the teenagers taking notes and answering a few questions the teacher would ask. During the last twenty minutes, the teacher allowed some free time to try and get the assignment done before the class was over. A simple set of ten questions and ten sentences to write out.

Sydney was quiet for the entire class. She took notes and absent-mindedly rolled her bracelets across her wrists while she watched the floor. Halius had no problem in English. He didn't need her in that class. She would look up for only a moment when she saw movement from the corner of her eye. Another Azure is being called up to the desk of their Master.

They were both thankful when that class ended and had ten minutes to cross the crowded halls to the next one. Sydney remained close behind Halius and had to make an extra effort not to bump into anyone lest she be shouted at by a Lycan who did not appreciate being touched by an Azure. Thankfully, because of Halius's large frame and high rank, he plowed a path through the crowd that she was able to stay in.

The next two classes were history and math. Though it always seemed like a mystery because his grades in science classes were generally good, in math, he could scramble for a D- at best. History didn't fair Halius any better, and it was the subject he had to crash-study the night before and left the table a mess for. It was three weeks into school, his first test was that day and Halius felt that he couldn't retain any of the information.

It was always the simplest things he couldn't hold onto. The history was something he knew. His mother had yelled at him about it nearly his entire life. The current study of the class was how the Lycan civilizations came to the Americas in the early centuries after the European Azure had lost their wars to the superior Lycan masters.

The Lycans had used the Azure they recently found a way to enslave to cross the vast ocean waters to new lands. A Spanish Alpha had a vision from the All-Immortal Fates to send ships across the seas and discover all the world had to offer.

When the ships had left the shore, there were 10 Alphas that served the Spanish and European Prime Alphas. They were Sub-Alphas with their own smaller packs, creating the layers of the first forms of government that would eventually overtake the world. The ships reached the new land, and the packs found the Azure, who had settled there. The original tribes had never met Lycans before and did not know how to push them back to the horizon where they had come.

Wars and battles broke out over land and freedom rights, with superior technology behind the slavery bracelets and the Lycan's ability to take the form of beasts at a moment's notice. Any fight the Azure had was not long-lasting. Reinforcements arrived from the European and African territories when word had spread about the abundant resources and powerful Azure bloodlines, creating a system of trade that made the Americas exceedingly wealthy. The descendants of the ten original Alpha sailors constructed the government that became the Highborn Court—the ruling body of the country—and the states of America the country knew as modern day. Their surviving crew members once spread out, made the fifty Nexus families that commanded each state. Within those states, the smaller counties formed, and it became the current day system of government.

Halius rubbed his temples as he sat in his chair, staring down at the paper. He knew the answers. He had the answers in his head, but his hand would not cooperate to write them down. The questions were even phrased to be nearly the same as the teacher's lectures. He could hear the old Lycan woman ranting at them about the importance of knowing their history. It was the same speech his mother constantly gave him about his education.

He looked up at the clock, feeling the color draining from his face when he saw there were only thirty minutes left in class. He felt his chest tighten. Thirty minutes? How had he already lost a half hour? He looked back down to his paper. He had managed to answer one question, but there were fifteen on the test!

He felt sweat forming on his brow as he glanced around. He had always tried to do his classes on his own. Using the Azure, to him at least, somehow diminished the progress Lycans were always taking credit for. Half of the students who had perfect grades had them because their Azure did the classwork for them. How smart were they really? He looked towards the clock again.

Fifteen minutes.

If he could have shouted a curse, he would have. If he brought home another F on his report, Gwen would surely kill him. He couldn't use his notes on the test, but there was something he could use...

Sydney had been looking out the window. She didn't sit as close to it as in some of the other classes. The large cushions were somewhat first-come-first-serve, so long as she was in sight of her Master to respond in case he needed help. She saw the teacher sitting at her desk; her nose stuffed into a history book as if it were the most interesting thing she had discovered, even though she had taught the subject probably a hundred times already.

The class was so quiet she could hear a pen drop.

And she did.

The noise snapped her to attention, coming from Halius's row. She saw him glance over his shoulder and point to the floor next to his desk as he dropped his head into his hand.

She understood the signal. Halius needed help, which wasn't rare in History class, but it was rare for him to ask. Thankfully, she wasn't far from him because that specific teacher did not allow Azure to walk the aisles of desks while the class was in session. Instead, she had to crawl.

Sydney picked up the pen that had landed on the floor. He was rubbing his eyes with his palms. Her voice was such a whisper she barely heard herself, "Halius." She tried a few times to get him to look at her. He either wasn't listening or was too frustrated to care. Against her better judgment, she touched his leg and said a bit aggressively, "Halius!"

He jumped when she did that and quickly looked around to see if anyone noticed. No one had. He whispered back to her to keep the volume in the room low. "Sydney, I don't know what to do about this test!"

She leaned up to look at the paper, "What question is bothering—" She gasped when she saw the nearly blank page. "You've answered one question? There's only ten minutes left!"

Halius leaned down, his teeth clenched. A growl lowly echoed his words as the yellow coloring threatened to shift his deep green eyes, "You think I don't know that? I can't get another F, Sydney! Just do *something*!"

She repressed her irritation and snatched the paper off the desk. She put the paper on the floor in front of her and took the pen from his hand. She frantically answered as many questions as possible.

Halius chewed on his nail as he watched her scribble across the test. He kept glancing at the clock, seeing the time tick down to the end of class. The *tink* noises of her bracelets hitting the tile floor were not helping his anxieties. He felt his chest tightening again, his heartbeat thrumming in his ears. He looked down at her, his words hissing through his teeth, "Hurry up!"

She didn't look up at him, continuing to write as she said, "I'm trying. I can only write so fast."

With nearly two minutes to spare, she placed the test back on his desk. "There. I don't know if it's right, but it's done. Try to relax." She crawled back to her place by the wall, having only enough time to collect herself before the bell rang, signaling the end of class.

The teacher's high-pitched voice echoed around the room as the students began to gather their bags, "Leave your tests where they are. I will collect them when you all leave. Grades will be posted at the end of the day."

Halius felt his breath returning to normal as they headed for his third class. Thankfully, he did not have a test in Math class. The lesson seemed easy enough, and he didn't need Sydney's help with the questions. However, he hadn't gotten them all done before the class ended.

During the last half of the class, all Azure, who served the students, were excused to go to the lunchroom. They were to use that half-hour to prep the cafeteria for their masters and set out the lunches for the Lycans.

The Azure would take the trays from those working in the kitchen and place them at the tables where their masters would sit. Rarely did the teenagers deviate from their normal tables, making it easy to lay out the food they preferred. They worked together to make it as efficient as possible. They were able to get the entire cafeteria set up in less than the time provided. Sydney worked with two other

Azure to place the trays at the table where Halius and his packmates would sit.

The first was Roderick. His sole responsibility in the pack house was to take care of the Alpha's son, Maddox. He had been responsible for his care since the prince of the territory was born; with Roderick himself being in his late thirties years old, he was assigned the sacred task when he was only nineteen.

The second Azure was a boy named Julien. He and his two siblings had been the Azure owned by Gwen, who were sold so she could secure her spot as the Prime-Beta's wife. Julien served the two prime omegas, Elliot and Ezra. He did not live with them in the pack house, instead living with the childless Omegas who had purchased him from Gwen. The Omegas who owned Julien and his siblings were quick to remind them of what they were but allowed them to go to the school and help serve those who may otherwise not have Azure help.

A way to mockingly "send the kids to school."

Elliot and Ezra only had one Azure between the two of them, which allowed Julien to have a place with them; due to the fact that he was closer to Ezra's age, the Lycan's parents had agreed for Julien to be his school attendant.

Julien's twin sister, Lyra, worked in the primary school wing. She had little to no education, unlike those who attended the higher education wing, like the middle and high schools. There were many Azure who couldn't write or read passed a third-grade level. Some Lycans believed it was better that way to discourage their Azure from having distractions from their lives of servitude. Lyra didn't need to learn how to read and write; all she was there for was to make sure the Lycan children were well-kept while in school. However, she did know how to help with some of their more basic assignments.

While they set the tables, the Azure was known to chat about events based on their master's lives.

Roderick approached the table with the final two trays. "Is everyone looking forward to the Annual Games? The training is supposed to begin this week."

Sydney shrugged one shoulder as she placed the cutlery around the trays. "Halius was very upset about missing boot camp again. Mistress Gwen didn't let him go this year either." She glanced around before she motioned for Julien and Roderick to lean in. She whispered with an amused tone, "He called her a *Gutter Hound.*"

Both Sydney and Julien suppressed snickers. Julien pressed his hand over his mouth to try and keep the shocked laughter down. He leaned onto his hand and asked, "Why would he do that? I remember Gwen; I'm surprised he's still alive."

Sydney nodded. "I know." She turned to the cart from where they got their table supplies. She picked up a water pitcher and filled the cups as Roderick placed them on the table. "I think he only survived because Master Liam thought it was funny."

Roderick clicked his tongue. He shook his head in disappointment. "Such insults are never funny." He didn't look up from the table but knew the expressions of the others. There were so many times when he took the humor out of situations they were in. Unlike some of the other Azure, who dropped their submissive servitude masks when Lycans were not around, Roderick always held the Lycans in high regard. He was proper in everything he did and served Maddox completely and without question. "As a Lycan, Halius needs to learn to appreciate the honor in his life. A Prime-Beta, no less. Such language is beneath him. Although admonishment is never due to a superior, Beta Liam should have known to chastise him for the remark."

Sydney sighed as she placed the empty pitcher on the cart. She knew she was privileged in how she was able to live her life, but she couldn't help but wonder how Roderick was treated to have such devotion towards the Alpha family. Did they treat him as well as he respected them? Or was he beaten into submission, as so many of them were?

The last thing that was brought into the main room of the cafeteria was brought in by the Azure, who had been working in the kitchen. They pushed one cart each that held two types of food. Small cups that held three ounces of meat, which varied but was usually cubed chicken, and small cups that held the same weight in random assortments of fruit. Usually, apples or grapes. Rarely some would find orange slices or berries, but it was extremely rare.

The Azure, who were allowed to eat, took one of each off the carts and ate them quickly before the Lycans got into the cafeteria. They would normally have five minutes after getting the tables set to eat themselves. The Azure had learned to rush their own meager lunches, for anyone who was still chewing when their masters entered the cafeteria would normally be struck. The food would be forcibly removed from their mouths, and the Azure would be harshly scolded for their disrespect.

The Lycans began to file into the cafeteria minutes after the bell had rung. The crowd of them finding their tables, with an ocean of chatty voices and clinking silverware, soon flooding the large, open room.

The four boys found their table. Closer to the back of the cafeteria, in an alcove that almost felt like its own hallway. With two sets of doors that were perpetually locked, both sets leading unadventurously to the corridor that would take someone to the Primary-Grade section of the school. There were only two tables in that part of the cafeteria, away from the main doors and all the windows, making it a less-than-desirable place to sit for lunch.

Sitting in the less-populated side of the cafeteria never bothered the young pack. It gave them the opportunity to have conversations and behave in a manner that would be considered "unconventional." There were times when they would offer Julien and Sydney to sit down with them. The offer was extended to Roderick also, but he always refused claiming it wouldn't be proper for him to sit with them.

He often looked at Julien and Sydney with disapproving eyes, but his concerns always fell on deaf ears.

The strange part was how opposite it seemed to be. Maddox was supposed to be front and center in the school. Not sitting in the corner in what would be considered "the reject table." He was supposed to be interacting with everyone as the next leader of the territory.

However, years prior, when the young pack was in middle school, he was swarmed by students who were trying to do just that. Halius had just moved to the territory, and working him into their pack gave Maddox such stress that it forced one of his earliest and most traumatic wolfen shifts. The stress behind his transformation triggered other students around him due to their growing connection and uncontrollable emotions. Young Lycans were incredibly difficult to control once shifted. The destruction to the school took years to repair and nearly forced Alpha Alex to announce to the students that his son was to be left alone unless he approached one of them directly.

Because the order came from their Alpha, there was no questioning. Rumors may have floated around the students and staff, as well as the other families throughout the territory and possibly the surrounding territories, but the Alpha's word was law. No one approached or bothered Maddox, and he was free to be a normal Lycan teenager.

They were about ten minutes into lunch, with the boys eating and chatting about the events they wanted to train for in the Annual Games. Maddox was speaking as he chewed, "When I went to the boot camp, Dad made me train for the Gauntlet. I think the Relay sounds like more fun."

Halius scoffed. Almost spitting his food back onto his tray. "Seriously? Who *picks* the Relay?"

Ezra shrugged a shoulder, "I mean… I would pick the Relay."

Maddox nodded as he motioned towards Ezra in agreement. He took a few moments to finish chewing what he had just stuffed into his mouth, swallowing a large bite before he said, "See, people like to do more than just hit each other, Halius. It's not that weird. We all go out for runs at least a few times a week. Especially here in the next two weeks because the moon is going to be full." He took a few more bites and said through the side of his mouth, "Besides, there's more to it than just running."

Halius sneered. "Not a fan of swimming either."

Elliot chuckled, "Why? Afraid of the water?"

Ezra added his own laughter and hugged his shoulders dramatically, "Oh no! There are snakes in the water!"

As the three others continued laughing, Halius shook his head again. "No—hey, shut the fuck up!" He continued as their laughter began to quiet down, "It's because the Gauntlet has more prestige. I don't know… it seems… higher caliber, I suppose." He chugged nearly half of his water before he added, "Why wouldn't you want to duke it out with someone in the Gauntlet?"

Maddox tapped his fork on his tray, "Maybe I don't think it's fun to get punched in the face. There's rock climbing, too, in the Relay." He glanced towards the Azure. The three of them had been silent, standing practically shoulder-to-shoulder as they waited at attention. "What do you think, Roderick? Think I can scale the wall in the Relay?"

Roderick flashed a smile. "You would do wonderfully in any event, Master. I have no doubt that whatever you are selected for, you will most certainly win."

Maddox laughed, his palm hitting the table as he said, "See? Suck it, boys."

Halius and Elliot exchanged a glance. The latter merely let the matter drop and turned back to his food while Halius muttered, "Kiss-ass." Before he began chewing on another forkful of food.

Silence overtook the rowdy bunch. With Halius being the one to break the silence, "I don't think my mom wants me to do it at all. I really want to be selected for the Gauntlet." He looked up to Sydney. "Think I can convince her to let me do the Gauntlet?"

Sydney opened her mouth but found herself too nervous to speak. She shifted on her feet and pressed her lips together. She could feel Roderick's sideways glance in her direction as if he knew how she was about to speak.

Maddox let his curiosity get the better of him and said, "Come on, Sydney. You are free to speak your mind here."

Sydney knew he hadn't moved; he would never move unless he were told he could. But it felt like Roderick was leaning down towards her. His eyes dug into her temple as he no doubt glared at her from where he stood. She knew the answer he was trying to press without speaking. Something full of praise and admiration, something encouraging that would boost the ego of her Master. Instead, the edge of her mouth pulled against a smile, and she said, "I think you have a higher chance of convincing her to hit Master Liam with a car."

The laughter that sounded off from the table made her smile grow. Ezra was theatrically hitting the table as he tried to compose himself. The others laughed so hard their faces reddened, Elliot nearly choking as he had just taken a swig of water. Halius had to slap his back several times before he could breathe properly.

It took a moment for them to realize Julien had not been laughing. He hadn't spoken the entire time. His eyes were on the floor, slightly tipped to the left as he was lost in thoughts.

Halius tapped Ezra's arm, motioning towards the Azure, which prompted Ezra to speak, "Julien, you don't think it's funny? You can laugh; I mean, we all know why Roderick isn't laughing."

That part was true; Roderick was not laughing. He considered nothing humorous about violent acts towards Lycans. He always believed that they should be grateful for their lives in servitude to the Lycans. They could have all just as easily been killed at birth.

Julien didn't respond right away. He didn't even look up until Sydney bumped him gently with her elbow. His head shot up, and he said, "What? Sorry, do you need something?"

Halius's brow turned down. The humor gone from his voice as he said, "Yeah, man, what's wrong with you? Sydney just dropped probably the only joke we'll ever hear in her whole life. You didn't react at all."

Sydney piped up without thinking, "Hey, I'm funny!"

Maddox shook his head. He let out a mocking laugh and took a drink of his own water. "No, girl, you're not." All four teenagers looked at Julien. Maddox realized he might not speak unless he was ordered to. "Speak, Julien. Tell us what's happening in that head of yours."

Julien took a deep breath. His gaze returned to the floor to hide the tears that were threatening the edge of his eyes. "You remember Malachi?"

Everyone at the table agreed. Malachi was the eldest brother of Julien and Lyra. He and Halius had been so close when they were younger due to how his father had treated the Azure he owned. They had been raised as brothers until his old Alpha attempted to flee the territory they had lived in. Halius tried not to think of that day, hearing the screams echo in the distance of his memory. Nothing about that day was clear, and he dared not ask his mother about details.

Julien took another few moments before he continued, "He turns twenty tomorrow. That's why he's not here today."

The silence that followed was thick in the air. The echoes from the other tables also seemed to die out around the group as their expressions fell. Maddox nodded once he looked at Halius for a moment before he looked back down to his tray. "I'm sorry to hear that."

Julien nodded as a thank you. Ezra and Elliot shared Maddox's sentiment and expressed it in nearly the same fashion. The Omega couple who purchased them from Gwen were known to buy Azure children of all ages for them to raise, as they were not able to have children on their own. Twenty years old was the minimum age that an Azure could be sold to work in factories and warehouses. Generally, to manufacturing work in another county. The work was long and grueling, with the factories always purchasing more Azure for their turnover rate. Although few Lycans ever wanted to speak of why they were always needing the help. The reasoning was clear: Azure went to those factories. Never did they leave.

The mood turned further down as the silence went on. No one would take the news harder than Halius. Maddox leaned his arm onto the table, "Hey, it's not like you'll never see him again. Just get the name of the factory he is going to. They're allowed visitors."

Halius's fists clenched. He threw his fork down onto the tray. His mind raced with a tumultuous wave of emotions. Rage at the couple who purchased Malachi, guilt for not fighting harder to keep them, and convincing Gwen to try and live somewhere else. It felt like he was losing his friend all over again. He knew what the insides of those factories looked like, no matter the industry. They were horrifying places where people went to die.

Without a word, he stood from the table. His motion threw his chair out behind him. It clattered against the floor, nearly drowning the sound of him snapping his fingers for Sydney to follow him.

She hesitated for a moment, but Roderick whispered to her, "I'll take care of the tray." She nodded once and darted after Halius.

He headed outside, not bothering to go back to his locker for the homework he might have needed for his other classes. After lunch, his pack, as well as half of the rest of the high school, would travel outside to the fields where they had their Rec Classes. They were across the property, far enough that Halius would normally drive himself and Sydney to the field. Many did that, as they would be so exhausted after training to walk back to the parking lot to get their cars. It also made it easier to go straight home afterward.

On that day, he kept walking. His strides were long and heavy, causing Sydney to have a difficult time catching him. "Halius!" She called to him as she hurried along, "Halius, can you wait for me, please?"

His pace slowed, but he didn't turn to look at her. He continued down the cracked sidewalk over the drop of the small hill that crossed the road. He could see the field, set up for a few different sports. It was divided into a football field circled by a track. A large baseball diamond and soccer field were used by all levels of the school. A second track behind the football bleachers was set for more of an obstacle course, with bars, log runs, and swing ropes that spanned a mud pit, a net parallel to the ground that they either had to navigate overtop of or under, depending on what they were ordered. And a slanted wooden wall to scale that dropped with a repelling rope on the other side.

Each area was separated by a four-foot chain-link fence and had its own sets of bleachers of varying sizes depending on how in demand the sports were. The school had several teams who would compete in seasons against the other counties. The games were just attempts to boast in preparation for the Annual Games.

Halius stopped at the top of the hill after they had crossed the empty road. He could begin to make out figures on the field; his mother was already there. A clipboard in her hand, while she grasped her wrist with the other and spoke to Luna Erika, the wife of the Prime-Alpha.

Sydney was finally able to catch him. She didn't try speaking, seeing where his gaze traveled. She didn't try to encourage him to speak, as much of their time was already spent in silence. He always seemed to only want to talk to her if there was someone else there with them who would carry the conversation.

She continuously wondered if it was something Maddox prompted him to do. Maddox had what appeared to be a good relationship with Roderick. It was expected that he, as Alpha, would want his pack to treat the Azure with the same behavior he used towards his servants.

When Halius did look at her, it seemed like he wanted to speak. She could see the turmoil in his eyes, his lips parting slightly as he let out a sigh. He did need to talk to someone, before his anger got the best of him. But he simply shook his head and continued down the hill.

His silence remained when he dropped his backpack on the bleachers and when his mother greeted him with a hug that he was forced to return. And when Luna Erika gave a colloquial "Good Afternoon," as she did with all the students who came across her path. Halius refused to make eye contact with his mother and sat on the bottom bench, away from where the women were waiting, while he waited for the rest of his pack to arrive.

Gwen took notice of his behavior. Her cheeks reddened when she had tried to talk to him again, but still received no response. Her eyes snapped to Sydney, who was getting ready to take her place sitting on the ground between the bleachers and the fence. "What did you do to my son to put him in this sour mood?"

Sydney hadn't yet sat on the ground, as she and the other Azure were made to during the training sessions. She shook her head and stepped back when Gwen advanced on her. She knew Liam had expressly forbidden Gwen from ever striking her, but would that stop her if he were not there and Gwen's anger got the better of her? She opened her mouth as if to respond, but before she could, the Lycan woman was screaming again.

"How *dare* you sully his mood with your deplorable presence!" The coloring of Gwen's eyes began to tint, the poisonous yellow pushing through the deep amber of her eyes. "Perhaps you should go sit in the car where you won't be such a nuisance!"

Sydney's jaw quivered as her back pressed against the chain link fence. Gwen wasn't much taller than her, but the ferocity in the woman was frightening. Her voice was small when she stammered, "M-M-Master Liam says I must stay by Halius… in… in… in case he needs something. I-I-I'm supposed to k-k-keep track of his studies."

Gwen leaned over Sydney as she shrank against the fence. Her face inches from the Azure's, the heat of her breath caused Sydney's cheeks to redden as she growled, "He doesn't need *your* help for his training. He has *me*." She couldn't deny her thrill in watching the young Azure cower. The way Sydney followed Halius around the school made Gwen think of how Liam spent an abundant amount of time with her.

They didn't need such a sorry excuse for an Azure. Liam needed a strong Lycan wife, and Halius needed a strong mother. She was both of those things and was not about to let some Azure trash take it from her.

Halius looked up when he finished switching out his shoes to his cross-trainers and saw the confrontation. His wolf growled, tightening his chest and rumbling his head with the thunderous sound. He stood from the bleachers, his anger fuming to the point where he almost tore off his shirt as he unbuttoned it, leaving him in just his A-shirt he wore to keep sweat off his body.

Usually, it wasn't wise for Lycans to dress in layers, and it wasn't something they even preferred. Generally, the young were discouraged from it because of their lack of emotional control. Unpredicted shifts would shred clothing and would enrage a young Lycan's parents once all their child's clothes were destroyed. Halius preferred his collared, short-sleeved shirts. He liked to look dressy, and they were easy enough to remove because of the buttoned-down fronts.

More students were arriving by the minute, but of course no one paid any mind to the situation between Gwen and Sydney. There would never be a time where a Lycan stepped up to protect an Azure, nor would any Azure dare risk a confrontation with a Lycan about the treatment of one of their own.

Halius finally broke his silence and pulled his mother back by her shoulder as he barked at his mother, "Will you give it a fucking rest, mother?" Through her glare, as the yellow took over her irises, he held his ground. He could feel the pressure of her command to back down, pushing on his mind. "Not everything in this Fate-forsaken county is Sydney's fault!"

Gwen's anger flared as she gave Halius a withering look. She yanked on his arm, shoving him out towards the track as she shrieked, "I've had enough of your attitude! Get running!"

Halius stumbled when she shoved him. Although he was taller than her, standing at a reasonable height of 5'9" and being much wider than her with his thick muscular build, she had strength behind her due to her rank. He longed for the day when his pack would mature, and he could finally step out of her influence.

He flinched when Gwen blew a whistle, and several others with him started running without needing to be told to do so.

Sydney steadied her breathing as she sat on the ground, her back against the fence; she took a minute and closed her eyes. How close had Gwen been to losing her control? Thankfully, Halius had stopped her. She would have to find a way to thank him later. She ran her hands through her hair, swiping one of her thumbs under her eyes before she pulled Halius's backpack closer to her and started going through his assignments.

It felt like an eternity when the rest of Halius's pack arrived. Erika and Gwen had been assigning the students, along with the typical gym class teachers, to areas of practice that they would rotate through each hour.

Erika smiled at her son, "Afternoon boys. Are you ready for some training?"

Elliot and Ezra returned her smile, with the eldest speaking, "Yes, ma'am."

Unfortunately, Gwen's mood had not improved. Even in Erika's presence, she spoke with a bit more hostility than she intended. "If you were ready, the three of you would have been on time!" She shoved both Elliot and Ezra respectively onto the track and screamed, "Get going!" Although she didn't touch the young Alpha, she tilted her head towards the track and attempted to order, "You too. Get running; you've lost too much time already."

Maddox heard the change in her voice when she addressed him. Her tone was softer than when she had screamed at Elliot and Ezra. It made him wonder if she was even capable of yelling at him. Something he thought the same of his mother, and the only person who could reprimand him was his father, the Prime-Alpha. Was that because he wasn't that bad of a kid or because he was further coming into his rank? Those who would be beneath him wouldn't be able to challenge him too easily.

Tensions seemed to be high enough, so he didn't fight the words of the Prime-Beta. He knew he was supposed to respect her anyway because of her marriage to Liam. While his father was still the Alpha, that meant something. But Maddox sometimes wished for the day when he would be able to overtake his father and assume control of the territory.

It was a conversation Maddox had several times with his father. When he was ready and had found his true mate, he and his father would engage in a ritualistic duel to decide if he was ready to assume control over a territory. It would be a fight that would take place both in and out of their wolfen forms. Centuries ago, the duel would be to the death. In the modern day, the fight would end in a yield from either party. Allowing the former Alpha to still consult with the new leader of the territory, and essentially "retire" the pack into a calm life until the end of their days.

Maddox touched two of his fingers to his temple in a jaunty salute before he started jogging in the mass of kids. He was half a lap behind Halius and nearly a third behind Elliot and Ezra. He would have to sprint for at least a quarter mile to catch up to his friend if he wanted to talk to him.

What should have taken half a lap took two full laps. By the time Maddox had reached Halius he was losing his breath. Sweat caked both of the teenagers, and Maddox had to gasp to try and speak, "Hey… man. You wanna… turn… your speed… down a notch?"

Halius didn't reply. His efforts to run off his anger were not working, either because he was too far into his rage or because each time he made a lap, he heard his mother's voice squawking at him and the other students.

At the end of the next lap, Maddox's chest was burning. He had sprinted nearly two miles and came to a stop near their start point. He moved to the grass, off the track, to not be in the way of the other runners, and leaned onto his knees as he watched Halius continue to run. Blessed Fates, how was he still running?

No sooner did he stop than he heard a whistle blow. His mother and Gwen were both sauntering over as his mother shouted, "Tired of running? How about some pushups, then?" She grabbed the stopwatch that hung at her chest and clicked a button. "It took you almost seven minutes to run that half-mile. Shame."

Maddox sniffed as he tried to catch his breath. He wiped the sweat from his forehead and stood straight, wobbling slightly as he continued to gasp for air. "I… it's… I'm not great at sprinting."

Erika rolled her eyes and mumbled, "It's as if I paid for that bootcamp for nothing." She pointed down to the grass and ordered, "Twenty. Right now."

Maddox groaned, "Mom, come on, I just need five minutes."

Erika shrugged one shoulder. "Fine, I'll count to twenty, and you can give me forty."

Maddox wanted to argue further, but he knew it would only lead to her raising the number. He dropped onto his hands against the grass and began his pushups.

As he struggled to complete the pushups, he realized his mother was correct. He shouldn't be *that* tired. They ran and exercised all the time. In their human form, they regularly used the gym built into the basement of the Alpha's pack house, and in their beastly forms, they would run at full speeds for hours on end throughout the early evenings through forests and fields.

When Erika was satisfied and allowed him to rest, he remained on his hands and knees and looked up to the track.

Halius was still running. Had his speed even changed? Around him, the crowd of other Lycans trotted along at their own paces; some were trying to beat their personal records, while others were just happy to be doing something outside. Ezra and Elliot were beginning to fall to the back of the crowd, clearly losing their energy also.

Ezra stopped as well. He fell onto his back on the grass not far from where Maddox was still trying to recover. His eyes squeezed closed in the glaring sun. But much like his young Alpha, he didn't have much rest time either.

A whistle blew, and a shrill voice shrieked at him, "Ezra Galloway! Get your ass up!"

When a shadow passed over him, he was able to open the slits of his eyes. Just enough to see Gwen's silhouetted form hovering above him. She could have been a blessed spirit sent by the Fates to guide him from his suffering into the peace of the next life.

Instead, what he got was a haggish demon that those same Fates would have forsaken into the void for sins committed during life. Her words pierced through the air as she folded her arms over her clipboard. "What is wrong with you guys today? Barely a mile in and already tired? Look at Halius, he is running fine."

Ezra breathed a few more times before speaking, "I'm sorry… Beta… but I… feel like my… energy is… being sucked out of me."

Gwen leaned onto her knees. Her tone was a condescending trill that accentuated a false, high-pitched, mid-Atlantean accent. "Well, if you want to spend time on the ground, how about some crunches?"

Ezra groaned as he interlocked his fingers behind his head. He had to force himself to breathe deeply as he started the sit-ups. His chest burned immediately, with the muscles in his stomach starting to feel like a cramp. "Great Fates… how many?"

Gwen pursed her lips. She tilted her head and mockingly thought for a moment. "Well, for the cursing and the attitude, I'm thinking of a number…" She let her voice trail off as she tapped her chin.

Ezra felt his irritation grow as his pain weakened his body. He slowly continued the agonizing crunches, feeling his shoulders beginning to shake from exhaustion. "Any… chance you… wanna share… that number?"

Gwen flashed a malicious grin. She straightened her back and said, "No. I'll tell you when to stop." She turned from Ezra, hearing his groan of displeasure without any sympathy from her.

Almost an hour had passed since the exercises for the afternoon group had begun. Many had run their required amount of time and were resting until their next assignment. Gwen and Erika allowed them to have water and electrolyte drinks as well as a few healthier snacks if they wanted.

Their groups' next rotation was to the obstacle course, with a ten-minute overlap for everyone to rotate.

Ezra and Maddox were still doing exercises for failing to continue the run. Luna Erika had switched up their exercise to include a ten-pound medicine ball they were to throw to one another. Maddox caught the ball against his chest. The weight slammed him down onto his back and pressed into his lungs as he struggled to breathe under the ball. "This is fucking ridiculous." His head tipped down to look at Ezra. "This ball is not that heavy; I didn't even make it the whole mile!"

Ezra grunted when Maddox returned the ball. He let the ball fall into his lap and took a moment to rest while Erika and Gwen were distracted by some of the other kids. His eyes trailed to the fence where Elliot was doubled over.

Whether it was the combination of the heat or what he had at lunch was unclear. Elliot dropped to his knees at the corner edge of the bleacher's fence. He violently retched several times; the revolting noise pulled the attention of Luna and Gwen.

Erika was running her hand across his back; she spoke to him gently, "Try to breathe, Elliot. Have you felt sick all day?" She raised a hand, ready to signal Roderick to come to her aid, but lowered her hand when Elliot shook his head.

Gwen arrived at his side not long after. She and Erika attempted to get Elliot to stand, and struggled to catch him when he nearly collapsed. Gwen waved a hand, her gesture called an Azure, who had been sitting on the ground, to her attention and helped Elliot to sit on the bench in front of the fence.

Gwen lifted his chin, "Tell me your symptoms, Omega."

Elliot was only able to look at her for a moment. His eyes closed as he struggled to push down the bile that was once again threatening to expel itself. "Um… dizzy… m… m… ugh…" He belched lightly, covering his mouth with his palm. After a minute, he was able to lift his head and looked at each of the women as he said, "Muscle weakness. Nausea." He was able to shake his head. "Not much else. The weakness is… is the big one."

Erika touched the back of her hand to his forehead. "No fever." She gave Gwen a single nod. "Likely not a diseased illness. Check the other two boys; this might be pack-related."

Ezra weakly rolled the ball from his lap onto the grass. "That's it. I'm done."

Maddox sat up onto his elbows, having watched Elliot be led to the bench after hurling his entire stomach contents. "Is that what it takes to get a break? Cause I'm willing to throw up all over this field."

Ezra shook his head and spoke more to himself than to Maddox, "This makes no sense." His eyes caught Halius, who was a quarter through another lap around the track. "Look at him; he's *still* running! I'm getting more exhausted just watching him!"

Halius's pace hadn't changed throughout the hour. He charged through his fifth-mile circuit, unaware of what kept him fueled enough to continue the run. It was excessive, he knew that, but he continued to feel the rage for his mother as he was unable to shake the thoughts of Malachi.

Halius only had one thought; he couldn't stop. He couldn't risk his mother saying or doing something that would put his rage over the edge. His wolf threatened him enough as it was. The vicious growls echoed through his head; his heart thundered in his chest. He had to run. He had to exhaust himself; that way, he would be too tired for his rage. He would be too tired to argue with his mother.

Too tired for anything.

Gwen watched Ezra and Maddox for a few seconds but seemed to shrug off their symptoms as simple exhaustion. She then clapped her hands for attention and shouted, "Alright, everyone! Rest up; we will be rotating to the obstacle course in five minutes!"

Ezra was able to stand and offered a hand to Maddox. "Come on, maybe a drink will make you feel better."

Maddox took the hand, but standing made his head spin. His legs nearly gave out, and he clung onto Ezra. The motion threatened to topple both young men. He was barely able to focus his vision as he felt a second pair of hands stabilize their movements. His voice waivered as he struggled to look over his shoulder, "Roderick? Where did you come from?"

The Azure pulled Maddox's arm over his shoulder. "I am never far, Master. It is my job to be attentive to you." He was able to help both Maddox and Ezra over to where Elliot still sat. "Rest here, Master."

Cautiously, he approached Erika, who had taken a moment to question a few other students about how they were feeling. However, no one else was having the problems the Prime Pack children were experiencing. "Great Luna."

She turned to him, seeing his head lower as soon as she glanced in his direction. "What is it, Roderick?" When the Azure motioned towards the young pack, her eyes widened in shock. "Maddox! What's happening? Are you all right?" She rushed to her son, pulling his head into her stomach as she attempted to console him.

Roderick turned when she dashed passed him. "Luna Erika."

When she looked over her shoulder, her eyes glared at him. The yellow pressed into the light blue of her eyes. Her words barked at him, "What is it, Roderick? Can't you see my baby is suffering?"

He nodded to the track where Halius was rounding the third corner. "Leech Syndrome, Mistress."

As soon as Roderick spoke the words, it became clear to all of them. The teenagers looked at each other in realization, then gently shook their heads in turn at their own idiocy for not recognizing it right away.

Leech Syndrome was one of many ailments that could afflict the Lycans. Packmates shared many things: thoughts and feelings, and if their connection was strong enough, even energy could be passed from one to another. It was a common condition for very strongly bonded packs.

Erika's jaw dropped. "Of course!" She waved a hand at Roderick. "Stop him this instant!"

Gwen heard Erika's order and screamed at her son, "Halius! Come take a break; we're about to head to the obstacle course!"

Halius heard her shouting. The shrill sound cut through the air, how was he not able to block her out? Was he not exhausted enough? He gritted his teeth as he continued to run, unwilling to break his pace as he heard his hag-mother's voice. His heart was hammering against his sternum. His ears burned from the blood that was forced through his body at a violent rate.

And still, he heard Gwen's voice shrieking, "Halius Usoro! I will not tell you again!"

Halius only felt his anger flare once more. A surge of hot energy erupted from his core. The skin around the sockets of his eyes began to darken as his wolf threatened to burst forth from his emotional turmoil. He felt tears streak his temples from the corners of his eyes. His mind kept flashing back to the horrible day, nearly ten years prior, when the three Azure Gwen owned were sold in order for them to remain in the territory.

He had tried to protest. Gwen literally ripped Malachi out of his arms when he tried to hold onto his closest friend. She had dragged him to the car, where Lyra and Julien had already been locked inside. She had left Halius at the hotel when she drove them off, having used her command to keep him from leaving the building while she was away.

And now, Malachi was being sold off once again. He was sentenced to die in a factory because Gwen had to have her way. She didn't even attempt to purchase him back; she hadn't spoken to Liam at all about it.

The dull yellow coloring seared through his irises. A growl boiled in his throat as the veins around his eye sockets darkened in black trails across his skin.

One day, he wouldn't have to listen to her.

One day, he wouldn't have to suffer under her command.

One day, maybe, he would be able to get Malachi back.

Fates willing, one day.

Erika's eyes narrowed as she continued to run her hand through Maddox's hair. Her head snapped to Roderick, and she shouted, "Roderick! Stop him now before he shifts!"

The Azure stepped out onto the track. He readied his stance as Halius charged towards them. He knew he couldn't let Halius get passed him; he wouldn't catch him in time to stop his inevitable shift.

When his timing was right, Roderick dashed across the track lanes. He collided with Halius; his shoulder slammed into Halius's side and launched both of them into the grass.

A silence fell over the field as Halius and Roderick rolled across the ground. Roderick recovered quickly and gracefully. He left Halius on the ground, turning his attention back to the Luna.

Erika looked down at Maddox. The color was returning to his face, and he was able to sit up. Elliot, as well, recovered his stability as the nausea receded from his stomach. Ezra seemed to perk up the fastest, seemingly affected the least by the whole ordeal. Erika stepped away from Maddox and gave Roderick a nod, "Thank you, Roderick."

He gave a bow, his head tipped down as he said, "The pleasure is mine, Luna. Anything for Master Maddox." He quickly returned to where he had been sitting with some of the other Azure on the ground near the opposite edge of the bleachers.

Halius was lying on the ground. His breath steadied as his rush of emotions faded. He stared up at the sky, almost unaware of what had happened. How much time had passed? How many laps did he run? The black and glowing yellow around his eyes faded back to their more human features.

Ezra stood up from the bench; he cupped his hands around his mouth as he shouted at Halius, "You feel better after sucking out our energy, you dick?"

Halius rolled onto his side before pushing himself into a sitting position. His eyes looked around, assessing where he was as if he couldn't remember how he had gotten there. He was just about to stand, just about to respond when something fixed his gaze.

Two men sat near the top of the bleachers. One, dressed in dark clothes with matching dark hair and shockingly white skin, was leaning forward. His elbows rested on his thighs, fingers folded thoughtfully between his knees.

The other, looking nearly the same but in features of white instead of black, with dark olive-tinted skin, had his back against the chain-link fence that blocked the edge of the bleachers. One arm rested on a knee that was bent from his foot being casually placed on the bench. Across his torso, leaning against his shoulder was a long staff that Halius was too far away from to see clearly. Only noting the shadow against the glossy white, casual clothes.

They could have been looking at anyone. The mass of kids readying themselves to rotate to their next course was a huge cluster against the edge of the track and bleachers. But Halius knew better. He could feel their eyes on him, and a strange familiarity began to nag against the back of his mind. A calm overtook the anger and rage like a gust of cold wind in the heart of the summer heat. Did he know them from somewhere?

Gwen marched towards him with heavy footfalls. "Halius!" Her shouting snapped him out of his trance. "How *dare* you ignore my instructions!"

He stammered, pushing himself up onto shaky legs as he steadied his breathing. "Uh… yeah… I'm… I'm sorry."

Gwen stopped. Her anger dropped from her face for a moment as it was replaced with shock. An apology was never something that her son uttered. He was constantly misbehaving, and she always attributed his bad behavior to not completely adapting to the move to Michigan. The scowl returned to her face to keep her reputation intact. "Oh, you are, are you?" The smug tone of satisfaction was genuine against her words. "And what would you be sorry for?"

He spoke as he began to walk behind Gwen, who seemed to be leading him over to where his pack mates had recovered. His three brothers looked up at him with glaring eyes. He spoke almost robotically as if someone else had put the words in his mouth. "I'm sorry. I didn't realize I was taking your energy. I… I was really in the zone for the run… I don't know what happened exactly."

Gwen nodded, and she and Erika shared a satisfied look. Before the young pack could respond to Halius, Erika clapped her hands and pulled the attention towards herself. "Alright, everyone! Let's make our way to the obstacle course!"

As the class began to head to the opposite side of the track, Halius looked up to the bleachers once again. But the seats, once occupied, were now empty. He felt Ezra knock against his shoulder when he moved past him.

Elliot was the one who stopped, his eyes following Halius's gaze. "What are you looking at?"

Halius shook his head, his eyes remaining locked on the spot for several more moments before he said, "Um… I don't… nothing, let's just go."

The rest of their time in class was spent on the obstacle course. They were supposed to rotate one more time; however, due to the delay with Halius's outburst, as Luna Erika was calling it, they remained where they were, and no set of students rotated again.

At the end of the day, Erika and Gwen dismissed the class as the buses arrived at the school. They waited for twenty minutes for the students to be loaded on before driving away full of unruly Lycans who were headed back to the Omega edges of the city.

Halius and Sydney walked back to his car, as he had not driven it to the field parking lot. He was putting his bag in the backseat when a vehicle pulled up to the open spot in front of his car.

It was Malachi who had picked up Julien and Lyra at the end of the school day. He had driven to the parking lot from the pickup lane in order to see Halius for what would be the last time.

Sydney gave a small wave and smiled from the passenger's seat. Malachi did give a slight smile and a nod, but his attention was quickly turned to Halius when the Lycan rounded the front of the car.

He wasted no time and slammed into the thin Azure with a tight embrace. Malachi returned the hug, and they stood like that in silence for a length of time that other Lycans would consider inappropriate.

Sydney watched as they stood together, her heart almost aching at the sight. It was a consensus around Lycans that the Azure were not supposed to have real affection shown towards them. They were property, nothing more. Something Liam had told her for as long as she could remember. Never expect affection; the Azure is not supposed to get it. They were to be used however their Lycan masters wanted.

Malachi spoke without breaking the embrace. "It's OK, Halius."

It wasn't until he spoke that Sydney noticed Halius's shoulders were shaking. He was crying. Nothing else would have made him shudder in such a way.

Malachi spoke again. "You have to believe me. It's going to be OK."

Halius pulled away from him. Tears streamed down his face. His voice cracked as he whispered, "It's not OK." He sucked on his lips, shaking his head and shifting uncomfortably on his feet. "It's not OK, Mal. We know what happens in those places."

Malachi tried to force a smile. His jaw quivered as he forced fear and sorrow from his face. His voice cracked as he stifled a sob that threatened to choke his words. "At least I'm not getting dropped in the wilderness to be hunted." A half-chuckle escaped him, with tears threatening his eyelids. "That happens too." When Halius wasn't looking, he swiped his fingers underneath his eyes. "At least I'll still have a place to live."

Halius continued to shake his head. He rubbed his hand across his mouth and said, "There has to be something. Anything we can do." His tone grew desperate, his thoughts voicing themselves before he realized what he was saying, "We can't let them do this. She promised!"

Malachi was able to chuckle at that statement genuinely. The depressive noise only worsened the tone of the space between them.

"Well… at least we learned what her word is worth, right?" When Halius looked at him again, tears fell from Malachi's eyes.

The sight of his tears made Halius's mood turn from grief to rage once more. It was almost as if a switch had been flipped in his mind. The hostile energy radiated the air to the point where it could have triggered a shift in an Omega if one was near enough.

Halius growled, his fists balling at his sides, and he began to pace back and forth across the front of his car. His voice rumbled with a growl as his rage got the better of him once again, "She just… she can't just… *Ugh*! She makes me so angry!"

Malachi let out a sigh. After watching his friend pace once, twice, three more times, he placed a hand on the Lycan's shoulder. "We have to accept this, Halius." He hugged his arms to his chest, keeping his eyes low when Halius looked at him again. "This is how it goes, right? Azure are bought and sold all the time. We… we, um…" His voice trailed off as he began to tremble.

Halius yanked him into another hug as Malachi started to sob. His fists pressed tight against Malachi's back as he tried to keep himself under control. "I'm going to find a way, hear me? I will find a way to get you out of there."

Malachi had to be the one to separate them once again. He nodded, taking several deep breaths as he quieted his weeping. "Richmond Plastics. The Ionia Territory."

Halius felt his heart stop. His wolf threatened to explode out of his body. Ionia? It was nearly two territories away, and getting to and from that county took almost three hours by train. There were many factories closer to Newaygo. It had to have been done on purpose. Why wouldn't they have tried to get an offer from a factory that was closer?

Malachi looked over his shoulder, seeing Julien and Lyra in the car. He cleared his throat and said, "I have to get them home. If I'm late… well… I'd rather not be late." He chuckled, but Halius did not share the humor. He began to head towards the driver's door and said, "I'll see you…" He stopped and forced down a choke to keep his voice from cracking again. "I'll see you later, right?" He waited for Halius to nod and got in the car.

Halius watched the road where the car had disappeared long after it had gone from his sight.

Sydney opened her door and stood from the car. She knew that anything she said would be the wrong thing, but she couldn't leave him in the horrific trance he seemed to be locked in. No matter how long he stared at the road, Malachi would not be returning. No one was going to come and say Malachi's purchasers had changed their minds or that Liam had agreed to purchase Malachi instead. "Halius… we need to get home."

Her words seemed to have worked. Silently, they got into the car together. Halius slammed his door so hard that Sydney was sure she heard the glass shake. For a while, he just sat there. His fists clenched on the wheel as he took long, steady breaths. His emotions swirled through his mind in a painful, torrential swarm. Tears rolled down his face as he looked straight out the windshield.

Sydney didn't want to break the silence, but she also didn't want them to spend all evening sitting in the parking lot of the school. She had evening chores to do, that Gwen would certainly try to punish her for if she didn't complete them on time.

What broke the silence of the car was her phone when it started to buzz in her bag. Without looking at the screen, she knew who was calling. Her phone was tracked, and anything that deviated from their normal schedule was questioned.

She didn't know Halius could hear the phone's noise, although she shouldn't be surprised due to his Lycan hearing. In a quiet, exhausted voice, Halius asked, "Is that Liam?"

Sydney stammered and pulled her phone from the bag. "Um… yes. He is probably wondering why we aren't on our way home. We really should get going."

Halius let out his final calculated breath. He leaned his head against the back of the seat, his grip loosening on the wheel as the buzzing from the phone stopped. "I don't want to go back there."

Sydney glanced down at her screen. She had missed the call from Liam. It was a strange sight to see the missed call notification on her phone. She never missed a call from him, knowing better than to disobey her Master in any form. She was under orders to never deny his call, but she couldn't ignore Halius's turmoil.

It seemed important. More important than trying to explain something to Liam.

Halius ran his fingers across his mouth as he spoke, "I don't want to go back there. I hate it there."

To that, Sydney didn't know how to respond. Was she supposed to tell him it wasn't as bad as he thought? That it was all in his head? She could try to spin something about Lycan's superiority, but because of what had happened to Malachi, she knew that was the wrong move.

For the third time, her phone started to buzz. Liam's caller ID came across her screen again. She looked down at the phone but stopped herself from answering the call. Instead, she looked at Halius and said, "If you need to, Halius, I will listen to anything you have to say."

He looked at her. His eyes blinked as he processed her words. He had never considered talking to Sydney about something that was on his mind. He feared how that might end, with her needing to be so loyal to Liam. He couldn't hide the shock from his voice when he asked, "Yeah?"

She nodded, speaking with as much confidence as she could muster. Her words sounded more like a whisper of encouragement. "Yes."

It was another silent moment, Halius's eyes flashed down to the phone she still held in her hand. "Answer that, it's probably important."

She obeyed, touching the screen and holding the phone to her ear. "Hello."

Through the quiet of the car, Halius could hear Liam's distressed voice. "Sydney! Finally! Why didn't you answer? Why are the two of you still at the school? You need to be on your way home."

She tried not to look at Halius when she answered. Was her voice shaking? "Well, Halius had… he had something he had to do at the end of the day. He's just about to start driving, Master Liam. I'm sorry for not informing you."

As she spoke, Halius started the car. He slammed the shifter into gear and mumbled, "Blame it on me. I'm the one who took so long." His volume increased so Liam could hear him say, "We're coming right now, don't worry."

Sydney heard Liam breathe a sigh of what seemed like relief on the other end of the call. "Alright. Tell him not to drive too erratically. I had a stressful enough day without needing to worry further about my assets."

The phone speaker beeped when the call was disconnected. She slouched against her seat, sliding the phone back into her bag, and knew Halius was judging her based on the conversation she just heard. It shouldn't bother her when Liam referred to her as an asset. By all accounts of legality, she was. An Azure.

Property. Nothing else.

When they arrived home, Halius was bombarded by Gwen as soon as they walked through the door. "Halius! Where were you? Do you know how worried we were? What in this sacred world could be important enough that you couldn't call your mother?"

Halius didn't answer. He scoffed and pushed away from the hug she was trying to give him. Her worry always seemed disingenuous, regardless of how sincere her voice sounded. There was something he couldn't trust about her barrage of questions like she was trying to pry information from him.

He threw his backpack on the table, seeing Liam sitting on the couch, tablet in hand, and had not responded to their arrival. He kept stern eyes on Sydney as she went into the kitchen after leaving her own bag by the door. Cooking dinner was on her list of chores for the evening, which would now have a late start due to their tardiness.

Gwen was quick to announce that to the already tense household, "I hope you feel good about yourself, girl. Your Master's evening schedule is completely derailed because of you."

Sydney bit the inside of her cheek and ignored the comment. Upon her silence, she turned her attention back to Halius and continued to badger him with questions as he sat at the table.

After what felt like an eternity of questioning, in a fit of rage, Gwen slammed her hands down on the oak table. "Halius! Answer me! Why were you so late? Did Sydney make you late? You can forget going out for a run tonight—if it was in your plans—because you are *not* losing sleep for this. Especially after the turmoil you caused at training."

Halius's eyes shifted to Sydney, who gave a worried glance to Liam. The young Lycan pulled his headphones from their case in his pocket and pressed them into his ears. The music effectively drowned out the ruckus Gwen was causing. He could only see her gestures as she threw a temper tantrum for his interest in her questioning. She even tried to pull Liam into the argument when she stepped away from the table.

He didn't hear what Liam had said, but he saw him speak only one seemingly simple line to his wife. Whatever he said caused her to stop, and the evening was allowed to go on.

The dinner Sydney made was a very basic chicken and noodles for dinner, it was as close to one-pot as she came most of the time. She left the kitchen dirty while she placed the bowls on the table at everyone's place.

By that time, Halius had finished going through his assignments and made sure they were all completed. He had packed up his books just in time for Sydney to begin setting the table. He slumped down in his seat with his head resting on his palm and toyed with the food he was given.

Sydney was the last one to sit, per usual. The dinner had a heavy silence over the household. More so than normal due to the sour mood of the day.

Gwen addressed Liam, attempting to break the silence. "Halius showed great promise for the Relay today. I can see him being selected by the Alpha."

Liam nodded, not looking up from his bowl. When he spoke, his words were dull, "Good job."

Halius didn't respond. He placed a chicken cube in his mouth and rolled it around his teeth. He couldn't figure out if he was angry at Liam or not that Malachi was being sold off to a factory. It was he who spurned Gwen's selling of Malachi, Julien, and Lyra. But she made that choice. No one made it for her.

Liam glanced up at Halius. "What's wrong, boy?"

Halius pushed his bowl away. "I'm not hungry."

Gwen let out a mocking laugh. She returned his bowl to where it had been and said, "Halius, don't be ridiculous. You're a growing Lycan. You have to eat."

He shoved the bowl away again and stood from the table. His chair slammed into the wall, causing Sydney to flinch, and he shouted, "Well, I'm not hungry right now, so can you just drop it?" Before his mother could respond, he stormed down the hallway and slammed his bedroom door closed.

Gwen's glare turned immediately to Sydney. "What did you do to him? What happened after school? He was fine until you two left the fields! I knew I shouldn't have trusted you to be alone with him!"

Sydney shrank in her seat, shaking her head. She looked at Liam with frightened eyes before she said, "Nothing, Mistress Gwen. He… He… um…"

Liam placed his hand flat on the table, almost reaching to her as he said. "Take a deep breath, Sydney." When she obeyed, he continued. His voice was calm, tone mild as he said, "Look at me. What happened when you got back to the car?"

Sydney took another breath before she spoke. It wasn't a secret, was it? But if it wasn't, why did it feel like such a shameful thing? It was definitely something that was going to spark an argument or at least hateful rhetoric from Gwen. She couldn't help but think of how Halius had looked at her while they were in the car. She didn't want to speak of it but couldn't disobey her Master so openly in front of another Lycan, especially when the other Lycan was his horrid wife. "We saw Malachi when he came to pick up Lyra and Julien. He turns twenty tomorrow."

Liam nodded slowly. A saddened expression flashed across his face before his features returned to neutral. He gave one side-glace to Gwen before returning his focus to his food. He didn't need to look at her; he didn't want to look at her to know what her reaction was going to be.

It was a disgusted scoff as she said, "Is that all? And here I thought it was something important." She shook her head in disbelief, "Teenagers." She took a couple of bites of food before she said, "Well, Halius will be fine. It's not like he saw much of Malachi anyway."

Sydney saw Liam give the slightest shake of his head. A motion that was unnoticed by Gwen, who dismissively focused on her food. Without thinking, Sydney mumbled, "Whose fault is that?"

The air in the room seemed to freeze. Sydney's eyes widened as she realized what she had done, but it was far too late. Liam looked up just in time to see Gwen's eyes flare the flaming yellow of her wolf.

What happened next seemed impossibly fast, faster than anyone might have perceived.

Gwen tried jumping the table, swiping a hand at Sydney in a thwarted attempt to snatch the girl by her styled hair.

In just enough time, Sydney had attempted to push her chair back from the table, but her motion rocked her back and caused it to fall against the wall before she rolled to the floor.

Gwen seemed to have appeared out of nowhere, her body shadowing the chandelier that hung over the large table. Her weight pressed Sydney into the floor; her teeth gritted as the skin around her eyes began to darken. She had managed to shove Liam back and scale the table just as Sydney had rolled from her chair. Her nails dug into Sydney's shoulders, threatening to break her skin. Her words hissed, "I think I've had enough of your mouth, you little *bitch*!"

Before Gwen could assault her further, she was pulled off the girl. Liam had jumped to his feet, his chair cracking the glass of the sliding door as he reached for Gwen. She had managed to push him back once, an error he would soon rectify.

His wife shrieked in protest as his iron grip crushed her biceps. Her legs kicked in the air, trying to pull herself from his hands. "Get off me, Liam!"

He bellowed over her furious screaming, "Sydney! Go to your room, now!"

She scrambled away from the table, hitting her shoulder on the corner of the hall as she ran by. She had no breath to sob as she bolted into her room and quickly closed the door behind her.

Liam wrestled Gwen down onto the table, knocking the dishes onto the floor in a shattering mess. His eyes turned a deep golden yellow as he yanked her wrists behind her back and forced her chest down onto the wood. He held her wrists tightly in one hand, his other palm pressing into her golden-dyed hair. "Guinevere! Stop!"

All her attempts to pull from his grip were futile. His grip tightened each time she tried, the small bones in her wrists grinding together and making her whimper. Eventually, she stopped pulling against him and screamed, "Why do you defend that *whore*? She has no respect for—"

Liam cut her off as he roared, "You will not speak of her that way!" He removed his hand from her hair. Swiftly gripping her body, he flipped her over on the table. Taking a wrist in each hand that he slammed down next to her shoulders.

Gwen attempted to breathe as he leaned over her. His weight pressed against her stomach as she hissed, "Nothing at all in my defense, hmm? That little *brat* gets away with everything!"

The color of his eyes burned into her. A deep, golden color that was always a few shades darker than it should have been. He watched the color recede from her skin, from her eyes as he howled, "Shut up!" He could see her trying to fight the order. Trying to speak again even though he had commanded her to silence. Rarely did he ever raise his voice, let alone put his hands on his wife, or any of them for that matter. But he would not tolerate Sydney's mistreatment.

His words were strong, as his Command always was. "You will not lay a hand on her! You will never lay a hand on her! Do you understand me?"

When she didn't reply, he lifted her from the table and slammed her back down again. The air was thrown from her lungs as he repeated in a thunderous voice, "Do you understand?"

She had no choice but to answer. The command burned through her mind, it heated up her skin, tightening her chest as her wolf whimpered in her head. Eventually, when the pain became too much, she gritted her teeth and responded. "Yes, I understand."

As soon as she spoke the words, Liam released her. He stepped back, keeping his golden eyes locked on her as he said, "For nearly a full decade, we have had this argument." He watched her slowly stand from the table and step away, her back to the kitchen as he continued. "I will not tell you again. Sydney is not yours. You will not lay a hand on her."

Gwen felt tears stinging her eyes. She echoed his words with an almost imperceptible whisper, "Ten years." She shook her head, watching the color finally disappear from his eyes. "I am your wife."

Liam's brow twitched. "Yes, you are. And?"

Gwen let out a trembling breath. She rubbed her sore wrists as she said, "You should hold me in higher regard than your *pet*." She saw him pause. Did he flinch? He often did with every insult that was thrown towards the Azure he owned. Every insult made his blood boil. Some of the twitches she could see, others she knew were there but didn't quite catch.

He stepped closer to her, nearly nose to nose. His eyes narrowed in a glare that nearly made Gwen choke out a sob. His teeth were clenched, his words hot against her face. "I don't."

With a slacked jaw, she watched him storm down the hallway. She silently prayed to the Fates that he would go into their master bedroom, and ready himself for sleep. A deep, sickening disgust twisted her stomach when he stopped at Sydney's door. He looked over his shoulder to Gwen and gave her a withering look before stepping inside and slamming the door behind him.

Gwen let out a shriek of frustration and rage. The sound echoed around the now-quiet house, but her screams yielded no attention from those who had already abandoned her. She felt her wolf roar behind her scream and knew she wouldn't be able to fight the shift. She threw open the sliding door, which cracked further under the force of the slam.

One by one, she took off her clothes as she walked with intensity through the back yard to the trees just beyond the property line, leaving a trail of cloth behind her as she stomped across the grass.

The veins across her body blackened as she entered the trees. She could feel her body morphing effortlessly as she began to run from her home. Without breaking her stride, two legs became four as her wolf grew from her human body. Shimmering bronze fur grew from her black skin, and she bounded through the woods on four paws, burning the aggression she had been trying to suppress.

Unbeknownst to the rest of the house, Gwen was not the only one to leave the house that night.

The next morning, the house did what all Lycan households did if there was a confrontation the night before. They all tried to act like it never happened. Lycans were never ones to hold much of a grudge and attempted to put all past events behind them in order to "look towards the future."

However, to some, it seemed like an excuse to deny terrible past actions and justified abusive behavior.

Sydney was the first one awake, per normal. She shut off her alarm quickly so it wouldn't wake Liam. He had slept in her room, on folded blankets on the floor next to her bed. Normally, when he and Gwen had a fight, he would have just spent a few hours with her before joining Gwen in their bed. That night, he slept in her room, unwilling to leave Sydney with Gwen in the house. As he did not know she had left.

Sydney crept passed him and took a set of clothes to the bathroom she shared with Halius so she could get dressed. The bathroom separated their bedrooms in the hall, giving some much-needed privacy to the teenagers. She looked towards Halius's door, wondering if she should try and wake him up so his day didn't start like the previous one. Quickly decided against it, as one of Liam's rules for her was that she was not allowed in Halius's room, especially if no one else was in the house.

She looked through the open door of the master bedroom. Gwen had returned sometime late in the night. Her dirty prints trailed across the floor. She had showered before going to bed and slept in her bed soaking wet. The clean sheets stuck to her naked, unconscious body.

Sydney went out to the main room, and seeing the destruction made guilt stab at her chest. It was her fault the night had taken such a horrid turn. She cleaned up what she could as she made breakfast and started the coffee they would expect when they woke up.

The morning went by as commonly as a normal day. Breakfast was served, they ate and the adults had their coffee. Sydney picked a set of ribbons that Liam weaved into her hair. He sat on the couch, with her on the floor.

Except for the morning TV, the house was silent. With the occasional one-tones questions and answers from the four people in the house.

Gwen's voice was flat when she asked, "Halius, do you have all your homework?"

He nodded. His eyes were puffy as if he hadn't had much sleep. He yawned, rubbing his eyes before he tossed Advil into his mouth to beat back a headache that was threatening his forehead.

When they were ready to leave, Halius threw his bag on his shoulder. He slid sunglasses over his eyes to combat the rising sun, even though it wouldn't crest the horizon for another hour. It wasn't until the teenagers were outside, that Halius asked Sydney to drive. He handed her the keys and flopped into the passenger's seat.

She didn't question him, but did pause for a moment before answering, "Yes." To his question about her driving them to school. She waved to Liam who watched them from the doorway before she drove away.

Sydney parked the car where Halius did each day. She couldn't see his eyes beneath the tint of the sunglasses, but it looked like he fell asleep on the way to school. When the car stopped, he took in a large inhale through his nose and stretched hard before getting out of the car.

Halius kept the sunglasses on as they headed to the building, seeing the others had once again already arrived, and were waiting at the door.

Maddox and Ezra were talking casually, as they normally did. Rambling about video game statistics from the night before.

Halius didn't try to join the conversation, usually joining them online with the gaming console he had in his bedroom. He slumped against one of the pillars that held the entrance awning aloft and let out a tired breath as he rested his head against the stone.

Maddox looked him up and down. "Damn, man, what is wrong with you now?"

Halius shrugged one shoulder without standing from the pillar. "Nothing. I've got a headache. Must be allergies."

Elliot, whom Sydney and Halius hadn't seen when they approached, piped up from the ground he sat on. "Yes, me too, allergies."

They looked down, seeing him also wearing dark sunglasses to shield him from the morning light that had risen from the horizon. He leaned against the base of another stone pillar, his backpack on his lap as he rubbed his temples.

Maddox looked between the two of them. Elliot had woken up groggy, weakened, and slow at the pack house. He had fallen asleep in the car on the way to school, which wasn't incredibly shocking but wasn't normal for him either. Elliot was known to have seasonal allergies at times, but it never seemed as extreme as it did that morning.

When the young Alpha looked at Ezra, the youngest member of the pack seemed to take their statements as truth. Maddox, however, was less convinced. A simple "uh-huh" escaped him before they started to move inside.

Thankfully for Halius, he didn't have any other exams that day. Sydney made sure to take detailed notes on each lesson, as Halius fell asleep in almost every class. Sydney could only hope that he began to feel better before his Rec classes, Fates knew what Gwen would torture him with, especially because she knew he didn't feel well.

*****

Malachi sat on his knees, on the floor of the living room that used to be his home. That morning, he had taken Lyra and Julien to school but they had arrangements to take one of the busses home at the end of the day. He had overheard his Master and Mistress, John and Lillian, speaking about how Lyra was the next one to learn how to drive.

They had no plans to have Julien learn, because he was the next one who would be sold off. Malachi knew he shouldn't have listened to their private conversation, but he had let his curiosity and worry get the better of him. He listened at their bedroom door a week prior.

The plan from John and Lillian was to keep Lyra, and to sell Julien not long after Malachi had been picked up by the "recruiters" from the factory that now owned him. Lillian, after years of trying, was finally pregnant. Because they would finally have the child they longed for, they didn't need so many Azure. Lyra would be kept as the nanny for the new baby, as well as doting on Lillian's every need to make sure she didn't strain herself during her pregnancy.

Malachi didn't have the heart to tell Julien he would soon suffer the same fate. He wanted his little brother to enjoy his last days in the house and hoped he would be sold to another family and not end up in a factory like he was about to.

He rubbed his sweaty palms on his jeans as he watched Lillian pace the kitchen. Her phone was held to her ear as she spoke to the recruiters, who were allegedly en route to them. John had already gone to work, with Lillian having the day off to be present for Malachi's pickup.

When she was done with her call, she placed her phone on the table and sat down in her chair. She absentmindedly rubbed her hand across her belly and said, "Well, they'll be here soon. Are you ready?"

Malachi lowered his eyes. She asked so casually, speaking as if he needed to be ready for something mundane like going to the park or a friend's house. Could he even speak without shaking? Should he respond at all? There were plenty of times when her questions were rhetorical, and when any of the three Azure answered her question, they were met with a brutal hand.

She pursed her lips innocently. Speaking with a nonchalant tone that set his teeth on edge. "Oh, don't be sad, sweetie. You always knew this day was coming. Just think of it as another adventure you're going on."

Malachi looked up at her, tears staining his cheeks. It was the exact line Gwen had used on them the day they were handed over. Lillian had led them to her car with that same winning smile as she said, "Just think of this as a new adventure."

And there he was again, getting the same line as he was being sold. The same line meant to pacify terrified children as they were ripped from their families. He let out a shuddered breath, "You don't have to do this, Miss Lill."

She chuckled, her eyes floating to the left, and she began to rub her belly again as she thought. "Oh, no? Where will we all fit, Malachi? We won't get a bigger house from the Alpha. John and I have priorities, you know."

Malachi tried to think as his mind started to spiral. Was there something he could say or do? Something *anything* that would cancel or stall his sale. "What about just selling me to someone else in the pack? I don't have to go to the factory. I can drive, I can cook. Maybe the school? Or…" His mind flashed to Halius. "What about Beta Liam? Halius could say something to him."

Lillian let out a single laugh. The sight of him begging seemed a bit more pathetic than usual. His comical desperation was almost cute. Sometimes, the children begging for something worked on her, but it had been too late. "Oh, baby boy, no." She stood from the chair, keeping an innocent tone as she shrugged, "The factory pays much more than the school ever would. Besides, if Beta Liam wanted any of you, he wouldn't have told Gwen to sell you to me." She patted the top of his head. "But you're a good boy. Remember that."

Malachi flinched when there was a hammering wrap sounded on the door. Lillian opened the door and allowed two men inside. They were strong and much larger than Malachi. Lillian gestured to him with a smile on her face, and the men advanced.

He knew it was over in minutes, but it seemed to happen so slowly in his mind. Each arm was grabbed. He was yanked up from the floor. Even though it was useless, he knew it was useless; Malachi attempted to pull away from them as they locked his bracelets with heavy magnets behind his back. In an act of absolute desperation, he attempted to beg one last time, "You don't have to do this! Miss Lill, please! I'll be good! I'll do anything!"

Her expression didn't falter as she watched him be pulled from the house, nor did she answer him as she placed her hand once again on her flat stomach.

Malachi was hauled outside, where a white van was waiting, with large words painted with the company font of *Richmond Plastics* printed on the side. The words were cut by the open rear sliding door when it was opened by one of the men who was taking him away.

Malachi didn't know what possessed him. He had tried to beg without success, and though he didn't have much of a plan if it worked, he couldn't help but try to fight. He swung his legs up, leaning against the Lycan who still held his arms behind his back, and slammed a hard kick against the one who opened the door, bashing the Lycan into the edge of the doorframe.

The grip on his arms loosened and allowed him to wriggle free. He jumped through his arms, never so thankful about how skinny he was, and attempted to run. He wasn't as fast as the Lycans and nowhere near as strong. The one Malachi kicked was still leaning against the van, holding his rib with one hand and rubbing his sore head with another. The Lycan who had held his arms caught him easily, with Malachi barely making it ten paces away from the van down the street.

Lillian leaned against the doorframe, folding her arms across her chest as she giggled and said, "I told you to bring three."

The Lycan who held him let out a roaring laugh. "You also said he only weighed 110 pounds. You didn't say he was slipperier than a catfish!"

Malachi clenched his jaw as he tried to thrash his way out of the Lycan's iron grip. Hearing Lillian and these men laugh like it was some kind of sick joke sparked a rage Malachi had never felt. It burned in his chest, twisting his stomach and making his hair stand on end as goosebumps waved across his arms.

His rageful glare turned back towards the house. He locked eyes with Lillian and screamed, "You'll pay for this! You hear me? You'll be sorry!"

Lillian waved a dismissive hand. "Oh, baby boy, the only thing I'm sorry for is not unloading your brother sooner than next week. Bye now." She nodded in thanks to each of the wolves and closed the door of the house.

The fist of the Lycan man Malachi had kicked slammed into his stomach, effectively silencing the Azure's screams of rage and vengeance." He coughed hard, gasping for air as he was thrown into the back of the van. His arms pressed against his stomach in a futile attempt to clutch his aching gut.

Whatever emotion he had for himself, fear, humiliation, and loss all faded from his mind. An overwhelming rage boiled into his blood as a single thought etched itself into his head.

Who was he leaving Lyra and Julien with?

It took almost three hours to drive to the factory. It was not in the city but in the manufacturing sector that was to the north and east of the city. Hidden from view so as not to obstruct the peaceful lives of the Lycans while they went about their days.

The van pulled up to the edge of a sidewalk that led to the building. The back of the van had been completely blackened, with no interior lights and a wall that prevented Malachi from reaching the drivers. He felt nothing but the hard floor and walls as he was occasionally tossed around from curves and the van stopping or accelerating through the twisting roads that led in and out of the other territories. It wasn't a far stretch for him to assume they would be tossing him around on purpose.

When the door had been thrown open, the white light of day glared in on him. He squeezed his eyes shut in an attempt to combat the light and was pulled from the van.

Surrounded by trees, undoubtedly there to muffle the horrid smell that seemed to linger in the air even outside, the building itself was massive. Pure white walls that stretched out almost farther than he could see in the reflection of the midday sun. There were no windows or doors of any kind to break up the concrete wall that loomed over him as he was pushed up the sidewalk.

Malachi attempted to survey what was around him. Any other doors, windows, perforations in the walls, or access to the roof. Anything he could grab within reach to fight off the men and get away.

No. There was nothing. Nothing was within reach as each man held an arm and continued pulling him towards the single, ominous door that nearly blended in with the surrounding wall.

What did catch his eye and held his attention longer than perhaps he even realized, was the sight of two men standing by the edge of the trees.

Their features were hard to see from the distance they were standing, and his eyes had not yet completely adjusted to the glare of the sun. What he could tell was the difference in their height, with one dressed all in white and the other in black. They were also watching him; he could feel the stare of their eyes. A mixture of dread and grief swirled through his head that was trying to be pushed back by a ray of hope. Was it coming from them? Was that possible?

Malachi couldn't shake the thought he had seen them somewhere. Where? Anything he tried to think of felt as foggy and distant as a dream. He looked up to the trees, their tops blown by a gust of wind that shot through the air. But the wind didn't touch the men. It threw grass and leaves from the floor of the forest, never moving a garment on either of the figures that watched him.

Malachi lost sight of them when he was shoved through the open door. His last sight was the Lycan men brushing off their own hands as the heavy, solid door closed behind him. He tried hitting it, pushing it open in several different places. It was as if the door had sealed into the wall.

The room he had been thrown into wasn't much bigger than a medium-sized closet. The walls were white, the same concrete material that made the walls of the outside. Two metal beams cut the white of the walls and stretched from floor to ceiling. When he turned from the direction he had come, he saw another similar crack in the wall in front of him. Another door?

A voice came from a speaker he didn't realize was there. A robotic, emotionless voice that sounded after an alarm that had made him jump. *Standby for decontamination and registration.*

Malachi didn't know what decontamination meant, but he did know what the registration would be. The process when his bracelets would be ground and stamped with the new information, probably the information of the factory, in case he was ever found and his owners needed to be contacted. He had done it once before and nearly suffered severe burns on his wrists because the smith who altered his information when he was sold by Gwen had been careless in grinding down her contact information.

Lyra had been scarred by the process. The lines, due to the age of the injury, had turned white against her skin and were barely noticeable. Although Malachi never forgot the sound of her wailing as she had been burned by the grinder.

A loud alarm blared over the speaker. Malachi clapped his hands over his ears, moving from the wall to closer to the center of the room. The noise seemed to be sounding from everywhere, reverberating through the empty walls that surrounded him. The lights, wherever they had been coming from, switched off for a moment before turning to a soft UV glow.

The alarm silenced, with it being replaced by a *whirring* noise that shook his chest. It vibrated the air, and he was able to discern its source from the metal bars that were on either side of him.

He felt a heat against his body as the vibrating noise intensified. He knew that feeling a little too well. The vicious, relentless heat that would normally emanate from his bracelets if he had tried to use too much of his magic. Once an Azure would stop the use of their abilities, the heat would dissipate, often leaving welts from the burns as a reminder to not use their abilities to a degree unbecoming of servants.

The sensation of the vibrations was starting to make him dizzy; just as he felt like he was going to fall over, his arms were ripped from his chest. His wrists slammed against the bars at shoulder level. Malachi tried to pull free, to no avail. He was weakened, but even at full strength, he knew the chances of him being able to pull free from what had to have been magnets would have been nearly impossible.

The alarm blared again, only for a moment that time, and from the speaker that was mounted from the center of the ceiling sprayed an aerosol liquid. It rained down on him as both a fog and a shower of fluid, burning his skin when it touched him. It soaked his clothes, stinging him like ants crawling and biting through his clothing. He sharply inhaled, quickly learning that was a mistake as the gas entered his body.

In the same moment, the heat turned to an electric shock that seized his body. Arcs of electricity rocked across his bracelets; the volts battered his nerves, tightened his muscles, and forced his back to arch painfully as his muscles tried in vain to pull away from what was causing his agony.

The gas burned his mouth and lungs, choking him on the air he attempted to consume in desperation. If Malachi hadn't known better, he could swear his throat had closed.

He couldn't scream, he couldn't breathe, he couldn't see. All he knew was pain. Immovable, intolerable pain that seared his nerves and boiled his blood. If the Fates had the capability to show Azure mercy, he would have begged for it.

Malachi felt a rush of cold air blast into his lungs, as icy and intense as a gust of winter air after stepping outside of a sauna. Upon his exhale, Malachi let out a hellacious scream that echoed around him in the enclosed torture chamber.

He wasn't sure how long the agony had lasted long enough for him to scream several more times in pain that forced his muscles to pull against his bracelets to the point where he nearly severed his hands.

Suddenly, it stopped.

The power in the room was cut. The lights went out once more before returning to the soft white glow that had been when he first arrived. His arms dropped painfully to his sides, and he collapsed to the floor, barely able to catch himself on his hands so his chest didn't hit the ground. He coughed hard, nearly retching as his stomach heaved with desperation to choke in as much air as possible.

A door opened in front of him; whatever lay on the other side offered no glaring light. The air seemed not to move at all as a middle-aged woman stepped through the doorway. She held a clipboard in her hands that she was studying. Dark-colored hair that was tied back in a tight tail against the nape of her neck and Sunkissed skin that seemed a little too pale. It was hard to see the shape of her body from the loose clothing she wore.

Without looking up, she asked, "Designation number?"

Malachi could barely lift his head. He struggled to speak, his throat barely rattling coherent sounds, let alone words.

The woman theatrically rolled her eyes. She bent down and snatched one of his wrists, nearly pulling him off his balance, and looked at the metal that was still warm in her hands. She read what had been newly printed and scribbled quickly on her paper. She read it to herself before she dropped her wrist once again, *"24M-1812. Right on time."* She straightened, making a few more notes before she said, "1812, follow me."

She took two steps from the door, looking back over her shoulder before giving an exasperated sigh. She stepped towards him once again, her voice barking at him, "1812, follow me, or I will have someone drag you."

Malachi managed to pull himself to his feet. He silently promised himself never to be thrown around again, should he be able to prevent it. He swallowed hard, his throat clicking against the strain. Carefully, he stepped out of the lit entrance into his new hellscape.

The woman spoke as she walked, "1812, my name is Whitney. I will be your liaison as you go through your probationary training period here at Richmond Plastics. I am here to orient you and oversee your training on the presses." She walked him through a series of rooms. Each one is seemingly worse than before.

A bathroom that was not segregated by gender. A row of open toilets and sinks stood across the narrow room from one another. The back of the room was a dozen or so open showerheads with single controlled knobs under each one. The tile was cracked and filmy, and the floor and lower walls were a dark tan that faded to a pale white further up the wall.

Whitney checked off her clipboard as she spoke. "This is one of the bathrooms you share with the other Azure. You get one shower a week with a ten-minute limit. Don't worry about exceeding your limit; the showers have an automatic shutoff and a sensor to make sure no one tries to double up. The sensor is triggered by the number on your bracelet."

They moved on, the next room being large and possibly more foul-smelling than the previous room. Large, dirty, and worn-down benches sat in several rows of equal distance on either side of the room. The center was just an aisle way to access the benches. A large heap of what could have been food at one time sat on a table at the far side of the room. It looked like overcooked, half-eaten meat, fruits, and vegetables that had been sitting outside of refrigeration for two days too long, and a variety of items that were no longer identifiable dripping a viscous liquid onto the floor.

Malachi resisted pressing his hand to his mouth in disgust. He watched an older woman with loose, tattered clothing pick through the pile before finding a piece she wanted.

Whitney glanced at him and saw the disgust starting to twist his face. "Something the matter with the rations?"

Malachi cleared his throat so as not to cough against the smell. "Um… no, miss. Of course not. I… I was just… wondering where it came from?"

Whitney pressed the clipboard to her chest as she folded her arms. Though her stance was harsh, her words were soft when she spoke. A gentleness to her voice that did not translate to her mannerisms. "Our gracious Alpa has gifted you with charitable food donations from the schools around the county. Unlike some others, we do not waste food here. The table is replenished when it is empty."

Malachi followed her out of the room; it seemed the smell was getting to her as well, for she stopped them just outside the breakroom door. "How often is that, may I ask?"

Whitney shrugged. She looked back down to her clipboard and made a few more notes. When she finally did answer, she sounded bored with the topic. "A week, maybe less. There are several hundred Azure working in this facility, so it happens… semi-often."

The further they walked, the louder the noise of the factory became. The hallway continued, with a break in one wall that showed a glimpse of the factory floor. Malachi kept his eyes low; the noise and smells were harsh enough; he didn't want to try and see what the rest of his life would look like.

The next doorless room they entered was like the rest. A large, open room with discolored, empty walls. Whitney hit a light switch on the wall, illuminating the dark with unevenly bright fluorescent lights.

This room was full of beds. Four rows of twelve beds were evenly spaced across the room. The mattresses were bare of any dressings and were heavily stained with fluids Malachi tried not to think of.

Whitney continued across the room and stepped through another doorway Malachi didn't realize was there. He hurried to catch up with her and met her again just as she was starting to speak.

She had turned on another light, and they stood in an incredibly small closet-like room that was lined floor to ceiling with shelves. The shelves were filled with even amounts of shirts and pants. The bottom of one shelved wall was stacked with thin blankets, although it didn't seem like there were enough for every bed. "These are your clothes. You may take one item at a time and wear it until the garment is worn out." She moved out of the closet and motioned towards the cloaked door they had entered through. "There is a chute out there for worn garments. If a garment is found at the bottom of the chute that is still wearable, the room the garment came from will receive harsh punishment."

Malachi nodded. His fear of what the answer was prevented him from asking what lurked all underneath the facility. Perhaps it was better that he did not know. He looked down to what he was wearing, "Um… I don't get to keep my clothes?"

Whitney glanced at his outfit before she said, "Oh, no, you can. Just remember where to get your new clothes when those wear out. Don't take another set until those wear out. It probably won't be long. I see others getting new pieces every week or so." She cleared her throat and regarded her clipboard before speaking again. Her voice was robotic and quick, clearly reading a script that was written on the paper she held in front of herself. "This is room four of twelve. Only sleep in your designated room. It does not matter which bed you take. You will get six hours of designated sleep, a break from work to not exceed fifteen minutes every four hours, and one-hour segments before and after your shift each day. Each shift is sixteen hours long. Shifts are staggered among the staff, so production never stops. Do not stop your work until relief comes for you. It is your responsibility to track where you are in your shift so as not to disrupt production. You are only allowed food and water during your designated breaks in designated areas. You may not take food and water out onto the production floor, nor can you take food and water out to the floor for someone else. Failure to follow the rules and regulations of Richmond Plastics will result in punishments to be determined by the severity of the indiscretion." She looked up at him once she was done reading and asked, "Any questions?"

Malachi blinked at her. It was so much information so quickly. Would he be able to remember everything? Would there be someone to ask if he forgot? He looked down at his wrists; his hands had been clutched together since she had started ranting at him. After an uncomfortable silence, he shook his head.

She nodded and checked a final box before she lowered the clipboard and said, "Alright, your first shift will start tomorrow."

Just as she had turned to leave the room, Malachi blurted out, "Wait! Um… do we… get days off? You know, for visitors?"

Whitney turned back to him. She held her composure for nearly a minute before she blurted out a harsh laugh. The noise echoed mockingly around the empty room until she was able to contain herself. "1812, this is a factory. This establishment runs around the clock; if we gave anyone time off, we would lose production. That is why you are here. Who would even visit you?"

The question punched his gut. It stole his breath, causing tears to flood his eyes. He looked away from her because she would expect him to avert his eyes after a moment, but he also did it to hide the bitter look on his face. He shook his head and managed to choke out the words, "Um… of course… I apologize, Miss Whitney. I should have been more considerate to the needs of the company."

Whitney's false smile returned. The unnatural pull against her mouth stretched her lips and did not travel to her eyes. "You'll get used to it, 1812."

Without looking up at her, he asked, "Do you want to know my name?"

She shrugged a single shoulder. "It doesn't really matter. You can tell it to me, but I probably won't remember it. All your shift assignments will have your number. 24M-1812. *24M* because you were brought here on the 24th and are male. *1812* because the factory hasn't been open for very long, and you are the one-thousand eight-hundred and twelfth Azure to work here."

He looked up at her again. His cold stare almost made her step back. His words were quiet in the empty room. "Malachi. My name is Malachi."

The corners of her mouth turned down. "Perhaps it was. Now you have a number." Her irritation began to grow. Her teeth clenched as she asked tersely, "Any more questions?"

Malachi's eyes twitched for a moment. He shouldn't provoke a Lycan, a superior, but he didn't know when he would be able to get any more information. Part of him wanted to know how long he could keep her there if he continued to ask questions. How many would she be required to answer before she walked away from him?

The thought of a Lycan being forced to interact with an Azure was almost humorous.

He kept his voice as submissive as possible when he asked, "You said you were a liaison. What does that mean for me?"

Whitney relaxed slightly. It must have been a question she was more accustomed to answering. "I maintain the Azure of this room. Keeping your shifts, making sure you have assignments, and you are on time, following the rules." She checked the watch she wore on her left wrist. "I have to go crossover with another liaison. Our shifts are only eight hours. So, I will see you on the floor tomorrow."

Without allowing him to ask another question, she turned on the balls of her feet and snapped back the curtain as she practically fled the room.

Malachi stood there for what felt like a long while. He turned, slowly taking in the sight of the room he stood in. He walked, almost in a daze, down one of the bed rows and chose a bed that was close to the corner of the room against the wall. The mattress was hard; he could feel the springs digging into his body when he lay down. He almost feared trying to move as the metal threatened to push through the thin layer of fabric and foam that kept them contained.

The air was still warm and sticky. He noticed one vent on the opposite side of the ceiling from where he lay. The only evidence of an air system there somewhere. It had to have been a heater and made him wonder what an icy winter, or blazing summer, would feel like in the factory.

Malachi remained on his back as he tried to listen to the sounds of the factory. He could hear machinery. High-pitched whirring and whining sounds of metal moving back and forth. A low, almost grinding, vibrating noise reverberated through the air and probably came from the heavy machines.

After some time had passed, a shift alarm sounded. He remained on the bed as more Azure began to shuffle in and out of the room he lay in. No one spoke to him, nor did he try to speak to any of them.

When the Azure's two-hour break had ended, they had taken as many beds as they needed. Malachi didn't try to look around and see how many of them there were. He heard bedframes creaking as others chose their places to sleep, and when the lights went out, and he heard the deep rhythmic breathing of people falling asleep, he finally let himself silently weep.

Malachi had to have fallen asleep at some point. The morning alarm jolted him awake as the blinding lights were turned on. He sat up, putting his legs over the side of the bed as he took a few deep breaths. He looked down at his bracelets for the first time since he had arrived.

Each territory often designed the bracelets of the Azure in a specific fashion. The Alphas oversaw the design, and it could be as complex or simple as they wanted. The Newaygo bracelets had a beautiful, intricate design that swirled and pattered like a river around the metal. Vines and flowers made the frame of the box where the Lycan owner's information was usually stamped.

The design that he had grown so accustomed to wearing had been effectively erased. Only against the metal's edge was there still a hint of what the picture had been. In its place was now just a flat, blank shine. No depth, no picture. It was smooth, plain, and emotionless with letters in all capitals that wrote, *Property of Richmond Plastics.*

Malachi jolted when someone reached down and grabbed his bracelet. His arm yanked upwards, which caused him to jump to his feet. His hand lurched out against his would-be attacker and grabbed a man by his shirt.

He appeared young, perhaps younger than Malachi, but he wasn't. Malachi could see it in his eyes, in his hands that continued to hold onto his arm, this man was older than him. But it was impossible to see how much older. His skin was pale and stretched across the bones of his thin frame. His clothes hung in rags around him, with a red tint to his hair and a dull hazel in his eyes. He grinned when Malachi's fist wrapped around his shirt. "Fast. Strong. Good." He let out a chuckle. Asking in a single word, "New?"

Malachi slowly released him, piecing together what the question would have been in his own head, and responded with his own single-word answer. "Yesterday."

The young man's smile never faltered. Using both hands, he lifted one of Malachi's bracelets again, his long fingers tracing over the newly printed words. "I like the shine. Like light we carry with us." He held up his wrist. "Mine are dull."

Malachi blinked at the strange man before his eyes moved down to the metal the stranger wore. When he was released, Malachi took the man's wrist into his hand. His bracelet was dingy, coated with a film that was undoubtedly caused by the dirty factory air. Unlike his own bracelet, this one held no hint of a pattern around the edge. "I'm Malachi."

The man echoed, "Malachi." He lowered his voice to a whisper, "She calls me Cato."

Malachi's brow furrowed. "She?"

But he didn't answer. His smile had faded, but the light and airy tone of his voice remained. "I'm hungry. Come on."

By the end of his first week, Malachi had learned all he wanted to about the factory. The first week was the most crucial, because it was used to determine those who would be unfit for work in production. Those who didn't meet the stressful and demanding requirements were "removed" from the floor. No one spoke of what happened to those who were removed, and Malachi never asked.

When he had made it past the trial of those beginning days, others in the room were more eager to speak to him. They were never told of news, weather, leadership changes, or anything that was happening in the outside world. Many of the Azure he spoke to didn't even know what month it was. Some would ask about the Games that were close, but not many remembered what the special Lycan event was.

He began to understand some of the strange behavior he saw in the Azure around him. There were no windows of any kind for them to see, with the only lights being the heavy fluorescent lights that shined down on them at all hours of the day. It was maddening not to see the sun, the stars, the moon phase. It was all gone from his world.

There was no night, or perhaps it was night all the time.

Was that thunder from a storm or a semi-truck pulling into the docks?

The world could have ended, and he would never have known.

The only saving grace inside the factory was Cato. The young, thin man he had met on his first day. He would ask the strangest questions, seemingly out of nowhere, with the same whimsical, almost sing-song voice of a child discovering the world for the first time. There were times when Cato's voice would flatten when he would talk more levelly and hold a deeper conversation, but those incidents were fleeting.

They were on a break after a shift, sitting on the worn-down benches in the room that wasn't quite a cafeteria. Cato had found half an apple in the pile that had been replenished the day before and was rolling it in his fingers. He stared at it with wide eyes as he spoke to Malachi. "Have you seen these before?"

Malachi looked at him, his eyes narrowing for a moment. "An apple? Yeah. You had a slice of one a few days ago."

Cato's smile grew. "It's so large. I've never seen one so large."

Malachi watched as Cato took a bite of the soft apple. The man hugged the fruit to his chest, which made Malachi chuckle for an unknown reason. "How long have you been here, Cato?"

He grinned before he continued chewing. "I was born here."

Malachi felt his mouth open and close. His mind spinning as he fumbled for a response. His face twisted with confusion, stammering until Cato began to laugh at him.

Although he laughed, his fingers dug into the flesh of the apple. When his chuckling stopped, his smile faded and took with it all the joy that was in his voice. A dark, almost venomous tone overtook him. His eyes locked onto Malachi's as he whispered, "It hasn't happened in our room in a while. But they come, sometimes, and take some of us away."

Malachi felt himself freeze. He swallowed hard on the old meat he had grabbed from the pile. "Away… what do you mean?"

Cato spoke matter-of-factly, with the slightest hint of sorrow behind his words. "Lycans are wolves. Wolves must hunt. They come for us, and we have to play with them."

Malachi didn't want to ask. He knew it would be an answer he did not want. But he couldn't stop himself from asking. "Play? Like…"

Cato leaned closer. His hand gripping the edge of the bench with such intensity his pale skin whitened even further against his knuckles. "Like, *play*. Run. Hide. Fight if you can. They like it. They like *us*, and sometimes, the girls have to go away for a while. I've seen them come back, though, much later. They don't last long afterward, though."

Malachi let his eyes sink to the floor when Cato straightened his back once more. It made sense, especially after he had learned that all the Lycans in the factory were Omegas. Just like the Azure, they were not permitted to leave the factory. It was never explained why that was. He had asked Whitney once, as she was much friendlier than most of the other Lycans. The only response he ever got from her was, "My Alpha has ordered I stay here."

He heard Cato continuing to eat his apple, his cares vanishing as his mind twisted itself back into the innocence he held so often. He didn't want the relief he felt, brought on by the knowledge that much of the time, their room was avoided for the selection of such activities. He didn't see many children in his area, but the rooms they were assigned to sleep in determined their placement in the factory, and there were no children who slept in his room.

It did make sense, if it was as horrific a situation as Malachi thought. Did they breed their own workforce in the factory? How would that be possible if most of the ones taken were women? Lycans and Azure were forbidden to reproduce across the country. With a shaky voice, Malachi asked another question he didn't want the answer to, "So when they take the men… do they…?"

Cato tossed his apple core into a metal bin against the wall. "They play with boys too. I've heard stories that they let the Azure play together in the basement." He shrugged his shoulder, answering a question that Malachi had yet to ask but knew it was coming. "I've never been down there."

Malachi lowered his voice to a whisper, "Have you… have they ever played with you?"

Cato's eyes snapped up to his. The sideways, icy glare cut into him sharper than any blade. His words were low and haunting, leaving Malachi unable to determine if he was upset by the question or the answer he provided, "Twice. I thought they liked me. But they don't come for me anymore."

Malachi let the silence overtake them. He didn't want to hear more; he didn't want to hear what he had already been told. Everything he saw, everything he learned, made his skin crawl with disgust. Everything about the factory was completely twisted compared to the world he had come from.

He longed for his family, his siblings, his parents. Malachi had a home once. He had fresh food, clean clothes, warm places to sleep, and windows that let in the sun and stars, the moon and clouds. The more he tried to remember his life with the Montana pack before things had gone so wrong for all of them, the more it faded. It began to feel like a distant dream. Details started to warp the more he tried to recall them. What did the house look like? What were the trees and plants that decorated the land? How thick was the snow in the wintertime? What had his parents looked like? The life he had lost was melting into obscurity.

A thousand miles away, a thousand years ago.

Malachi followed the others out of the room when they needed to head out onto the floor for their shift. He was able to push back his feelings as he headed out onto the smelly production floor and attempted to focus on what he had to do in that moment.

Survive and work.

One night, Malachi had been lying on his side, trying to sleep. He was half-conscious when it happened. It all seemed to happen so quickly.

The curtain that made their door was thrown. Heavy footfalls echoed around the room, accompanied by several sets of loud laughter. The lights remained off, but the intruders knew their way around the room.

Malachi kept his eyes closed, maybe it would be better if he pretended to be asleep. How many Lycans were there? It was impossible to tell.

What he heard sounded like a scuffle. Azure were ripped from their beds, their mouths quickly covered if they impulsively screamed. One of the she-wolves pulled an Azure from her bed. She grunted softly against the pull, wincing under the grip of her captor's hand.

Her shrill chuckle echoed through the dark room. The sickeningly sweet voice hissed through the air, "She's cute. What do you think, boys?"

There were murmurs of agreement from the others. A shuffling of fabric as the Lycan woman snaked her fingers underneath the clothes the Azure wore. The Azure whimpered as the Lycans' hands found her chest. The woman laughed again, "Nice. Just as I thought."

The Azure woman was taken away, with similar things happening to several others as the raiders moved around the room.

Malachi felt himself start to shiver in fear. He pressed his palm to his ear, trying to block out the violating sounds; whimpering, laughing, the rustling of fabric, hands across sensitive skin.

If the Fates had cared to hear him, he would have prayed for the Lycans to move on. However, the Fates did not care for the Azure and did not answer prayers from them or provide protection of any kind.

His fear was manifested when his arm was grabbed and he was ripped from his bed. He was yanked to his feet and pushed back. The Lycan that caught him was a large shadow against the dim light that glowed from the other side of the curtain door. Heavy hands held him by the shoulders tight against a muscular, intimidating man. The deep voice boomed through the commotion of the room. "What about this one?"

The woman's hands were on him in seconds. Her fingers slid underneath his worn-out shirt. Her hands were cold against his ribs, trailing ice up his torso and over his chest. Malachi saw her grin, the dull shine of her teeth in the minimal light. "Oh, this one's still fresh."

Malachi attempted to fight back but was held firm by the two Lycans. He didn't recognize any of the voices that invaded the room that night, finding himself thankful that Whitney didn't seem to be among them.

The woman's breath was hot on his neck as she lowered her head; she took a deep inhale before running her tongue against his skin. She rested her head against his ear and looked up to the Lycan who held him. When she spoke, her words were a moan. "Ooh, baby, he still smells like outside. Let's have this one too."

Malachi tried to pull against the man's grip. His efforts quickly halted when the woman grabbed the waistband of his pants. Her hands slid down his hips, pulling the thin fabric away from his pelvis. He managed to beg, "Please… don't."

Both Lycans giggled. The woman spoke, "That's right, boy, you're going to beg me." Her sharp nails pressed against his groin. "And then, you're going to beg *him*."

A hand left one of Malachi's shoulders and twisted into his hair; at the same time, the woman's fingers wrapped around his shaft. Her other arm slid around his body, grabbing the belt of the man who still held him and pulling them closer together. Before Malachi could fight, her mouth pressed onto his.

Between the hard grip on his hair, the woman's fingers around his flesh, and the two bodies he was pressed between, it was impossible for him to pull away from the assault. He felt her moan as her tongue prodded his mouth. His heart pounded in his chest with wave after wave of fear and shock, heated his blood, and slicked his skin with a layer of sweat. His body betrayed him as his mind went blank. Unable to resist, though, what would be the point? He was only an Azure; Malachi couldn't do anything against a Lycan superior. No one would help him if he tried to fight or speak out against her actions. His body wasn't his. At that moment, for as long as she wanted—whatever she wanted—it was hers, and he could do nothing. He *was* nothing.

The woman then let out a painful gasp, and she was pulled away from him. Her head yanked back, and her body followed. The hands and mouth left him, and a cold vacuum of air hit the sensitive flesh that was now exposed from her molestations.

Malachi gasped heavy breaths once he was able to breathe again. The outline of the woman thrashing against an assailant he could barely see as his eyes refused to focus in the dark.

He heard Cato's voice; the deep, almost growling tone sounded loud against the muffled shuffling that was slowly dying out as the others who were chosen were taken away. "Drop the boy."

Malachi let out a quiet whimpering scream when the hand in his hair tightened its grip and pulled his head back at a painful angle. The other hand of the Lycan man gripped his throat, cutting off whatever he might have tried to say. He attempted to loosen the man's fingers from either his hair or his throat, but both attempts led to failure.

The Lycan man's eyes glowed yellow in the dark, and his words growled in response, "Let her go."

Cato grinned. His teeth flashed in a sadistic smirk that glowed in the coloring of the man's eyes, and his hold on the woman was illuminated. His back was against the wall; the weight of his lean forced the woman up onto her toes from Cato's superior height. A small, corded rope was wrapped tightly around her neck. He gave a pull, the skin puckering around the braided cord that had to have been a shoelace.

Her fingers clawed at her neck, desperately attempting to pull it away. She gasped for air; any attempt at speech only escaped her in ragged coughs.

Cato's words hissed through the air. "Remember the last time they played with me? That one didn't last too long. Do you think yours will last longer than him? I'll take that gamble if you will." He pecked a kiss on the woman's temple. "Then the fun begins, hmm?"

The man did not hesitate; his hands released Malachi, who collapsed to the floor.

In a swift move, Cato pulled the cord away from the woman and shoved her into the Lycan man. He took hold of Malachi's leg and pulled him away from the wolves while the man awkwardly caught the woman who stumbled into his arms. Cato crouched over Malachi, wrapping his arms around the young man who curled into his embrace as he struggled to regain his breath between growing sobs.

The two Lycans glared down at him, and Cato spoke with an unearned confidence and calm the Azure were not privy to. "You'll not have this one. Pick someone else."

The woman gritted her teeth, her eyes sharing the yellow glow of her mate. She grabbed the man's hand and pulled him along with her; she pointed to a different bed. Her voice was hoarse, "Grab that one, and let's go."

It was another man who was taken from his bed upon the woman's request. That time, they didn't stay long enough to be fought off. The Lycan man was able to lift the Azure with one arm and carried the terrified slave from the room.

Malachi clutched onto Cato as he started to sob. Cato shushed him gently, running his hand gently across Malachi's back as he whispered, "Shh, it's OK. It's OK, Mal. You're OK. I'm here."

With Cato's help, Malachi was redressed and climbed back up onto one of the beds. He was shaking when he laid down and felt Cato lay down with him. Malachi's breath slowed as he felt Cato's body wrap around him. He hugged Cato's arm to his chest and heard his friend continue to coo at him with a gentle, whispering voice.

"It's alright. I won't let them take you. You're safe now."

Hours later, the stolen Azure was returned. One at a time, they were thrown through the curtain door. Each of them attempted to catch themselves on whatever they could grab before their skin smacked against the concrete floor.

Silently, they returned to bed. Malachi was awake when he heard the squeaking of the bedframes as they all lay down. Some of them were weeping quietly. He focused on the smooth sound of Cato's breathing as his friend slept, his arms still wrapped protectively around Malachi's body. He used the gentle sound to try and lull himself to sleep and found success not long after things had calmed down.

All were asleep except for one of the other young Azure had climbed out of his bed. The one that was taken in Malachi's place. He had been at the factory for almost eight months and had been the victim of the raids three other times since his arrival.

He crawled underneath the bedframe, quietly working one of the thin, metal support rods from under the mattress off the frame with a quiet *snap* sounding when he pulled it free. Finally, after almost a month of working on it, the rod had come loose.

With as much silence as he could muster, he rolled onto his stomach and placed the tip of the metal against his wrist. He pressed hard against his skin, feeling the metal open his flesh in the dark of the night as he pulled the rod up to his elbow. He felt warmth against his stomach as his blood pooled underneath him on the floor. Slowly, he no longer felt the pain in his body. He no longer felt the fear of the Lycans returning for him, as they had done so many times before. The deep, quiet pull of peaceful darkness beckoned him. With a final breath, his eyes closed, and he let himself fall into the comforting embrace of death.

When the buzzer went off for them to awaken, Malachi and Cato rose from the bed. Malachi rubbed his dry and reddened eyes. He tried to push the night's events from his mind. He couldn't linger on the thoughts when he had to focus on getting some food and getting to his molding presses on time. He was about to stand when he saw the blood that had pooled underneath a bed a few feet from where they had laid.

The young man's hands and feet were visible from underneath the bed. Malachi could see the piece of metal he used in an inch of blood underneath his palm. The young man who had been taken when Malachi was spared, thanks to Cato.

Cato had sat up and stretched his arms up high before standing. Neither of them spoke, but he saw where Malachi's eyes were fixed.

Cato reached down and gently pulled on Malachi's arm, coaxing him to stand.

Malachi walked with him, his mind still in a haze as he mumbled, "Could we have helped him?"

Cato looked at him curiously, the light tone contrasting the scene in such a way it could have given Malachi whiplash. "I'm not sure what you mean. He did a fine job on his own. We don't have to clean it if that's your worry."

Malachi shook his head, keeping his eyes low as he allowed Cato to lead him from the room and mumbled, "It's not."

Malachi wasn't sure how many days passed. Could it have been weeks? Months, maybe? He only knew work and sleep. He once tried to use it to mark how many days had gone, to try and keep track of the days of the week. When it all blended, he had to give up before the task drove him mad.

Work. Sleep.

Work. Sleep.

He would eat when he remembered that he felt hungry. He had lost a lot of weight, now looking thin and almost emaciated, much like the Azure around him. He wasn't even sure if he ate enough, but his stomach refused to growl around the slop he had grown semi-accustomed to. He was alive, so it must have been enough.

He often felt like he was turning into a zombie. A dead, barely mobile creature that trudged its way through what meaningless existence it had. Something without purpose or drive.

But he did have a drive. He did have a purpose. Malachi reminded himself of that as he worked on his press. Unloading hot, plastic molded parts that came down a conveyor belt into proper bins that were stacked and then taken away by another Azure to a different part of the factory. He had a purpose. He made a promise to himself the first time those Lycans raided his room.

It happened a few more times while he was there, but they never tried to take him, not after Cato's attempt on the Lycan woman's life. Malachi violated the often-strict religious following of the majority of Lycans; he prayed to the Fates before he slept each night. He prayed for Them to protect his siblings. He prayed in thanks for Cato saving him the night he was at the mercy of the Lycans.

He prayed for a way out of the factory.

Cato caught him praying once. He had waited until the lights were out and most people were sleeping. Malachi had slipped off his bed and sat on his knees with his palms turned upwards, head bowed down, and murmured words that were forbidden to the Azure.

Cato rolled on his bed, and when he witnessed Malachi's position, he reached out and swatted Malachi's shoulder. "What are you doing?"

Malachi didn't stand. He turned his head slightly and said, "Don't worry about it, Cato."

Cato leaned forward off the edge of his bed. His voice was deep, level, flooded with concern as he whispered, "You cannot practice *any* form of worship. You know that. If they catch you, I cannot help you."

Malachi let out a sigh. The name of the religion was not used often, but all practices of the Lycans's religion, Artiria, were forbidden to the Azure. They were not worthy of the Fates and were not allowed to worship them. He finished his prayer and sat up on his bed. "What if I told you the Fates are going to help us get out of here?"

Cato chuckled. He shook his head in disbelief, and as he rolled onto his other side, he said, "Yup. I'm sure we are at the top of their concerns."

Malachi was running his presses. His mind grows more determined by the day in his efforts to leave the factory. There had to be a way out. He coughed against the fumes of the presses and watched the Azure with pallet jacks pick up another stack of crates and quickly whisk them away.

He saw Whitney making her rounds and wondered how much information he could get from her that day. She was nice enough and would sometimes be able to bring Cato better food that he would share with Malachi.

When she approached, Malachi smiled at her. She returned his grin and said, "Well, at least you seem chipper today. Did you sleep well?"

He leaned on the edge of the conveyor belt railing. "It's easy to be happy with you around." He saw her try not to smile; her cheeks reddened as she ran her hand across her bangs. "How full is the moon tonight, do you think?"

She faltered for a moment. Malachi could see the hesitation in her eyes. She had no idea where the moon was in its phase. After an uncomfortable moment, she replied, "It's as powerful as it needs to be for us."

Malachi quickly touched her hand when she rested her fingers on the conveyor belt railing. He met her eyes, his gaze as intense as he could muster while he attempted a tactic he had yet to try on her. "Wouldn't it be nice if you could see it? Just once? Isn't there somewhere we could go after the sun sets?"

She faltered, looking away from him for a moment. Which was a strange action, considering she was a Lycan and him an Azure. When she looked at him again, her words were rehearsed. A tinge of pain in her voice as she said, "You are bound to the work in this factory. There is no place in the factory where you can see the outside. There are no windows or doors." Her eyes trailed down one of the aisleways that seemed to stretch on forever, even glancing upwards for a moment as if she could see the sky through the metal of the roof. "The Azure cannot leave this place. I don't even know how one would try." She pulled her hand away and gave his arm a gentle pat. "Don't fret, 1812; this is honorable work."

Malachi dramatically lower his head, knowing the action would be expected from him. "It is ma'am. Thank you. I won't ask again."

She kept her eyes on him for a long while as she walked away. He saw her smile to herself as her head turned away from him. She relished the kindness he gave her, as it was not often received from the other Lycans.

That night, Malachi slipped out of his bed. He moved slowly, his eyes on Cato the entire time to make sure his friend would not stir in the night. He desperately wanted Cato to go with him should he make an escape. But he needed to find the way first before he attempted to drag another along with him.

Once he was out of his room, it was easy to walk around. The factory was still in full production, as it always was. The Azure who worked on the floor were only ever recognized by their liaisons. To the rest of the Lycans, they were just workers. Not being recognized gave Malachi an advantage, as the others wouldn't stop him from walking because they thought he would be there on official business. It was also worth noting for him that the Lycans barely spoke to one another except for a quick passing of information.

It was the most disjointed pack system Malachi had ever witnessed. Then again, how much of a pack could they be if they were all sealed inside the factory.

The Azure had rumors of the Lycans having windows that would open high up in the offices of the factory. But Malachi knew that was false after Whitney's dodge of the moon phase question.

They, just like the Azure, had no windows. No doors. No way to escape the factory.

Malachi made his way down the aisles he knew. Passing an unattended pallet jack that was stacked with empty totes. He caught the handle and pulled it behind himself as he walked down the aisle. His head on a swivel as he made his way to the more unfamiliar parts of the factory.

When he was out of sight of his area, he dropped the pallet jack. It was hard to pull and would be difficult to hide if he needed to.

And he did need to.

He heard the voices of two Lycans as they approached. Malachi recognized one of the voices, the man's voice from the horrid night Cato had protected him from. A chill ran up his spine, and he panicked. He dashed from the aisle, quickly crouching behind stacks of products waiting to be moved to their next step.

Once the Lycans had moved past him, not giving a second look to the stack of product he hid behind, Malachi stood and followed them at a distance. From where he walked, he could see the two men shared the same Omega symbol tattooed on their necks.

He had seen the same symbol on a few of the other Lycans also and saw it on Whitney not long after he had arrived. He stopped when the men did and were speaking as a third Lycan walked up.

The newcomer also had the same Omega tattoo. Malachi glanced down and touched his bracelets. He wondered for a moment if it was their version of the bracelets.

The men spoke together for a few moments regarding the third Lycan, who had come up in a huff. "By the Fates, can't we go one fucking day without a bird getting stuck on the roof?"

One of the others rolled his eyes, "Come off it, man. They see the panels and crash into them. Just go clean it off. Be lucky you even get to do that. You know how many of us would kill to have your job? It's because you have that Beta blood, you know."

The roof! Malachi almost cheered aloud as the men split off from one another. The realization distracted him from the rest of what the

Lycan had said. He had Beta blood but had the Omega tattoo and was locked with them inside the factory.

A mystery for later, Malachi thought to himself.

He followed the one who had been cursing about having to go up on the roof. He turned corners and walked between machines and products through paths that Malachi didn't realize existed. Between and around presses, under conveyor belts, they walked over hoses, huge wires, and pipes. Malachi nearly lost his footing twice while trying to keep the Lycan in his sights.

It didn't take long for the Lycan's path to come to an end. A ladder was mounted to the concrete wall and led up to the roof, where Malachi could see a hatch door. The ladder was surrounded by round metal slats. Evenly spaced, they trailed the entirety of the ladder and were spaced just wide enough to fit between.

The Lycan hit a button on the wall near the ladder. After a moment, the roof opened at the top of the ladder. Malachi could barely discern the difference between the roof beyond the lights and the sky. However, he could see some of the smog start to lift into the air.

The Lycan slid between the metal bands and climbed the latter quickly and efficiently. He made it out of the hatch door before it closed.

Malachi quickly moved off the path he had walked upon. He wedged himself underneath one of the large presses he had been standing behind and waited for the Lycan to return.

It felt like hours later, but he did return. He was huffing from the climb and coughing as he tried to reacclimate to the smog inside the building. He brushed his hands off on his clothes and went back down the path he had come.

Malachi emerged from his hiding place, waiting only a few more minutes to make sure no one else would walk up to him. When he was confident that Lycan was the only one who took care of whatever was on the roof, he approached the ladder.

He pressed the button, just as the Lycan had. He climbed in between the railings, just as the Lycan had. But as soon as he touched the rungs of the ladder, he realized why the roof would not be a viable option.

An electrical surge pulsed through him. Malachi gritted his teeth, suppressing a scream as he groaned under the pain and forced his hands to release the bars. The electricity arced between him and the metal slats. It spread through his body, spasming his limbs until he was able to escape through the slats and fell away from the ladder.

He caught himself before he smashed his head against a support leg for one of the many conveyor belts. His breath heaved his chest, his heart racing as he tried to put his thoughts back together. He carefully sat himself down, feeling his body continuing to seize for several minutes afterward.

Malachi cursed to himself as he watched the top hatch close. There had to be another way. There was always another way. He made it back to the main aisleway and had to pause as Azure passed him. He thought of hiding but realized he would never be recognized by them. A different shift, in a different section of the factory; these were not people he had ever seen before.

While they passed, Malachi caught fragments of the conversation and heard one of them mention a shipment that was being expedited from the factory.

Malachi let out a heavy breath as he continued walking. "A shipment, you *dumbass*." He admonished himself as he walked. Everything that was shipped out of Richmond Plastics was sent out in semi-trucks. They also *received* containers and materials from those same semi-trucks.

They couldn't load and unload the trucks without doors.

It wasn't hard to find the shipping docks, although it seemed quite hidden. Rows and rows of products ready for shipment were stacked and waiting to be loaded on the scheduled trucks. Malachi pressed himself between two of the rows that were barely wide enough for him to squeeze through and said a silent prayer that the product he hid between would not be moved so as not to be discovered.

Surprisingly, the number of workers at the docks was scarce. Only three or four were trying to manage the in and out of at least ten shipping lanes. He needed a way to distract them, the plan piecing itself together in his mind.

Distract the workers and make a break for one of the doors.

Each of the massive dock doors had a small sheen-covered window near the top. Malachi guessed they were for showing if there was a waiting semi in the dock, or if it were empty. The liaison for the dock, a gruff-looking woman, oversaw the opening and closing of the doors. Opening the door too early meant they were able to have a glimpse of the outside; they couldn't let that happen.

Malachi watched how she did it half a dozen times. The doors didn't seem locked in any way; she would just walk up to one of the doors and hit the button that allowed access to the truck trailer. He wondered what kept the Azure on the forklifts from taking off as they loaded and unloaded the trucks.

They were so close to the outside but didn't run. Were they that loyal to the factory? Were they brainwashed?

No. They were prisoners just as the rest of them were. One drove by, and Malachi received his answer. They were handcuffed to the steering wheels of the forklifts. They were unable to leave their positions until the liaison released them with a key that hung from a cord on her wrist.

One of the forklifts came to a stop, the back only a pace away from where Malachi was hiding. While the Azure on the truck checked a bundle of papers he had on his forklift, Malachi crawled over. He could hear papers flipping and high-pitched beeping from the other machines backing up.

He slid under the forklift as far as he dared to and grabbed anything he could reach. A pulled plug, a ripped wire, he was able to cut one of the small tubes with his nail and felt a fluid pour onto his hand.

Malachi quickly returned to his hiding place and watched the forklift drive away. For a moment, he feared it hadn't worked. It needed to work. He silently begged for it to work.

He felt his heart skip when he heard the crash. The forklift smashed into one of the waiting stacks, suddenly unable to stop, and spilled parts across the floor. The liaison started screaming at the driver, running from the dock so she could unlock the driver and force him to clean the mess.

Malachi didn't wait; he didn't check to make sure no one was looking. That was his chance. He bolted to the closest door. Seeing the light of dawn discoloring the black of the empty dock window. He managed to crack the door; the noise was quick and hopefully hidden from the Lycan, who was still shrieking.

The drop was four or five feet to the ground, and he was unprepared for the drop. When he crossed the threshold of the dock, he felt the familiar buzz of the electricity. Thankfully, he didn't touch the metal long enough to feel the shock he did at the ladder. The buzzing in his bracelet dispersed as quickly as it had arrived once he crossed the other side.

He hit the ground with an audible cry and froze. He waited to see if anyone was going to catch him. But he heard no alarm; he saw no flashing lights. No electric shocks followed. He heard the Lycan woman turn her howls to the door, admonishing her Azure and no doubt confused as to how the door had opened.

Malachi pushed himself to his feet, and without thinking, he dashed away. Away from the building, he crossed the concrete lot, leaped the curb that separated the asphalt and the grass, and found himself in the woods that surrounded the factory.

He didn't make it far when his legs gave out from under him. He fell to his hands and knees, palms scraping the rough ground. Malachi's chest heaved as he gasped at the fresh air; he was outside. *Outside.* For the first time in how many weeks or months, maybe? There was no way for him to know until he made it back to…

A realization crushed his shoulders. He sat back on his heels, eyes turning up to the pale morning sky. They would be waking up soon.

Cato would be waking up soon.

Malachi realized then that he had left Cato. His one and only friend in the hellscape his life had turned into. He closed his eyes as tears threatened to fall. If he went back inside, he might not be able to get out again.

If he and Cato did get out, where would they go? Back to Newaygo? How would they explain the text on their bracelets? If they were found by any Lycans, they would be sent back to the factory.

The factory that owned them.

Malachi pushed himself to his feet, trying to formulate some kind of plan that could work in their favor. No scenario was acceptable.

When he straightened himself, he leaped back with a scream.

A young man stood in front of him. His black hair and clothes faded into the shadows of the trees that kept the morning light at bay. His pale skin looked even paler compared to his dark features. He smiled warmly, and Malachi could feel his anxiety slowly melting.

Malachi jumped in shock, letting out another fearful scream when he backed into another man. This one was older, maybe forty, with the same style of loose robe clothing. His features were light, with dark olive-tinted skin against white hair and cloud-grey eyes.

He held a staff and did not smile when Malachi looked at him. "Hello, boy." His words were deep, almost haunting. He walked around Malachi and stood next to the man in black.

Malachi stared at them, his eyes shifting back and forth as his mind tried to right itself. Had he seen them somewhere before? Yes. He had. They had stood at the edge of the forest, watching him get thrown into the factory.

But was there something else?

A sense of dread crept into his mind as he tried to back away from them. He knew them. He had spoken to them. Faded images worked their way back into his mind. Malachi thought of Montana; he tried to imagine the houses and the roads. But it felt… wrong.

The more he tried to think, the more his memories warped themselves. The houses changed; the landscape morphed. His head began to ache as he thought back, farther… and farther… into a time impossibly long ago. A life he had never lived, in a place he had never seen.

…But he had seen it…

A ring of mountains.

A village of huts used as houses.

A family?

What snapped him back to the reality he stood in was when he had backed into the man in white once again. He had tried to turn and run, but the heavy hand caught his shoulder. The man in white urging, "Don't run. Don't make me chase you."

Malachi managed to stammer a question, "A-A-Are you… Are you going to… to… to k-k-kill me?"

The man in black simply shook his head, his smile never faltering. "No, Malachi. We would never kill you." He gave one nod to the man in white, and Malachi's shoulder was released. "You're actually going to help us."

Malachi turned, trying to keep both men in his sights as they continued to advance towards him while he backed away. "With… with what?" His eyes flashed down to the wrists of the men. Their arms were covered in the heavy fabric that nearly enveloped their hands. Were they Lycans? The power the man in white radiated made Malachi believe he was from Prime blood, but he was not an Alpha he recognized, not that he had met many.

The man in white smiled. It was a more genuine smile and made Malachi's apprehension diminish enough to where he stopped retreating. His words echoed with something Malachi couldn't place. Whispers of a thousand voices spoke as he did when he said, "You're going to help us preserve the world."

Malachi wanted to ask what that meant. He wanted to ask ten, a hundred, a thousand questions as the fragments of his memory waved across his eyes. Could he imagine these men in different clothes? With different colored hair?

With names?

The man in black took his attention; a sense of peace and calm cooled his anxieties like water on a fire. Malachi felt himself able to breathe once more as the man in black reached out. "Just keep your eyes on me. Do this for us, and see your family set free."

When his hands came to rest on Malachi's shoulders, Malachi felt truly at ease. He felt the peace, the light, and all the reverence and marvel the Lycans would put towards their beliefs.

He heard the words of the man in black echo around him and had never heard a voice so angelic. "Look at me."

Malachi stared into the eyes of the man in black. Although he was an Azure, and unworthy of Their love, he knew in that moment he stood in the presence of the Fates. The dark irises of the man in black seemed to glow. Even throughout the pupils, which were difficult to distinguish from the dark irises, they sparkled with a shimmering beauty that rivaled the starry night sky. Fixing Malachi in a hypnotic stare he felt a spiritual peace beyond anything he knew in the world he lived.

What broke his trance was when two large, bony hands came down on him. The fingers felt like they nearly wrapped around his neck, stretching down over his collar and back. The iron grip was painful and cold and sent a chill down his spine that would have made him shake if not for the weight of the hands.

Fear froze him, unable to turn and look at whatever void-dwelling demon held him in place. He tried to focus on the peace given to him by the man in black, but the image of him seemed unfocused. Unreal. As if tranquility itself was unobtainable.

A pulse of energy radiated through the air; it seemed to emanate from Malachi himself. Had there been clouds, he would have believed it was thunder from an oncoming storm. The soundless wave vibrated his body, his soul—if the Azure had such a thing. The very *essence* that tied him to the world was rocked; it shifted and twisted into something unrecognizable.

The hands left him all at once, and he collapsed. When he looked up again, he was alone. He tried to stand, but his legs would not cooperate. He had to shake his head to steady his thoughts as his eyes shifted in and out of focus. The memory of the experience faded nearly as fast as it had happened. His heart pounded as he struggled to get his feet under him. Alone, once again, in the woods.

Pain shot through his nerves, and he fell to his side. His body convulsed uncontrollably in tight gyrations. The agony burned his skin, boiled his blood, seized his muscles, and strained his bones.

He couldn't move.

He couldn't scream.

He couldn't breathe.

He couldn't think.

His head ached; the light shined through the trees and cut into his eyes. His mind felt as if it would split open. His veins pushed against his skin; his body crawled with an unyielding anguish that rivaled any punishment he suffered at the hands of his old Masters. Any torture he endured whilst trying to survive the factory. Nothing was equal.

Malachi allowed himself a final thought and reached for the peace that was given when he stood in the presence of the Fates. He relented to his end and wished for the death that would allow him to end the torment. A proper death for an unwanted Azure, alone in unfamiliar woods.

But he did not die.

It came to a stop, and he was able to breathe. His movements were slow and smooth, and he stood from where he lay on the ground. A strength he had not had, that he *never* had, helped him balance with ease. Malachi's panic settled as waves of calm moved through his body. He touched his hands to his torso. Did he look the same?

He didn't feel the same. He felt strong, powerful, and *alive*. He blinked through the shadows that were shrinking beneath the autumn sun. He could see farther and deeper than he ever had with a great saturation of color. There was no moon in the sky, no stars that he could see. But he knew they still shined down on him. He could *feel* them, the sun, moon, and stars that blanketed overhead. The eyes of the Fates as they watched the earth.

He looked down at his wrists; his bracelets were warm against his skin. A strange thing, as the metal was only ever warm when he was attempting to use the gifts that had been given to him. Though he had little practice, and most of the time, his mark of imprisonment was as cold as the world he lived in.

Malachi knelt and placed his hands on the earth. The magic flowed around him, through him, and he closed his eyes. He thought of Cato, his brother who had protected him and helped him through his time in the factory. He thought of Whitney, of her kindness that perhaps helped him more than he had realized.

And he found them. His mind found them. As his bracelets continued to heat up to an intolerable degree, he reached out to them and felt them reach back. With gritted teeth, he forced his magic into his bracelets and felt his skin burning against the metal. The bracelets began to redden. A smell of seared flesh assaulted his nostrils as he focused on pouring the magic into the copper and iron.

Malachi let out an intense cry as he felt his skin burn. It blistered and split under the heat, with some of the wounds cauterizing almost instantly, but it didn't stop the blood from flowing down his hands. It trailed across his fingers and soaked into the ground.

He didn't know how long it lasted, but his efforts were rewarded when he heard the metal snap. The welding of the bracelets gave way and fell to the ground. He sat back, staring at the metal as it sizzled the small pools of blood that had formed in the shallow pits of the earth.

Malachi stood and felt his newfound energy overwhelm him. He stretched out his arms and breathed deeply. Thin trails of blood snaked down his arms, but he didn't care. He felt invincible. He could do anything, *be* anything. He could make it back to Newaygo and get his siblings away from those horrid creatures.

He could get Cato out of the factory.

A smile came to his face as he watched the sun's rays shine through the leaves. The words of the Fates returned to his head like a ghostly whisper: *Preserve the world, and set your family free.*

His eyes found the smokestacks of the factory as he dissected the words. To preserve the world, he needed a world *worth* preserving. His smile remained as he reached out to Cato again and felt a nudge in return. It was weak, but his brother was still chained. He could unchain him; he could unchain all of the Azure in the factory. The Lycans as well, there had to be some who would help him. They couldn't all feel the same way about the Azure.

What would the world be like if they didn't have to be enslaved? If they could all be free and live and work in a society that didn't look down on them as lesser. The Lycans were slaves to each other, just as the Azure were slaves to them. Locked into their own ranks and forced to obey those above them.

He could fix it. He could fix all of it.

*****

For Halius, a little over a month had passed since Malachi was sold. His mother would constantly shout at him that his behavior was getting worse. That he needed to shape up for the Qualifiers where the Alpha would decide who was going to represent the Newaygo territory in the Annual Games.

Halius's most recent delinquent behavior, however, could not be fully blamed on the selling of his former best friend.

The Qualifiers had come faster than the young pack had expected. The Alpha had arrived at the school with Liam, as well as Elliot and Ezra's father to assess the senior students in the school. A series of grueling tests that lasted nearly six hours and were far more rigorous than any of the training Gwen and Erika had put them through.

Constant running, climbing, fighting, and even swimming in the pool that was inside the preschool wing of the school.

All to find out that the only one out of the Prime pack who was selected for the games was Maddox. The young Alpha was furious at his father, for he wanted to compete in the games with his friends, his brothers, by his side as they all rose to glory.

Maddox had threatened to drop out of the games, leading to a series of fights between himself and his father that did not end until he was Commanded to let the topic drop. He would be competing with ten other Lycans from Newaygo, with the rest of them being Lesser Omegas and Betas from across the county. While Halius, Ezra, and Elliot would be attending the games as spectators.

One evening, Halius sat on the edge of his bed and waited to hear the gentle opening and closing of bedroom doors, signaling Liam had left Sydney's room. Sometimes it took hours and made Halius wonder what he could be doing in there, although some of the thoughts were so sickening he would immediately regret the images that entered his head.

He often attempted to force himself to believe that Liam would never abuse Sydney. Although it wouldn't be looked at as abuse. Liam could do what he wanted to Sydney. A thought that made Halius's stomach twist in disgust. He went into that bedroom every night; sometimes Halius could hear their voices but couldn't piece together the words they were saying. The house was well-insulated and didn't offer much in terms of snooping.

Halius stood from his bed, knowing it was probably better that he did not hear whatever Liam was putting Sydney through. But it was too late. He kept imagining Liam entering her room. Would he force her to undress for him, or would he rather remove her clothes himself? Sydney often wore sleeves or sweaters; was she hiding bruises? Did he prefer to throw her around a little before he forced himself on her?

Halius felt a growl rumble in his throat. He squeezed his eyes shut and shook his head in a pitiful attempt to throw the thoughts from his mind. If it were true, there was nothing he could do about it.

Finally, he heard the sound from the hallway, a door opening and closing, quickly followed by another door farther away opening and closing again. Halius carefully opened his bedroom window and pulled in the screen. He slowly slid out the window, carefully landing his feet on the small rocks that traced the edge of the house. Without replacing the screen, he gently closed the window.

He didn't risk walking through the house in case someone left their bedroom and couldn't leave earlier in case he was seen outside Sydney's window.

When he stepped away from the house, he couldn't stop himself from looking towards her bedroom. The lights were off, but he could see the glow of her phone against the walls. She was awake. For a moment, he debated if he should try to take her with him. Give her something that was outside of the house that she almost never left, save to go to school or accompany Liam somewhere else.

Halius turned from the house and headed off into the night. It would be too risky to take Sydney with him, and he wouldn't have a good reason for doing it. The truth was, the fewer people who knew where he was going, the safer he would be.

He cut through several yards of the scattered houses that lined the streets in the Omega sectors of the outer city and found himself on a road that held one of the numerous bus routes that went through Newaygo. The buses ran throughout the night and, of course, were driven by Azure drivers.

When he boarded the bus, the Azure gave him a cordial, "Good evening, sir."

Halius tried to act as passive as possible and ignored the driver. The Omega, especially the Lesser Omega, often treated the Azure poorly. Often worse than the other ranks of Lycans because there was no one else below them. Depending on the territory, Alphas were known to consider their Lesser Omegas and Azure in the same manner.

Halius also had to play the part because a Beta would never take something as low as the bus. If anyone recognized him, word would spread, and his cover would be blown. When he took his seat, the bus started to move. He quickly pulled up his phone and sent a text message through a group chat he had with the others. *I'm on my way.*

The only response he received was from Ezra, a street address he was supposed to meet them at. After the disappointing Qualifiers, the young pack decided to blow off some steam by partying throughout the Omega sectors of the city. They had yet to be recognized and made sure to stay in areas where members of the Prime pack would generally not go.

Halius got off the bus two blocks before his meeting point and walked the remaining short distance. All the buildings on the Southeast side of the town were tall, old brick buildings that often had a minimum of three floors. Many upper floors were empty, with only the street level being occupied by small businesses that had varying levels of success depending on the funding they were provided by the Alpha. Many others had broken and boarded up windows and doors, some even having condemned signs hanging on what used to be the entrance doors.

When Halius rounded the next block, he started to hear music. A pulsing bass that let him know a club or bar was nearby. Through the air rose a blanket of voices, and Halius could see a small collection of people forming outside one of the alleyways between the buildings.

The club had a steady stream of people wandering in and out. Kept by a doorman who seemed not to be enjoying his job that night. Halius couldn't help but note the clothing worn by those waiting to enter the club or lack thereof. Each of them looked like they were heading to work at a strip club; it was almost silly.

He stopped at the corner of the neighboring building. He stepped into the shadow of the bricks, away from the streetlights, and waited for the rest of them to arrive.

Ezra arrived first and greeted Halius with a one-armed hug. "Elliot and Maddox will be here soon. We thought it was better to not get here all at the same time." True to his word, the other two arrived and gave Halius the same greeting Ezra had.

Maddox took a deep breath, always too excited to break the rules on the nights they decided to go out. "Alright, everyone ready?" When they agreed, he turned to Ezra. "It's your turn to pick the spot after you."

Ezra smiled wide and led them to the entrance of the club. They didn't have to wait long until they were at the front of the line and were promptly stopped by the doorman.

Before the doorman could speak, Ezra caught his hand in a handshake the doorman was not prepared for. Ezra spoke quickly, "Hey man! Good to see you, buddy! It's been a while; listen, we'll catch up later, alright? We're gonna head inside, but I'll be back around to talk to you, alright?"

When his hand was released, the doorman looked down at his palm. To the shock of the other three boys, the doorman smiled and said, "Alright, man, I'll see you later." And he motioned for them to enter.

They walked in, each of them keeping cool until they sat down at a table after someone had gotten up and left. Maddox grabbed Ezra's shoulders with exuberance as Halius laughed. Elliot ruffled his brother's hair and said, "Way to go, little brother. I'm gonna see if I can score us some drinks." He left the table and headed towards the bar.

Maddox looked around, shaking his head as his amazement had not worn off. "How did you get him to let us in? Dude, that was so smooth."

Ezra shrugged one shoulder, his eyes giving away the false bashfulness he was trying to portray, "Maybe I just have a way with words." He grinned and took a liquor drink Elliot had returned with.

He looked down at the colorful drink and added, "And a hundred bucks I took out of Luna Erika's purse."

Maddox spat some of his drink across the table. He coughed hard as he choked from the shock of Ezra's statement. Halius hit the young Alpha's back in an attempt to help him clear his throat.

Elliot spoke with a hushed voice, although it was hardly necessary in the loud establishment. "You *stole* from the Alphas? What is wrong with you?"

Ezra waved his hand dismissively. "Relax, they're so loaded she probably won't even notice. Besides, look around you, man. A little petty theft is probably the tamest thing we'll be doing tonight."

Halius took a large swig from his own drink. "What's the worst thing? We aren't doing anything wrong."

Maddox, finally able to speak, took Ezra's side. "Halius, we are all underage, drinking in an Omega Bar on the Southeast side of the city. What are we doing here that *is* legal?" He slammed a heavy hand on Ezra's collar and shoved the Omega back a step. "But don't *ever* steal from my parents again."

Halius took a moment to think before his brow raised and he nodded slowly, consigning to Ezra's way of thinking.

The night went on, with the boys taking turns getting drinks and dancing to the heavy music that thrummed the air. Rainbow lights flashed along to the beat and swirled around the half-naked bodies that were sweating and pulsing against each other in a swirl of drunken flesh.

Halius was trying not to drink too heavily; it generally didn't take much for a Lycan to become drunk, and he wouldn't be able to explain his drunkenness to his mother the next day.

Lycans, as a whole, lacked a true ability to heal themselves. Simple scrapes and bruises often took weeks to heal. More severe injuries, broken bones, ruptures, and muscle tears required the assistance of an Azure who had the ability to heal. Hospitals were always equipped with dozens of Azure who were healers, led by a Lycan doctor who had a medical degree from a university.

Roderick was one such Azure.

Maddox had brought Roderick along on several occasions when they had first started going to the clubs at night. However, Ezra had spoken to Maddox about reservations he had with the Azure joining them, believing that the Azure would blow their cover, and they would receive some kind of punishment for their actions.

Or at least, Ezra claimed to have those fears.

Halius stood at the bar, waiting for the bartender to come back with his next order of drinks for the group. He felt his balance sway a bit as he leaned onto the slick, wooden counter. He watched the Azure bartender dash back and forth as she was barked at by a fleet of drunk, demanding Lycans.

He tried to ignore the Azure's turmoil. Such a thing wouldn't help his decreasing mood as his intoxication began to rise. It made him think too much about the arguments he had with his mother, the way Sydney had been treated by her, as well as so many others. He had never figured out why Gwen seemed to hate Sydney so badly.

Perhaps Gwen blamed her for having to sell Malachi, Julien, and Lyra. If it were true, at least that would mean she had some regrets about what she had done.

Halius was pulled from his thoughts when a Lycan leaned against the bar next to him. He was large, thickly built, with muscles and scars that made him look like he was from the Old Wars, long before civilization took over the earth. His voice was chipper, with a gruff undertone like he was speaking with a sore throat, "Well, well, well. You look like you know how to scrap."

Halius gave him a sideways glance. He reached over the bar and stole a full shot glass the bartender had filled, "What makes you say that?"

The man shrugged. His eyes moved away from Halius as if he were assessing the others in the bar. "You don't get that big by jogging, is all I'm saying." He paused, running his thumb across his nose before he continued, "You ever put those muscles to the test? With something a little more rugged than some weights?"

Halius leaned onto his elbow, facing the stranger as the bartender finally placed his four drinks up on the bar in front of him. He glanced at the dance floor where the other three teenagers were dancing with a group of girls they had all picked up. Halius let out a sigh when he saw them all dancing together and having a good time. It seemed like they didn't even notice he was gone; even the woman who feigned interest in him looked like she was having a better time with the others.

It made him wonder who else he was impeding. Who else would benefit if he wasn't there? He looked again at the stranger and asked with caution, "What did you have in mind?"

The Lycan grinned and slid a business card across the slick bar. "Should you decide to join us, the entrance fee is $20. Round one starts at dusk if you think you can handle it, big guy." He lightly wrapped Halius's shoulder and walked away without ordering a drink.

Halius looked at the card, flipping it between his fingers as he read the information. It was for a lumber mill not ten miles south of where they were. The back of the card was blank, with the lower corner having a poorly written *86* indelible ink that had already begun to fade.

With his interest peaked, he slid the card into his pocket, grabbed the tray of drinks that he had ordered, and returned to the table as the guys and girls they picked up returned when they saw him.

Elliot and the woman oozing all over his side slumped over the table and grabbed two shots off the tray. Elliot laughed and said, "Don't try to keep up with me, sweetie."

The woman laughed and rocked back her glass before she spoke, "Boy, I'm gonna lap you around this bar!" She dropped the glass hard onto the table. Her hands were awkwardly flopping about as she tried to move. She looked over her shoulder and shouted to the friend who had briefly danced with Halius, "Maria! Come with me; I have to go to the bathroom!"

The women linked arms and stumbled away from the table. Elliot watched them walk away and grabbed onto Halius's shirt; he hung on him to the point where Halius had to take hold of the table to steady himself. His words were slurred when he said, "She's so hot, Halius! Don't you think she's hot?"

Halius could have rolled his eyes. "Honestly, no, not really."

Elliot threw his arm over Halius's shoulders. His heavy limb pressed hard against Halius, his face turning sour as he said, "Hey man, that could be my mate. Don't you think?"

Halius let out an audible sigh. Each time they had gone out, Elliot had gotten drunk. Each time Elliot got drunk, Maddox generally followed his lead, and both would think every woman they interacted with would be their True Mates. "Elliot, she is not your mate. You do this every time we go out."

Elliot blew a raspberry from his lips. His breath made Halius turn his head with a sneer as he said, "Those other girls were *nothing*, man. This one," He jabbed his finger into Halius's chest, "This one I feel in *here*."

Halius shook his head once more. Gwen had tried to explain to him once what it would feel like when he found his True Mate.

When his mother had originally known his father was her True Mate, she said the world had slowed down.

He remembered her words as he watched Elliot lean his head down onto his shoulder, a pitiful doe-eyed look on his face as he rocked back and forth. His mother had said, "When you see your True Mate for the first time, even if it's someone you've known your whole life, the world will stop. The only thing you'll be able to think of is them, your life with them. Maybe you'll be able to picture your children or your future. Your wolf will want to stop your heart because once he sees the other half of your soul the Fates have made in this world, everything else will feel pointless. You will want the moment never to end, and you'll have that feeling every day you wake up next to them."

The more Halius thought of it, the more ridiculous it sounded. The gooey, oversaturated description his mother often gave him when he was younger made him think of those chick-flick movies she loved to watch. Where a woman would live a stressful life, and her True Mate would show up and whisk her away to a life of luxury.

It all sounded so excessive. Even though they were all approaching the ages where finding their True Mate would become possible, it wasn't too far a stretch for Halius to believe he wouldn't have one.

What Halius also couldn't believe was the sight of Maddox, and the woman the young Alpha had been dancing with, in a twist of limbs and lips against one of the walls on the opposite side of the dance floor. Halius couldn't hide the visible shock that rocketed through his body; a wave of disgust twisted his stomach. His wolf growled within his head, sharing Halius's feelings on the abhorrent behavior.

In the lower Omega ranks, it didn't always matter if they found their True Mates or not. It was favorable if they did, as the matchups yielded the strongest children. But it was incredibly common for

Omegas to have several lovers, both emotional and physical, before finding their mates. Prime packs, however, had strict and often obsessive, rigorous rules regarding the importance of purity. Alphas could even lose their claims to a territory if the bloodline was questioned, and the credibility of the Alpha—or Luna in the case of promiscuity in women—would be destroyed. Lycan parents and children were known to be killed for such indiscretions. There was no fraternization with *anyone* who was not a True Mate for Lycans with Prime blood. The lesson had been nearly beaten into them, into every Prime Lycan, for their entire lives. Purity, over everything else.

Halius knew by looking at them that Maddox was not in the thralls of love with his new mate. If he were, Halius would hope he wouldn't be filled with such rage at the sight. He left Elliot at the table and pushed his way across the crowded dance floor.

Maddox had his mouth pressed against the lips of the woman he held against the wall. Her hands were underneath his shirt with one leg wrapped around his waist. Maddox had one hand bracing him against the exposed brick with his other hand against the woman's breast. He had unfastened her shirt, a flimsy laced bra the only fabric that separated her bare chest from the humid air of the club.

With a swift and rough hand, Halius ripped Maddox away from the woman. He crashed his Alpha against a nearby table, where Lycans screamed in protest. Although their largest concern seemed to be the newly spilled drinks.

Halius spoke before Maddox could attempt to berate him, dragging him across the club as Halius snarled, "What the fuck are you doing?"

Maddox's words didn't slur as heavily as Elliot's, but Halius could smell the overconsumption of alcohol as soon as the young Alpha began to talk, "What the hell, dude? Why are you trying to ruin my game?"

Halius pulled him up from the table, rage burning his eyes as his hands gripped tighter on Maddox's t-shirt. "Your *game*? You think that kind of act is a *game*? How far were you going to let that go if I hadn't stopped you?" He released Maddox with a shove.

Maddox stumbled and caught himself on the table that Elliot was leaning against. "She could have been my mate! How am I supposed to know if we don't, you know?" He thrusted his hips as Elliot began to laugh at the crude gesture.

Halius threw out a hand and rapped Maddox's shoulder. "You would throw away your purity on some Omega harlot you met in a bar? We are not here to meet our mates!"

Elliot was leaning his cheek on his hand. His legs barely kept him standing as he grinned stupidly and slurred, "The Fates decide when and where we meet our mates, man. Who's to say, not here?"

Maddox leaned forward, his center of gravity compromised, and he fell into Halius's chest as he tried to poke at him with a finger. "Yeah! Don't forget you… you, dude! I'm your—"

Halius clapped his hand over Maddox's mouth before he could speak the word, *Alpha*. "That's it, we're done here. You guys are too drunk; this was a mistake." He pulled Maddox and Elliot, although the latter didn't fight him as much, and headed for the door. On his way, his eyes caught Ezra who was sitting at a lower table with a woman who was giggling at something he had said. Halius's thunderous voice roared over the music, "Ezra! Let's go! We're leaving!"

The girl was trailing her fingers against Ezra's forearm. "I guess that's your cue, hmm?"

Ezra placed his head on his fist and said, "Oh, naw, that's just them going to warm up the car." He flinched when he heard Halius's booming voice a second time.

"*Ezra!*"

He nodded, dropping a few dollars on the table as he softly said, "OK." He gave a slight wave that she returned with hesitation, and he followed Halius out the door.

He had fought his brothers all the way to where Roderick was waiting in the car, they had arrived in. Halius had never felt more relief than to see the loyal Azure getting out of the car upon their arrival, so Maddox didn't leave him home after all. Halius should have known; Roderick almost never let Maddox out of his sight.

Halius explained the drunkenness but left out the immoral acts committed by at least two of his brothers. Roderick had assured him they would be taken care of and offered Halius a ride home, which he refused.

Roderick tried to insist, "It's no trouble, Master Halius."

Halius let out a sigh, "How many times do I have to tell you it's just *Halius*? Roderick, please. Just Halius." He saw the Azure smile, the smile that told him it was never going to happen. "I'm fine just taking the bus back; I don't mind it."

Roderick gave a single nod; he couldn't fight Halius's will. It would be improper for an Azure to question the wishes of a Lycan. "Of course, sir. We will see you at the school tomorrow."

Halius nodded and walked away; school was undoubtedly going to be rough the next day as his body tried to process not only the alcohol but the lack of sleep also. Although it didn't seem to bother him as much, he was getting used to functioning on lesser sleep.

The next morning, Halius once again had a late start.

Sydney didn't know the extent of what Halius had done when he went out, but she knew he left the house. She had seen him leaving the yard but said nothing to his mother or Liam. She was expecting to be the one who drove them to school and monitored him again as she had a few other times.

Gwen let out a huff as Sydney placed her breakfast in front of her. "I'm going to get him up."

Liam let out an audible sigh as he watched his wife get up from the table.

She spun to face him and quickly snapped, "Something to say, Liam?"

He placed his tablet on the table and pulled the plate Sydney had placed in front of him closer to himself. "Halius has plenty of time to get ready. The new moon is close; just let him sleep."

Gwen ran her hand through her artificially blonde hair. She gripped the back of one of the wooden chairs, her hostile eyes turning to Sydney as she barked, "Are you ever going to learn to serve the head of this household first?"

Sydney lowered her head as she backed away. She mumbled a pitiful, "I'm sorry,

Mistress Gwen." Her eyes flicked to Liam. "I… I will serve you better tomorrow."

Liam was more focused on his food and seemed quite uninterested in what was happening. Was he deliberately not looking at Gwen? It could certainly appear that way. As he began to eat, he said in a very nonchalant voice, "I look forward to it, Sydney."

Gwen huffed and roughly sat herself down in one of the chairs. She pulled her plate across the table to herself and stabbed her food so aggressively that it was amazing the plate didn't crack.

Liam's eyes finally looked up to her. A smile pulled the edge of his mouth as he spoke in a plain voice, "Oh, something to say, Guinevere?"

That made the woman's blood boil in a heated rage. Her face reddened as her fingers gripped her silverware to the point it started to warp. He only called her *Guinevere* in two scenarios: when he was being passive-aggressively cruel to her or when he was forcing her to submit to his Command. There was no Command in his voice; it would have shaken the air with a terrible force, as it did in their heated arguments.

Gwen felt her strength draining with each second that passed; the absence of the moon drained her as well as any wolf. It made them irritable, tired, and quick to mood swings. She was still drowsy from the day before, dealing with the students from the Rec classes at the county school. Even though the rankings were already posted, and the competitors for the Annual Games were chosen, the students had to continue their training. The Alpha believed in training above almost all else and believed if they were to stop, even for a couple of weeks, they would become soft. He couldn't allow that.

Gwen let out a sigh as she looked down at her food in defeat. "He needs to get up, is all."

Sydney could feel the tension in the room. Did they even enjoy being around each other? She couldn't remember a single moment since they had married when Liam enjoyed Gwen's company. Perhaps in the beginning, before her contempt for Sydney started to show. It constantly amazed Sydney that Halius didn't seem to hate her as much as Gwen did, though he did have heavy resentment towards his mother for a variety of reasons.

She knew she shouldn't offer but was hoping to break the tension by proposing, "I might be able to wake him, Mistress Gwen."

Both Gwen and Liam's eyes turned to her. A silence fell over the house that could have convinced Sydney that time had stopped. If not for the loud ticking clock that hung on the kitchen wall, they seemed frozen for a moment. Gwen spoke first in a gentle tone she did not expect from the woman. "That…" It started almost aggressive, floating to a gracious tone as she continued, "That would be… mighty kind of you, girl."

Liam immediately shook his head. "Absolutely not. You are not allowed in Halius's room, you know that."

Gwen looked at him with wide, pleading eyes to see how the new moon changed the dynamic of the house. "Do you want to go get him, then? If I try, he's going to make my morning miserable." She dramatically swiped her fingers across her forehead. "I just don't have it in me to deal with him this morning."

Liam looked towards the hallway; he could just barely see the edge of Halius's bedroom door. He ran through the scenarios in his head, trying to imagine what kind of backlash he would get from Halius if he were the one who attempted to rouse the young Lycan. He had very little strength as well and knew what kind of hothead the teenager could be. He let out an exhausted sigh and looked up at Sydney. "You think you can get him up without putting him in a bad mood?"

Sydney wasn't sure why she believed it but nodded confidently.

Liam's voice was firm, he responded as soon as she had confirmed his question. "Into the room. Shake him awake. Leave the room. Do not close the door."

Sydney lowered her head, "Of course, Master." She stepped up to Halius's door and wrapped the wood. "Halius, it's time to get up. Breakfast is ready." Silence was the only response. Slowly, she opened the door and stepped in. "Halius, are you awake?"

He wasn't awake. He was lying on his side, his blankets in heaps against the wall behind him. It was strange to see, but he seemed to sleep deeply with dreams that evaded wolves during a new moon. No Lycan slept well during that time; their wolves and bodies were weak, hormones dropped and caused irritability, and their bodies often betrayed them.

Sydney stepped around the mess on the floor. Clothing littered the carpet, and a desk table in the corner was cluttered and disorganized. His closet door was ajar, with scrunched clothing piled on shelving and various pieces of clothing half-dangling off hangers.

She crouched next to his twin-sized bed. His arms were pulled tightly to his chest as he slowly breathed. When she took a closer look, she saw his top bed sheet had been twisted around his legs, so he had done a fair amount of tossing and turning. She touched his shoulder and rocked him gently. "Halius? Halius, it's time to get up."

He jolted awake. The sudden motion caused Sydney to jump back while repressing a shocked scream. She covered her mouth quickly, composing herself as she glanced towards the door to see if the adults had noticed, but there seemed to be no reaction.

Halius blinked hard; he rubbed his eyes with one palm and groaned, "Huh? What time is it?" His eyes focused slightly, and he could see the shape of the young woman standing just in front of his entertainment system. "Sydney? What happened? Are you OK?" He pushed himself up, hanging his legs over the edge of his bed. He kept the bed sheet pulled across his waist. After a moment of his mind piecing together where he was, he looked up at her with groggy, swollen eyes. "Why are you in my room?"

Sydney spoke quickly as she backed towards the door. "It's time to get up, Halius. Gwen and Liam sent me in here to get you."

Halius raised a brow at her, a smile pulling the edge of his mouth as he asked, "Liam allowed you to come in here?"

She nodded. "That was my order. You need to get up; breakfast is ready."

He seemed to pause but nodded after a moment and spoke with a calm voice. He was much too calm for his normal morning behavior. "I'll be right out. Let me get dressed first."

Sydney left the room, a sense of pride swelling in her chest. She was able to get him up, and he was not irate in the slightest; at least, he didn't seem so. She was only able to step into the main room for a moment, after she reported that Halius would be out momentarily, Liam had her fetch the ribbons for her hair.

When Halius emerged, he was finishing the buttoning of his shirt. He adjusted his collar as he sat where the plate of food was waiting for him.

Gwen threw back the last swig of her coffee before she snipped, "Well, finally." When Halius didn't respond, she sniffed theatrically and leaned back in her chair as she folded her arms. "Were you ever going to get up on your own?"

Halius shook his head without looking up. "Not if I could help it."

Gwen's response was sharp. "Why are you so tired? You went to bed at a decent time last night."

He shrugged at her, continuing to look down at his plate, and said nonchalantly, "New moon, right? We're weaker than normal. I guess I just needed more sleep."

Silence overtook the house. A cold wind ruffled the outside as the ticking clock continued to be some of the only noise from inside. The wind was a sign that winter would be on its way.

Gwen huffed and shook her head. Her eyes moved to where Liam had sat in the living room with Sydney on the floor in front of him. She saw her husband smile at the wretched girl, he leaned down and whispered something to her. A term of endearment, no doubt, that Gwen never heard from him.

Halius could see her indignation towards Sydney. The irritation tugged at his head, threatening to fuel his rage that he had little energy for at that moment.

When his mother's eyes turned back to him, her words were icy. "You shouldn't need any more sleep since you failed the Qualifiers."

That was enough to start the fire of his anger. It was as if she was intentionally prodding him to make him angry. Any calm he had when he had awoken was overtaken in that moment. Unable to suppress a weak growl that echoed his words when he said, "That was your fault for not letting me go to boot camp *again*."

Gwen's body tensed. Was it really worth him fighting her that morning? Couldn't she have one day where he didn't try to make her miserable. Was this all a revenge for something ridiculous from the past? "It's your fault because you don't have any manners! I was sick of your derogatory comments towards me. I am your mother!"

Halius practically jumped from the table. His chair slammed against the wall as he stormed around, grabbing his backpack from the chair at the end as he shouted, "If you're such a good mother, you won't act like such a *cur*."

Gwen took a shocked breath. She dramatically placed a hand on her chest, as she often did when he spoke to her in such a fashion. Her voice nearly shrieked as she declared, "Halius Usoro!" She stood from her own chair and moved quickly, stepping in his path towards the door. "You apologize right now!"

He threw his bag over his shoulder. "Or what? You'll ground me? I'm not five anymore, mother. I don't care if I have to sit in my room for a few days."

Gwen's eyes flashed a faded yellow. She was weak, her wolf was weak, and her threats fell flat. Unable to force an apology, she reached over to her son. With a quick motion, perhaps too quick for a woman her age, she snatched the phone from his front pocket.

Halius dropped his bag when he tried to snatch it back from her. "Mom, hey! Give me back my phone! Mom, seriously?"

Gwen evaded each one of his attempts. "No. Until you learn respect for your elders, for your mother, you don't need this kind of distraction." She dashed into the kitchen with Halius behind her. "You need to focus on your training! You need to do better! You need to *be* better!" She threw the phone onto the countertop and grabbed one of the large cast iron pans Sydney used to cook for them each morning. "Until you are, you don't deserve this!"

With as much force as she could muster, she slammed the pan down onto the phone. The screen shattered, and shards of glass bounced across the marble and onto the floor. The metal cracked and split around the ports as the protective case disintegrated from the force.

Halius stared at her with wide, horrified eyes as she dropped the pan back onto the stove with a loud *clang*. He felt his hands shake and balled his fingers into fists. His voice was cold and quiet when he spoke, "Mom… why did you do that?" His tone grew louder when all she did was shrug. "What if I need to call someone? What if something happens?"

She moved passed him with a dismissive wave of her hand. "Well, you'd better make sure nothing happens today. Cause now; no one can come to help you."

At his silence, she believed she had won, whatever that meant to her. Halius felt himself running away from her when he dashed back through the house. He snatched his bag from the floor and threw open the door.

Liam had ushered Sydney out of the house before things had gone completely awry. Sydney had already gotten into the car when they saw Halius storm from the house. Liam approached him and attempted to ask, "Hey, what happened?"

Halius shook his head as he rounded passed Liam. He threw his bag into the backseat, slamming the door with such force the car rocked. He screamed at Liam, "Your *cunt* of a wife broke my phone!"

Liam let out a mournful sigh. He should have questioned Halius further, but the young Lycan got in his driver's seat, and the car rocketed down the driveway.

It didn't take long for Sydney's phone to buzz; a message from Liam appeared on her screen. *Keep me updated.*

Sydney didn't expect him to talk. He was often quiet for some time after being angered to such a degree by Gwen, or anyone for that matter. She fidgeted with her nails as the car sped down the freeway. The silence was heavy between them, with only the hum of the engine for noise.

Halius's enraged voice suddenly thundered through the car. "I don't understand why she has to be like this!" He saw her jump at his outburst. Regret twisted his face, and he let out a sigh. His voice calmed, and he said, "I'm sorry. I didn't mean to scare you."

Sydney let her breath slow down before she looked up at him. She felt her heart racing in her chest but was able to keep her voice steady when she said, "It's… um… it's OK. I know what you mean."

Halius rubbed his tired eyes. He switched the hand that was on the steering wheel. "Yeah, you know better than the rest of us." He gave her a sideways glance. "Look… I'm… I'm sorry for the way she treats you."

Sydney looked at him with a furrowed brow. Either she didn't know why he was apologizing for his mother's behavior, or she was bewildered at the thought of someone apologizing. "Um… thanks."

For another few minutes, the silence returned. Halius gripped the wheel tight as a question burned the back of his mind. He could hear his wolf snapping its jaws in agitation. He cleared his throat and shifted uncomfortably in his seat. "Listen, Sydney, I… I really want to ask you something. I… I feel like I *need* to ask you."

She looked at him, once again, with confusion but remained silent. She responded with a nod.

They rode the rest of the way in silence. Halius didn't speak again until he parked the car in the school parking lot. He began with a stammer, "I, um… I just…" He looked out the window for a moment, his eyes looking everywhere except for her. "I really need you to answer the question, even if you've been ordered not to."

Sydney felt her heart start to race again as her anxieties grew. She knew what was demanded of the Azure from some of the other teenagers, especially in times of stress. The Azure who served them would never be allowed to refuse.

Liam told her she had to obey Halius while they were at school; he trusted Halius enough to tell her that. But to what extent would she have to obey him?

Halius finally met her eyes; he ran his palms across his pants before he was able to speak. "At night… when… At night, Liam goes into your room." It was a statement, but Sydney nodded in response. "Does he… does he make you…" He growled in frustration and ran a hand down his jaw. He looked away from her once more. He didn't want the answer, but he couldn't stop himself from asking, "What does he do to you when he goes into your room?"

His question shocked her. Sydney blinked at him, her fears lessening as she mumbled, "I'm… I'm not supposed to say."

Halius breathed deeply. His teeth were clenched when he responded, "Yes, I know." He bit his lip and looked at her once again. "Just… answer the question, please. Does he… does he… *touch* you?"

Sydney pursed her lips as she considered whether she should answer. Liam had expressly forbidden her to speak of what happens inside their home. She was never supposed to talk about what went on between them, especially from inside her room. However, when she looked into Halius's emerald eyes and saw the desperation behind his questioning, she felt almost compelled to answer. She also knew exactly what he was asking and saw the relief come across his face when she said, "No. Nothing like that. He would never lay a hand on me."

Halius did seem to relax. He asked nothing else as they left the car and headed to the school.

The classes didn't make Halius's day any better. He ended up with a quiz in his history class—a class he loathed on his rotating schedule—and knew he had failed. The teacher forbade the use of their Azure in class, which they were permitted to do if the quiz was worth less than 10% of an overall grade.

The bell rang at the end of class, and Halius practically jumped to his feet and left the room. He didn't even wait for Sydney, who rushed to catch up to him in the hallway. When she passed his desk, she saw he had not even finished the quiz and knew his grade would drop even further. Undoubtedly, the declining grade would spark yet another fight between him and his mother.

As they walked through the hall, Sydney could see Halius beginning to sweat. His fist was still clenched at his side, his hand on his backpack strap was tight, his knuckles turning white against the force of his hand. His stress level was still too high, which meant he was at risk of shifting into his wolf at school.

Young Lycans were not as adept as the adults in controlling their changes, largely due to factors involving their ever-swinging hormones and heightened emotional state. One change could spark a dozen or more others to do the same.

Sydney had never needed to try to calm Halius down. He was usually good at controlling himself and had ample amounts of practice from dealing with Gwen.

To make matters worse, Halius was shoved by a boy who was walking by. He lost his balance and collided with the lockers before he could see who did it.

The boy in question was Gregory Wiliker. A lesser Beta from a lower-ranking family. He always had it out for Halius since his arrival, as Gregory was set to be the Beta for Maddox's pack before Gwen had married Liam. It would have put Gregory's family on a higher standing with the Alpha, but Halius had edged him out.

Gregory let out a ruckus laugh. "Walk much, half-breed?" He slammed his fist on his own chest. "Best clear the way for a *real* Beta."

Halius pushed himself up from the locker. It was an insult he didn't hear often. It referenced a difference in rank between his parents. Liam, although not his real father, was a Prime Beta by birth. His mother, however, was born an Omega. Her rank only changed because of her marriage to Prime Beta men.

Halius lunged forward and shoved Gregory back. "Fuck off, Gregory! And if you were a real Beta, you wouldn't live in the outer ring."

Their fight had drawn a crowd, a ring forming around them in the hallway. Sydney attempted to shrink behind the first row of people. Gregory snarled and waved his hands as he spoke, "We only live out there because of rats like you! Coming in here like you own the place, disrupting our ranks. Why don't you head back to the hovel you crawled out of?"

Halius shoved him once again. "Why? I seem to fit right in with all the trash around here!" He let out a mocking laugh. "If I'm the best the Alphas had to pick from, I guess your Daddy's influence only goes so far."

Gregory's lip curled. A growl echoed his words as he bellowed, "Well, at least my daddy's influence didn't go up in smoke!" He attempted to shove Halius again, but Sydney was trying to get Halius to continue down the hall.

Her actions caused Halius to sidestep Gregory, and instead of Halius getting shoved, the Lycan knocked into Sydney. The force was hard, and she was slammed against the lockers. She felt her head bounce against the metal, and she collapsed to the floor. Her vision was obstructed by an explosion of stars. With little strength, she pulled one of the pencils from her bag.

One of Liam's strict rules for her was never to use her ability. She was forbidden from ever speaking what it was. Thankfully, she almost never needed to use it. But she couldn't risk Halius shifting in the school and had no way to calm him down. He needed his pack; they would know how to calm him down. Maddox would be able to take control of the situation.

Sydney snapped the pencil in half and rolled up her sleeve. She didn't even know if it would truly work. She reached out and was able to grab hold of Halius's ankle while he and Gregory continued to yell at one another. Her pupils swelled across the irises and whites of her eyes, turning her eyes into endless black voids. She looked down quickly before anyone could see and held the shard of the wooden pencil to her bare arm.

It hurt when she pulled the wood across her skin, scratching into her arm in a desperate attempt to call for help.

Halius exploded in rage; he tackled Gregory. The two boys hit the floor; landing blows on each other as they rolled across the floor while the circle of kids cheered them on. Gregory was on top, his fists slamming into Halius's gut several times. Halius managed to wrestle Gregory onto his back. He straddled Gregory's chest, landing blow after blow on Gregory's face.

Blood poured from Gregory's nose and his mouth. It coated Halius's hand as he struck him over and over. He felt the bones in Gregory's face crack and snap the longer he continued to strike.

There were hands on him, trying to pull him off Gregory, and then there wasn't. He was able to push them back with ease.

Word had spread about the fight, with staff unable to break up the assault that was currently taking place. Halius's pack forced their way through the crowd. Ezra and Maddox pulled Halius from Gregory with extreme difficulty as the staff of the school dragged Gregory's limp body away from Halius's reach.

Maddox looked up at Roderick and ordered, "Calm him down, Roderick, now!"

The Azure obeyed without question. He stood over Halius, his irises turning a bright and shining white. He placed his hand on Halius's chest and gently said, "Halius… sleep." For a moment, Halius's eyes shined with the same white as Roderick's eyes. A calm overtook his body; his limbs were suddenly heavy.

The green returned to his eyes before his lids closed, and his body went limp.

The staff ushered the rest of the kids to their classes. Maddox and Ezra dropped Halius and assisted the staff, with Roderick checking on Gregory, who was continuing to bleed onto the tile floor.

Elliot seemed to be the only one who noticed Sydney. He knelt next to her as her vision finally returned. She shied away from his touch, and he quickly retracted his hand. "Hey, it's OK. It's just me."

Sydney allowed him to help her stand. She had very little interaction with the other members of the pack and generally only spoke when a question was directed towards her. But Elliot seemed kind, at least in that moment he was.

When she stood, he stepped back from her and asked, "What happened? Did you see how it started?"

Sydney nodded. "We… Halius was trying to get to his next class. Master Gregory came up on him, and they started to fight."

Elliot nodded and left her at the locker. He walked up to where Maddox was still speaking to a few members of the school staff. He relayed the information Sydney had given him.

Sydney couldn't see what Maddox had said to them, but Elliot and Ezra quickly gave a nod of their heads and rushed off, presumably to their next class. Maddox then turned his attention to Sydney and approached her with a rush that made her cower back.

His words were hushed but forceful as he asked, "What did you do to me?" When Sydney opened her mouth and began to shake her head, Maddox interrupted her. "Don't you dare lie to me, girl." He stepped closer, towering over her as she shrank back against the lockers. "We all felt Halius turn on Gregory before word reached us about the fight. But just as we were about to come here, what did I see?" He held out his arm to her.

When Sydney looked down at his arm, she saw welts that had formed. The welts spelled the faded word *help*.

Maddox's words were still hushed when he ordered, "Tell me the truth, girl. What did you do to me? What did you do to Halius to make him turn on another Lycan?"

Sydney stammered, shaking her head as she hugged her hands to her chest. "N-N-Nothing. Please, Alpha. I'm sorry. He-He-He needed help…"

One of the Matrons of the school caught Maddox's attention before he could question her further. She had shined a light into Halius's eyes before looking at the young Alpha. "His Rec classes are in the afternoon, I am assuming, Alpha?" When Maddox nodded, she said, "OK, if you'll permit us to borrow Roderick, should it not inconvenience you, Alpha."

Maddox kept his eyes on Sydney as he spoke. "Of course." The crowd around them had dispersed, with Roderick following the Matrons as they wheeled Gregory and Halius away after the gurneys had arrived.

When he spoke, he was forceful. "Serve Halius's food to him in the nurses' station. And call your Master. Tell him what you have done to me today. I will call my father and do the same; that way, they can decide what to do with you."

Sydney scrambled to collect hers and Halius's bags from the floor before she darted away. She headed to the cafeteria, knowing it wouldn't be long before she could collect the food for Halius.

When she stepped into the empty cafeteria, she covered her mouth as a sob escaped her. She finally looked down at her own arm; blood had soaked through her sleeve from where she had cut with the pencil. She was thankful that the injury was not as prevalent on the Alpha, but that did little to quell the turmoil she found herself in. She had to call Liam and tell him to come to the school because she had performed magic on the Alpha's son.

How was she supposed to tell him that?

*****

Liam and his Alpha spent the whole morning in the office complex downtown. They were 45 minutes away from the school, in a high skyscraper that had windows on all sides, allowing full views of the city.

When the latest meeting ended, a discussion about construction projects for infrastructure improvements, Liam leaned against the back of his chair. He ran his hands down his face and through his hair, letting out a bored sigh.

The Alpha, Alexander, patted his friend's chest with a heavy hand as he walked by him. "What's the matter, Liam? Too boring for you?"

Liam reclined his chair. "Oh no, it's great. I really want to know more about how our freeways once again need an upgrade. Even though we upgraded them last year and two years ago. And a year prior to that, if I remember."

Alex chuckled. "Last year was the north segment. This is the south. The tourists from Kent are complaining our roads aren't up to par. Besides, when it's done, the traffic here downtown won't be so bad."

Liam swiveled in his chair, facing Alex, who was looking out the massive window of the conference room. "Tell Kent we're more in touch with the earth. So much so, we let it grow through our roads."

After a pause, he could see Alex's shoulders moving as he chuckled. "Besides, it will never not be busy downtown. What we need to do, instead of trying to focus on roads that are working just fine, is re-blaze the territory markers on the eastern trails. Last time I tried going for a run out that way, I ended up in Montcalm without even realizing it."

Alex's laugh was short, "Well, I don't think Felix will go for that excuse on the roads. He would use our infrastructure to force us to travel to Kent for a meeting." He nearly shuddered and looked over his shoulder with a raised brow as he said, "And you should know your own territory bounds without the blazes. You've only lived here your whole life."

Liam shook his head in disgust at the mention of Kent. He let out an *ugh* noise that scratched the back of his throat and checked the time on his watch. "Are we going to try to make it to the school today?"

Alex checked his own watch. "I was hoping to. Maddox seems to prefer it when I am there to see his training." He grinned, an airy tone coming over his voice. "Erika does a phenomenal job with them. I think Maddox is trying to impress me."

Liam stood from his chair and joined Alex at the window. "You are a hard man to impress." He was silent for a moment, looking down slightly before he said, "Halius was quite upset about not getting a place in the Annual Games."

Alex gently patted Liam's shoulder. "Ah, tell him to buck up. He won't age out till he's 23 when he graduates from university. He's got a better chance next year." He innocently shrugged his shoulder. "Perhaps Gwen will settle down a little and let him go to Bootcamp like he's supposed to." It was brief, but Liam detected a bitterness in his voice. It was gone as soon as he spoke again. "How are things going with her?"

It was Liam's turn to shrug. Any lightheartedness drained from him faster than pulling a plug in a tub. "Fine, I guess. She is a wife like you always wanted me to have."

Alex let out a sigh; his gaze returned to the outside. He shook his head and stepped away from the window, leaving Liam where he stood. "You gave me little choice, Liam." He turned his attention to the papers and folders that were still stretched out across the large conference room table. "You needed a wife and children to strengthen your wolf and your claim as my Prime Beta. Be thankful the one I found you had a son who held such a rank." After a moment of silence, he added. "You need to live in the pack house."

Liam's jaw hardened. "You know I can't do that."

Alex sighed again, this time in frustration. It was a conversation they had numerous times over the years. He snapped his fingers, and an Azure rushed over and placed a drink in his waiting hand. "It was damn near 20 years ago now." He sipped the drink and looked at Liam's back as he still faced the outside. "It's all been rebuilt and upgraded. It's like it never happened."

Liam refused to turn and look at Alex. He dismissed the Azure, who tried to offer him a drink. "Sixteen years, three months and eighteen days." He shook his head and spoke more to himself when he added, "I lost too much in that house."

Liam could almost hear Alex rolling his eyes. "Close enough to twenty years, man. We all lost property that day, I get it." He even let out a chuckle. "A third of my house burned down." He walked up to Liam and had to push him on his shoulder to get the Beta to look at him. "You know, I lost almost ten thousand dollars in assets that day. What did you lose, five hundred at best?"

Liam had to fight himself to keep the rage from burning his eyes. Everything came down to money for the Alpha, and Liam knew exactly what he was speaking of when he said the word *assets*. It made his skin crawl at just the mention of it.

Alex kept talking. He seemed to ignore the unrest that was starting to inflict on his friend. "I know she served your family for a while, and you seemed to have a strange kind of attachment to her when your mother passed on, but we have plenty more that I have offered you free of charge." He took another drink, smacking his lips before he said, "Besides, you have a wife now, Gwen, remember? You also have Sydney still to use if you want; she's close enough."

Liam had to step away from the Alpha before he made the mistake of lashing out at him. He heard Alex chuckle as if what he said was so clever. He gripped the back of one of the leather chairs, his fingers threatening to tear the fabric when he squeezed it.

It wasn't worth the fight. Liam had to tell that to himself over and over. It wasn't worth the fight to defend the Azure. Alex would never see them as anything other than property, and Liam knew that he lost more than Alex would ever realize the day the pack house burned.

Thankfully, they were offered a distraction when his phone started to ring. He reached into his suit coat and pulled the phone from his pocket.

Alex's brow furrowed as he watched Liam's expression turn to worry. "Who is it?"

Without looking up from the screen, Liam said quickly, "It's Sydney." And he answered the call.

*****

It took about an hour for Halius to wake up.

His head was sore, his vision blurry as he struggled to blink heavy eyelids. Rolling to his side was difficult. Someone could have told him his limbs were made of stones, and he would have believed them.

Suddenly, there was a woman in front of him. The Matron Halius recognized her after a moment of blinking. She assisted him in sitting up as she said, "Easy there, boy."

His throat was dry; his words croaked when he tried to speak. "Where am I?"

The Matron removed her hands from his back when he braced himself on the edge of the bed. "You're in the Medical room, dear." From the small fridge, she pulled a pouch that she promptly tore the top off. "Drink this, dear."

Halius's movements were slow. He regarded the fluid with curiosity before he decided to drink it. It was thicker than water and tasted like salt. He hadn't planned on drinking the whole thing, but it was cold and coated his throat, which made it even easier to swallow. Before he knew it, the pouch was empty. His headache had subsided, and the irritation in his throat had gone.

The Matron moved to another bed that was close by; she busied herself with folding sheets that had been messed up by someone who had already gone. "What do you remember, dear?"

Halius gasped his breath and lowered the empty plastic pouch. "I… um… I had a quiz in History." His eyes widened when the memories returned to him. "Great Fates, I… Gregory tried to fight me… and…" He looked around the room. There were three other beds in the small room that lined the walls. All three beds were empty. "I didn't kill him, did I?"

The Matron suppressed a smile and shook her head. "Of course not. You were stopped." She let out a sigh and turned from the sheets she was folding. "Gregory. One day, that pup is going to end up in the hospital with how much he instigates." She shrugged one shoulder, speaking matter-of-factly, "But I suppose he'll deserve it if it's the only way he will learn."

Halius clenched his jaw as the recollection of how it began came back to him. He saw Sydney trying to usher him down the hall. He saw Gregory slam her into the lockers. Halius managed to and spoke through his teeth, "I'll be sure to put him there."

There was a light tapping on the door, and when the Matron answered, Sydney stood on the other side. The Matron looked her up and down, a disdainful sneer coming to her face as she motioned into the room, "You should have been here with that ten minutes ago. Come on, girl, he needs nutrition after an incident like that."

Sydney stepped into the medical room and placed Halius's tray of food on a small rollaway table. No sooner did she move it over to him that she was prodded on the arm by the Matron.

The woman barked at her. "Don't linger, girl. Sit down there if you must stay in proximity of your Master."

Sydney quickly sat on her knees in a space between two of the beds. There was no cushion for her there, not like in the classrooms, just an empty part of the cold floor. Not a moment later, a wrapped granola bar was dropped in front of her.

The Matron folded her arms when she saw Sydney's reaction or lack thereof. Her contempt for the Azure filled the room as she tapped her foot and glared down at Sydney. "What's the matter? Alpha Maddox said you were allowed rations. I am being quite generous by giving you some of the few that I have here." She leaned down, her words biting through the air as she hissed, "You do look a little fat."

Sydney quickly took the bar off the floor and said, "Of course, I apologize, Matron. You are most kind." She unwrapped it carefully and ate the crunchy granola as quietly as she could. She was much healthier than most of the other Azure. Liam constantly made sure she ate real meals, which was another thing that caused fights from Gwen at the beginning of their marriage. She made sure not to eat with exuberance, feeling her stomach growl as she began to eat.

Sydney hadn't seen him because her eyes had been lowered, but Halius had been watching the interaction. He glanced up at the woman and said, "Matron, she's allowed to eat real meals. She's going to need more than just that."

The Matron rolled her eyes, she had gone back to smooth out the freshly remade bed. "Young Beta, she clearly has enough meat on her to last until she gets home. My Azure rations are for emergencies."

Halius let an irritated snarl escape his mouth that caused the Matron's body to tense for a moment. "Fine." He said tersely. He took the chicken sandwich from his tray and held it down to Sydney. "Here, eat this."

Sydney began to shake her head when the Matron spoke before she could. "Beta Halius, you need that food for your training."

Halius held Sydney's eyes until she reluctantly took the food he offered. He stood, grabbing the muffin and fruit bowl his lunch came with. "Oh, don't worry about me, Matron." He took a large bite of the muffin and patted his hand against his chest. "I've got plenty of meat on me. Right?" With a swipe of his hand, he knocked the tray from the table. The remaining food splattered across the floor. Halius smiled as he watched the Matron's face twist to horror at the sight of a mess in her medical room. "Oops." He shoved the rest of the muffin in his mouth and motioned towards the Azure. He chewed his mouthful as he said, "My bad. Come on, Sydney, I have training to get to. Let's not be in Matron's way."

The Rec Classes had already started by the time he got out to the field. To Halius's dismay, the rumor of the incident had already spread. Of course, Elliot and Ezra could never keep their mouths shut. When the questions about why Halius missed his last class *and* lunch started to float around, the brothers were all too happy to provide the answers.

As soon as he set foot down on the track, Gwen rushed over to him. Luna Erika was nowhere to be seen; of course, all Halius could see was his mother obsessing over him. She held his face in her hands and moved his head back and forth at a painful angle. "Are you OK? I heard about what happened! Don't worry, baby, I'll make sure Gregory pays for that!"

Halius removed her hands. Why was she trying to be sweet to him? Was it because they were outside where others could see them, or did she truly feel bad about the morning? "I think he's paid enough. Mother, stop it. I'm fine. Fights happen."

Gwen wrapped his shoulder. "Not to my son, it doesn't!" When he tried to push her away from him, she caught his wrist. "Halius Usoro! What is *this*?"

He hadn't realized it, but there were welts running down his arm. Some were straight, and some were at funny angles. It stung slightly as if he had been scratched by something. "What? Nothing. I have no idea. Will you let go?"

Gwen ran a finger over one of the lines. "Nothing? *Nothing*? Do you need to talk to someone again?"

Halius attempted to step back, nearly knocking Sydney over when he ripped his arm out of his mother's hand. "What? No! Shut up, mother!" He turned to Sydney, but before he could apologize for bumping her, he saw blood staining her sleeve. His words were halted, and when Sydney noticed what he was looking at, she hid her arm behind her back.

Before he could formulate any kind of speech, the attention was taken as Halius caught sight of Erika. She was pulling Maddox by the arm over to where two men had just arrived.

Alex and Liam.

The men looked completely out of place in their suits as they walked down the path to the track fields. Alex stepped through the main gate first, with Liam quickly behind him. Erika was speaking frantically and was too far away for Halius and Gwen to hear what they were saying.

Liam only stood there for a moment and listened to Erika scream and gesture at Maddox's arm. Liam nodded at her and stepped away from them, walking towards where his small family stood near the bleachers.

Gwen practically ran to him. "Liam! Thank the Fates! Halius he—"

Liam cut her off; he stopped the hug she was attempting to inflict upon him. He caught her by her biceps and rubbed her arm gently as he continued to walk towards Halius. "I know. Sydney had to call me." He watched as Gwen snatched Halius's arm and held it out.

Halius attempted to explain. "Liam, I have no idea how those got there. I swear I didn't do it to myself."

Gwen began ranting at him again. "Don't try to lie to us, Halius! We can see the marks plain as day! Is this why you've been so tired? Do I have to take the door off your room again?"

As she continued to obsess over her son and his possibly questionable mental state, Liam turned his eyes to Sydney.

Sydney visibly shrank away from him; she stepped back, carefully folding her arms over her chest to hide her stained sleeve. She didn't try to speak; there was nothing she would be able to say. No lie, she could attempt to weave. Liam knew. He knew because he knew what she was able to do.

Liam looked over his shoulder in time to see Roderick trotting up to the Alphas. It didn't take but a moment after the Azure started to speak, that Erika exploded in rage.

She screamed and was pointing in their direction. Erika kept ahold of her son's arm as she stormed over with Alex and Roderick behind her. When they got close, she released her son and screamed at Halius, "Look at what you've done to my son!"

Gwen and Liam could feel the rage radiating from the Alphas. When Erika held up Maddox's arm, Gwen's hand went to her chest and she took in a dramatically horrified breath, "Maddox! You too? Is this some kind of pact you two have?"

Maddox and Halius began to scream simultaneously. Talking over each other about the fight, about how Maddox knew something was wrong, and how the message came across his arm.

Alex had one arm folded over his chest, his elbow resting on his arm while he pinched the bridge of his nose, clearly irritated at the babble and shrieks that were echoing around them.

Gwen and Erika had begun shouting about how the other's child was a bad influence. Insults were thrown back and forth as their arguments escalated.

After five minutes of the conglomeration of noise, Alex's voice roared a command. "Alright, everyone, stop!"

It ended immediately. The eyes of all the Lycans lowered the arguments had halted. Alex adjusted his tie around his neck. "Roderick already told us what happened." His eyes went to Liam. "Your little *witch* used the connection that Halius has with Maddox to signal him that Halius was in distress."

Gwen's jaw dropped. She turned her glare to Sydney and shoved the girl away from Liam as she screamed, "What? How? That is one of the forbidden abilities!" She looked up at Liam. "Did you know she could do this? Are her bracelets defective?"

Liam stepped between her and Sydney, who had begun to quietly sob. "Gwen, stop. There is nothing wrong with her bracelets."

Alex stuffed his hands into his pockets. "The ability is not forbidden if the bracelets contain it."

Erika folded her arms with a huff. "She violated a sacred bond between Lycans. Her bracelets will be tested later; right now, I want her admonished."

Liam nodded towards the Luna. "I will reprimand her when we get home."

Gwen's jaw clenched when she was pushed aside by Liam. She should have torn Sydney apart right there. "Halius and Maddox have marks on their skin! Caused by that *thing,* you protect so heavily." The hint of a smirk pulled at the corner of her mouth. "Punish her right here."

Erika immediately agreed. "Yes, that way, she can be humiliated properly. Discourage this behavior in the future."

The coloring of Liam's eyes began to turn as he looked at Gwen. He tried to keep his voice as level as possible when his eyes moved to his Alpha. "I will take her home right now, and I will punish her when we get there." He felt relief when Alex gave him a shrug in credence. He was just about to leave with Sydney when the shrill voice of his wife cut through the air.

"He'll never do it, he's lying."

The air around them stilled. Everyone seemed to exchange nervous glances as the Alpha's eyes fell on the she-wolf. His voice was a shard of a whisper when he asked, "What did you just say?"

Gwen squared her shoulders. Her eyes locked on Liam, who was drilling fire into her with his glare. She could feel her wolf starting to whimper, wanting her to submit to him with how angry she had just made him. The only thing that kept her strong was the fact that the Alphas were there and her hatred of Sydney. She wanted to see the girl punished for the first time in her life. "He never punishes her. He lets her get away with all sorts of punishable behavior, and if you let him leave with her, he'll just brush it off because that thing is his favorite." She lifted her chin towards Sydney, who was hiding behind Liam.

Liam looked over his shoulder at Sydney. The girl was beginning to take small steps back. Her sobs had stopped, although she continued to shake in terrified anticipation of what would happen. He wouldn't hit her, right? He wouldn't.

Alex folded his arms and stood tall next to his wife. "You know what, you're right. Do it right here."

Liam rolled his neck, his eyes closed as he began to feel the itch of Alex's command over him. "Why?"

The Alpha shrugged with indifference. "Why not? We all want to see her punished." He took steps forward, standing chest-to-chest with the Beta. He could see Liam's fists clench as he fought the order. "Maybe not entirely; I know how… private you are." He spat the word. "But let us at least see the beginning of it. So, I know you're serious about punishing her."

Liam met his eyes for a moment. He managed to shake his head slightly, almost imperceptibly, clenching his teeth as he begged in a whispered voice. "Alex, please don't."

The Alpha glanced at his son, who stood frozen with Halius as they watched the interaction unfold. His eyes moved to his wife. The Luna gave him an expected look. His gaze turned back to Liam, and he said, "My son has been injured. The sacred bond between Lycans was infringed by the creature behind you." He stepped closer to Liam as the Lycan began to back away from him. "Hit the girl, and you can take her home." A smile that churned Liam's stomach twisted onto the face of the Alpha. "If you don't, I will take her and see that she is punished properly." He leaned forward, whispering in Liam's ear, "Consider it a favor to me, as keeping her was my favor to you."

Liam fought back furious tears as he broke the stare with Alex. His breath quickened when he looked back to Sydney. Her eyes were wide and pleading. He had to fight it; there was no way he could strike her. He never had before. His head began to throb as his wolf's thunderous barks slammed through his head.

He heard her voice, her petrified voice. "Master… please… I'm sorry."

Liam took in a deep breath and managed to whisper, "I am too." He knew he couldn't fight Alex's words. Either he obeyed, or his wolf would tear his mind apart. Either he obeyed, or she would be taken by Alex and would suffer beyond imagination.

She would understand. She had to. She knew the risks if he disobeyed.

In a swift movement, Liam whirled around and threw up his hand. His wedding ring cut Sydney's lip when he struck her. The impact knocked her to the ground, and a shocked scream of pain escaped her mouth.

When he turned back to the audience he had, Liam expected to see satisfaction from Alex and Erika. The smug and endearing look on his wife's face was the most disgusting thing he had ever seen. He managed to look at the boys that were still standing near their mothers.

Maddox and Halius didn't share the amusement their parents did. Halius had a hand rubbing his forehead as he looked down at the ground. Maddox shook his head at the cruelty of the situation.

Alex looked at Erika, "There. Now we know she will be further punished when they get home." He gave a horribly friendly grin to Liam. "Right?"

Liam looked away. "Yes, Alpha."

Erika and Gwen looked at each other and nodded in agreement. They were satisfied and turned their attention towards their children. Gwen screamed, "Now get running, you two; we've lost too much time already!"

The boys took off with Gwen and Erika following behind them. Already beginning to shout orders at the rest of the class.

Liam took in a shaky breath when the women and children walked away. He refused to look at Alex as he asked, "Are you satisfied?"

Alex tipped his head as he looked down at Sydney. He watched as the girl silently cried and sat up on her knees. "I don't know. If what Gwen said is true, maybe I need to see one more."

Liam finally met his Alpha's eyes. Now that they were alone, he let the painful tears fall and silently begged the Fates not to have Alex ask why he cried. "Alex, please don't. She knows what she did. She is sorry; I do not need to hit her."

Alex nodded. "You're right. *You* already did." He saw Liam's eyes widen as he continued, "You got a hit for your son; I get one for my son." Before Liam could attempt to stop him, Alex shoved Liam aside and swiped his hand at Sydney. The back of his hand clapped against her cheekbone with an audible *crack*.

Sydney sobbed as she feebly tried to hold up her hands. She knew how other Azure were beaten when their Lycan Masters were angered. It was never just one hit. And she was right; he struck her again as she tried to pull herself further away. Her back hit the chain link fence, and she was trapped.

Liam managed to fight past the hold Alex would have on him. Seeing her cower against the fence as the Alpha stepped towards her again. He had seen enough, even if it meant the worst; Sydney didn't deserve that.

Liam put his hands on Alex and pulled him back before he could strike the girl again. "Alex, stop!"

The Alpha spun and snatched Liam's shirt. The blazing yellow shone through the hazel of his eyes, a growl emanating from deep within his chest that made Liam's own wolf whimper inside his mind. His voice was quiet, echoed with the growl that vibrated the air around them, "Why is she so important to you?"

Liam managed to keep his composure and attempted to diffuse the hostility. "Alpha, you're angry, I know, but Halius was in trouble. Had he turned inside that school or allowed his anger to kill Gregory, there would have been chaos."

Alex's eyes flicked down to the Azure. The yellow receded from his eyes as he watched her wipe blood from her lip and cheek onto her already blood-soaked sleeve.

Liam finally felt the aggression lessening. The air calmed as a cool breeze blew across the field. "There was no other way for her to quickly signal Maddox and Roderick. She has been punished here adequately, I would say. Let me take her home, and I will make sure this never happens again."

Alex stepped back after he released his grip on Liam. "You'd better." He knelt in front of Sydney. His words were kinder than before as his eyes trailed up and down the frightened girl's body. "Put a mark on my son or his pack, infect their sacred bond with your Fate-Forsaken curse one more time, and I will make sure you never see Master Liam again. Am I clear?"

Sydney nodded quickly. Her movements were shaky, her lips trembling as she said, "Yes, Alpha. It will not happen again."

Alex stood, adjusting his coat before he said, "No. It won't." He walked passed his friend, knocking into Liam's shoulder as he said, "Get out of my sight."

Liam lowered his head, making sure Alex was walking away before he pulled Sydney up onto her feet. He walked her quickly away from the field and took her home.

Liam and Sydney were quiet the entire car ride home. He helped her into the house; her dizziness from the impact of the hits was concerning, and he was going to have to check her for a concussion. He sat her at the table and went into the kitchen. Over his shoulder, he heard her begin to speak. Thankfully, her words were not slurred.

"It's not your fault."

He silently filled a bag with ice. Suppressing the rage that was building when he saw her press the bag to her swollen cheek.

It didn't take long before she spoke again, "I know it had to be done."

Liam only looked into her eyes for a moment before he pulled the ice away from her face and wrapped it in a towel. He handed it back to her, seeing the bruise already coloring the skin beneath her eye. Her lip was fat and broken from his ring. His voice cracking as he whispered, "I'm so sorry, Sydney."

She half-smiled, pulling the side of her face that had not been beaten. "I know you are, but this is what I get for misbehaving, right?" She shifted the ice as he pulled a chair close to her. He began wiping the blood stains off her mouth with a wet cloth. With a small voice, she added, "I'm supposed to be hit."

Liam spoke insistently, "No. You're not." He took a breath and lowered the cloth. "That's why we don't live in the pack house. These Lycans they're… they're…" He groaned as he searched for his words.

Sydney finished his sentence. Although it may not have been what Liam wanted to hear. "They're your pack. Your family. Alex is your Alpha, and you are bound to him as your superior. You have no choice against his wishes."

Liam lifted her chin when she lowered her eyes. "No. They are monsters who think themselves evolved. I am ashamed to be part of this cult they have used to twist what the world should be." He turned his attention to her arm. He gently rolled up her sleeve; the fabric had begun to cling to the scabbed wounds. "You are my family." His words turned to a whisper as he spoke more to himself than to her. "You're the only thing I have left."

She tried to give him a smile that he did not return and winced when he began to clean off her arm. It had bled more than she expected. The letters muddled together in a mix of welts and scabs.

After a moment, he asked, "You want to tell me about this?"

Sydney felt tears beginning to fall down her face once more. "Um… I was… I was trying to signal Maddox for Halius. I was hoping Roderick would come and stop the fight before Halius… you know."

He pulled her into a hug and felt her start to tremble again as she quietly sobbed. "It's alright. Just try to breathe." He kissed her head and whispered, "I love you, baby girl."

Sydney's eyes closed as she settled into his arms. Her own breath finally settled as she listened to the rhythmic drum of his heart within his chest. Finally able to speak the words she knew he was desperate to hear, "I love you too, Dad."

Liam let out a relieved breath. Hearing those words always calmed him. Since Gwen and Halius had entered their lives, he heard it less and less, as she could only address him as her father when they were alone. Lycans and Azure were never allowed to breed, with any conceived children being immediately destroyed by the Alpha of the territory. Either after birth, if the mother was a Lycan—which usually followed the woman's imprisonment—or while the child was still inside the womb if the mother was an Azure.

Liam had successfully hidden his relation to Sydney from his Alpha and treated her like his daughter whenever possible. Although, those opportunities were lessoning as she got older. He stood from his chair, "Stay here; I'm going to get something to wrap your arm with."

When he returned with their home medical kit, he cleaned her arm with antiseptic and covered the worst of the cuts with large bandages. "Why did you do it to yourself?"

Sydney shrugged. "I linked with Halius before the worst of the fight broke out. I wouldn't have been able to do it without everyone seeing me. I honestly didn't think it would work." After another moment of consideration, she said, "It… it shouldn't have worked."

Liam pulled her from wherever her thoughts were threatening to spiral towards. "How did it start, the fight?"

Sydney placed the ice bag on the table. "Gregory and Halius were arguing. I tried to get Halius to move, to get to his next class. I ended up pushing him out of the way, and Gregory pushed me against the lockers." She lowered her eyes, recalling the events to the best of her ability. "When I fell before Halius lunged at Gregory, I grabbed ahold of his ankle and… you know the rest." She ran her hand across her forearm.

Liam nodded. He sat for a moment in contemplation. He knew Halius's temper; the boy was also known to be unpredictable. His Alpha always thought it amusing how wild Halius was. Alex would often tell him that it was what his son's pack needed. A little rebellion to keep them from becoming stagnant. "Do you believe Halius was trying to protect you from Gregory?"

Sydney shrugged. "Kinda hard to tell. They were already fighting." A smile pulled the corners of her mouth. "You don't have to worry about him, Dad. He's nice to me."

Liam's brow pulled together. His eyes narrowed and he leaned his elbows onto his thighs. "What do you mean? What does he do?"

Sydney spoke with her light and innocent tone, she suppressed a giggle as she retold the story. "He gave me the chicken sandwich off his lunch tray today." She continued when Liam tipped his head in confusion. "The Matron in the medical room wouldn't give me any food. She threw a granola bar at me, so Halius gave me his sandwich in front of her and then threw his tray on the floor and forced her to clean it up."

A single laugh came from Liam as he pictured the scenario. A wild one, indeed. What made his smile vanish was the next statement that came from his daughter.

"I think we can trust him, Dad."

Liam let long moments pass as he tried to consider her words. At one time, he could have agreed with her and tried to test the theory when Halius had first moved in. Gwen, however, was so obsessed with Halius doing and saying all the right things. The boy was never truly able to express what he thought in front of Liam. Eventually, Liam had to accept the fact that Halius would never get out from under his mother's thumb.

But what if he could?

Would it be worth the risk?

Liam eventually shook his head. His words escaped him in airy whispers, "I… I really." He let out the rest of his breath. "I don't know about Halius, sweetie. I would need to have a conversation with him, a real conversation. If he can't give it to me, then… I don't think he would be trustworthy."

Sydney nodded. She understood, and whether Halius ever learned about what she was to Liam didn't matter to her. What she did care about was how alone Liam felt within the pack. How isolated he was even within his own house. Having one Lycan, one other person that he could call a friend, would be something that could take some of the burden off his shoulders.

Sydney gave Liam a small smile. She tried to keep the prospective joy from her voice when she said, "I hope you get that conversation, Dad. For both our sake."

By the time Gwen and Halius got home, Sydney was halfway through making dinner. Halius didn't speak; he stormed into his room and slammed the door. Not even dropping his shoes when he entered the house, as Gwen preferred them to go barefoot.

Liam had been lying on the couch, his attention on the TV. When the door had flown open, he sat up and attempted to speak to Halius as he stormed by without a word. His eyes turned to Gwen, and he asked, "What's wrong with him?"

Gwen sauntered up to Liam. She threw her arms around his shoulders in a forceful hug he did not want, nor did he reciprocate. She kissed his cheek before she straightened her spine and said, "Oh, he's just angry because I told him there was no way I would ever allow him to be selected for the Gauntlet in the games."

Liam let the expression on his face speak to his confusion. "I thought he didn't qualify for the games. Alex didn't select him."

Gwen sat heavily on the couch. She kicked her legs across his lap, practically pinning him to the sofa. She spoke with a condescending tone. "He was asking me about *next* year. I simply told him if he didn't shape up, he was never going to compete. Now he's mad." Her voice was sickeningly sweet as she looked in Sydney's direction, still speaking to Liam when she asked, "And how was your afternoon, my love? Did you fulfill our Alpha's requests?"

Liam almost flinched when she said, *my love*. His disdain for her sometimes felt a little unjustified. He knew her behavior was no different from any other Lycan. He could have picked any woman off the street, she would act nearly the same. He leaned against the back of the couch and called, "Sydney, come in here." He quickly stopped himself from saying, *please*, as he normally would.

Sydney walked around the couches, her head low when she stood in front of them. "Yes, Master."

Liam waved a hand. "Show Gwen the punishment you received."

Gwen folded her arms impatiently. She didn't expect anything much. He never punished her like he was supposed to. The fact that he struck her at all in front of the Alpha was nothing short of a miracle by the Fates themselves.

Sydney hesitated at first, then slowly lifted the side of her shirt. A bruise, possibly the size of two hands, was painted across her ribcage in a blended mix of dark reds and browns.

A smile grew on Gwen's face. The thrilled, wicked smile made a chill run up Sydney's spine. She reached out, grabbed Sydney by the belt of her pants, and pulled her towards the sofa. Her fingers were cold on Sydney's skin, the girl letting out a small gasp of pain and shock as her ribs were prodded by Gwen's witchy fingers. Her voice sang with a horrifying glee. She looked at her husband and asked, "You did this?"

Liam gritted his teeth and gave a single nod.

With a thunderous laugh, Gwen shoved Sydney away. A blast of pain surged through Sydney's body when her bruised ribs were squeezed. The girl almost couldn't catch herself before she crashed into the coffee table, but she was able to recover quickly and only bounced her leg off the wood.

Gwen sat up on her knees and hugged Liam's side on the sofa. She buried her face in his neck before she kissed his jaw. "I'm so proud of you, Liam! Didn't that feel better? To get out some of that aggression from her horrendous behavior?"

Liam kept his face turned away from her as she continued to kiss the side of his face and neck. Her arms were tight around his chest, squeezing his ribs. If he closed his eyes, he could have believed a snake wrapped around him. He had to force himself to answer her joyous question, "Yes. Yes, that feels much better. I suppose I should do it more often."

Halius had attempted to emerge from his room, stopping in the hallway in just enough time to see Sydney collect herself and hide her damaged skin beneath her shirt once more. She met his eyes for only a moment before she returned to the kitchen. He stepped from the hallway, getting the attention of his parents on the couch. "Liam… did you really put that bruise on Sydney?"

Gwen was the one who answered. Her voice squeaked with glee, "He did!" She stood from the couch after kissing his cheek once more. "I'm so glad we can finally start to move on from this and get passed all this nonsense!" She sashayed across the room and sat at the table. "Halius, come sit with me. I want to hear more about what happened in your fight with Gregory."

Halius hesitated; he glanced at Sydney before he shook his head. "No, no, I'm… I'm not feeling too good. I'm just going to go lay down."

Gwen let out a sigh. She rolled her eyes and leaned onto the table. "So dramatic, that one. I don't know where he gets it. Hopefully, he'll grow out of it soon."

Liam joined her at the table when he heard Sydney plating their dinner. To his surprise, which he worked hard to keep from his face, she placed the plate in front of him before serving Gwen.

His wife, once again, seemed overfilled with her nauseating joy. She clapped her hands together and shouted, "Finally! See, I knew you would get it eventually." She patted Liam's arm, "Look at how well-behaved she is with just a few marks. I told you it wouldn't take much for her to learn."

Liam forced a smile, and they began to eat. He felt himself forcing the food down his throat when he saw Sydney sitting on the floor against the wall. She didn't eat with them; she didn't sit at the table. She kept her eyes down and remained silent. A proper Azure after a punishment. He kept looking at her, unnoticed by his wife who was more focused on her food and yammering on about something he was not listening to.

Halius didn't leave his room for the rest of the night. He ignored Gwen when she knocked on his door, begging for attention that he didn't want to give. She had shouted at him to go and eat, which he did not want to do if she were out there. Nor did he want to see Liam; a newly found contempt formed inside his head as he thought of the bruise he had seen on Sydney's ribs.

He heard Gwen scream at Liam to break down the door. The request was denied by his stepfather, who had told her to step away from the door and let him be.

Hours passed, and well into the evening, Gwen had tapped on his door once again. Her voice sounded through the wood, "I love you, Halius." Upon his silence, she said, "Halius? Anything to say to your mother, who loves you?"

Halius sighed; he was lying on his bed, staring at the ceiling. She rapped the door two more times with the same insistent tone. Stopping only when he responded with a quiet and irritated, "I love you too, mother. Goodnight."

Gwen shook her head and looked at Liam as he passed her down the hall. "Alright, let's go to bed."

He stopped at Sydney's door; the Azure had already gone into her room hours prior. Gwen thought it was a good thing that she dismissed herself upon finishing her chores. Liam looked over his shoulder and said, "Not until after my time with Sydney."

Gwen arched her back slightly as she turned in over-dramatized anguish. "Liam, come on. Didn't you learn anything from today? She's just an Azure. You finally punished her for the first time." She stepped towards him and took his hands sweetly. "I'm proud of you for finally breaking her spell over you. Come to bed with me. I would love the extra time with you."

She made a sad face when he wouldn't move after she tried to pull him forward. She leaned against him and hugged him around his waist. "Come on, sweetie." She stood up on her toes and gently brushed her lips against his neck beneath his jawline. "You don't need her."

Liam removed her hands from his body. He watched her expression fall as she was forced to step back when he put pressure on her arms. "Yes. I do." Without letting her try to seduce him further, he entered Sydney's room, practically slamming the door behind him.

He ran a hand across his tired face as he crossed the bedroom. Sydney was sitting on her bed, a hairbrush in her hands as she waited for him. The sight of her nearly made him weep. Her bruised face was swelling beneath her eye, her lip puffy and scabbed.

He did that.

He allowed Alex to do that.

She gave a half-smile when he approached. Undoubtedly, all she could manage without inflicting pain on herself. Silently, she moved to the side and handed him the brush when he sat next to her.

He hugged her, gently wrapping his arms around her for several long moments. "I'm so sorry." He spoke the words, although they didn't seem as comforting as he wanted them to be. "I didn't want any of this to happen."

Sydney stood from the bed. She took one of the large pillows off her mattress and placed it on the floor before sitting between Liam's knees. Her back against the bedframe as she said, "I know." She winced as she settled and hoped he didn't notice.

He began unweaving the ribbons and braids that decorated her hair. "How are your ribs?"

She would have shrugged if she could have done so without pain. "Fine, I suppose. I just hurt myself for a second when I put pressure on that arm."

Liam brushed her smooth hair after taking out the decorations. It always calmed him. One of the only ways he could show her love in public was by styling her hair. They used to spend hours in front of the TV when Sydney was younger, watching movies or shows while he brushed her hair before Gwen and Halius had moved in.

In the quiet of the room, they heard Sydney's stomach rumble. Both let out thin chuckles as Sydney said, "Oh… I guess I forgot to eat dinner. I was so focused on acting like I learned my lesson."

Liam's laugh faded quickly. "Yeah… I'm…" He stopped himself from apologizing again. He kissed the top of her head and said, "I'll go get you something. Hang on." He stood and quietly left the room, keeping the bedroom door open when he went into the kitchen.

Some time had passed, and Halius emerged from his room. Not hungry enough to justify eating the full dinner that had been plated for him. He instead rummaged through the refrigerator, attempting to find something else.

When Liam entered the kitchen, Halius stared at him with wide eyes. It was as if he was back to being ten years old and was caught rooting through the cupboards for snack cakes. The sight made Liam chuckle, "Finally got hungry, did you?"

Halius awkwardly shut the fridge; he held an apple in his hand. He rolled it in his palm before he said, "Yeah, I guess. Not a lot though… just… just thought I should get something, you know?" He let out a tense breath and moved around Liam. "Well, goodnight."

Liam watched as Halius stepped around him; the wide berth he was given seemed more awkward than the hesitation in the young man's voice. "Hey, Halius." When he turned and looked at Liam, he asked, "Is there something on your mind?"

Halius feigned a laugh. "What? No. No… I…" He attempted to shake his head, though his words faded when he tried to speak again, "I'm fine. I'm… I'm fine… I just…" He groaned and placed the apple on the table before he crushed it in his hand. A moment of silence passed. Halius tapped his palm on the back of one of the table chairs. "I know I asked you this earlier… but… I really need to ask you something." When Halius saw Liam give a single nod, he spoke with a deep and quiet voice, "Did you really put the bruise on Sydney's ribs?"

Liam let the silence loom over them once more. Instead of answering, he moved into the kitchen and walked back with the plate of food Halius had ignored. "Let me take this to Sydney first, then we can talk."

To his shock, Halius held up a hand and blocked the entrance to the hallway. "I… really need you to answer me… I would prefer it if you did before you went back in there with her."

Liam held his eyes with a firm gaze. "And I would prefer she eats, which she didn't tonight because of *your* mother." At the mention of Gwen, Halius broke their stare. Looking away with a slight flicker of shame in his eyes. "Would you rather her go hungry tonight?"

Halius didn't meet his eyes again before he stepped aside. He leaned both hands against the back of the chair. The wood creaked against his grip when he heard Sydney's door gently close.

When Liam returned, he sat at the table. He didn't speak until Halius looked at him again. Liam took another moment to assess Halius's icy glare. His voice broke the deep silence, "No. I did not bruise her ribs."

Halius visibly relaxed at the words. He pulled the chair from the table and sat down. His whispered words held an elated tone. "I didn't think you did."

Liam resisted the urge to smile. "She told me about the fight; I thought it happened when she hit the lockers." He watched the scowl return to Halius's face, and after another long minute of silence, Liam dared ask the question, "Why do you care so much about Sydney?"

He expected silence or another spout of emotionally fueled rage and began to think of things he could do or say to calm the rageful teenager. To his surprise, Halius gave him nothing of the sort. The young Lycan shifted in his chair and eventually ended with his eyes gazing out the slider door into the black of the night. His chin rested on his fingers as he contemplated whether to answer the question. For a moment, he wondered if putting his feelings into words would make them more real, more difficult to ignore. Did he really know why he cared about Sydney? The ticking of the kitchen clock made him grind his teeth before he settled with the words, "Because… she didn't deserve that." He looked down at his forearm; the marks on his skin had yet to fade completely but were slowly disappearing as his body struggled to heal the light marks. "Did you see her wrist?"

Liam only nodded and silently begged the almighty Fates that Halius would not ask further questions on the subject.

Halius tapped a finger on the table; he didn't know why he blurted the question; he just wanted to change the subject. "Did you ever find your True Mate?"

Liam blinked at him. The abrupt question almost halted his mind; his jaw slacked as his eyes moved around the room. As if the answer would be there for him to find. He countered the question with one of his own. A smirk threatened to stretch his mouth when he asked, "Why would I be married to your mother if I had found my True Mate?"

Halius gave an exaggerated shrug. He let out an exhausted sigh. "I… I… I don't know, man." He began to speak quickly; his frustration raised the pitch of his voice. "I just… I just don't… you know what, just forget it." He stood and scratched his fingers through his hair.

Liam reached out, stopping him from storming off. "Hey, hey. I'm sorry, alright? You just caught me off guard a little bit with that question." He managed to get Halius to sit back down, and he continued, "I'm guessing you have a few more questions about this? I can imagine what your mother has told you."

Halius nearly rolled his eyes. He muttered, "Yeah, a whole lot of sappy chick-flick stories." He sighed, his eyes fixed on the table, where he rubbed his nails against the polyurethane. "So… how would… is she gonna know?"

Liam's brow furrowed. "What do you mean?"

Halius groaned again. "Let's say I find my mate. When I see them, and I feel all the things mom says I am supposed to feel, are they going to feel it too?" He saw the hint of a smile pull the corner of Liam's mouth. "My dad told me once that when he saw Mom, she was all he could think of. It's like she infiltrated his brain or something."

Liam let out a chuckle and shook his head. "I'm sure it can feel that way." He paused, considering his words before he said, "I would say… for many, it's more of a pull. My parents, before they were killed, would tell me something similar. They began to share activities, interests, and things like that. It really sounded like a classic love story." His smile began to grow, his eyes fixed on the distance as his mind drifted to somewhere far from where they were. "The infatuation would… definitely be part of it." He chuckled looking to Halius for just a moment before his eyes shifted away again. "You may dream of your mate, too. You'll start to see them everywhere…"

Halius leaned onto his knees as Liam continued to speak. It was a strange array of details that seemed more than just something he would have heard. The way he was talking, how his voice quieted as if he were remembering something he had pushed from his life. Liam's voice sounded heavy like he was hiding something important that he didn't want to say. Could Liam be hiding something? Halius had never tried to detect if Liam was ever lying to anyone. Would he be able to tell if he tried? When Liam stopped speaking, Halius asked, "So… it's not like a true obsession, then?"

Liam shook his head, his hand dropping to the table as he took in a contented breath. "No. No, it's… it's much deeper than that.

Trust me, you'll know. And when you meet your True Mate for the first time, they'll know it too."

Halius allowed himself to smile. The prospect of someone *wanting* to be around him gave him a flutter in his chest. He had his friends, but he always knew that he was not originally from the pack he found himself in. He often wondered if his friends really cared for him or if it was the pack bond they were trained to respect.

Halius couldn't help but ask again, "So… have you ever found your True Mate?"

Liam's smile vanished in a flash. His eyes hardened to a stony glare that felt like it cut through Halius's soul. His wolf whimpering in the back of his mind when Liam simply said, "No."

Halius leaned his back against the chair; his breath was hard as if he had been pushed. The sudden change in Liam's mannerisms was jarring, even if he had been suspecting it. Halius attempted to recover, "It's just… you describe it so well… I thought…"

Liam shook his head, his voice calming, and he asked again, "Halius, how would I have been able to marry your mother?"

Halius shrugged his shoulder, "I don't know. She or he, I guess, could have died. It happens sometimes." He watched Liam carefully. Did he just flinch? "I was just curious."

Liam was quiet. His eyes fixed on the table as he considered how he should react. He imagined himself getting up, storming away in screams of anger at being questioned. He even saw himself striking Halius. Would it have been an appropriate reaction? It was certainly something Alex would have done and had done whenever he was questioned.

Very quietly, the words slipped from Liam's mouth before he realized he was speaking once more. A mournful longing nearly choked his throat. "Yes… sometimes they can die… it very much happens."

Halius nodded and asked nothing else. The nod made it seem like he agreed with Liam's statement, and the boy said, "Thank you, Liam. I think… I think I understand now."

Liam nodded in return and stood from the table. He made his way down the hallway, hearing Halius stand from his own chair.

Halius watched as Liam cracked open Sydney's door, but by that time, the girl had crawled into her bed and was fast asleep. A growing question burned inside his mind. He shouldn't ask. He knew he shouldn't ask. If he was wrong and he asked, he could provoke Liam's anger at not trusting his words. If he was right, and he asked… he wasn't sure what would happen. Halius couldn't think that far ahead. "What was her name, Liam?"

The Lycan stopped in the hallway midway into a step that led to the room he shared with Gwen. He let out a heavy sigh and turned, meeting Halius's eyes when he said, "Her name was London."

Halius couldn't help but smile at him. Having learned a secret of Liam's, even if the man wasn't fully aware of what he had told that night. "So, you did have a True Mate?"

Liam breathed once, twice. Long, drawn breaths that made Halius's palms start to sweat. He shook his head and said in a whisper that Halius almost struggled to hear, "No." Without another word, he stepped into his bedroom. The door closed gently behind him.

*****

Miles away, the factory had been overtaken. It was easier than Malachi had thought to liberate them. He wasn't surprised when nearly all the Azure joined him and revolted against the Lycans. He wasn't surprised when some of the Lycans refused him and suffered the consequences for it.

What he did not expect was what it took to liberate the Lycans and some of the Azure who wanted to cooperate. The removal of their bracelets became easier when the first few were freed. An

Elemental Azure—one who could control water, earth, and fire—was able to melt and snap the metal without forcing the Azure to injure themselves by overloading their own shackles. Malachi's one regret was the fate of Azure who were not willing to join him. However, he needed to respect their choice, and ensured they died quickly.

The Lycans were not freed so easily. Their bond with the Alpha, who had locked them in the factory, was weak but was present. It kept them from accepting Malachi's way of thinking, but he was able to break those bonds; although it caused such discomfort in the Lycans, those who resisted him entirely did not survive the severing.

Strangely enough, there were some Azure who had a bonded energy with the Lycans. They were all willing enough to be released from their bondage; the severing was easy enough.

Malachi's wrists were heavily damaged from his own unchaining. He did what he could to act uninjured despite the cracked and weeping wounds that dripped blood onto the floor as he paced back and forth. The smog from the molten plastic still lingered heavily in the air, a constant reminder of their struggle for freedom. He inhaled deeply through his nose and reached out to his new followers.

He could feel them, their presence within him and his in theirs. They had completely overtaken the factory; the machines had been turned off. The noise that had buzzed their ears for longer than anyone wanted to speak of was finally still. For the first time in ages, the absence of sound felt louder than the machines ever had. Many of the liberated were scattered around the factory, getting in one last look before they would finally be truly free.

What Malachi paced in front of was a Lycan woman. The same woman who had tried to grab him from his room—the one Cato had saved him from. He learned her name was Katherine, and she was the last one alive who refused to cooperate.

Malachi stopped his pacing. He leaned forward and rested his hands gently on his knees. He kept himself from flinching at the pain that shot through his arms, his blood soaking into his pants.

Katherine, too, was stained in blood. Hers, and the blood of others she fought against. She bled from wounds across her body, one shoulder dislocated, and made her posture slant as she sat on her knees. She had watched her Mate die at the hands of Malachi's followers.

Cato had caught her amongst the chaos and had taken her to Malachi. He was crouched behind Katherine. He rocked side to side on the balls of his feet with both elbows resting on his knees. A knife, found in the upper offices of the factory, was being rolled in his palm as he watched Malachi.

Katherine's breath shuddered; she spoke first, trying to sound strong. "I will not betray my Alpha."

Malachi continued to stare into her eyes. His unblinking gaze sent a chill down her spine, and he said, "No. I imagine not." He straightened and swung his arms as he paced a few steps back and forth. He flicked his fingers, sending blood droplets sprinkling to the floor around him as he continued, "Not when you watched your Mate be torn apart. Not when we broke into the cages you called homes." He heard Cato let out a mocking laugh when he referenced what they had found in the so-called *offices*. He stepped closer, watching her turn her head away from him as he looked down upon her. "Not when you would enter the rooms of the Azure and take them from their beds." He stopped and bent down behind her. His voice was deep and rough, an echo of a familiar sound shook his voice, "Not when your *precious* Alpha put you in here."

Katherine kept her eyes straight. She felt his lips brush against her ear when he spoke to her. She gritted her teeth and said, "My Alpha is just and fair. My actions put me here; I will not deny that."

Her voice grew, as did her trembling when she declared. "I. Will. Not. Succumb. To. You."

Malachi chuckled as he moved around her. He knelt, matching the height of her eyes as he said. "No. You're not." His eyes flicked to Cato, whose smile grew across his face. "You will to him."

Katherine let out a frightened yelp when the edge of Cato's knife moved down her spine. In a swift move, he cut her shirt in several places and tore it from her body. Tears fell from her eyes as she whimpered from the shock of her undressing. She hugged her arms to her chest to cover her brassiere.

Malachi tipped his head, "What? Something to say, Katherine?"

She tried to steady her shaky breathing. Her wolf was weak since the death of her mate; the pathetic mewling whimpers were barely audible in her head. She opened her mouth, her voice trembling as she said, "You… you don't have to do this. I won't say anything." She saw Malachi's brow raise, and after a hesitation, she whispered, "Please… I don't want to die."

He nodded understandingly before a smile wormed onto his face. "That's right, girl. Beg me." He straightened once more and nodded at Cato. "And then, you're going to beg him."

Cato gripped the woman's hair and yanked her down. He laughed when she let out a shriek of pain as he pressed her chest against the cement floor. He held her in place with his knee crashing into the small of her back. Her lack of strength and defeated willpower left her unable to push him away. He hunched over her, rubbing his cheek on the side of her head. His voice was light, airy, and hauntingly playful as he hissed, "You've always been so pretty." He touched the tip of the knife to her scapula.

Katherine whimpered again; her eyes found Malachi, who watched with an expression of disinterest. "Don't… please… don't let him do this."

Malachi gave a simple shrug; he pursed his lips and gestured towards Cato with his bloody hand. "Cato is a free man now. He can do what he likes." Cato looked up at his friend, and they exchanged smiles. "Right now, he likes you."

Cato chuckled, his mouth inches from Katherine's cheek when he looked down at her and whispered, "You've always had beautiful skin." He pushed the tip of his knife into her shoulder and let out an innocent-sounding laugh when she started to cry out. "I think I'd like to have it."

Malachi watched as a pool of blood formed around where she lay. The woman cried and begged for mercy as Cato peeled back her flesh. Her shrieks echoed around the silent machinery and rows of plastic totes. The sound abruptly stopped when Cato plunged the knife into her exposed spine.

After a moment, Cato stood. Leaving the knife where it was in her fileted back. He stared down at her; his whimsy and joy left his voice. The tone was replaced with a seriousness that almost made him sound compassionate. "They are supposed to be Children of the Fates." He looked at Malachi with confusion. "They're just… like us?" He looked down at himself, still soaked and dripping long strands of blood and viscera from the woman's body and several others he had stripped apart. "Blood, bones. They're supposed to be different, right? They're supposed to have power and magic beyond our understanding."

Malachi reached out and touched his shoulder. "No. *We* are the Children. They are demons. Forsaken monsters that wear human skin." He took a deep breath; his irises flecked with marks of crimson red that nearly matched the pool of blood on the floor.. He reached out, his mind connecting with all those who followed him. "Hear me, brothers, sisters! The final choice has been made. May the Fates accept those who rebuke their Children. And allow them to find peace."

As he spoke, they emerged from the stacks of products and machines and approached the bay doors where Cato and Malachi stood.

"This choice is what I have offered all of you. And you have chosen freedom!" He held up his hands, stretching his arms out wide as he declared in a booming voice, "Freedom from your captors!" He motioned to the body of the woman, splayed out on the floor. "Freedom from your burdens on this earth." He began to pace in front of the crowd that had formed. "You need not suffer in any form. We will tear down the walls of those who have tortured us."

From the crowd, Malachi began to hear hoots and hollers of approval and agreement.

"The Azure have suffered in their chains long enough! The Lycans have suffered in their ranks long enough!" The cheers grew louder as Malachi's voice roared through the quiet of the factory. "We will no longer bow! We will no longer suffer the tyrants! With the will of the Fates, we will set the world free!"

The crowd exploded in a thunderstorm of cheers; rallying cries began to sound, and they clapped. In a moment no one expected, Malachi let out a loud howl.

It was never done in a civilized society. Lycans, in their wolf forms, often howled to one another through the moonlit night. While in human form, however, howling—or any other animalistic sound that was not a threatening growl from a superior—was considered incredibly low class. Not even Omegas ever howled in human bodies, even in their most indecent moments.

Malachi howled again, and slowly, the others joined in as they were liberated from yet another rule that had held them down.

With the Azure bracelets broken, the Omega wolves wanted their own form of symbolic liberation. It was Whitney who conceived the idea, and using her own knife she had pilfered from supplies, she carefully carved a mark overtop of their tattooed Omega symbols. The cuts would take an excessive amount of time to heal on their own, as there were no healers in the factory. Of course, there wouldn't have been; no Lycan of sound mind would sell something as valuable as a healer to a factory.

Overtop of the Omega symbol, she carved the ancient mark of the Alpha. Alpha and Omega. The beginning and the end of everything they knew. No longer the last, nor was anyone the first. They were all one.

When she was finished, Malachi signaled the Lycans, and they opened the large dock doors. Evening sunlight and cool autumn air poured into the factory. After a moment of hesitation, the crowd jumped from the docks and ran into the light.

Many of them dropped almost immediately and rolled in the manicured grass. Soft and cool against their skin. They breathed deep the clean air and rolled with one another in playful wrestling, exploring the outside world for the first time in ages. For some, in their lifetimes.

Malachi and Cato jumped from the dock, with Cato having to stabilize Malachi due to his inability to catch himself. Cato shielded his eyes against the glare of the sun as they walked away from the only world he had ever known. Every step he took felt like walking in a delicate dream that might break at any moment. A headache from the shock was starting to form, but it was a sensation he wouldn't trade as he took in the beauty around him.

The sky was a brilliant blue in the afternoon. The sun shone low as the autumn days grew short. Leaves of flaming colors danced in the chilly wind against the vibrant evergreen. He took a deep breath of the fresh pine and earthy smell, which was so different from the stuffy air he was used to. The trees stand taller than the building, making Cato's eyes go wide with amazement. He could hear songs in the air, the rustling of the breeze that made goosebumps run up his arms.

Cato sank to his knees, his eyes fixed on the top of the trees that split the sky. White puffy clouds floated across the blue and sank into a distance that Cato had never dreamed of. It seemed to go on forever. There was no top, no cap like the ceiling in the factory. The grass on the ground swayed and rippled, dotted with colorful flowers that were low in the grass, colors Cato had never seen. The wind was gentle on his skin, not rough from the fans. And it was clean. He could see, he could hear, and with his bracelets now removed, he could feel.

It was as if power was radiating from the ground. Did the earth pulse in some way, or was it just his heart beating from his chest? As the power was within him, he realized he could feel things. Where things were and how far away. Malachi had told him once that he would have a special skill that he would be able to perfect now that he was unshackled. Was that his skill?

He was distracted by the strange sensation in the air. It was cold, but the light that touched him was warm. The mix of hot and cold made him shiver, but he didn't mind it. The sun radiating its own power down on them soaked into his skin. The warmth made his pale skin glow bright in its light.

He had no words. His emotions choked him as he pressed his eyes into his hand. He felt Malachi's arm wrap around his shoulder when his friend, his liberator, crouched down. Cato leaned against him, overcome with emotions he had never felt in the twenty-seven years he had been alive, and he wept.

*****

Weeks passed for the young Newaygo pack. Tensions had died down; the moon had returned, and the events around the fight between Gregory and Halius were forgotten nearly as fast as it had started. The leaves had all turned, and the majority had dropped. Autumn wind and storms had cleared most of the leaves that had blazed with color just a few days prior.

No one, however, was feeling down due to the weather. Spirits were high, and it was time for the Seasonal Games. The opportunity was rare for the whole of the territory leaders to gather for anything other than business. However, some wouldn't miss an opportunity to discuss the issues between feuding packs. The once-a-year congregation allowed them to gather under their Nexus for the best of reasons. A chance for each territory to fight for glory while also giving the packs a chance to fight as peacefully as possible. Sport, it seemed, was an excellent substitute for war.

The Newaygo Prime pack arrived in the state capital, Clare. They were not the first to arrive but were hardly the last. The city was mostly made up of hotels, parking garages, bus stops, and everything a tourist city could have. There was even an airport for those who chose to fly if their territory was far across the state. The streets were full of excitement as different groups showed up, making the city even more lively and fun. Only one Lycan family lived in the capital of the state. The Nexus family. The house in which they lived was hidden somewhere within the city, the location generally not shared with the public for multiple security reasons.

In the state of Michigan, only one Lycan lived in Clare. All others were merely visitors.

Halius was on the road, driving himself to Clare. He begged and pleaded with his mother for permission to drive himself. Everyone was astounded when she consented. Even more surprising, in the car that contained the rest of the small family, Liam, Sydney, and Gwen, there were no fights on the three-hour drive.

Sydney was in the back of the car, silently enjoying the ride by either looking out the window or playing on Liam's phone. Her phone was loaned to Halius for the drive-up, as Gwen had still not replaced the device she had broken.

The parking garage for the hotel was massive. Liam found open spaces side by side on the sixth floor. Many of the parking structures around Clare were higher than five levels, and during the four days all the Prime Families would be in the capital, they would nearly all be full. This city was one of the only tourist spots in Michigan. Other territories could boast beaches, rivers, trails, and excellent forests, but the rigidity of the Alphas determined their level of traffic in and out of the territory. The Nexus allowed open travel throughout the territory. With only one segment of the forest that surrounded the city closed to the public.

When Liam parked the car, Gwen got out of the vehicle and stretched. Liam turned in his seat and said, "Alright, Sydney. I need my phone back."

She ended her game and smiled as she placed the phone in his waiting hand. "I got to level eleven."

He returned the smile. "Good job. But you had to make it to thirteen to get a soda." He heard her audible, *aww*, from the back seat, and he got out of the car. He quickly dialed a number and held the device to his ear.

After a few rings, Halius answered. "What's up, Liam?"

"We're here. Are you parked?"

The wind was rustling over the phone as Halius's car continued down the freeway. "Not yet. I had to stop for gas and ran into the guys. We're not far."

Liam nodded to himself and let out a verbal, "Alright." He should have known Maddox would want them to ride together instead of taking the train, as was the most common practice for Lycans to travel. "Are you riding in their car?"

Halius replied quickly, "N-No! I'm still in my car. I'm following them so we can park next to each other. You can tell Mom I didn't let any of them get in my car. I am safely driving by myself, behind Maddox's Lexus, while talking on the phone."

Liam chuckled. "OK. We're in Garage 15." The parking structure was one of the furthest away from the arenas where the games would be played. The subway systems in Clare went to each of the parking structures and hotels, allowing easy transportation.

He could hear the smile in Halius's voice. "We'll be there in a bit; try to save us two spots." When Liam agreed, stating he would do his best, Halius finished the call. "Thanks, Liam. See you soon."

Sydney opened her door while Liam was on the phone; he had walked to the back of the car and was watching the driveway as he waited for Halius's car. Just as she was about to stand from the backseat, Gwen leaned on her open door.

Gwen didn't smile, but for a moment, she didn't seem harsh either. She looked at Sydney and saw her nervousness growing the longer she looked at the Azure. Her eyes narrowed for a moment; her hand rested on her hip as she leaned on the door. Her question was genuine when she asked, "Are you afraid of me, Sydney?"

Sydney looked up at her and blinked at her in confusion. Should she lie? Would Gwen be angrier if she did? She looked to Liam, who was still on the phone, and tried to sound truthful when she said, "You have not been kind to me, Mistress Gwen." She saw Gwen's brows furrow and added, "You made Master Liam hit me."

Gwen folded and unfolded her arms several times as she adjusted her stance. Did she seem sorry? The way she looked away from Sydney, throwing her false-blonde hair over her shoulder, it was difficult to discern. The majority of the time, the only emotion Gwen emitted towards her was rage. She spoke with quick words, "He had to punish you under the command of his Alpha. I didn't make him do that."

Sydney lowered her eyes and knew she shouldn't speak further on the subject. Liam would have told her to remain quiet. Halius probably would have told her to remain quiet. She told *herself* to remain quiet. Why did she have such a problem listening? "You instigated a situation that provoked the rage of the Alpha and made him force Master Liam to strike me." Her voice was calm, but her hands shook slightly until she balled her fists. Her eyes flicked up to Gwen and waited to speak again until the woman finally matched her eyes once more. "Then Master Liam took me home and finished my cruel and unnecessary punishment in private."

Gwen huffed as she shifted from one foot to another. They both turned to see the two cars they had been waiting for take spaces not far from where Liam had parked them. A flash of what seemed like regret came across her eyes. Her voice was quiet, barely audible, as she mumbled, "Well… I was… I didn't mean…"

Sydney felt her heart skip. Was that the start of an apology? It made her wonder if Liam had said something to Gwen about the way she was treated. Liam had tried before to tell Gwen to back off and never had it worked. Did something change in that shrewd brain? Finally? For a moment, Sydney almost believed that there was some kindness hidden behind Gwen's harsh words. But just as quickly as that thought came, it vanished.

Gwen saw Halius step out of his car. Her shoulders straightened, jaw clenched. Her whole body seemed to tense as her usual demeanor resurfaced. She leaned down and whispered in her classic, horrid tone, "Such big words for a creature like you." She stepped back and spoke with a dismissive voice, "I don't control what the Alpha does with his pack. His actions are his own."

Gwen turned from the girl and rounded the back of the car to greet Halius. She gave him a hug that lasted longer than he wanted it to, only releasing him when he hugged her with one arm. She slapped his chest and said, "Where have you been? You were supposed to be right behind us!"

Halius shrugged as Elliot and Ezra joined the small group. "My car needed gas. What do you want from me?"

Roderick emerged from the car and quickly opened the back door, allowing Maddox to step out easily.

The young Alpha was on his phone. He shook his head with a groan as he got out of the car. "I was just texting Dad, Roderick. You don't need to open doors for me."

Roderick's smile was brilliant. He bowed slightly with his hand on his chest. "It is my purpose to serve you, sir."

Maddox shook his head as Roderick closed the car door. The young Alpha properly shook Liam's hand and said, "Good to see you, sir."

Liam returned the smile. "Always a pleasure, young Alpha. I am surprised you didn't take the train with your father."

Maddox let out a sigh and stuffed his hands into his coat pockets. "Honestly, there's only so much I can take of that man."

The adults seemed to ignore the statement, with the young pack all exchanging looks. Maddox kept his smile and said, "Their train left about an hour ago. He gave me the name of the hotel if you wanted to head over there."

Liam's smile dropped from his face. "The… wait, what? What hotel?"

Maddox tried to keep the confusion from dropping his expression. His eyes narrowed for a moment before he said, "Yeah… Dad said we're all getting a hotel for the weekend. Because of the games." His smile slowly vanished as he looked between Liam and Gwen. "H-H-He said it was stupid that we would keep driving back and forth when we can just stay here."

Liam didn't attempt to keep himself calm. His face reddened slightly as he stepped back. He paced as he ran his hands down his face. He knew the answer without needing to ask, but spoke the question regardless, "Did he say who was staying in the hotel with him?"

Maddox let out a frustrated breath as he pulled his shoulders up to his ears. His hands turned into fists at his sides, his irritation growing at Liam's unfounded distress. He opened his mouth to speak, but Liam stopped him. The air between the men tensed, the answer was clear without either of them needing to speak.

"No, you know what, I'm just going to call him." He snatched his phone from his pocket and found his contacts with shaky hands. He glanced up at Maddox, "Go find a place for lunch; I'll catch up."

The young Alpha nodded and waved a hand; the small crowd followed him. Gwen kissed Liam on the cheek before she walked with the teenagers. Only Sydney lingered behind and waited for his instructions.

Liam held the phone to his ear and said, "Go with them, sweetie. Stay by Halius."

Sydney nodded. It was still shocking that she could go anywhere without Liam. For so long, unless they were home, she was only permitted to go to school with Halius. But in the last couple of weeks, Liam was giving her more freedom so long as Halius was around. It seemed appropriate that the Prime-Beta would have an Azure attendant, although it still made her nervous. With a whisper, she asked, "Are we trusting him?"

Liam let his eyes trail to the group who were walking away. He could hear the voices of the young men in rowdy conversation echoing across the concrete structure. He stepped closer to Sydney and pecked a kiss on her forehead. "I trust him. For now."

Sydney gave one nod and trotted after the group. Her hands were tight against the zipper of her coat to block out the bitter wind. She felt warmth flood her face and hands when she caught up with the group. It was a strange feeling to know Liam trusted Halius. He trusted no one. Not even his Alpha. It was the whole reason they didn't live in the pack house.

Liam watched her disappear into the elevator. His inner wolf growled with irritation as Alex finally picked up the phone.

"Hello, Liam."

Liam didn't return the greeting. He had planned on restraining himself, on trying not to speak with such an aggressive tone towards who was supposed to be his oldest friend. His voice snapped like a rubber band when he started to speak, "I am not staying in a hotel all weekend."

He heard Alex give a gruff snort of annoyance. Liam's finger tightened over his phone; his jaw clenched in frustration. "Why not? For Fates' sake, Liam. It's one weekend. I got us all set up in one of the Pack Suites. You should have seen the pictures, man. It's like the size of a house. Everyone will have their own room." But that wasn't the problem, and they both knew it.

Liam rubbed his eyes, his tone cooling as the wind cut through the parking garage. "Come on, Alex. I don't mind the drive. We don't need a hotel room."

Alex was quiet for some time. The silence made Liam's palms sweat, and his wolf started to whine as he waited for his Alpha's response. When he finally spoke, his tone would have sent a chill down Liam's spine if they had been facing one another. "Are you part of this pack, Liam?"

He closed his eyes. "Yes."

There was shuffling on the other side of the call as Alex moved away from who he sat next to on the train. His tone started to rise when he said, "Are you? Because I have done nothing but fight you for the past fifteen years. You didn't want a mate, you won't live in the pack house, you let your Azure run wild, and your stepson is acting like a delinquent." The growl echoed through the phone, causing Liam's skin to run cold beneath the layers of clothing he wore. "What is it you are wanting? Would you rather not be part of this at all because I am getting tired of your attitude."

Liam couldn't answer. He stammered, his throat choking with his words. He had nothing he could say to Alex without risking Sydney. His bumbling silence gave Alex all the answers he needed.

The Alpha's voice barked through the phone, "My pack is staying in one of the hotels this weekend, per tradition. We are going to be a unified front as we support our players in the games, and this is the last time I want to hear any complaints from you. You will make sure your family is properly behaved, and if you don't—"

Liam nearly held his breath. He knew what the Alpha would threaten him with. After all the years, all the things he and Alex had done together or *for* one another, would it all end because he didn't want to sleep in a hotel with them? "Alex… please don't…"

He heard Alex's growl through the phone, as close to a command as the Alpha could muster without being in the same place. "If you don't, Liam, you will be Exiled." Upon Liam's silence, he continued, "I am tired of this. You have constantly taken advantage of my generosity for years. This separation makes my pack look weak, and I will *not* look weak in the presence of the Nexus! Shape up, be part of this pack, or get out!"

Liam clenched his jaw, his fingers tightening around the phone as a cold weight settled in his chest.

Before he could respond, Alex disconnected the call. Liam held the phone against his cheek long after the conversation ended. His arm finally dropped; he looked up to the concrete ceiling with tears burning his eyes. Alex was not a man to make threats. His words were promises, and if Liam did not do as he said, he would face the consequences and be removed from the pack.

Liam rubbed his fingertips against his forehead and began to walk. If he faced Exile from Alex, it would turn him into a Rogue. It hadn't happened in decades within Newaygo, long before Alex had taken over the territory from his father. A disobedient wolf would have their connection severed from the pack in a painful and often torturous procedure using an Azure who held such powers. The power was rare, but each territory had at least one locked away somewhere secret in the event they needed to ostracize someone.

If he were a Rogue, he would be forced from his station. He would be chased deep into the woods, forbidden to ever return to Newaygo for any reason. If he could make it to another territory that would accept him, he would have a chance to at least live among them, which was rarer still than a wolf ever becoming a Rogue.

With no connections and no family, a wolf would easily succumb to disease or starvation. Liam hit the elevator button as his fingers squeezed his phone to the point he feared it might break. If he was made a Rogue, he would be forced to leave Sydney. She would be confiscated as property of the territory and would either be kept in the Packhouse to be used at Alex's whim or be sold off to anyone who was willing to pay for her.

Neither of those scenarios was acceptable.

Using the tracking app he had for Sydney's phone, Liam was able to catch up with the group, who had stopped for a bit of food at a cart vendor that Maddox had insisted upon. He approached just as Gwen was trying to smile.

The woman is unable to hide the disgust on her face as Roderick handed her a pita stuffed with shredded meat she couldn't identify. She looked at Maddox, almost nervously, and said, "Um… thank you, Maddox. This is… um… I'm really not that hungry."

Maddox had taken a large bite of his own food, speaking from the side of his mouth as he chewed, "Oh, whatever. You guys didn't even stop for food on the drive. It's really good. Just try it."

Halius and Sydney exchanged an amused look as Gwen forced herself to eat the vendor's food. Sydney smiled at Liam who gently touched the back of her arm before he stuffed his hands in his coat pockets. He cleared his throat, getting Maddox's attention before he asked, "So, where are we meeting your father?"

Maddox ushered everyone with a hand. "At the hotel. It's like a block from here."

The building was huge and lavish. The ground floor was large and open, with a meditation pond in the center and an open ceiling that allowed one to look up to nearly all thirty floors. The roof was glass, allowing light to shine into the hotel. Glass elevators rose and fell against the open columns of floors that carried Lycans to their rooms.

Roderick quickly checked them into the hotel. The group collectively ignored Gwen's not-so-quiet comment about how much easier her life would be if Sydney was as well trained as Roderick. The only one who seemed to attempt to agree was Ezra, who was silenced quickly by a venomous glare shot at him by Halius.

The Azure returned to the group and held up a card key. "So, the suite is the entire fourteenth floor. This is to unlock the door, and so long as this key is kept within the room, it remains unlocked. Take the key into the elevator, and the door will lock." He looked at Maddox while he spoke. "This is because of how many guests usually stay in one room in the hotel. Which is comprised of mostly Pack Suites, as they are called."

Maddox took the card, turning it in his hand as he said, "Awesome. You wanna head back to the car and grab our stuff?"

Roderick bowed, hinging at his waist with his eyes on the floor. "Anything you wish, Master. Would you like me to see you to the room first?"

Maddox rolled his eyes. He heard Elliot and Ezra chuckle, "I think we can handle it." He gently patted Roderick's bicep, "Thanks, man."

Liam was about to walk with them when Roderick stopped him. "Sir, I can bring your bags too if you like."

Liam rolled his head in irritation. "We didn't bring anything because I thought we would be going home."

Roderick's eyes shifted to the side, catching a glimpse of Sydney, who was walking slightly behind Halius as the boys looked around the extravagant lobby. "Well, we will be here for about four days. Sydney could return to your home and pack bags for you." He checked the watch he wore on his wrist. "She would return well before we had to start preparing dinner for the pack."

Sydney had overheard Roderick's suggestion. Her eyes moved to Liam and Gwen, trying to gage their actions to the new task without showing emotion of her own. Gwen inhaled an overly dramatic breath. She leaned against him, one hand on his shoulder while the other pressed against his chest. "That is a *wonderful* idea! Isn't it, Liam?"

He immediately shook his head. "She's not driving by herself all the way home and back. It's too far."

Gwen stepped back. She huffed and folded her arms over her chest. "Well, *I'm* not going to do it, and I am not spending all weekend in the same outfit."

Liam closed his eyes for a moment. "If you wanted, I can—"

Gwen cut him off with a wave of her hand. "No, that's ridiculous. There is no reason for you to go home when we have a perfectly good Azure to run this kind of errand." Sydney exhaled quietly, as she continued to listen, already calculating the fastest route home and back in her mind.

Liam rolled his tongue across his teeth. His irritation threatened to color his eyes as his wolf snarled at Gwen within his head. He saw her step back, her aggression faltering slightly at his anger.

He looked to where the group of teenagers had stopped. They were all standing at the coy pond, laughing as Ezra was luring one of the fish around the water with what looked like his phone charger.

Sydney could have looked like any other Lycan. Standing and laughing with the rest of the pack. She was well fed well dressed, in styled hair, and clean clothing. Just as he was imagining what her life could look like, he saw the glint of light reflected against the bracelets that slid from beneath her coat sleeves.

Liam let out a sigh. What he would give to have those taken off. Alex had told him to behave or be cast out. He would need to be sure to play the part and not look suspicious. Lycans were supposed to use their Azure in any way they wanted. Right now, his wife wanted her to fetch their luggage.

There were worse things she could have asked for.

When Liam nodded, Gwen spun with glee and screamed, "Sydney! Get over here!"

Her sudden shout made the young pack jump; eyes went to Sydney, who quickly walked from the pond. "Yes, Mistress Gwen?"

Gwen smiled her nasty, toothy grin. "You have to go home and get some things from the house for this weekend."

Sydney nodded; she quickly pulled out her phone and started taking notes as Gwen rattled off her demands. When Gwen finished speaking, Sydney glanced at Liam for confirmation. "I… you want me to go home? And…"

Gwen waved her hand in front of Sydney's eyes. The action pulled the Azure's attention back to her. "Yes, that's what I said. Don't you ever listen? Do you need to be admonished again?"

Sydney could see Liam's anger rising when Gwen stepped towards her. The reminder of what happened burned her cheek and lip. Sydney shrank back, lowering her eyes and shaking her head. "N-N-No, Mistress. I will do as you ask."

Gwen stepped around her and spat the words, "That's what I *thought.*"

Liam watched as she shoved the boys away from the pond and demanded they head towards the elevator. Keeping his eyes on her, although she never looked back at him. He didn't look down at Sydney until Gwen had boarded one of the elevators. "Are you up for this?"

Sydney gave a half-hearted smile and took the car keys that were offered to her. "Do I have a choice?" She tried to keep her smile as reassuring as possible. "I'll be as quick as I can."

Liam glanced around before he gave her a quick kiss on the forehead. "Call me the minute you arrive at the house." He added in a whisper, "I love you."

She returned in the same whispered tone, "I love you too." She quickly left the hotel and headed back to the car.

Liam watched her leave; his heart ached once she was out of sight. His wolf whined in his head, nearly giving him a headache as he headed for the elevator. Sydney was eighteen and fully capable of driving a few hours to pack some bags and return.

He leaned against the railing attached to the glass wall as the elevator closed. Liam couldn't help but think it was all an elaborate plot to get Sydney away from him. Alex had no love for Azure; to him, she would only ever be property. Would Gwen and Alex have plotted together to get her away from him? Was this all some kind of test to see if he would have gone with her? To test if he would have chosen her over his pack?

Liam knew he couldn't risk it around any of his packmates. He had been kind to the Azure his entire life. How much of a leap would it be for Alex to think he was a full-blown sympathizer?

When the elevator doors slid open, he saw a thirty-foot hallway ahead, where Gwen and the teenagers were just about to enter a room. Elliot had snatched the key from Maddox, and they ran to the door. It unlocked automatically with a signal from the card, and they all dashed inside.

The room was massive, looking like a floor of a packed house. With a full galley kitchen and a large island fully stocked with dishes. A large U-shaped couch in front of an entertainment system that boasted a TV almost as big as the wall. Two gaming systems and dozens of games. There were so many choices that it was clear this place was meant for staying a long time, not just a short weekend. There were separate chairs and end tables around each piece of furniture. A dining room table that was surrounded by 16 chairs, and a hallway that led to the eight different bedrooms and six bathrooms that circled the rest of the floor.

Liam tried not to look astounded at the vastness of the room. Suddenly missing the coziness of the small home he had become accustomed to.

Gwen sat on the large sofa as she asked, "So how are the bedrooms assigned? Who is supposed to be joining us?"

Maddox also flopped onto the couch while Elliot, Ezra, and Halius began to search the kitchen. "Um… let me think…" He started naming people he knew Alex had picked to be there. It was basically half of the prime pack, the Alphas, of course. Elliot and Ezra's parents, who were Prime-Omegas, and three other Prime-Omega families that lived in the pack house.

Liam quickly counted them. Even with so much space, it was easy to see how quickly the rooms would fill up. "OK, so you kids are gonna have to share rooms. What do we do with the Azure? There aren't enough bedrooms."

Gwen had begun scrolling through TV channels as she said, "Oh, I'm sure there is a spot for them to sleep. Alex said each family gets one to bring with them. There has to be a place with bedrolls for them."

Halius spoke with a mouthful of chips he had found in the cupboard. "We have to share a room?"

Ezra wrapped his brother's shoulder. "I'm going to find which one is ours! I'm getting the bed by the window!"

Elliot chased him down the hall as he screamed, "I'm the oldest! I get the window!"

Maddox leaped from the couch and hollered, "Fuck no! I'm the Alpha, and I'll kick your ass if you take the window bed!"

Halius laughed, carrying the chip bag with him as he walked down the hallway and followed his brothers.

Liam joined Gwen on the couch. At first, he leaned onto his knees while rolling his phone in his hands. He kept looking at the screen, waiting for Sydney's call, even though he knew it would take hours.

Gwen noticed him continuing to look at his black phone screen. She pulled back his shoulders so he leaned against the back of the sofa. "Hey, she's going to be fine, you know?"

He looked at her, his brow furrowing in confusion.

Before he could speak, she said, "You seem nervous about Sydney going back to the house. I know she's never had a lot of time by herself, but this is a simple task, and she should be able to do it correctly."

Liam's expression softened when Gwen leaned against his chest. It was almost kind. He let her sink into his side as he put his arm around her. Thinking for just a moment that it was possible for Gwen to be kind to Sydney, and how amazing it would be if she could keep it up for more than five minutes.

Sydney shut off the car when she parked in the driveway of the house. A wave of relaxation washed over her, to be home and not have to try to keep herself together in public. She didn't like going into crowds; school was bad enough. Being forced to spend the whole weekend with a pack she knew would see to her death if they knew the truth was nearly enough to make her scream.

It had to be a way for Alex to punish Liam for something. In all the years they had been going to the Seasonal Games, Alex had never demanded Liam stay with them in the hotel. Alex didn't even get a hotel most of the time they attended. Something must have changed.

Sydney called her father when she got out of the car. The conversation was quick and a bit one-sided, but she could hear the packed crowd in the background and knew Liam wouldn't be able to talk to her. He had to be passive, and she could hear the turmoil in his voice when he did so.

She tried to move quickly through the house as she packed everyone's bags. She started with Liam's, knowing it would be the fastest bag for her to pack since what he wanted was simple. A basic array of his nice clothes and a phone charger.

For Gwen's bag, Sydney couldn't help but take the opportunity to grab some of Gwen's less-favorite outfits. A basic grey dress that Gwen never wore, claiming once that it was too boring for a woman of her station. A puffy-sleeved blouse that had ruffles down the sides and was shorter than the woman preferred, and a turtleneck with synched short sleeves that hung at an odd length over her arms.

She giggled to herself as she packed the ridiculous outfits. The ugly clothing was gifts from Lycans across the territory throughout the time Gwen had been in Michigan, and she never specified what clothes she wanted. It could be seen as a tribute to those families who had given her the clothes when they saw her in the televised games wearing the clothing. When she slipped into Halius's room, she realized his bag was the hardest one to pack. Sydney tried to take some extra time to consider what he would genuinely want. She knew his preference for his buttoned shirts and didn't have much else for tops. She also packed one extra pair of his pants, even though he probably would spend all weekend in his jeans without complaining, and grabbed his pillow.

She was searching for his phone charger, she pulled open his side table drawer, but when she remembered Gwen had smashed his phone and wouldn't need the charger, she was about to close it when something caught her eye.

It was a business card. Harmless enough. But it seemed drastically out of place in a teenage boy's bedroom. Halius didn't have cards, and Sydney had never known him to openly take one from someone. She wondered for a moment if anyone used cards anymore; it seemed like a practice that had died out years prior.

She sat on the edge of his bed and examined the card. Why would he have a card to the Lumber Mill? Nothing about the card seemed strange, and she found no other answers. Carefully, she put the card back where she had found it and finished gathering the family's belongings in the living room. She didn't pack a bag for herself; most Azure didn't own much, and if none of the others brought clothing with them, it would look suspicious. If the others did have clothing with them, she could just tell them Liam didn't permit her to bring any extra outfits. Simple enough.

When she got into the car, she sent Liam a text at his request, saying that she was on her way back. She turned on the vehicle and began the long drive back.

The hotel room was chaotic in the late afternoon. The small children from the three other Omega families were running around, playing with toys provided by the hotel and squealing as some of them were chased about by their Azure attendants.

Halius was sitting on a barstool at the kitchen island finishing his dinner and would pass chocolate squares to whichever small child ran up to him.

Elliot, Ezra, and Maddox were all focused on the TV. They were screaming over the loud entertainment system as they played a competitive shooting game on one of the consoles.

The adults were all sitting on the huge sofa and the nearby chairs. Despite the chaos around them, they managed to keep their conversations going. They spoke of what the games would entail and who they thought would win.

Alex pulled Erika onto his lap and kissed her collar. He let out a roaring laugh and declared, "Of course, my boy will win all the competitions!"

Erika, as well as several others, shared the laughter. She put one arm on his shoulder and said, "Alex, darling, he's only competing in one event."

Alex scoffed. "Even so! He will win!" He looked to where Maddox was, the boy hammering buttons on the controller he held. "Too bad he didn't seem ready for the Gauntlet. Maybe next year."

Elliot and Ezra's mother, Evelyn, smiled kindly. "Plenty of glory will come to Maddox when he wins the Relay, Alpha. Scaling that wall is no small feat. I hear this year the contestants must run the whole thing."

There was a moment of silence as some of the Lycans exchanged looks. A few nodded in agreement with Evelyn as if they, too, had heard the rumor. Liam was the one who asked, "What do you mean?"

Desmond, Evelyn's husband and True Mate, was the one who answered. "Some of the other Omegas in the lobby were talking when we arrived. The Nexus changed the course this year. Instead of four different racers for the segments of the Relay and their time being averaged for the winner, the four will run one at a time. They will have to cover the length of the course against eight other territories. The winner of each bracket must then run the track again against the other winners. The fastest runner will be declared the winner."

Erika gave Alex a worried look, but her mate seemed more impressed than concerned. His voice maintained his confidence when he said, "Huh, that will be interesting. I wonder why he did that."

Evelyn gave an innocent shrug. "The events are ever-changing, Alpha. It is the will of the Nexus as to how his games are played."

The group of adults nodded in consensus, and the subject changed.

Sydney was sitting with her back against the opposite side of the sofa. One of the younger girls was painting her nails, each one a different color. While the girl giggled and sang a little ditty to herself, Sydney had been listening to the conversations. It worried her a bit more than it worried the adults, it seemed. She kept the fear from her face as she continued to smile for the girl, but it crept into her mind.

Maddox could run; he was fast. He could climb; his arms were strong enough that he could climb the rope at school nearly without using his legs. But part of the relay involved swimming, and Maddox was not a powerful swimmer.

Just about when the girl was finished painting her fingernails and much of her fingers in several sloppy colors, it was late into the evening. Each Azure, save for Sydney and Roderick, took the small children they were responsible for and tucked them into one of the rooms set up for the smaller children. Maddox, Elliot, and Ezra had finished their game and headed into their own room with Halius. Sydney was headed for the hallway when Liam called to her. She turned and saw Liam motioning for her to approach him as he stood from the couch. She whispered to him, as if it were a secret, "I didn't bring my hairbrush."

Liam nodded. "That's alright. Do you know how to put the braids in your hair with the ribbons, like I do?" When Sydney nodded, he continued quietly, "OK, because you're..." He felt his words threatening to choke him and forced himself to speak, "You're going to have to do it this weekend." His attempt at a comforting tone did not fool Sydney. "It's only for a weekend, right?"

She smiled at him and gave a nod. Her smile seemed to relax him; she closed her eyes when he brushed his fingers over her cheek.

He removed his hand quickly when Erika walked back into the main room from the hall. Liam squared his shoulders and spoke firmly, "Remember the rules while in the presence of your superiors, and I won't have to punish you publicly."

Sydney quickly lowered her eyes. She didn't see that it was Erika, but his sudden change in tone told her all she needed to know. They weren't alone any longer. Her voice was meek, her hands clasped in front of her body. "I understand, Master. I will keep your rules; you will not see a deviation in your daily routine."

Liam's eyes flicked to Erika, who was fixing a drink for herself. "Good. I don't want any lax from you just because there is more Azure to help with the chores. You still have duties to my family."

Sydney lowered her chest in a deep bow, hinged at the waist in proper fashion for an Azure. "Of course, Master. Sleep well." She quickly turned on the balls of her feet and disappeared into the hallway.

Erika gave him a smile when she walked from the kitchen. "He is so glad you decided to stay, you know."

Liam let out a sigh. "Is that so? On the phone, he threatened to toss me out if I said no."

Erika swirled the spoon in the mug of tea she held in her hands, shaking her head as if she had heard the most ridiculous thing. "You are his best friend. His Prime-Beta. Do you really think he would be capable of casting you out just because you didn't want to stay in a hotel for one weekend?" She patted his arm when she walked by. "Loosen up, Liam."

He watched her walk down the hallway until he was alone. Erika would never see anything but good in Alex. She was his mate, after all, and he was her Alpha. There was nothing he could do that would cause her to think his actions were anything but justified and truthful.

But Liam knew what she was capable of; she was devious in her own way, and because of that, Liam did not trust her word. He knew when she was speaking to keep the peace, or perhaps it was so he would let his guard down, and she could give Alex a reason to banish him.

The quiet filled the air; it pressed on him like a warm blanket. The Pack house was nearly always as loud as the hotel room was. He took an extra moment in peace, marveling in the quiet. The Pack house was always loud, always chaotic.

Liam tried to take a deep breath as he headed towards his room. He would have to be on his best behavior and say a silent prayer to the Fates that Sydney would be able to keep her head down and survive the weekend.

When he entered the room, Gwen was readying herself for bed. She smiled at him as she removed her shirt. "There you are. Help me with my bra, will you?"

He managed to smile at her and crossed the large room. His hands moved slowly across her smooth skin to the clasp against her spine and undid the fasteners.

She turned and faced him, her hands snaking up his waist. He didn't resist her when she pulled off his shirt. Her palms came to rest on his chest, and she pressed her lips against his neck. She smiled when he allowed her to remove his jeans. He sat on the bed in nothing but his shorts, seeing the joy come across her face when he removed her denim as well as her laced panties. She straddled his lap and let out her breath when his hands settled on her bare hips. "I'm glad you agreed to stay here." Her breath quickened when his lips teased her collar. "Doesn't it feel better to be with your pack again?"

Liam managed to smile before he pulled Gwen's face down to his. The kiss was passionate and rough, causing Gwen to moan against his mouth. Liam didn't answer her question. Instead, he flipped her onto her back and settled himself between her thighs. "It doesn't feel as good as you."

Liam kissed her again as she removed the final barrier of fabric between them. It didn't take as much effort as he thought it would, probably because of how long it had been since the last time he had lain with her. It was bad enough that he had to behave around Alex, but in such proximity to the Alpha, he couldn't trust Gwen either. With the full moon shining down on them, he had to behave the way they would all expect. He had to be a proper Lycan to Alex and a proper husband to Gwen, even if he didn't want to.

Gwen's body shuddered underneath him when he entered her. Her back arched, moaning when Liam's tongue found her breast. He thrusted hard against her, sending wave after wave of pleasure through her body. She made only one attempt to pull up his eyes, but he kept his face turned away from hers as his mouth was preoccupied with her neck and chest. She took it as a sign of passion that he seemed more interested in her flesh and allowed ecstasy to overtake her as her husband ravaged her body.

Liam was more interested in her flesh. He knew her body and what she enjoyed. He knew where and how to touch her to finish with it as fast as possible. Liam knew what she thought of him, she thought him a quiet and loving man who took what he wanted. He did, but there was a time when his actions wouldn't have appeared so cold. A time long ago he would have given himself completely, body and soul, but that time had gone. It was nothing more to him than a physical obligation.

Gwen had fallen asleep shortly after they had finished, a contented look on her face as her mind sank into a deep and satisfied slumber.

Liam was awake long after. He lay on his side, his back to his wife, who rested undisturbed by what they had just done. It shouldn't be troubling, but to him, it was. His wolf whined in his head, but he forced the creature back. Deep into the depths of his own mind until the beast knew to be silent.

Liam closed his eyes. Tears soaked his pillowcase until he finally made it to sleep.

The room for the Azure was an open space at the very end of the long hall. There was a doorway where the room opened but had no door, nor were there any windows. There were thick mats neatly stacked in a pile at the back of the room. No pillows, no blankets.

Roderick smiled at Sydney as he handed her one of the mats. It was heavy and rubber. Sydney unrolled it and pressed her finger against the mat as she said, "It's like a yoga mat."

Roderick's smile never faltered. "It kind of is, isn't it?" He continued to pass them out and added, "This is going to make me miss sleeping at the foot of Maddox's bed."

Gracie, the Azure attendant for Ezra and Elliot, seemed to agree and said, "The young Alpha knows where to find you if he needs something, Roderick."

Sydney should act like she understood. She should act like she does something similar. But she couldn't; shock appeared across her face as she asked, "You really do that?"

Roderick nodded. His voice was chipper, elated to a strange degree. "My charge is to serve the prince. I have a small mattress on the floor at the end of his bed I sleep on."

Gracie placed a gentle hand on Sydney's arm. She was much older than many of them, with a smile that wrinkled her face. "The beds in the lower levels are lovely. My pillow is one that used to belong to Master Desmond." She giggled as if she were sharing a schoolyard secret. "Can you imagine? Me, having something that was owned by a Lycan."

The statement sparked a conversation throughout the small group of Azure about how they all loved their bedding in the pack house. Sydney was silent as they all lay down on their respective mats. It didn't feel cold until she stopped moving. Trying to debate if she should use her coat as a blanket or a pillow.

She looked around after the lights were turned off. Her eyes adjusted to the dark as silence overtook the room. No one else seemed bothered; perhaps it was just her that didn't care for the open air. It made her wonder what kind of sleeping conditions they were used to. She tried to push those thoughts from her head, hoping she would be able to sleep without kinking her neck.

In the room the young pack had chosen, the four boys were settling into their beds.

Halius had his back against his headboard, hugging the pillow Sydney had brought him from home. He looked around the room and asked, "You guys think we'll find our True Mates here?"

Ezra let out a heavy sigh. He flopped down onto his bed without pulling back the covers. "Oh, I've seen mine." His words caused Elliot and Halius to look at him with excitement. "She was walking by the falafel place. And I saw her again in the lobby… and again when we got on the elevator."

Elliot sat up on his elbow. "That was three different girls. They can't all be your mate."

Ezra snorted. "You don't know, shut up."

Elliot and Halius laughed as Elliot asked, "Why are you guys so obsessed with finding your mates? Just let it happen when it's going to happen."

Halius rolled his head against the headboard, looking towards Elliot with a scoff. "Awful big talk from a guy trying to pick up Omega chicks in nightclubs."

Ezra answered before Elliot could. His words snapped hard in the otherwise silent air. "Hey! How are we supposed to know if someone is our mate if we don't talk to them?"

Halius rolled his eyes, his gaze turning to Maddox. "We're supposed to know by looking at them. Isn't that what our parents always say? What do you think, Maddox?"

Silence befell the room as Maddox did not answer.

Halius sat forward. "Maddox?" Silence. "Maddox! Are you listening?"

The young Alpha was not listening. Maddox lay on his back with one arm behind his head. His eyes were fixed on the ceiling in a trance-like state. Images formed in his mind's eye as he stared at the swirling pattern above him. The world seemed to fall away as the feelings enveloped him. He could hear a laugh, a soft and sweet laugh, from someone he knew he had never met. A light perfume dusted the air around him. Maddox took long, deep breaths, trying to fill his lungs with the scent. The shapes in the ceiling morphed and twisted like mist against a street lamp. He heard the laugh again, his chest tightening as the form of a featureless woman began to take shape.

Elliot grabbed his pillow and tossed it across the room. The pillow struck Maddox's face and knocked him from the trance before the features of the woman could appear to him in the misty vision.

Maddox's fist tightened around the pillow; he sat up with a venomous glare and hurled the pillow back at Elliot. "What the fuck, man? What's your problem?"

His immediate hostility shocked his packmates. Elliot snapped back at him, catching his pillow and nearly shouting, "What's your problem? We were just having a conversation, and here you are screaming at us now!"

Maddox huffed as he laid back down. He put his back to his friends and faced out the window. His chest ached with longing, he tried to recall the sound of the laugh, the smell of the perfume. But he couldn't. It had vanished from his mind and left a black void in its place. The sudden emptiness frightened him, and because of that fear, he kept the reasoning behind his daydreams to himself. Instead, he said, "Maybe I am trying to prep myself for the Relay, ever think about that? I'm going to need to concentrate, you know."

The other three boys exchanged worried and angered looks. Ezra got off his bed and turned out the lights; the attitude from Maddox told them to end the conversation. In silence, they soon fell to sleep.

In the morning, all the Azure roused themselves at the same time. Sydney made her way to the kitchen with the rest of them. It was strange for her to have help with what she was used to doing alone. The others were efficient, having most of the breakfast made and the table set not long after the large pots of coffee were done brewing.

It didn't take long for the Lycans to start to appear. The small children were quickly sat at the table and fed before they became too rowdy and woke the adults prematurely. The adults also started to emerge, some fully dressed and some still in their sleeping clothes.

When Gwen and Liam emerged, they, too, were fully dressed. Gwen was still running a hairbrush through her long hair as she took a seat at the table. She seemed rested and chipper as she took a coffee and breakfast from Sydney.

Liam did not have the same eagerness at the beginning of his day. His eyes were ringed with red. A tired heaviness surrounded him as he sat at the table. He didn't look up at Sydney when she placed a plate and mug in front of him.

The young pack was the last to emerge from their room. Ezra gave an exaggerated yawn as the teenagers spoke their good mornings to the adults.

Erika looked around the table, "Where is Maddox? He needs to be up so he can ready himself for the Games."

Halius yawned before he said, "He's still asleep. Hang on, I'll go get him."

Maddox's dream had pulled him into a deep sleep he had not experienced in quite some time. Images flashed quickly across his eyes as he tossed around on his bed.

He stood in a forest. The familiar trees swayed and creaked in a gentle wind that rustled the leaves. He knew those woods; he was in Newaygo. The southern side towards the boarder of Kent. The lovely laugh echoed around him, causing him to turn around again and again as he looked about the trees.

One thought, one drive filled his mind as he heard her laughing. He needed to find her. He needed to be near her. He didn't fight the overwhelming feeling that warmed his limbs and possessed his mind; he picked a direction and gave chase.

Each time he felt as if he were close, he would hear her laugh coming from behind him. Each time he turned, he would see her disappearing behind another tree. Just out of reach every time. He never saw her face, just a flare of her white dress or a shadowed arm that was shadowed by the sunlight that pierced through the trees.

The game lasted an eternity, to the point where it should have made him angry. He caught up to her and saw her shadow cast on a large oak tree, but when he turned and the sun, she was gone one more. But he found himself still smiling; he wasn't angry. The game was fun, and Maddox felt as if he could chase her forever. He even wanted to. The freedom and joy he felt running through the woods with the mystery woman he was determined to catch rivaled anything he had ever felt in his normal life.

He stopped running when her laughter grew quiet. The forest calmed, and his smile vanished as he looked around the trees. Where could she have gone? Did she leave?

His heart skipped when he felt a hand gently touch his back. His stomach fluttered, hearing her voice whisper in a playful, sing-song tone, "I caught you."

Maddox spun around, but the forest was gone. He was lying in his bed, the glaring light from the window blinding his eyes as his shoulder flopped down onto his bed. Halius stood over him, shaking him awake.

The world crashed back down on him with a heavy reality. His chest was heavy; a depressing realization came over him as he remembered where he was. He didn't mean to sound angry, but his words bit the air as he tried to speak with a rough, dry throat. "Halius? What do you want?"

Halius took a step back, confused by his sudden outburst. "Dude, it's like 8:30, you have to get up. You're the last one still in a bed; let's go."

Maddox threw Halius's hand away from him when the Beta offered to help him stand. "No, fuck off, man. Can't I get some fucking sleep anymore?" He yanked up his blanket and pulled it tight across his shoulders.

Halius tried to insist. He attempted to pull on the blanket, but it only tightened Maddox's grip. "Seriously? You already slept! You woke me up with your snoring like twice!"

Maddox leaned back as he looked over his shoulder at Halius. "You want me to put my fist through your fucking teeth? Piss off!" He slapped his head down on his blanket, putting his back to Halius once more.

The Beta threw his hands up in defeat. "Fine! Stay there for all I care!" He turned from the bed and stormed towards the door as he muttered, "Punk-ass cur. Why you gotta be such a dick in the morning?"

Eyes fell on Halius when he stormed out of the hallway. The conversations were hushed as the adults looked his way. He took the plate Sydney had offered him at the table and sat at one of the barstools in a huff.

Erika spoke, "Is he on his way?"

Halius's voice barked at her, "No. He yelled at me and told me to fuck off."

Erika's gaze snapped to Gwen. Hostility fuming behind her Luna's eyes. Gwen knew why she was being glared at. As Halius's mother, she was responsible for making sure he behaved himself. Constantly, she had to prove herself worthy of raising a son who was technically above her station.

She made her voice as tough as she could, "Halius, remember who you're speaking to. You'd best quell that attitude right now."

Halius let out a heavy sigh. He closed his eyes for several minutes. If he spoke, he would snap at her. They would fight and would have to deal with whatever consequences befell him and his mother once they did. He unwrapped the muffin that sat on his plate and shoved the majority of it in his mouth to give himself as much time as possible before he needed to speak again.

Somehow, he felt himself calming down. Maybe it was the muffin, he wasn't sure which of the Azure made it, but it ended up being his favorite blueberry flavor. He glanced at the floor next to the kitchen countertops. There was an open space of wall between it and the hallway where the Azure were sitting on their knees and picking through the pots and pans of extra food on the floor.

The sight appalled him. Was that what it was like in the pack house? Did they only get the scraps, living on their knees waiting to be called upon? His eyes met Sydney's for a moment. It seemed easy for her to be on the floor with the rest of them. She didn't behave that way when they were home. She didn't behave that way when Halius was alone with her in his car on the way to school.

She did it because she knew it was how she was supposed to behave. And Halius knew how he was supposed to behave. He finished swallowing the muffin and spoke with a cooler voice, "I'm sorry, Mother. Maddox's hostility impacted me; he refused to leave his bed and threatened me if I did not leave him alone."

Alex shook his head with an irritated sigh. He looked at Erika and grumbled, "He does know this isn't a fucking vacation, right?" He snapped his fingers, looking to the group of Azure, whose eyes immediately rose in attention. "Roderick, go get him."

Roderick placed his palms on the floor as he bowed to the Alpha. "Of course, Master." He quickly got to his feet and headed down the hall.

In the bedroom, Maddox had his eyes squeezed shut. He mumbled to himself, "Come on! Go to sleep. Go back to sleep!" He cursed at himself several times. He wanted, no he needed to go back to the dream. He had to catch the woman. He had to see her face, touch her skin, hold her, and learn her name.

But he couldn't.

The light was too bright, the sun's rays sharp through the morning as it bounced from the other glass-covered skyscrapers that cut through the open air. The memory of the forest, the light and shadows he had run through, and the smells and sounds all faded the longer he lay in his bed.

Maddox didn't turn when he heard the bedroom door open. He didn't need to turn; he knew who it was. Who it always was whenever he needed something.

Roderick placed a gentle hand on Maddox's shoulder. "Master, it's time to get up. Your family is waiting."

Maddox sighed. "I just want to sleep. Is that so bad?"

Roderick's hand coaxed Maddox to roll and face him. "There will be plenty of time for rest before the Relay begins. Today we are going to the arena so you can see the course and see where you are on the roster. Then, I am sure you will be allowed to return to the hotel and sleep if you so desire."

Maddox looked up to the ceiling, hoping he would be able to once again see the woman's form swirling in the plaster above him. When nothing happened, he sat up. "Fine. This bed is stupid anyway."

Because of how late he got up, Maddox didn't have a lot of time to hang out with everyone else before his parents decided it was time to get going. The apartment-sized hotel room was buzzing with activity as the Azure cleaned up and got ready while also getting the Lycan children ready to leave the hotel room as well.

Sydney was getting side glances from some of the other Azure as she took the time to style her hair. Twisting and retwisting the ribbons she wore through braids tightly bound to her head. Everyone had heard Liam order her to style her hair; none questioned him, but a few of the other Azure couldn't hide their irritation that Sydney was not helping them corral the small children.

The Alphas, Liam and Gwen, Halius, and Maddox, and their two Azure attendants all left first. Alex gave the Omegas in the hotel room free reign of the city of Clare as tourists, as they were there mostly to cheer on Maddox while he competed.

It was easier for Alex to boast in front of the Nexus without the chaos of the rest of his pack around him. To the Nexus, Alex had one of the unruliest packs in the state. He was still well respected by the Prime Alphas of other counties, but there were some things he allowed that many of the other, stricter Alphas would consider unorthodox.

Liam, not living in the pack house, was one such matter. As were the living conditions for most of the Azure owned in the territory. The children who came from Newaygo were often considered to be loud and obnoxious.

The large group walked to the elevator. The Alphas and Roderick all boarded the elevator, with Erika taking Gwen's hand and pulling her on. They began chatting to one another like teenagers. Even though Halius could have stepped on with them, Liam put a firm hand on his shoulder and held him back.

When the elevator door closed, Halius looked at Liam and asked, "Is there a reason we're not riding with them?"

Liam kept his eyes on the numbers above the elevator door. "Because we didn't get a chance to talk before all this began. I figured we should go over the rules."

The elevator returned to them, and they all stepped inside. Liam stood near the door with Halius and Sydney behind him. He took a few deep breaths as the elevator started to move. "Alright. Let's take this chance to go over the rules of the weekend. Sydney, rule one."

She kept her eyes on the floor and said, "Do not speak unless you are spoken to. Eyes down, formal addresses only."

Liam glanced over his shoulder. "Rule two, Halius."

Halius was adjusting his shirt underneath his coat. "Do not engage Mother's attitude. Consider anything she says as clout for the Alpha's approval."

Liam took his own coat from his daughter and pulled it on. "Sydney, rule three."

She slid her hands into her own pockets after zipping her coat together. "Stay close, never go out of sight in a public place."

Liam stuffed his hands in his coat pockets. Without turning, he said, "Last rule."

Halius glanced at Sydney, the two exchanging a quick smile before he answered, "Do not attract attention from the other Prime families. Unwanted questions lead to unspeakable answers."

The elevator came to a stop. Moments before the door opened, Liam whispered, "Good." And they stepped out from the elevator and rejoined the Alphas who were waiting.

The group was heading across the lavish lobby when Maddox stopped in his tracks. His stomach fluttered, his wolf yipping in excitement inside his head. The smell struck him like a bat. The smell from his dream was there. If only for a moment.

His head spun on a swivel, his eyes searching the lobby as he turned on the balls of his feet. Could she really be there? He tried to concentrate on his hearing, but a sea of voices rose in his head. What did she sound like? All he knew was her laugh. Could he pick her voice just by her melodious laugh?

He felt a pull on his arm; attempting to pull himself free only caused the assailant to tighten their grip. When he finally pulled his mind from the frenzy he found himself in, he met the eyes of his mother.

Erika was trying to coax him towards the door. A gentle expression on her face when she said softly, "Maddie, are you OK? What are you looking at?"

Maddox stammered as a terrifying thought wormed its way into his mind. It plagued whatever happy announcement it would have been for him to tell her what he was looking for. "I... I was..." He looked around one last time; the sensation faded as fast as it had arrived. "I thought... Just give me a minute."

Erika continued to pull on him, "We don't have a minute, sweetie. We need to get to the arena."

He relented to the will of his mother and followed her outside. They only had to walk a few blocks to reach a staircase that led down to a train station. As they walked, Maddox could hear them all talking about nonsense. His mind was too distracted to engage with them, even when someone would try and pull him in. It didn't matter who, his mother or father, Liam, even Halius couldn't get his attention. He couldn't help but think of the girl—no, the woman—who had slithered her way into his psyche without him ever seeing her.

Maddox began to watch the faces of the people as they walked along the street. Were any of them her? Something seemed wrong about each of them. He judged their features, the way they walked, the shape of their shoulders. None of them were right, none were the woman from his dream.

That realization as they headed down the subway stairs made Maddox's brow furrow in confusion. How could he be so critical of her appearance when he had never seen her? Did he even know how tall she was? He tried to imagine the color of her skin or the length of her hair. But he couldn't; he had no details. All he did know was that all the women he walked past were not her.

Roderick placed a hand on his back and guided him onto the train. Good thing, or he probably would have remained there on the platform. He found a seat next to Halius. Their respective parents were sitting in the row behind them, continuing to chat about a cluster of topics that he did not pay attention to.

Roderick and Sydney had to stand on the train, taking hold of nearby bars and rails as the train rocketed from the station.

It was mostly quiet as the passengers enjoyed the ride along the smooth tracks. The bracelets on the Azure tapped the metal poles they hung on to, making an almost windchime sound through the train.

Roderick kept his hand on the pole as he knelt in front of Maddox. "Master, are you unwell? Do you need something?"

Maddox's eyes were fixed on the floor. He was running his fingertips across his bottom lip as he leaned on the arm of his seat into the aisle. "I don't know."

Roderick looked towards the adults, "Maybe your parents can—"

Maddox immediately silenced him. His words snapped in a whisper that made Roderick pause, "No! You will not tell them. Not until I figure this out." He saw the confusion growing on Roderick's face and knew the next question he was going to be asked. But he couldn't tell him, he couldn't tell anyone. Not until he figured out who it was. The thoughts finally pieced themselves together in his head.

His mate was somewhere in their hotel.

The problem he had was he didn't know who his mate was. He, as a Prime-Alpha, had to find his True Mate in order to take control of the territory from his father, lest his father were to die unexpectedly. His mate was also supposed to be an Alpha. Many Lycans preferred their children not to accept mates from lower ranks, although the lower-ranking Lycan was always thrilled with the matchup. To a traditional Lycan, mates who had different ranks were considered "unclean." If his mate was a Beta or Fates forbidden and Omega, he wasn't sure if his father would honor the bond bestowed upon him.

It hadn't happened in quite some time, at least not publicly, but if his mate was a lower station, there was a risk Alex would kill her and force him to mate with someone who matched his Alpha rank.

He rested his palm on his forehead as he tried to push out the thoughts. The faded images of his dreams crept into the forefront of his mind like ghosts, the sing-song voice filling his head as he remembered her words, I caught you.

He had to find her. Before anyone found out what was happening to him, and before the end of the Games. If they all went home, he may never see her again. Maddox tried to focus on the Relay, knowing that in order to meet his mate by the end of the weekend, he would have to survive the race.

The arena for the Relay was the only one not located within the City of Clare. Against one of the great lakes in the Bay Territory, it was built centuries prior and maintained by the Nexus.

Rows and rows of stone bleachers lined the length of the track, tracing nearly every inch except for the water. The swimming would take place within part of the Great Lake Huron that traced the entire side of the state. A floating line of buoys showed where the edge of the swimming section was before the water swept out to the horizon.

The track started with riding a sand-board down a dune while slaloming poles that were placed as obstacles. Once down the dune, they would run to the water and swim half a mile across the shore of the lake. From the water, they had to scale a rocky cliff that was the only way they left the lake and navigate a course of ropes that would lead them back down to the bottom of the bluff. Ended with a mile-long run over flat land that would take them to the finish line.

Normally, it was divided among four runners. One to slalom the sand, one to swim, one to climb the cliff and descend on the rope, and one to run the last mile.

Maddox stared at the 3D map of the arena as Erika and Alex went to the registration counter. Halius stood next to him as he leaned forward on the table.

Halius patted his shoulder. "You'll be fine. It's not going to be that bad. You're a good runner and… stuff."

Maddox couldn't take his eyes off the model of the lake segment he would have to cross. The blue paint tipped with specs of white to symbolize waves almost looked pretty. His voice was quiet when he said, "I hate water."

Halius folded his arms across his chest. "It's only a half a mile; it's not that far." He managed a chuckle, "That's like crossing your house, right? You do that every day."

Maddox blew out an irritated breath. "There's no risk of sinking through my floor and dying every time I go from my bedroom to my kitchen."

Halius smirked. "You're not going to die, you know? I've seen you swim; your house has a pool."

Maddox scoffed and stepped away from the map. "My pool has a bottom that I can see and walls I can grab onto."

Halius knew there was nothing he could say that would ease Maddox's panic. He debated for a moment if he should try a joke, although it probably wouldn't work. "There is a wall you can grab onto. It's the one you have to climb in order to get out of the water."

Maddox didn't laugh; he wasn't even angry when he heard Halius chuckle at his terrible attempt at a joke. He felt Halius pat his shoulder as he looked back toward the model for the Relay track. His mind drifted away from the task at hand. Once again, enveloped by the thoughts of the woman. "Hey, Halius… what do you think it will be like when we find our mates?"

He slid his hands into his pockets. "I think I asked you this question yesterday, and you yelled at me for it." When Maddox shot him a glaring look, he answered, "Well… I have it on good authority that the woman will infiltrate our thoughts until we are mindless zombies that will kill upon command and eat the flesh of her enemies at her will."

Maddox looked at him with a raised brow. "Dude, what does that even mean?"

Halius shrugged his shoulder. "You'd have to ask my mother. She knows how to make it all gooey sounding."

Roderick and Sydney approached. The man was holding a purple strip of cotton cloth that was maybe two feet long and a few papers with information printed on them. "Master," He bowed slightly when Maddox turned to them. "These are for your registration. The Relay starts tomorrow, and you are in the third bracket."

Maddox let out a nervous breath. He took the cloth and said with a bit of resentfulness, "Yeah, thanks."

Roderick bowed again. "You will be able to practice the segments today if you choose, Master. The Arena is open to competitors for them to get accustomed to the terrain."

Maddox nearly rolled his eyes. He was already tired of hearing about the Relay, and it hadn't even begun. His voice was tired, "Yeah, I guess. Take me there." He looked at Halius and Sydney, waving a hand as he said, "You guys go do whatever you want."

Halius nodded once, seeing Sydney give a small bow as Maddox and Roderick walked away from them. They watched as Alex and Erika met the young Alpha across the large open room, giving words of encouragement before Roderick led him out a different door.

As other contestants came and left to look at the track, other territory leaders were gathering in the main room. Liam and Gwen were speaking to two such Lycans.

When Halius and Sydney approached, Liam took the lead to introduce the boy to the Alpha family, who stood before him. "Halius! There you are. Ryan, Carly, this is my stepson Halius Usoro." He patted Halius's shoulder as the boy gave a disheartening smile. "Halius, this is Ryan and Carly Hart. Alphas of the Ionia Territory."

Halius's eyes snapped up at them. "Ionia?" He caught sight of Gwen from the corner of his eye. Her face started to stiffen at him from the mention of the territory. He tried to keep the malice from his voice as he asked, "A lot of… um… manufacturing on your side, isn't there?"

The Alphas clearly didn't notice his discomfort. Carly was a petite woman with a chipper and annoying high-pitched voice. She almost squeaked when she laughed, "Yes! We boat some of the most diverse manufacturing in the state! Car parts to apple orchards. If you want it, chances are, we make it."

Halius forced himself to chuckle as the others laughed. Gwen roared with laughter as Carly and Ryan cackled like hyenas. Halius bit the inside of his cheek, using the taste of blood to force himself to remain silent.

When the laughter died down, Ryan narrowed his eyes to Halius. "Usoro… I feel like I know that name from somewhere."

Halius's fabricated smile faded. He felt his chest tighten as Carly seemed to agree.

Her high voice squeaked, "Yeah, yeah, that's right. Didn't you guys live in Montana?"

Gwen tried to recover from the shock of it being mentioned. She blinked rapidly and stammered, "Well… yes, we… it was such a long time ago."

Ryan nodded, shaking a finger toward Halius. "Oh! I remember now! Yeah, Terrance. That was your dad's name, right?" He and Carly looked at one another and nodded as he continued, "One of the higher-ups from that new city. What was it? Yeah! New Salem, before it fell to pieces."

Sydney could feel the tension rising in the air. Lycans only ever talked about situations like Montana for one reason. To remind whoever could be sympathetic to remain loyal to their packs. The destruction of New Salem was never something that just came up in idol conversation. Sydney couldn't even remember the last time it was mentioned, even with Halius and Gwen present.

Halius had to stuff his hands back into his coat pockets as his fingers twisted into fists. His heart began to thrum in his ears. He did not want to talk about his father. Certainly not with the disgusting wolves who ran the territory that Malachi was told to. He looked at Liam, fear flashing across his eyes as he was unsure of what to do.

Liam didn't want to have the conversation either. Attempting to end the topic when he said, "Yes, that was his father. Terrance was a great Beta and fell to… unfortunate circumstances."

Carly let out a shrieking laugh. "Unfortunate? He was a Sympathizer! Those dogs got what they deserved." She tossed her false platinum-blonde hair. "Ionia doesn't have a Sympathizer problem. We quell that behavior long before it develops. Our Omegas know not to be too comfortable, and the word spreads throughout the ranks." She continued with her hubris tone, "Those who think they're not better than the Azure can be treated the same way."

Ryan hugged his arm around his wife's shoulders. "Absolutely, my love. If they want to eat with pigs, we'll treat them like pigs." They laughed again.

Halius wasn't sure if he was breathing. The shock of hearing how they treated their own Lycans was bad enough. If they didn't care about their own pack to the point where they would throw them in with the Azure… it was sickening. How was Malachi being treated if they were so willing to toss away their Omegas?

Somehow, Liam and Gwen continued a conversation with them as Halius took a couple of steps back. Liam matched Ryan's gesture and put his arm around Gwen's waist. When he did, Gwen leaned into him as she said, "If they're foolish enough to throw away their station then why not? Keep the others toeing the line."

Carly nodded. She reached out and gently squeezed Gwen's arm. "Exactly!" Her eyes turned to Ryan as she continued. "You know, before we leave, we're going to have to talk to Newaygo about getting more Azure."

Ryan agreed, "That's true, my dear. Which one of you deals with the Azure transactions?"

Liam felt his arm tighten around Gwen. He spoke quickly, attempting to conceal his growing nerves. "Desmond, the… the…" He cleared his throat, feigning a cough before his smile returned. "Excuse me. Yes, Desmond Galloway oversees such transactions. I can pass a message to him and set up a meeting if you'd like."

Ryan nodded. "That would be kind of you. We recently had an incident at one of our factories that cost us millions."

Carly's smile finally vanished, and the high-pitched squeak to her voice settled to a more acceptable tone, "All the Azure, and even some of our own Lycans, were lost in the incident.

From the corner of his eye, Liam could see Halius turn his head from where he had moved to when he no longer wanted to be part of the conversation. Before he could ask, Gwen spoke, "That's quite a bit of loss. Do you know what happened?"

Carly let out an exasperated breath. With a dismissive wave of her hand, she said, "Oh, there was an explosion at Richmond Plastics." She placed her palm on her husband's chest. She leaned her head on his shoulder almost sympathetically. "That was the very company Ryan's grandfather had started before he had to take control of the territory when the last Alpha family fell to Moon Fever."

The corners of Gwen's mouth turned down with a shake of her head. The sad expression is not nearly as fabricated as the others, "A terrible disease. I'm so sorry for all your losses."

True to her words, it was a terrible disease. Azure was immune to many of the illnesses that could ravage a Lycan community in months, weeks even, depending on the strain and severity of illness.

Liam nodded, his expression of sorrow matching Gwen's as best as he could. He kept a sharp eye on the actions of Halius and Sydney, who had turned back to the map of the Relay track. "I hadn't heard about the explosion. To lose your family's legacy, that's—"

Carly nodded, interrupting Liam with an overly dramatic, wispy voice. "It destroyed everything. Almost three months' worth of product." She snapped her fingers together. "Gone. Just like that."

Liam knew the teenagers nearby could still hear the conversation. He knew the question that would probably be burning in Halius's head. He could see the grim expression from the corner of his vision. Liam held his composure and asked, "So if it went up so suddenly…"

Ryan assumed the rest of the question and answered it without Liam having to finish, "None survived, Liam. We lost almost fifteen good Lycans." He let out a heavy sigh and hugged his arm tight around his wife's shoulders. He kissed the top of her head and spoke matter-of-factly, "Well, they did make their choice to be there, I suppose. Didn't they, dear?"

Carly nodded and turned a smile up at him. "We are rebuilding immediately and will need Azure to staff our new facility. If Alex has any for sale, tell him we will pay the top price for them right away. We are even willing to negate the age restriction if you have teenagers available who can work."

Liam removed his arm from Gwen. He struggled to keep his last smile and said, "I will… I will tell him you want to meet before the end of the Games."

Gwen's eyes trailed to Halius and Sydney. Her venomous stare locked on the girl as she grinned wider and said, "I know a few that may be ready for shipment. The Newaygo Pack will be happy to help contribute to your rebuilding."

With that, Liam broke them away from the Alphas. Speaking a quick "Goodbye" before he shoved Gwen away from them. His grip was tight on her arm as they crossed the room away from the groups of other people.

She threw his hands off her. Her voice hissed in a whisper when they faced each other. "What's your problem? We were just starting to talk business with other Alphas!"

Liam's glare burned into her as his irises flashed the yellow light. He snarled and spoke quietly, "I saw you look at Sydney. Don't even think about it."

Gwen folded her arms. "If you're worried about the housework, we can get another Azure. Maybe we can buy Julien back from Lillian and John; that would make Halius happy."

Liam leaned down to her eye level. The curl of his lip harshened his voice and echoed with his wolf's growl. "If you try to take Sydney from me, I will kill you." He stepped closer to her, their faces only inches apart. His voice quieted further, if that were possible, and he hissed, "And I promise you, that would make Halius happy too."

At the sound of the threat, Gwen felt herself freeze. Her breaths quickened as her eyes looked towards her son. He was standing with Sydney, constantly shaking his head and looking away from the Azure as she tried to speak to him. Gwen refused to believe Liam's threat, her deal wouldn't make him happy. She tried to sound strong, but the tremor in her voice was clear. "He's already lost his father. He would never recover if you took away the only family he had left."

Liam straightened his spine. His eyes looked to the teenagers just in time to see Halius slam open the doors. A blast of air shuddered through the open room. When Sydney looked back at him, Liam gave her a single nod, and she followed him out of the building. When he looked back to his wife, a disturbing smile stretched his face. "Do you want to take that chance?"

Gwen held his eyes for as long as she was capable. Eventually, her gaze turned down with a mix of shame and defeat. A soft "No" escaped her mouth. She didn't wait for his response before she moved away from him and rushed away to find Erika.

Sydney almost had to run to keep up with Halius. He was almost jogging through the small game trail path that led deeper into the trees at the edge of the Arena's boundary. She shoved passed undergrowth that he seemed to traverse easily.

It wasn't long before he stopped. He leaned against one of the massive oak trees with his back to her. His breaths were long as she approached. "Halius?" She stepped closer and gently touched his back. "Halius, look at me, please."

She expected him to be furious. She braced herself for the possibility that she would need to try and pull him back from letting his wolf tear through his body and disappear into the woods. She expected him to face her, eyes yellow and crazed.

When he turned to her, he was none of those things. He wasn't holding himself back because he wasn't angry. He slumped against the tree, sliding to the ground as he slid his fingers into his own hair. His breath shuddered as he pressed his palms into the sides of his head. His voice whispered, "I can't take this."

Sydney knelt on her knees. She couldn't hide the confusion. His anger she was ready for, but not whatever his emotions were twisting into. "What is it?"

Halius dropped his hands; tears streamed down his face as his head fell back against the tree. "Why are they like this? Why are they always like this?" He tried to steady his breathing, closing his eyes for a moment as he said, "Don't look at me like that. You've seen them. How they behave."

She rested her palms on her knees. The cold from the ground slowly seeps into her skin from her legs against the earth. "I'm just… I don't know where this is coming from."

Halius rolled his eyes in irritation, never lifting his skull from the bark of the tree. "You know exactly where this is coming from." His tone harshened as he tried to whisper, "Those are the wolves whose company bought Malachi! They threw him into that factory, and now he's dead!" He leaned forward, his voice shuddered against his suppressed sobs as tears continued to fall from his eyes. "They lock up their packmates, Lycans if they even try to support the Azure. What kind of system is that?"

Sydney's eyes lowered. Her voice was almost robotic when she responded. "It's their right to treat us, however—"

Halius cut her off when he snapped, "Bullshit!" He snatched her arm in his hand, feeling her try to pull back to no avail. He shoved back her coat sleeve, exposing the metal of her bracelet to the afternoon sun. "Think about how you have helped me. How you could help others if these fucking things weren't on you all the time!"

When he released her hand, she hugged her arms to her chest. She saw a flash of guilt come over his face when she cowered down. Her cheeks reddened as her nervousness increased. She spoke with a shaky, uncertain voice. "I… I think that… it's to make it so we don't hurt anyone. Don't you remember your lessons about the old wars? I should be restrained. I am a threat to the sacred bond between Lycan packs. If we were all on the loose, there would be chaos."

Halius ran a hand down his cheeks to clear away some of the moisture that felt even colder against the bitter wind. He leaned against the tree with heavy breaths. His voice was calmer than it had been when he said, "I know you don't believe that shit. Don't try to make yourself think it's just because I'm here." His eyes looked to the ground, where he began to fidget with a few small twigs. "We should be passed that by now."

Sydney didn't have to put much thought into his statement. They were past it; she didn't have to act like the perfect Azure when it was just her and Halius. She knew that. After several long moments of silence, Sydney said, "I'm sorry. I know Malachi meant a lot to you."

Halius tossed the twig fragments he had been fussing with. He didn't look up at Sydney when he started to speak, "For a long time, I thought he could be my brother. I didn't understand that I was supposed to be his superior. My father didn't treat him differently than me. He didn't treat Malachi's parents any different." His voice was soft and distant as he recalled what was possibly the only joyous point in his life. "No one did. Not even Mom. She was… better, better than she is now." He finally met her eyes, adding quietly, "Dad wouldn't have wanted this." He looked up, seeing the bare branches of the leafless trees beginning to still. The air turned pleasant without the icy wind cutting against them. His voice cracked as he bit back a violent sob, "At least Malachi can see him again."

Sydney felt herself suppressing sobs of her own. Somehow able to contain herself as she watched Halius break down. She pressed her sleeve into her eyes for a moment before she cleared her throat to speak, "Halius, I don't know what to say to make you feel better. But I do know that um… the house really wouldn't be the same if you weren't there. You and… Gwen, I guess… there are times when we feel like a family." She knew she shouldn't have said it, but Sydney couldn't stop herself from saying quietly, "Until she threatens to sell me off all the time."

Halius licked his dry lips. His breath steadied as he whispered, "I have lost everything because of that woman." He leaned forward and placed a gentle hand on her arm. His eyes were firm when she met his gaze. A hard determination in his voice when he said, "I will not let her take you too."

It seemed like such a strange thing to say. The care, the calm in his voice that signified what he said was a promise and not a hope. It took Sydney far too long to realize why it was striking her as astonishing to hear it and to hear it said in such a way. People weren't supposed to care about her; she was only an Azure.

Her breath caught in her throat as she was pulled into an embrace, which she expected even less. She felt a heaviness in her chest as she realized she had never been hugged before by anyone other than Liam. She fell onto her hip as he wrapped his arms around her torso. Her head rested on his chest as she settled into his warmth. She could hear his heartbeat in her chest, a deep and powerful rhythm she could have used to lull herself to sleep.

Halius felt a strange relief when she curled into his side. She was shivering against the ground, which made her pull in closer. He felt her arm wrapped around his torso, her cold hand radiating through the fabric of his shirt. He touched his cheek to her soft, dark hair. He tightened his arms around her as he took in a deep breath, her scent filling his lungs and washing him with a calm he had never felt.

For a moment, it was just them in the quiet of the forest.

His world shattered when they heard the bellow of Liam's voice.

"Halius! Sydney! Where are you?"

It was as if they had been caught breaking a law. Sydney gasped, scrambling away from Halius as she covered her mouth in shock.

He blinked at her in confusion, as if he didn't understand what had just happened. Did he force her to lay there with him? She didn't pull away. Had she wanted to? Was she afraid resisting him would make him lash out at her somehow? Feared crawled into his mind at the thought of her telling Liam he had forced her to do something. "Sydney—"

She shook her head, her words quickly silencing him. "I'm sorry! I'm sorry, I didn't mean…" She stammered, unable to formulate a thought. What was she trying to say? Should she apologize? She had quickly gotten to her feet, nervously rolling her bracelet in her palm against her wrist. "Forgive my indecency, Halius."

Halius couldn't believe what he was hearing. What was indecent? Unless she thought he was angry at her for something. He pulled himself to his feet, bracing against the tree as he asked, "What? What's indecent? We didn't do anything!"

She continued to shake her head feverishly. "No! No! This is inappropriate."

Liam's voice sounded through the still trees again. "Sydney! It's time to go! Halius!"

Just as she tried to turn away from him, Halius caught her arm just above her bracelet. He wanted to speak; he wanted to tell her he didn't think what they had done was improper. That she had nothing to fear, he wanted to ask if she had felt any of it, or if it was just his imagination.

But he couldn't speak. His throat felt cemented shut as his eyes fixed on the metal of her bracelet. The golden shine sparkled against the sun's light. Realization struck him like lightning. His wolf whimpered in his head.

She was an Azure.

Anything he felt, anything he thought he felt, was an insult to his pack. A travesty towards the Fates. His heart sank, his stomach twisting into knots at the reality of his situation. He was a Lycan and was supposed to be her superior. He released her arm and forced himself to speak with a croaking voice, "Yes… you're right. This is inappropriate." With each word, he felt his will draining. Each step she took as she backed away from him caused a pain in his chest. "I'm sorry for forcing you into that situation."

Sydney paused. Her tongue parted her chapped lips before she bit down on her own mouth. She could see the torment growing in him and quickly whispered, "You didn't." Without allowing him to speak again, she slipped back through the colorful undergrowth towards the sound of Liam's voice.

Halius told himself he had to wait for her to leave to make it look less suspicious. If he and Sydney emerged from the trees at the same time, there would be assumptions and rumors about what they did… wouldn't there? Liam would ask questions, and Sydney would never lie to him. But how she told the story could determine Liam's reaction. But if nothing happened, there was nothing to ask about, right?

Halius began to shake himself out of his thoughts. The confusing and frustrating feelings were disappearing quickly. It should have brought him back to a sense of normalcy, but all he felt was emptiness. Was that better? Was it favorable to not feel anything, if the alternative was confusion and suffering?

He collected himself, pushing back the thoughts as best he could. It must be nerves from the full moon. Being cooped up in the hotel room with all the others certainly wasn't helping. Halius steadied his breath as he ruffled his hair. He never really hugged people, either. Other than the forced hugs impended on him by his mother. Maybe that's what it felt like to hug someone else; there was no way for him to know.

Sydney emerged from the woods. She hailed Liam, who approached her as she walked towards the building.

He tried to keep his voice steady, but she could hear the frustration in his tone when he asked, "Where were you? Did you lose Halius?"

Sydney could see Gwen watching from the sidewalk. The usual irritated and bored expression from the Lycan woman as she stood with her arms folded at her chest. Sydney lowered her head, as all obedient Azure did when speaking to a master. "I'm sorry I didn't come when I was called. Halius ran into the woods; I did find him. I had to console him."

Liam's eyes narrowed as he echoed, "Console?"

Sydney nodded. "He was upset about Malachi. I was attempting to talk him out of... of..." She looked over her shoulder when she heard Halius emerge from the trees. He didn't look tense, perhaps a bit tired when he walked past her and was immediately berated by Gwen about how he had run off. Sydney looked up to Liam and said, "He wanted to leave before he got a chance to see Maddox compete. I talked him into staying."

Liam kept his eyes narrowed, fixed on Sydney even as he heard Gwen and Halius approaching them from behind him. Liam leaned down, whispering in Sydney's ear, "Is that really what happened?"

The girl inhaled a deep breath through her nose. She didn't want to lie. She couldn't do that to him. Everything Liam did, she knew, was in her best interest. Trusting Halius was something that Liam was starting to become surer of. A secret, even a minor one, would rupture whatever trust was building between the two men, and for some reason, Sydney couldn't allow that to happen. Her voice whispered back to him, "No. I'll tell you later."

Liam took the answer and turned towards his wife. "Ready to go? I want to make sure we know where to sit for the games. We're supposed to meet Alex and Erika by the entrance to the seating area."

Maddox slid his hands into his coat pockets as he walked. He was trying to imagine what the track would look like with any of the other men and women from across the state as they all attempted to traverse the obstacles.

He had started his venture from the finish line. He knew what the straightaway run would look like; what he wanted to see was the ropes course down the bluff and the dreaded Great Lake. He came to the edge of the ridge, a tangle of tossed rope twisted and knotted down the steep bluff's edge. The woven mass snaked in and out of the trees that grew from the steep rocks that jutted out from the ground. The ropes seemed to be an unintelligible mass that had no rhyme or reasoning. The cluster hanging loosely a foot off the ground.

He looked over his shoulder; Roderick was standing a few paces behind him. His usual place while he waited for his Master to act. Maddox looked up once more to the tangle of ropes before he walked the shallow slant against the edge of the bluff. The underbrush was thick, but there was a small natural path—a game trail, more likely—that he was able to follow.

Roderick kept up with Maddox with ease. He moved almost silently through the brush as he kept his back to the steep rocks.

Maddox looked back at him and smiled, "You move so silently through these woods; it's as if you're a Lycan yourself."

Roderick smiled. "Never, Master, would I ever consider myself your equal."

Maddox looked onward as he began to see the edge of the water. The brush cleared out, giving way to a few feet of sand and rocks that separated him from gentle waves that lapped on the shore. It was water to the horizon, with land stretching to eternity on either side of him. The curve in the bay allowed him to see the dune of sand he would surf down. His eyes followed the red buoys that stood out against the dark water, marking his path for the race.

The water was dark, even against the sun. The shadow of the cliff he would have to climb cast an indigo gloom into the deep water. Maddox could only see a few feet of land underneath the water before it disappeared into the abyss.

He felt his heart quicken as he tried to step forward. The sand slid from where he stepped; it fell into the water, causing graceful streams of silt and rock to drift down into the dark. Maddox inhaled sharply and backed away from the shoreline. He fell into Roderick, who held his shoulders when his legs felt weakened. "Nope. No. I can't do this."

Roderick gave his shoulders a gentle squeeze. "You can, Master. It's just water."

Maddox continued to shake his head. He stepped out of Roderick's hands, nearly falling as he struggled to walk with speed in the sand. "I don't care. I don't care; I'm never going to be able to do this." He sat down before he could fall. Looking up at the looming rock face that he would have to climb to escape the water.

The small strip of sand where he sat and the accompanying small trail seemed to be a way for the racers to remove themselves from the competition without death.

Roderick sat next to Maddox as the young Alpha tried to catch his breath. The Azure placed a hand at the center of Maddox's back as the teenager pulled his knees up to his chest and pressed his thumbs into his eyes. His eyes flashed white.

Maddox felt the relief flood his body through where Roderick touched him. His breath evened as he was able to calm down finally. The warmth of what Roderick gave him allowed him to stretch out his legs, leaning back on his hands as he stared out into the water. When the Azure removed his hand, Maddox asked, "Why do you do this, Roderick?"

The Azure seemed confused, "Do what?"

Maddox's gaze was fixed to the distance. His voice was almost saddened as he said, "Serve, and with such enthusiasm all the time. Everything the Lycans do to you, to your people. And yet, you cook for us, comfort us, and you seem unbothered. Why is that?"

Roderick leaned his elbows onto his folded legs. He rubbed his hands in contemplation before he answered. "The Alphas gave me an order, a duty to—"

Maddox crossed his ankles as he shook his head. "No, no. Shut up." He sighed in annoyance. "If you're not going to give me a serious answer, then don't talk."

Roderick pressed his lips closed, obediently silencing himself. Although that, too, seemed to irritate the young Lycan. Did he want him to speak even though he had just ordered him to be silent? He opened his mouth and saw Maddox look at him in anticipation. After a long breath, he said, "Maddox, you know it's my job to take care of you. I do not have shame in that."

Maddox repeated his question. "How, though? How do you serve us with the way your people are treated?" He saw Roderick tip his head, considering how he should answer. "No, I want you to speak freely."

Roderick ran his tongue against the back of his teeth before he responded. "I do not consider the Azure to be 'my people.' We may be of the same race, but I have loyalty to you, and you only. I do it because I care about you." He had Maddox's full attention when he continued, "I have served your father for my entire life. I was there when your grandfather was challenged by Alex. I was there when Alex had to try and navigate his new role as Alpha. I cared for your mother when she became sick while pregnant with you." His words hardened, a firmness to his tone that Maddox had never heard, "I was nineteen years old when you were placed in my arms after your birth, and Alex told me you were my only concern going forward. I am loyal to you and to your family. I will serve you as I have served my Alpha. Not because I have to, because I am an Azure, but because I want to."

Maddox sat in utter awe at his words. He knew many Azure who suffered during their service. True, some of them acted happy, but it was clear when their enthusiasm was fabricated. He spoke with airy amazement. "I… I thought you were fifteen when I was born?"

For a moment, Roderick smiled as he said, "I was nineteen. I'm 37 years old." Roderick could see the troubling thoughts infecting his Master's eyes. He debated if he should speak further, but Maddox did order him to speak freely. "If it means anything, Master, my loyalties have been greatly rewarded."

Maddox's brow furrowed. "Rewarded? What do you mean?"

Roderick looked down at his wrists. He could feel the metal against his skin underneath his old and tattered jacket. "I… I don't know if I should say." When he saw Maddox glare at him, he chose to continue. "When your mother was pregnant, she fell sick. I was the one who was able to heal her; because of my actions, Master Alex had my bracelets recast." He pulled up his sleeve, showing the metal to Maddox as he continued, "Most of the time, our bracelets are made of a special combination of copper and iron. The usual mixture is 50% copper and 40% iron. With the other 10% being stainless steel, to give a bit more rigidity." A smile crested his mouth when he said with hidden pride, "Mine are 60% steel."

Maddox stared at the bracelet. Could he see a difference in Roderick's versus any of the others? He felt a pang of regret when he realized he had never paid attention enough to see what their bracelets looked like.

Roderick patiently waited as Maddox processed the information he was given. If he reacted poorly, Roderick would have no choice but to go to Alex and confess that he had spoken of a secret that Alex made him swear to keep.

After a bout of silence, Maddox said, "Thank you for telling me." He saw a hint of a smile pull at Roderick's face. "Want to know one of my secrets?" When Roderick nodded, he added, "You cannot tell Mom and Dad. Seriously. You need to promise secrecy; this is an order if it has to be."

Roderick paused a moment before he answered. Why did it feel like a test? Was Maddox testing to see if he was more loyal to him or to his parents? It made him wonder which would be the right answer. Maddox would split from his father's pack one day, would Roderick have to make his choice then? "Yes, I will keep your secret."

Maddox bit his lip in excitement. "My mate is somewhere in the city." When Roderick's eyes went wide, he nodded. "I dreamt of her. She is somewhere in the hotel we are staying in. I just… I just can't see her yet."

Roderick's grin almost made Maddox laugh, as if the Azure was happier than he was. "Wow, what makes you so certain?"

Maddox playfully wrapped Roderick's shoulder. It was starting to feel like he was talking to one of his friends. The formality had all but gone as if he were no different from Halius or Elliot. "I just… I just know. I heard her laugh in my dream… hmm." He closed his eyes and fell onto his back in the sand. "I could hear that laugh for eternity. But I haven't seen her face."

Roderick patted Maddox's thigh. "We still have three more days here. Fear not, Master, you'll find her."

When Maddox finished the course, he met up with the rest of the group, and they headed back to the train. Maddox would not stop talking to Halius. He was rambling about nonsense to the point where he didn't notice Halius wasn't talking back. The topics pouring from his mouth switched faster than the buildings that flew by as the train made its way back to Clare.

It was the relay track, and then he was talking about food, then how well he felt because of the full moon, then he was excited about climbing the wall but was still nervous about the swim.

On and on and on.

The adults, of course, didn't notice because they were wrapped up in their own conversations. Halius was trying not to look up at Sydney, who was standing in the aisle with Roderick.

She was leaning against the pole she held onto. Clutching both hands to the metal pole, her cheek rested against her knuckles as she kept her eyes on the floor. Her long braid fell across her shoulder as she braced herself against one of the train's many stops along its route. Stepping closer to the metal pole to be as out of the way as possible for those moving around her.

Halius watched as she readjusted herself on the pole when the train moved again. He let his hands fall between his knees and rubbed his palms together. It took all his will not to take her hand and have her sit with them. She shouldn't have to stand just because she was an Azure.

The lights flashed across her face from the streetlights that had begun to light up in the late afternoon. Her skin glowed with a golden radiance that Halius couldn't look away from.

He shook his head, trying to break his trance, and looked at Maddox, who continued to babble on about nothing. He leaned onto his fist. His elbow pressed against the armrest of his seat. He tried to pick up what Maddox was saying, but he had been disinterested for far too long.

When they returned to the hotel, Maddox was still talking. Halius gave him an audible sigh, wondering to himself how long Maddox would be able to keep it up and how long Halius could hold out before he slapped him for rambling more than a pre-teen girl.

Just before Halius could scream at him, Maddox finally quieted down. A laugh rang out through the air that stole his words. The familiar, elegant, floral smell swirled around him. His eyes suddenly fixed across the lobby.

Walking towards them were two Lycan women. One was speaking as the other listened and laughed along to a joke that had just been told. When her eyes met Maddox, her pace slowed.

Maddox's eyes widened. He had never seen a creature more gloriously beautiful. She was lean and muscular; her dark skin accented the light pastel-colored clothes that hung loosely around her frame. Her hair was a masterpiece of lemonade braids that flowed down across her shoulders like black water. A silver necklace chain hung around her neck with a white moon-shaped pendant.

It was her. The woman from his dream.

Her pace slowed when she saw Maddox, the taller woman, as well, seeing her friend's reaction.

Maddox felt his heart stop and couldn't help but wish she felt something, too. He could see the way she looked at him, her chest rose with an inhale that answered his question. He opened his mouth to speak, but his words never made it out of his throat.

Instead, the noise he made was a short, grunting scream. He had still been walking, and because of his momentary distraction, his foot caught the edge of the decorative rocks that lined the coy pond. He tripped over the stone and crashed into the shallow pool.

The splash was the loudest noise in the lobby, with a wave of silence following the noise before a chorus of laughter could be heard from several surrounding families. Hands wrapped around his arms, and Maddox felt himself being pulled from the water just in time for him to gasp for air.

Sydney and Roderick had pulled him from the pond. The water was quite shallow, but the fury now emanating from the Alphas made them act without being instructed.

Embarrassment reddened Maddox's face as he saw the woman, his woman. She had jumped back, covering her mouth with her fingers to keep herself from laughing aloud. But he could see her shoulders shaking.

His dorky smile was accentuated by the fact that he was suddenly soaking wet.

With guidance from her friend, the girls linked arms and continued towards the elevator on the opposite side of the lobby.

Maddox barely had time to see her step into the elevator when he was ripped to his feet by his father. His mother's voice hissing at him, "Where's your head, boy?"

He couldn't collect his thoughts as he was pushed into one of the elevators. The Alphas were so enraged that they forced everyone, even Roderick and Sydney, to cram into one elevator. Maddox had no answer for his mother. It felt ridiculous that he couldn't trust them enough to tell his own parents his mate was there.

The thought felt surreal. She was there, standing before him. He almost spoke to her.

Erika spun to him in the crowded elevator. "Well? Are you going to speak?"

Halius, who had not spoken one word the entire way back, could see the look on Maddox's face. He felt the uncertainty and nerves radiating from him like unwelcome heat. His eyes kept moving out of the glass wall Halius found himself again. It was all strange behavior.

Even stranger, Maddox was never one to trip over his feet. He was careful, especially when his parents were around, to say and do all the right things. To suddenly be so distracted, coupled with how moody he had been lately, made Halius wonder if something else was going on.

He took the rage from the Alphas, pulling their attention away from Maddox as he said, "It was me, Luna Erika."

All eyes turned to him as he pulled Maddox behind him in the cramped space. Standing between his Alpha and the adults, Erika's eyes began to burn yellow with his anger. "You? Why?" That was all Erika managed to ask.

Halius nodded. His tone was plain when he responded. It should have been a submissive tone. He should have known to cower towards their anger. But he didn't have the energy to behave at that moment. "I had been giving him a hard time because of the swimming portion of the Relay. I saw the water in the lobby and thought it would be funny."

This time, it was Alex who spoke. His words echoed around the small space, making his voice all the more threatening as he bellowed, "You just embarrassed us in front of the Kent County Prime-Alpha's daughter!"

Maddox leaned against the railing of the glass elevator. The Kent Alpha! Of course! That's why, in his dreams, he was in the southern forest of Newaygo, which was close to the Kent border. Was the next Alpha of Kent truly his mate? If she were, he would have to decide if he would move to Kent and rule her territory or if he should force her to move to Newaygo.

The thought twisted his mind, could he force his mate to do anything she didn't want to? Of course, his parents would tell him to have her move to Newaygo. Otherwise, when it was time for Alex to step aside, Liam would be the one to take the territory. That could cause problems. But if she had no other siblings, it would leave Kent's territory in the hands of its Prime-Betas to step in as the new Alphas.

No, he still had to keep it to himself. Even if she was an Alpha, he needed to talk to her first. If she was his True Mate, she would have felt it too, and would soon seek him out as well.

Halius kept his hands at his sides. His eyes never looked away from the Alphas as he said, "I didn't realize she was an Alpha. It was a mistake."

Halius's shoulder was pulled by Gwen. When he turned to face her, he felt her hand strike against his cheek. He closed his eyes as his skin began to sting.

Her voice cut into his ears, "Your antics will not be tolerated. When we get back to the hotel room, consider yourself grounded to your bed for the rest of the night!"

Halius didn't reply to his mother. There would be no point in trying to fight against her. It was a ridiculous punishment in any regard.

When the elevator finally stopped, everyone filed out. Maddox held Halius back, and when everyone was far enough away for him to speak. "Halius, why did you do that?"

Halius didn't meet his eyes. His voice was miles away when he said, "I panicked." After a moment, he added, "I didn't know how angry they would be. Remember, you're supposed to be the perfect son this weekend."

Maddox scoffed, his voice sounding more unsure than he would have liked, "That's… that's ridiculous."

When Halius finally met Maddox's eyes, they were full of concern. He responded quickly, "Is it?" He watched Sydney and Roderick disappear into the room, leaving them alone in the hall before he said, "That woman you saw, the one whom you swooned over, was not the Alpha's daughter. How do you think they would react to that?"

Maddox remained in the hallway as Halius walked around him and entered the room. His body felt heavy as he considered Halius's words. She wasn't the Alpha's daughter? Who was she then? How did Halius know which one he was looking at? Would he have been able to feel something as well because of their connection?

Maddox knew he wouldn't be able to figure it out if he just stood there. He tried to refocus his mind and entered the hotel room.

After dinner had been cooked and consumed, Sydney was helping Gracie wash some of the dishes. Most of the adults were in some kind of chatter, with Maddox explaining what he thought his time would be and what he saw on the track.

Halius had gone into the bedroom, doing what his mother said, and laid on his bed without speaking to anyone else.

After dinner, Liam followed Gwen into their room in a huffy voice when she finally had time to go through the bag that Sydney had packed for her.

In what seemed like an effort to make small talk, Gracie smiled at Sydney, "Must be nice to have some help, isn't it?"

Sydney gave a small shrug, "I guess so. There are only three in Liam's house; it's not hard to keep up with them. Halius doesn't like me to do everything for him, nor does Master Liam. Gwen is really the only one I have to wait on."

Gracie smiled in the direction of Elliot and Ezra. The boys were helping feed some of the smaller children who had yet to finish their food. "Well, I really only have those two. We just divide all the chores in the house."

Sydney nodded as if she thought Gracie's situation sounded better than her own. A few minutes passed, and she could feel Gracie's eyes lingering on her as she continued to wash the dishes. "Um… Gracie, do you need anything else?"

The old woman's eyes narrowed on her. "He seems to really care about you, doesn't he?" She leaned closer and whispered, "I've seen you in school; your hair never looks the way it does now. He does your hair, doesn't he? He looks at you whenever he is deep in thought. You must mean a great deal to him."

Sydney gently placed a dish in the sink in front of Gracie. Her voice quivered as she whispered, "I… I guess he does… it never really occurred to me."

Gracie stepped closer to Sydney, causing the young woman to step to the side. Gracie's voice turned dark. The malicious whisper hissed through the air between them. "How is it you don't get punished for anything?"

Sydney glanced over to where the Lycans were spread across the hotel room. She wanted to call for Liam, although he was already back in his room with Gwen. Would it look suspicious if she tried? Should her safety be a bigger concern? How soundproof were their rooms? Her voice was quieter still when she said, "I… I don't know what you mean… He punishes me… all the time. Just a few weeks ago, he put a bruise on my ribs after beating me at the track. I know you saw it… Gwen was so happy about it she took pictures… you can ask to see them if you want…”

Gracie pressed in closer to Sydney. Their stomachs pressed together, forcing Sydney to lean back against the counter. “I heard it from the boys. It never happens. The only reason he hit you that day was because Alex forced him to.”

Sydney shook her head, trying to turn her face away from Gracie’s glare. She felt her wet palms almost cutting into the sharp edge of the granite countertop. She whimpered when she felt Gracie’s fingers suddenly on her ribcage. Her wet hands soaked into Sydney’s shirt, her bony fingers pressing against the bruise that had yet to heal fully.

Gracie squeezed Sydney’s ribs. “I get punished all the time, you know. We all do. Except for you. I wonder if he would punish you here.”

Sydney felt tears welling in the corners of her eyes as she was forced further against the countertop. The granite crushed into her lower back, and she was beginning to lose feeling in her fingertips from how hard she gripped the counter. Gracie’s hands constricted her breathing; she tried not to gasp for air and call unwanted attention.

Gracie suddenly released Sydney’s ribs, allowing the girl to take deep breaths for the first time in what felt like hours, even though only a few minutes had passed. Sydney fell, quite ungracefully, from where she had been trying to balance on the edge of the countertop. In a move faster than Sydney could stop, probably due to her eyesight darkening around the edges from the sudden gust of oxygen, Gracie took two of the clean plates from the rack in her hand and smashed them against the floor.

The shatter rang out like a gong had been struck. Silence befell the room as everyone's eyes turned to the Azure in the kitchen. Gracie had already backed away further from Sydney.

Sydney had to take hold of the edge of the sink to steady herself; before she could say anything, Gracie screamed, "Sydney! Why did you do that?"

She shook her head, panic swelling in her mind as she tried to stammer a response.

Too late, Desmon rounded the corner of the kitchen island to see the source of the ruckus. His voice was loud and demanding, "What are you two doing in here?"

Gracie immediately bowed. Her perfectly submissive display only made Sydney look worse due to her having no time to process what was happening. All it would do was further the claim that Sydney had no manners. Gracie's voice was calm, too calm, as she explained what events took place. "Forgive me, Master Desmond, I tried to stop her. Sydney smashed these plates because she was angry about having to do the dishes?"

Sydney looked at Desmond with terrified eyes before she shook her head, her head snapping back to Gracie as she screamed, "What?! No! I didn't!"

Gracie bowed again; the submissive gesture hid the smile the was pulling the corners of her lips. "She declared that she doesn't have to do them at Master Liam's house. When I asked her to speed up, she threw the dishes at me."

Alex stood from the couch, he glanced around the kitchen island and let out an exhausted sigh when he saw the shards of the dishes. "Is this really what I have to deal with tonight?"

Sydney tried to step away from Gracie, doing her best to avoid the shards of porcelain as she said, "I'll… I'll go get Master Liam. So-So-So he can… punish me for what I did. I'm very sorry, Gracie."

Alex rubbed his tired eyes. He shot a glare at Desmond and said, "I'm really tired of the dysfunctional behavior of the Azure in my territory." When Desmond turned to him, Alex poked a finger into Desmond's chest. "You oversee the Azure in Newaygo. Punish them now, and I will tell Liam about it later." He turned his attention to the rest of the pack. "Everyone clear out; this doesn't concern any of you."

The rest of the pack and their Azure quickly gathered the children and disappeared down the hall.

Erika remained on the sofa; when Maddox attempted to get up, he was stopped by a stern look from her.

Desmond grabbed Gracie, pulling her over the shards of the plates by the back of her shirt. From his pocket, he pulled what looked like a small flashlight. With a flick of his wrist, the handle he held extended into a thin baton, over a foot long with a shrinking diameter to a tip that was shaped like a small marble ball.

Gracie tried not to struggle too harshly against his hold. "Master Desmond! I'm not the one who broke the dishes!"

Desmond forced the old woman to her knees. "Well, you didn't stop her either, did you?" He slammed the baton against her back, a loud snap sounding with each strike before he pushed her down onto her stomach. "You're supposed to make sure the rest of them behave! Isn't that why we keep you around?"

Gracie was gasping for breath. The strikes had knocked the wind from her before he had thrown her down. She never cried out, gritting her teeth as she groaned against the impacts that happened four more times as she lay on the floor.

Desmond looked to Alex for confirmation, already forgetting about the Azure he had put on the floor and pointed the baton at Sydney as he asked, "This one too, Alpha?"

Alex sat back down on the sofa. His glare made a hint of fear appear on Desmond's face. He threw his arms over the back of the couch and said harshly, "If I must repeat myself again, Desmond, you'll be up for it next. Just do it so we can move on, please."

Maddox was the one who protested. He tried not to sound too insistent, "Dad, I really think we should go get Liam to punish Sydney. She is his property. We need to respect that."

Alex leaned forward, his sharp eyes turning to his son. His words prodded Maddox's mind, a growl echoing in his voice as he said, "Liam is part of my pack. When someone in your pack doesn't behave as they are supposed to, you are going to have to pick up the slack. I have had enough of everyone thinking there are no consequences to their actions." His voice quieted slightly, the threat looming over his words when he added, "If you think something else needs to be done and are questioning my choices, then you can be the one to go get Liam."

Maddox pressed his hands into his knees. He was ready to jump from the couch and run to Liam's room. But it was a test. He could see it when he looked at his mother.

Erika sat with her back straight against the sofa. Her fingers delicately folded together on crossed knees. She looked at her son with her brow slightly raised.

He knew that look. She was waiting for him to do or not do something.

Maddox debated it in his head for longer than he should have and came to the worst conclusion. Halius had already saved him from the wrath of his parents; the smallest slip-up would surely spark their fury that weekend. He didn't want to have to be saved again by one of his brothers. What would that look like if an Alpha was always having to be saved by his packmates?

He leaned back against the sofa, looking away as his mother's smug face turned to Desmond. Her voice snapped the command, "Do it, Desmond."

The Omega seemed to smile. He reached Sydney in three steps and snatched her by her arm. She tried to pull against him, squeaking in pain as she tried not to cry. His grip tightened on her as she resisted. He pulled her across the floor and forced her to kneel against the wall.

When the first strike came down on her, she felt the sting and gasped in pain. The second strike split the fabric of the old shirt she was given, from Gracie of all people. The old woman gave her the shirt when she learned that Sydney had no other clothes for the weekend. Sydney whimpered as she felt air stinging her skin and knew a welt was forming.

The third strike made her cry out; the thin, rigid plastic snapped against her back. Desmond expertly struck the same place each time as he whipped the baton against her.

Every strike that followed sent shockwaves of searing pain throughout her entire body. She felt her skin split open. Blood ran hot down her back and soaked into her clothes. When she could bear the pain no longer, with tears painting her reddened cheeks, she cried out in agony.

When Liam had gone into his bedroom, he saw Gwen throwing her clothes all over their bed. He repressed a laugh as he said, "Gwen, what are you doing?"

She huffed, folding her arms after she threw down the powder-blue puffy shirt in disgust. "Do you see what that little wretch packed me to wear?" She pulled on the plain grey dress she had been wearing that day. "I had to wear this burlap sack while we went to the registration center today!"

Liam didn't react to the name Gwen used for Sydney. Forcing himself to try and direct the conversation in a positive direction, "It's… not a bad dress."

Gwen almost smiled; she brushed her hair behind her ear shyly at the compliment. "Really?" She shook her head, the irritation returning as she said, "No! It's ugly and I had plenty of good clothes that she could have picked from. Why did she bring me these?" She held up the same shirt with two fingers as if touching it would harm her somehow. "Is this what I have to wear tomorrow during the games? Everyone will be there! Photographers, Liam!" She gasped dramatically at the thought, "Am I supposed to act normal while looking like a parachute?"

Liam couldn't help but laugh. It was the first time in a long while that she didn't seem unnecessarily cruel. It made him remember that there was a time when she wasn't as vicious. He wondered what had changed. Although she was responsible for her own choices, Liam knew he did little to help her.

He approached the bed and arranged a few articles of clothing into an outfit that didn't make his wife want to claw her eyes out looking at him. When he finished the arrangement, he stepped back. "There. Wear that, it won't be that bad. Besides, you'll have your coat on. Just keep it buttoned for most of the event."

Gwen sighed thankfully. "Oh, Fates, thank you, Liam. I don't know what I would do without you." She stepped in front of him. She had to stand up on her toes to wrap her arms around his neck in an embrace.

Liam smiled and returned the welcoming hug. He felt a warmth growing in his chest as he held onto her. Genuine moments between them were rare, but they did happen. Occasional times when he could see her kindness and could return her softness with some of his own.

A sound then echoed around them. Faint, from the living room. A series of noises and voices made the hair on the back of Liam's neck stand on end.

A scream.

A scream that he knew and wished he never had to hear.

Gwen stepped back, sincere concern across her face as she looked up at him and asked, "Was that Sydney?"

Halius had been lying on his side, staring out the window where the sun had set. The color spray across the sky painted hues of pinks, oranges, and violets across clouds that were moving in over the horizon.

He may have heard the initial shattering but didn't react to it. There were lots of noises that were coming from the main hotel room. He was trying not to concentrate on them, not to encourage him to leave his bed. He wanted to try and behave as much as he could.

It wasn't until Elliot and Ezra entered the room that he knew something was wrong. Elliot explained the beginnings of what was happening. Broken dishes, Desmond's orders from Alex. To them, it was something that happened every day. Elliot seemed more disturbed than Ezra ever did when it came to matters of the Azure.

Halius sat up, about to question them further when a scream sounded through the hotel room. Without being able to think, he jumped from his bed and ran through the hallway. He had thrown Ezra aside when he refused to move; his sudden aggression prompted Elliot to follow him, hoping for answers when he would catch Halius again.

He dashed passed Liam and Gwen, who were also emerging from their room. Halius didn't hear Gwen screaming after him as he charged into the main room. He didn't hear Alex snap his fingers and command Desmond to finally stop his assault on Sydney.

He didn't hear anything except for Sydney's screams that had turned to whimpering sobs when the violence against her had finally ended. He couldn't see anything except Desmond stepping away from Sydney, who remained against the wall. The Lycan man was still gripping the baton that dripped her blood.

He couldn't feel anything except the unyielding rage that burned through his skin. His irises flared the deep golden yellow. The skin around his eyes darkened, with the black trailing down his face as his wolf took control of his body.

With a scream of rage, Halius tackled Desmond. The men hit the floor, wrestling against one another until Halius pinned Desmond to the floor. He straddled Desmond's torso, hammering his fists anywhere he could.

Liam stood, shocked at what he saw. His glare shot towards Alex, who remained on the sofa, looking quite irritated at the event as it unfolded. To his surprise, Gwen rushed to Sydney before he had the chance. His wife caught the girl as she fell, sobbing hysterically as Gwen tried to console her.

Gwen looked in horror at the state of Sydney's back; multiple gashes had opened in a diagonal line from her right shoulder to her left hip. She couldn't hold the girl properly without staining her own hands with blood. It had completely saturated Sydney's shirt, soaked through her jeans and even trailed on the floor when Gwen managed to get her away from the wall.

Liam, with Sydney being held by Gwen, was able to turn his attention back to his Alpha. As Erika stood from the couch, Liam screamed, "Why is Desmond beating Sydney? What the hell is happening?"

Erika only shrugged as she stepped forward. She folded her arms and said, "Look at my kitchen. Sydney did that; this was her punishment."

Liam suppressed the snarl that threatened to echo his voice. "Why didn't you come get me?"

Alex remained on the sofa. His irritation was shifting to disinterest as Erika took another step towards Liam. Her voice screamed over the fight that was still underway on the floor. "Why would we waste the time? Desmond supervises the behavior of the Azure. He is qualified to discipline them when necessary."

Maddox had finally gotten off the couch; he and Elliot were both attempting to pull Halius from Elliot's father.

When he felt their arms wrap around him, Halius snapped his arm back. His elbow collided with Maddox's nose; blood poured down the young Alpha's face as he clapped his hand to his nostrils.

The distraction wasn't enough for Desmond to go free. Halius had beaten him to the point where a pool of blood had formed underneath his head. Streams poured from his mouth, from his nose, and from a gash above his eye where Halius's fist had slammed his head into the tile floor.

It was Elliot who was able to wrestle Halius off his father. His body was still when Halius was pulled from him. Elliot threw Halius down the hall. He pulled Maddox to his feet, who screamed for Roderick, who emerged from the Azure's room and followed his Master into the bedroom.

A silence fell as the door slammed closed.

Alex finally rose from the couch. He slid his hands into his pockets and approached Desmond. He nudged the man with his foot until he heard a soft groan escape his friend's mouth. He looked down at Gwen, the woman still holding onto Sydney. Her arms protectively tightened as she tried not to touch the open wounds on the girl's back.

Alex huffed a breath, looking at his wife as he spoke plainly, "Alright, Erika, we're done."

Gwen stood, supporting most of Sydney's weight as she pulled her up. The shock plain across her face as she looked at the Alphas and asked, "Is that it?"

Alex held out one hand, motioning to the destruction left behind by Halius's onslaught. "You want more?"

Two of the kitchen chairs had been broken when the men crashed into them. The tiles on the dining room floor had cracked from where Desmond's head had collided with it. The side of the kitchen island was broken inward from the initial tackle. One of the only hits Desmond had landed on Halius was slamming his shoulder into the kitchen island before Halius overpowered him.

Alex scoffed as he shook his head, "If you had an Azure who behaved properly and didn't smash dishes, perhaps this wouldn't have happened."

None argued with Alex. There would be no point in trying. Nothing they would try to counter with would change anything that happened. Liam turned from his Alpha and helped Gwen take Sydney into their room.

When they heard the door locked, Erika let out a disappointing sigh. "Well, that didn't work, did it?"

Alex looked at the destruction that littered the room. He spoke in a condescending tone, "Oh, I don't know, Erika." He turned his eyes to Gracie, who was still cowering in the corner she managed to pull herself into.

Alex's eyes turned down; he nudged Desmond again with his foot as he asked, "Did it work, Desmond? Did we find the Sympathizer?" He stepped over to Gracie, each step closer making her flinch. He knelt in front of her, his eyes drilling into her soul as she started to whimper. "Do you think it worked, Gracie?"

The woman trembled violently. Her words shook from her throat in harsh gasps. "I… I swear… they… you saw him!"

Alex let out a hard breath through his nose. "You said you knew he was a Sympathizer. You said he would pick Sydney over his pack, and he would attack me to keep her safe. Wasn't that it? Wasn't that what you swore would happen?"

Gracie tried to look towards Erika. The powerful woman is standing just a pace behind her husband. Hands-on her hips, the same enraged glare shot down at her. Her fortitude drained as the reality of the situation began to crash down upon her. "He-He-He did! He has shown, multiple times, that he is a Sympathizer!"

Alex quickly snapped, "When?" He paused, but she did not respond. His voice rose when he asked again, "When did he? When he had his Azure, drive three hours back to his home to pack their bags and stay with us in the hotel? When he engaged Ryan and Carly in conversation about their bastard treatments of their pack mates and property? Or now, when his so-called precious pet was lying on the floor as I allowed Desmond to wail on her for no reason because you promised me," He began to scream at her, quickly quieting his tone so no one else could hear, "That one of them was a Sympathizer, and this was how we could weed them out!"

Gracie couldn't speak as her sobs shook her frail, old body. Her breaths heaved in her chest as she struggled to say, "They are! They are Sympathizers, both of them! There's something around that one, that Sydney. I don't know what it is, but it's there. She's bewitched them somehow!"

Erika tipped her head. A murderous look flashed across her face as she asked with a lighthearted voice, "And how do you know that? What evidence did you have, again? As you put my husband's— your Alpha's—reputation on the line, did you have some kind of intuition, perhaps?" Gracie started to shake her head as Erika questioned her. "Some kind of… connection, perhaps?"

The word hung in the air long after it had been spoken. Gracie's mouth dropped open as she looked up to her Luna in shock. What she was implying, the connection between Lycans that Sydney was able to tap into, was something she could not do. Her voice was almost aggressive as she said, "Great Luna, I would never—" Her words faded as a thought came to her. "Halius! Halius is the Sympathizer! You saw him, he attacked—"

Alex cut her off as he spoke with a quiet and powerful tone. "Desmond. He attacked Desmond. A true Sympathizer would have attacked me. Or Maddox, for not interfering. He would have chosen to protect Sydney and would have gone after one of us, his Alphas, to try and get her to safety." His eyes narrowed. "Which brings us back to you, Gracie."

Gracie whimpered when Alex's hand twisted into her hair. His words cut into her, making her flinch with every sentence. "You swore to me that you had witnessed a moment that proved Liam was a Sympathizer." He wrenched back her head to a painful angle. "You, who would have me cast out my oldest friend for a hunch you were unable to prove."

Erika leaned over her husband's shoulder. Her voice whispered to him as her eyes shot daggers at the Azure. "Perhaps this is her plan, darling. Perhaps she was coerced to divide our pack and make you weak. What have Liam and Halius done other than be the bull-headed men they are supposed to be?"

Alex seemed to agree. He yanked Gracie to her feet, his hand still tangled in her hair as he pulled her towards the door.

She was shoved into the hallway and fell to her knees as Alex closed the door behind them. Gracie turned but did not stand and clutched onto Alex's pant leg as she sobbed, "I have served this pack for over thirty years, Alpha!"

Alex rolled his eyes. He grabbed her by her arms and pulled her up to her feet. "You did. Until you didn't. Your actions almost caused me to ostracize the one man who would have defended you against me on baseless accusations that you couldn't even prove."

Step by step, he forced her backward. They stepped into a stairway that served as access to every floor. It wasn't until she hit the railing that she even realized they had been moving. The open well loomed below her, the staircase spiraling down the walls to the bottom floor that was barely visible from the height they stood. Her voice steadied for a moment when she said, "You'll be sorry. He is a Sympathizer. They both are."

Alex's jaw hardened. His irises sparkled with flecks of yellow. "I hope you're right. Otherwise, I have just nearly destroyed my relationship with my best friend for nothing." A smile pulled on his lips when he added, "Think about it when you get to the Void."

In a swift move, Alex grabbed onto Gracie's hips and threw her over the railing. The shock of his action left her incapable of screaming before her head collided with one of the rails on the lower floor. One by one, she crashed against the metal and concrete that supported the open staircase. Alex heard the final thud of her hitting the final floor, he adjusted his collared shirt as he looked over the railing.

Trails and splats of blood painted the railing and concrete where her mangled body had struck before crashing to the floor. He saw the crimson lake forming around her twisted limbs, the look of shock still visible on her face as her lifeless eyes stared up into nothing.

Alex tapped the railing, feeling satisfied with the results he gained from the little test he had put on Liam and Halius and returned to the hotel room.

Elliot and Ezra had been blocking the bedroom door after the former had dragged him inside. He tried charging passed them, but rage continued to burn through his limbs; the darkness around his eyelids marked his wolf as the one in control of his body.

Maddox, still bleeding from the hit to his nose, stormed into the room and shoved Halius back. His blood had begun to dry against his skin; it stained his shirt nearly down to his stomach and had coated half his face. "Halius! Get a grip!"

But he couldn't stop; he wouldn't stop. The never-ending scream echoed through his head and made him grit his teeth. He saw her crying, the image of her skull pressed against the wall by Desmond's hand. The blood that stained her pale skin.

When he tried to run again, hands wrapped around him. He couldn't move; he was forced down. All he saw was Maddox in front of him, still holding his bleeding face. Was this his doing?

Then there was another, older, thinner. Roderick? Where had he come from? He saw the man kneel before him. Halius tried to pull from the grip that held him in place, his vision still shaded in rage that only allowed him to focus on one thing.

He felt hands on his chest, a flash of white against the eyes of the man in front of him. His anger began to drain. The darkness faded from his eyelids as the yellow receded from his irises. His wolf seemed to retreat as the calm soothed his head. He felt the creature settle, seeming to fall asleep within his head.

The calming white light vanished from Roderick's eyes. The Azure stepped back, turning his attention to Maddox as Elliot and Ezra released Halius's arms.

Without their hold, he found himself quite unsteady. He fell forward and caught himself on his hands before he collapsed completely. Halius was finally able to look up, his mind clear for the first time since it had started. A gaping hole in his memory began when he leaped from his mattress and ended when he looked up to see Ezra and Elliot standing over him, waiting to see what he would do next.

Halius pushed himself back to sit on his heels. His eyes looked around the room as he asked, "What… what happened?"

Maddox had started wiping the blood from his face with a damp cloth Roderick had quickly fetched for him. His glare shot towards Halius as he screamed, "No! You tell us what the fuck just happened, man?"

Halius shook his head, trying to recall anything he remembered. But there was nothing. "I… I don't know." He looked towards Elliot and Ezra. "I don't remember… I don't remember anything."

Ezra shared Maddox's anger. "You flew into the living room and beat the piss out of my father, that's what!" Elliot had to hold back the young Lycan when he tried to step towards Halius. "And what for? Because he was punishing that little witch for something she was clearly responsible for!"

Halius flinched when he heard the derogatory word. To call an Azure a witch was one of the lowest insults that could be spoken. They hadn't been called "Witches" since the time of the Old Wars. He continued to stammer as he struggled to pull his mind together. "I… All I remember is… is Sydney screaming and… and…" His words choked when he saw the bloody state of his hands. "Oh, Fates!" He looked up at Maddox with terrified eyes. "I… I didn't… did I?"

Maddox was about to respond, but Ezra spoke before he could. Elliot had forced Ezra to sit on his bed. Ezra had once again tried to jump from the bed as he screamed, "You did, you asshole! You could have killed our father!"

Elliot once again shoved Ezra down onto the bed. He spoke as calmly as he could, considering the situation. "Alright, that's enough. Clearly, he wasn't in control of his faculties."

Maddox had the majority of his blood wiped off his face. "Alright, so you heard a scream, and you ran out there. Then what? You just saw Desmond admonishing Sydney and lost your cool?"

Halius gave a shrug; he pulled himself up onto the nearest mattress. "I… I guess." He shook his head. "Why would Desmond even do that?" As he looked around the room, his eyes halted on Roderick.

The Azure seemed to shift uncomfortably. He rubbed his palms against the waist of his pants as his eyes looked around. When he saw Maddox staring at him, his face reddened in fear. He did know what happened. He knew why Desmond acted the way he did.

And in that moment, Roderick saw that Maddox could tell he knew something. He stepped back when his Master asked him, "Roderick, do you know what happened?"

Roderick shook his head, quickly stammering, "I… um… I, uh." He couldn't decide if he should lie or not.

Halius looked up at him. All his rage was gone; Roderick had pulled it out of him. His wolf was calm, asleep in some trance that left him with a strange ability to think without his emotions. He could hear the tone in Roderick's voice, the guilty look in his eyes, the way he switched uneasily on his feet. The man was a horrid liar. His voice was a whisper when he asked, "You knew?"

Roderick closed his eyes for a moment. He could feel their eyes on him, the anger from his Master radiating outward without him even having to look upon his face. He let out a breath he didn't realize he had been holding. "Something had been… mentioned to me. There were rumors that Liam was a Sympathizer."

Halius stood from the bed. Even though he didn't have his anger to overpower him, his size made him an intimidating sight. His voice filled with disbelief. "You let me assault a superior Lycan because someone had a hunch that Liam was Sympathetic to the Azure?"

Roderick nervously looked at Maddox. He watched as his Master's face twisted in horrified confusion when he spoke. His voice started to shake as he said, "Yes… it was a test to see how far he— erm, you—would go to protect an Azure. Alex suspected that if Liam were a Sympathizer, he would attack him for letting Sydney get beaten by Desmond." He licked his lips, feeling sweat forming across the back of his neck as he continued, "When… when you acted out, Master Halius, and attacked Desmond… well… I can guarantee Alex's suspicions were put to rest."

Halius scoffed. "Oh, you can, can you? Why is that?"

Roderick swallowed hard. "Well…" His eyes moved from Halius to Maddox and back again before he continued, "Sympathizers, as I'm sure you're aware from your lessons in school, are known to lash out at their Alphas. Often attempting to kill them for letting injustice take place towards the Azure. Since neither Alpha Alex nor Maddox were attacked… it would…" He took a moment to take another breath before he finished, "It would have proved to Alex that the suspicions were unfounded."

A silence befell the room. For a moment, one could believe that time had stopped. None moved, nor did they even seem to breathe. Roderick was the only one visibly shaking. The servant sank to his knees, ready to accept whatever punishment was due.

After an eternity of silence, Maddox's voice split the air. His tone was quiet, almost plain, as he looked down at the man before him. "Get out."

Roderick looked up at him, tears flooding his eyes. "W-W-What? Master, I—"

Maddox's words snapped harshly. "You lied to me. A lie of omission is a lie nonetheless."

Roderick stood, attempting to approach Maddox, and was met with Halius's heavy hand against his chest. "No! Master! I never lied!"

Maddox looked away from him. "Your inaction caused the incapacitation of a Lycan superior. As well as the unnecessary admonishing of an Azure owned by Liam." After another silent moment, Maddox's eyes returned to Roderick, and he said, "Get out. I don't want to see you right now. Go help the others and leave us be."

Roderick felt regret stabbing into his chest. The order felt worse than if he had been beaten. Was he not worth the energy it would take for Maddox to punish him? He backed towards the door, giving a shallow bow before he slipped out the door. His decision solidified within his head as he moved to where Desmond was still unconscious in the living room.

Within the choice between Alex or Maddox. Choose Maddox.

Maddox had closed the door behind Roderick, shaking his head in disgust. Unable to process what had taken place. How quickly the night had turned sour.

Halius sat heavily on the nearest bed. He was studying his knuckles, trying to recall something, anything that would give him a semblance of what took place. The shadows of anger were still there, dim, flickering like coals that had been sprayed by water. Angry at what? He closed his eyes, hearing the scream echo through his head once again. He saw blood-staining porcelain skin.

Sydney's scream. Sydney's blood.

The picture was starting to form within his head, but he found himself unable to properly react to it as Roderick had pressed back his emotions when he calmed his violence.

Maddox was able to get his attention when he asked, "Halius, you alright, man?"

He nodded, standing from the bed as he said, "I've got to check on Sydney."

Before anyone could try to answer, Alpha Alex opened the bedroom door. He held onto the frame as he leaned into the room. "We're going on a pack run tonight, boys. To blow off some steam."

The young men all exchanged looks. A shallow wave of uncertain agreement rose from each of them. Although Maddox did agree, he took a step toward his father and nervously asked, "Is that wise?"

Alex's eyes fell for a moment. He seemed to be considering Maddox's question for far longer than they had expected. In his silence, his eyes were tired, shoulders slumped slightly as his fingers tapped against the doorknob he held. "Would it be wiser if we didn't?" His power returned to his voice as he continued, "I'm sick of this fucking hotel. It's going to be a nice night, and I'm not wasting the Beaver Moon because we're in a different county. It's still Public Forest Land; we just have to remember the laws. No shifting within the city; don't hunt any of the animals. We'll have the Azure drive us out and wait for us."

No one protested before Alex left the doorway. He left the door open and returned to the living room. Desmond had been moved by two of the other Omega men to the sofa. Roderick was crouching at his chest as Evelyn held his bloody and beaten head in her lap while she sobbed quietly.

After several long, quiet minutes, Roderick removed his hands and looked up to the Alpha, who had walked up behind him. "This is going to take considerable time, Master. The process has been started for him, but he will need several treatments."

Alex let out a disappointed sigh. "Why? It's just a beating. Just stitch him together, or… have him stitch himself together." He waved a hand as he insisted, "You know what I'm talking about."

Roderick lowered his head. "I do, Master. But healing bones is far more difficult than just regenerating flesh. If you want him to look the same," He looked at Evelyn, "And I assume that you do will take some time." One hand returned to Desmond's chest. The slow rise and fall of his breath had already increased in strength. Roderick almost sounded impressed when he said, "Halius dealt… significant damage."

Alex's head rocked back. His eyes closed as he collected his thoughts. "That kid's built like a wall. Stop any internal bleeding, get his bones working, and go check on Liam's Azure."

Within the walls of Liam's room, time had stopped.

The two men looked down at the Azure, who had been laid across the bed. Niklas, clad in black, stood away from the people positioned in the space they had arrived in as he watched his counterpart crouch down.

The man in robes of white, Atlas, shook his head sadly. His voice was quiet, but Niklas could hear the echo of voices behind his words. "It wasn't supposed to be like this." The ghostly sound had been Atlas's attempt to reach out to the world, barred by Niklas, who folded his arms in irritation.

Niklas saw Atlas reach out to the Azure. He spoke before Atlas could touch her. "Atlas, don't! It won't help them."

Atlas pulled back his hand and stood. He faced Niklas. His knuckles turned white against the staff that he was never without. "Will leaving them like this help them?"

A smile formed on Niklas's face. He stepped towards Atlas with an enthusiastic tone, "Think about what this means, Atlas." He reached up, his fingertips touched Atlas's cheek, and pulled his eyes towards him. "This is good."

Atlas's eyes looked toward Gwen, her body frozen in place midway through a step. The smile was small, but it was present. A rare thing for Atlas to smile. "They've never been this old before."

Niklas nodded. "Exactly. We're so close. I can feel it." He turned from Atlas, his palms rubbing together as he said, "I have a good feeling about this one."

Atlas could hear Niklas continuing to speak. However, he had stopped listening to the words. It was a speech like so many other speeches Atlas had heard throughout their attempts. While Niklas was wrapped in his thoughts, Atlas stepped over to where Gwen was. Through his ramblings, Niklas didn't hear him when he said, "I'm sorry, Guinevere."

Atlas reached up and placed a hand on her shoulder.

When Niklas turned to him, he was several paces away from Gwen. Leaning against his staff like a supportive crutch. Niklas held out his hand, the smile still on his face as he said, "Come on, we need to check on the Anomaly."

Atlas nodded in agreement and took the outstretched hand. The thick, black mist rose around him, growing and swirling in the absence of moving air. It enveloped them both, and they had vanished.

With their absence, time continued unimpeded.

In the bedroom, Liam was kneeling next to the bed where Sydney had been laid. Her breath was shuddering, and she whimpered every few breaths.

Gwen returned from the bathroom that was attached to their bedroom. A towel was wetted with warm water in her hands as she climbed onto the opposite side of the bed. She pulled on the torn edge of what had been the back of Sydney's shirt. The fabric was saturated and sticky with blood; she looked at Liam and said firmly, "We're going to have to take her shirt off."

Liam didn't attempt to argue. Still found himself in shock after what he had witnessed. He helped support the girl enough for Gwen to start removing the shredded fabric.

Sydney's whimpering grew louder. She attempted to move her arms against the stinging in her back. "Stop. I'm… I'm not allowed to undress for anyone."

Liam gently shushed her. "It's alright, Sydney. I'm right here; we need to get to your back, OK?"

Her struggle calmed, but she continued to mumble about the rules she had to follow. They managed to remove her shirt and lay her down on her belly.

Liam reached up and grabbed Gwen's wrist when her hands moved to the clasp on Sydney's bra. "Hey! What are you doing?"

Gwen shot him a withering look. "Seriously? Look at her! Are we worried about modesty at this point?" A moment of silence passed between them, and he removed his hand. She unclipped the bra and tucked the straps in at the girl's side.

Sydney's elbows pressed tightly to her ribs. Voice weak and broken from sobs she was unable to suppress, "No... I'm not... supposed to..."

Liam felt his chest tighten as Gwen began cleaning off the blood that had dried onto Sydney's skin. He looked up at his wife, "What's wrong with her?"

Gwen didn't meet his eyes. She was focused on the wounds that were painted across Sydney's back. Many of the welts were nearly as thick as her fingers, ranging in color from red to a deep purple. The number of marks where her skin had split open was hard to count, the marks cutting down in all the same direction thanks to Desmond hitting nearly the same place with each swing. "She might be going into shock; just try to keep her calm."

Liam nearly bit the inside of his lip to keep himself from weeping. Tears had soaked the sheet where Sydney had been sobbing silently as Gwen washed the blood from her skin. With the cleaning, the wounds were not as deep as they appeared, made worse by the swelling and bruising around the splits. Liam continued to stroke Sydney's hair and repeated, "It's OK, Sydney. You're going to be OK."

Gwen left the bed and rinsed the cloth in the sink under warm water. When she returned, she placed the towel flat across Sydney's back. She sat back on the bed, looking at Liam who had not taken his eyes off her in quite some time. "Am I doing something wrong, Liam?"

For what felt like a while, he didn't answer. He didn't want to fight with her, certainly not with everything that was happening, but anything he said would undoubtedly lead in that direction. Sometimes, it seemed all they did was fight. Until… very recently. Liam blinked a few times, finally averting his eyes as he said, "I just…" He looked down at his daughter. Under the warmth of the towel, she had stopped trembling. "I've never seen you care so much."

Gwen stood from the bed once again. She folded her arms over her chest. "I… I don't care." She purposefully looked away from her husband when she felt his eyes on her. She had no good reason for her sudden change of heart.

At that moment, she hadn't considered Sydney an Azure. Perhaps she hadn't been a Lycan either. What she saw being held against the wall by a man over five times her strength was a young woman being beaten. Screaming for mercy and receiving none of it.

Gwen turned to Liam, who was still watching her and waiting patiently for her to finish her response. She thought of a thousand ways to respond. She could snap at him with her usual aggressive tone; she could lie about how she thought Desmond had no right to admonish an Azure that wasn't his—even though all Azure transactions and ability reports went through him.

To her own surprise, she did none of it. She dropped her arms and chose honesty. "I do care about Sydney. She is your property, and I don't want her mistreated in a way that would displease you." She watched Liam's face twist into an irritated disbelief. "I just don't understand why you care more about her than you do me. I'm your wife. You should care about me."

He stood from the bed and approached her. She expected anger, the same anger he always gave her when she questioned why he loved her so much. The only look in his hazel-green eyes was disappointment. A debate went through his head as he considered sharing the true reason.

Liam had rolled the idea in his head so many times throughout the years that he eventually gave up on it. Although Gwen seemed softer at that moment, and learning Sydney was his daughter would answer some—if not all—of her questions, he feared her gentleness was either temporary or a ruse. He breathed, deep and slow, holding her eyes as he said in a hushed tone, "There is no possible way that you could ever understand."

Gwen stepped closer to him, their bodies only inches from touching. Her voice was as quiet as his when she desperately said, "Then please, make me understand. Make me understand why. I can handle it, I promise."

Liam's head tilted slightly. His wolf had been quiet, only whimpering when they were trying to help Sydney calm from her trauma. He felt uneasy stirs inside his head as he questioned whether Gwen could, or should, be trusted. Eventually, he said, "Years ago, I moved out of the pack house. I moved out because…" He paused, closing his eyes for a moment and continuing when he looked upon her again. "Sydney is the only thing that stopped me from ending my life."

Gwen held her hands together in prayer, touching her fingers to her lips as her mouth opened in shock. Suicide was considered an affront to the Fates themselves, as well as a mockery of the pack a Lycan was part of. It was common among Rogues, whom some considered to be Fate-Forsaken, but to hear of a civilized Lycan considering such a drastic action was shocking. Her voice was muffled by her fingers when she whispered, "Liam, I had no idea. I'm so sorry."

Liam shook his head as he looked away from her. Memories he had worked to repress began to slowly surface. He wiped his hand across his mouth and stepped away from Gwen. "Only Alex does. It was why he let me move out of the house." He returned to Sydney's side, giving his wife one last look before he said, "I'll talk about it when I'm ready."

Gwen shifted on the balls of her feet. Her words almost squeaked with desperation as she said quickly, "I'm not an evil woman, Liam. I… I want you to believe that."

Liam didn't look at her again. He ran his hand through the hair against Sydney's head and said rather dismissively, "Well, you haven't given me anything else to work with."

Without another word, she turned from him. She entered the bathroom and closed the door behind her. Tears flooded across her face as she was swarmed with guilt and shame for events that traced back nearly her entire life. Everything she had done was for her and Halius's benefit. Every angry outburst, every fight with Liam, every time she mistreated any of the Azure out of anger or jealousy. She convinced herself it was for her so she could keep her son lest he be taken from her due to her inability to control his actions.

Gwen put her back against the large tub as she sat on the floor. The confusion and conglomeration of emotion crushed her like a steamroller. Her wolf retreated into the back of her mind, frightened of the outburst with no tangible source. Gwen pulled her knees up to her chest. She rested her forehead against her legs and silently wept.

Halius slowly entered the room, only able to take a few steps forward before he was forced to stop. His legs weakened at the sight of Sydney. He saw Liam, who had moved himself to a chair he dragged closer to the bed.

The man leaned against the arm of the chair, his hand to his mouth as if he were chewing on his nails.

In the silence, Sydney's slow breaths could be heard. It was the only thing that gave Halius any sort of relief as he felt his emotions slowly returning from what Roderick had done to him. Halius managed to keep his voice from shaking when he asked Liam, "Do you think Alex will be angry about Desmond?"

Liam didn't look at the young man. His fingers brushed against his own chin as he spoke with a gentle tone. "Desmond is a vicious and often irrational man. He was overdue for a beating." His eyes flicked to Halius for a moment and caught a distressed and worrisome look on the teenager's face. "Had the Alpha disagreed, he would have done worse to you."

Halius could feel his palms start to sweat as his wolf slowly rose to life in his mind. Whatever Roderick had done was beginning to fade, the rage creeping back up when he mentioned Desmond's name. Halius cleared his throat, his voice as calm as he could muster. "I… guess… I should… apologize to him."

Without either man realizing it, Alex had entered the room. "That won't be necessary, boy." His sudden appearance made Halius jump. The young Lycan barely caught himself on his hand before crashing into the wall, his palm gripping his chest in alarm.

Alex was calm as ever. His eyes fixed on Liam as he said, "Desmond very well deserved what he got." He gestured towards the bed. "If not for this action, maybe for a dozen others I'm sure you can think of." He paused as if Liam was supposed to answer before he continued, "We're going for a pack run in a few hours, but before that, Liam, we need to speak."

Liam stood from the chair. He felt himself torn as he watched Alex turn and begin to leave the room. He rubbed his palms together, unable to fight his Alpha, and stepped away from the bed. When he walked passed Halius, Liam eyed him carefully and whispered, "Do not leave this room."

In the living room, Roderick was still working on Desmond. Alex snapped his fingers at the Azure. "Roderick, that's enough on Desmond. Sydney could use your attention."

Roderick stood from where he knelt in front of the sofa. Although he didn't want to question his Master, it was a strange request for him to make. "Master Alex, you want me to heal an

Azure?" When Alex halted his steps, Roderick's eyes dropped to the floor, and he quickly said, "I've never attempted such a thing, Master. The Azure… don't usually need healing, we can start our own regeneration. It just takes time."

Alex let the yellow flash across his eyes, making Roderick cower further. "They don't usually get lashed that intensely either. Perhaps we should try it on you and see how long it takes you to regenerate." When he felt his point had been made, the color receded, and Roderick rushed down the hallway.

Desmond had been able to sit up. Pain throbbed his face as he tried to look towards Liam and Alex, who were still headed towards the door. "Seriously? Look at my face, Alpha! I'm not going to be able to go on the pack run!"

Alex threw open the hotel door and ushered Liam out into the hall. His words were sharp, cutting through Desmond's injured ears as he barked, "Looks like an improvement to me. If you disagree, I can have Halius come even you out."

Before he heard any further protests, Alex left the room, slamming the door behind him.

They were alone in the hall. A strip of caution tape blocked the doorway to the stairs. Liam scrunched his nose before he ran his thumb across his nostrils. The hallway reeked of bleach. He could hear the scratching of hard bristle brushes scrubbing the cement and tile in the stairwell. It made him almost curious enough to slip behind the caution tape and see what they could be washing so intensely. He coughed against the odor and asked, "What do you want, Alex?"

The Alpha was silent for a moment. Letting the question hang in the contaminated air, knowing Liam wouldn't ask again. He could hear the thrum of Liam's stressed heart and wished he would have calmed in the solitude of the smelly hallway. He ran his tongue across his teeth before he confessed, "There was a reason why I ordered Desmond to abuse Sydney."

Liam's brow turned down. Not because of the revelation from Alex but because of his choice of words. Abuse. That word stuck out to him like a black line of paint against a white canvas. The way some Azure were punished was called many things; punishment, behavior correction, reforming practice, and admonishments were always popular words. No self-respecting Lycan ever called it abuse; it would humanize their servants, suggesting they were mistreated.

Alex continued before Liam could question him. He took control of the tone of conversation as he said, "I heard a rumor that you could be a Sympathizer. It was the reason why I wanted you to stay in the hotel with me. In truth, I wanted to watch you because I was almost convinced you had turned to their side."

Liam tried to keep his breath steady. Was he sweating? He couldn't wipe his forehead and check; that action would look guilty. Wouldn't it? He felt panic growing, his wolf whining as his chest constricted against his breathing. Was this where it would be finally brought to light? Could he manage to fight through the entire pack and get Sydney out of the hotel in her condition?

Alex kept talking, seemingly unaware of Liam's turmoil. "Gracie, the Azure who looked after Elliot and Ezra, was the one who first brought it to my attention. She claimed the only reason you moved to the Outer Ring was because you were a Sympathizer and it's easier around the Omegas. Away from the center of my city." He clasped his hands behind his back, taking a step closer to his friend. "So, I allowed Desmond to reprimand Sydney because I wanted to see your reaction."

Liam was confident he was sweating. His temperature rises with each agonizing breath. Alex's powerful stare was impossible to break. He could feel the pull of his Alpha trying to coax some kind of response from him. How would he respond once he started speaking? Would he scream? Would he fight?

He began to question the behavior of everyone he had interacted with. Were Ryan and Carly in it, too? Was Gwen? He would never trust her again if she had anything to do with the events of that night. Perhaps that was why she was trying to be sweet on him with Sydney.

It felt like hours when really it hadn't been a full minute of silence. Liam licked his dry lips, his throat clicking when he attempted to swallow. He had to clear his throat, whispering because if he spoke in volume, his voice would certainly break. "And... what did you find out, Alpha?"

Alex's face remained unchanged. He had a stony expression as he waited for Liam to siphon through his thoughts. A smile pulled the Alpha's face and broke the tension. Alex leaned forward and wrapped his arms around Liam's shoulders in an unexpected hug. "I'm sorry for doubting you."

Liam felt his heart stop when Alex's hand patted his back. When the embrace was released, the only thing keeping him grounded was Alex's hands that remained on his shoulders. He smiled in return and chuckled in an airy exhale. "I... um... don't... don't worry about it."

Alex let out a breath of his own as if the tension was all on him. He wrapped Liam's shoulders twice before lowering his hands. "Also, know I took care of Gracie. Don't worry about any rumors; the air is clear as far as I'm concerned."

Liam felt a weight lift from his chest. He breathed deeply, almost dizzying himself from the sudden inhalation of oxygen. Without being able to stop himself, he asked, "What made you think I was a Sympathizer?" He regretted it immediately and hoped Alex's cheerful mood wouldn't turn sour from the prodding.

Alex placed his hands on his hips. He shook his head, almost in disbelief, and began to pace, "Honestly, I never did. But too many others were starting to tell me differently. Gracie made the claims based on Sydney's weight and how clean she always is when she is at school with Halius. I heard once that you style her hair each day, but I've seen her do her own hair while we've been here. And there was that mess from when Halius almost shifted at school, and she performed the forbidden magic like you hadn't been keeping up on her bracelet registration."

Liam's smile grew as Alex spoke. Waves of calm washed over him, his heartbeat finally calming down. He managed an innocent shrug, knowing what he had to say to pacify his Alpha. "I like her clean. What can I say? And when it comes to her magic, she never has an opportunity to practice. I saw burn marks on her wrists afterward; it was a strain for her to do what little she had done." He saw Alex nodding slowly as he continued, "I think it was only because she was under great stress that she managed it at all. She's never even attempted something like that before."

Alex smiled once more, his tone satisfied when he said, "I figured as much. Now, can we please put this mess behind us?"

Liam agreed. He gestured for Alex to enter the hotel room first, which would be expected of him after a private meeting. When he turned and faced the door, he paused. The bleach gave way for a moment, and an aroma rose in the hallway around him. For only a moment, it cut into his nostrils, sending an icy chill down his spine. It was a sharp, stabbing reminder of who Alex was and what he would be willing to do. He looked back towards the stairway entrance as he recalled Alex's words, *I took care of Gracie.*

There had been blood, a lot of it, in the stairway where the Azure was still aggressively cleaning.

www.ingramcontent.com/pod-product-compliance
Lightning Source LLC
Chambersburg PA
CBHW041042310726

48978CB00011BA/402